PRAISE FOR

PHOENIX RISING

"The writing is clear, the pacing is fast and the story is visually arresting...the morality and ethical conflicts of the story will intrigue fans...the engaging characters will sweep the readers from the first page to the last."

—**Mark Rein-Hagen**, creator of *Vampire: The Masquerade*
and Lostlorn Games

PHOENIX RISING

THE LAST WARLORD CHRONICLES VOL. 1

PHOENIX RISING

ALEC PETERSON & CHARLOTTE FARIS

A RUIN WORLD NOVEL

KEYLIGHT
BOOKS
AN IMPRINT
OF TURNER
PUBLISHING

Keylight Books

An imprint of Turner Publishing Company

Nashville, Tennessee

www.turnerpublishing.com

Phoenix Rising

Cover design: GetCovers

Book design: William Ruoto

Library of Congress Control Number: 2024940083

9781684426256 Paperback

9781684426270 Hardcover

9781684426287 Epub

Printed in the United States of America

1 2 3 4 5 6 7 8 9 10

DEDICATION

I'VE ALWAYS BEEN A PERSON OF TWO WORLDS. SO, IT IS FITTING that I Thank both the Heavens...

Odin All-father whose trials kept me strong.

Athena who inspired my craft & gave me wisdom.

Tyche who brought me luck.

Bastet whose children & delights always provided comfort.

....and Earth.

Charlotte: my once and always sister & partner without whom this book would not be possible.

Kira: my dear friend and editor who shined during my times of darkness and followed me through her own.

Shelley: my wife and wizard.

And finally, to all those who seek to read this story hoping to find a moment's sanctuary in its pages. This one is for you. –AP

To THE FAMILY THAT LOVES ME, THE FRIENDS THAT SUPPORT me, and the God that sustains me... Thank you from the bottom of my very grateful heart. To all my doubters, critics and naysayers... go waltz with Chirak —CF

FOREWORD

A LITTLE OVER A YEAR AGO, I WAS STARING AT ONE OF MY stand-alone stories and hated it. Hate might even be a gentle word— loathe may be more appropriate. I looked at it, lived it, breathed it until there was nothing it hadn't shown me before and I was bored to tears. I needed a change...so I turned back to fanfiction. I slammed out a story about one of my favorite people and had some moderate success with it, enough that it caught the eye of a much better writer than me. She invited me to an online fanfiction writer's group that she was moderating. And as I read the posts, one caught my eye. This guy was looking for a Beta reader for a work in progress and I figured, why not?

That was when I fell deeply and irrevocably in love with Captain Drachaen Sul. I couldn't get enough of him, of Ceyrabeth, of Pellinore and Maul and the rest. Even only three chapters in, I had moments for these characters, lives and dreams. But...the man called Deacon, who I would later call my adopted twin brother, was burned out. I fangirled like hell, desperate to save my Legion from apathy, and he gave in. I was invited into their world, not just as a reader or even an editor anymore, but a full partner.

We wrote the hell out of the story and here it is. It's a first novel for me, and even if it never gains any sort of critical recognition, I call it a triumph. It showed me the power of passion, how you should never hold yourself back from admiring something even if you think that someone is going to think you're a weirdo because of it. It showed me how much power is in words, both spoken and written, and how you don't need to be physically with someone to be part of their world. I will always be grateful to these characters, and their creator, for pushing me and showing me that perseverance is strength, and that sometimes being a fangirl is just another word for being brave.

Cheers, all. See you in book two.

For the Legion!

Charlotte Faris 12/1/2019

"The old world is dying, and the new world struggles to be born: now is the time of monsters."

—Antonio Gramsci

PHOENIX RISING

A LESSON IN HISTORY

"Battle is not a matter of chance, but a measure of dedication. The novice seeks battle. The master claims victory."
—A passage from *Victor Vinguardis* (Way of Victory) translated from Daymorian. Author unknown. Currently banned by the Church of Imperius

MORNING MEANT NOTHING TO THE MAN IN THE IMPECCA-ble black uniform. It had been many years since he had seen the sun, in any conventional sense at least. But it mattered much to the others who shared his world if the bustle from the camp was any indication. Horses whinnied, people chattered, the forge began with a whoosh of fire and clang of steel. And as Captain Drachaen Sul readied himself for his day, he realized he was not alone.

"Renala," he stated calmly, "what a pleasant surprise."

"Surprise! Pah!" An old woman emerged from the shadows with a derisive sound. "Nothing enters the bounds of this sanctuary for cast-offs without your knowledge." The woman faced the man; he stood just over six feet, gray hair and solid build, middle-aged but lean and still strong. The confines of the tent cloaked the remainder of his features in shadow. A dim light flickered from a long pipe held in his strangely graceful fingers. "I suppose I should thank you for not setting one of your pet monstrosities on me the moment I stepped foot in your camp."

"The day is still young."

Renala chuckled. "Spare me your witty threats, young man. You never exterminate anything that may prove useful to you."

"Indeed." Sul stepped into the light. A pair of long white strips of fabric crossed over his eyes, concealing them from view. The remainder of his face bore the weight of his years well, marked only by slight lines around the mouth. He inclined his head to her. "Something that was taught to me by my wise teacher, long ago."

"Flatterer."

"Would you like some tea?" He motioned to the pot set on the table. Renala shook her head.

"Your civility is…unexpected," she mused. "After how we parted, I thought…well, every now and then life manages to surprise even an old crone like me.

"I detest rudeness, even within the confines of a *strained* relationship, and so my civility should not come as any kind of surprise. Though if you would be so kind—dispense with the illusion. It's distracting, and the 'harmless old hermit woman' countenance does you little credit."

"There are times, my friend, when there are more important things than credit but very well." Renala raised her hands above her head and brought them down. Within seconds, her drab robes were replaced by scaled armor in shimmering shades of violet and plum. Her face elongated, her cheekbones becoming high and sharp. "Better?" She ran her gauntleted hand through her long white hair and peered at him with yellow eyes—the only feature that had not changed.

"Thank you. It was giving me a headache."

Renala reached out and touched the man's temples, tracing the outline of the lengths of fabric that masked his eyes.

"Are the visions getting worse?" she asked with a touch of matronly concern.

The man smiled slightly. "Yes, but these bindings you supplied work much more effectively than the others. Things are not so...bright."

"You see too much, old friend."

"A burden we both bear, wouldn't you say?"

Renala laughed, "Come and pour me some tea."

They sipped for a moment in silence, until Sul put his cup down on the table. Renala correctly interpreted the gesture. "You want to know why I am here?"

"It is time?"

"It is. She makes her way to you even now, thinking that it's her own idea, silly girl. I give you that which I value the most in this accursed world, young man. See that you value it as much as I do."

"Has she been made aware of your...unique predilections?"

"Ha!" Renala crowed, "Are you certain you are not an aristocrat? You are so adept at decorating your words in flowers and ribbons."

"I shall speak more plainly then: is your daughter Tarah aware what it is that she is seeking so earnestly?"

"Now then, that will depend entirely on whether or not you lived up to your end of the bargain."

"Of course, I did. I learned long ago that it is unwise to fail in one's obligations to you."

Renala raised her cup in acknowledgment and took a measured sip, golden eyes boring into the man's face. "Speak plainly."

"The tome you requested has found its way into the hands of the Winter Queen's advisors, as you specified. It could hardly be more conspicuous. I imagine she will be most vexed by its presence."

"Bah! The girl will have more than that to vex her if the rumors of the Farcold are to be believed."

"And what manner of rumors are those?"

"They are the sort that one does not share with charming, devious former students." she smiled broadly. "As if you should be anything else."

"I am what you taught me to be."

"Of course you are. What a mage you would have made."

"Would I have been an asset to you or a liability?"

"As if you could only be one or the other."

The man with the covered eyes stared in her direction for a few moments with an air of quiet amusement before proceeding. "No doubt, once it is discovered, the forgery will send Tarah into a frenzy of self-righteous indignation at the thought of whatever plot she believes you are concocting against her. And of course, once the contents of that tome take hold of her imagination."

"Silly girl, I thought I had taught her better than to make such rash assumptions."

"You did, but the manuscript is especially convincing."

"Of course it is. You wrote it."

"At your behest." The man's lips curled up in amusement. "You truly have her convinced that you simply 'lost' a priceless tome of lore somewhere to be absconded with by some fool trader as if it were a random trinket?"

"Oh yes, my performance was quite convincing. I must have ranted and raved about that silly grimoire a half dozen times."

"You did not overplay your hand?"

"If I did, it was by necessity, to get through that hard head of hers."

"And to make certain that it never occurs to her that anything valuable enough to have you in such a state over its loss would have sooner been destroyed than fall into another's hands."

"Just so."

"Then I'm fairly certain your daughter's reaction is likely to be volatile."

"I should certainly hope so," Renala scoffed. "So, what will your next move be?"

"That remains to be seen. And yours?"

"That remains to be seen," she mocked. "Though perhaps you would be willing to lend your vision to an old friend?"

The man put his cup down. "Oh, anything for an old friend." His tone was dry as he gently unwove the cloth from his eyes and placed it neatly folded on the table.

He possessed no eyelids and inserted into the sockets of his eyes were shards of multicolored glass. A latticework of scar tissue emanated from each wound, and it surged and flickered with traces of energy. He reached into the folds of his coat and removed a small, wrapped bundle.

"I see you're still sentimental." Renala motioned toward the item in his hands.

"It came at a great price. I always tend to keep such things close to my heart." He slowly unwrapped the bundle to reveal a set of black cards which he slowly fanned out in front of himself in a single, practiced motion.

"What do you see?" Renala whispered.

He reached out and turned over one card.

"It's a crossing; a village. Filled with bears and spiders and wolves feasting on a pasture of red hair built on the graves of dead kings."

"Torvalen. I know the village. Please continue."

He turned over several other cards. "The inhabitants are lambs to the slaughter for the most part, but there are three cages that hold something interesting." He ran his hands over the cards. "A lily grows in briars, a red-breasted nightingale captured in a rose bush, and"—he turned over a final card—"a dragon bound with chains."

"A lily, hmm?"

"Yes. She will require your assistance."

"When?"

"Shortly. My sentries have reported that the Taintbrood horde have almost finished hauling off the corpses of the slain in Velasgate."

"Pray that they all did indeed die in the battle. One does not wish to be taken alive by the Brood."

"Any of my forces that are sent into their territory carry two vials of poison; one for any survivors they find and one for themselves should it become necessary."

"Prudent." Renala nodded approvingly. "How long until the Horde consumes Velasgate?"

"If they are not delayed, sooner as opposed to later."

"And I assume your forces are nearby?"

The man nodded. "Outside Velasgate with scouts in the Wilds and the surrounding territories."

"Then have your forces delay them and I shall see to the safety of our little flower."

"And the one other item?"

Renala held her hands out in front of her. Whispering a few words, a portal of light came into being, widened, and a small chest dropped into the tent from midair. At her hissed command, the portal disappeared. The lid of the chest glowed, then popped open. Reaching in, she removed a small, wrapped object that caused the air around it to hum.

"You're...certain about this?" Renala asked cautiously as she eyed the object with grave apprehension.

"Entirely. The effects of this artifact have been most promising."

"By 'promising,' I assume you mean horror and madness?"

"Which is precisely what I require." The man took the object from her and unwrapped it. A small half-mask adorned in blue and yellow jewels rested in his palms. "Where there is magic, there is life. And where there is life..." he ran his fingers over the edges of the mask, "...

there is power."

"So, you plan on going through with this insanity?"

"A change is coming, and it would appear I am destined to be its herald."

"And if that change has to come on the broken lives of an entire world?"

"Sacrifices must be made." The man gestured towards his eyes.

"Perhaps you have sacrificed too much, my friend."

The man only smiled and turned his attention back to the artifact. "The knowledge gained from unlocking this artifact's secrets will serve me well and provide me with the information I need to further my goals."

"And then...?"

The man simply held up his hands. "Change will happen."

"On your head be the consequences, old friend." She warned, "Some things once seen, cannot be unseen."

"How like a cloistered sister you sound; parroting the words of the church."

The old woman cackled. "Very well then, go and do what you please, as you always have." She gave him a steady look. "You know, I could simply kill you and spare the world your antics."

The man tied the wraps back around his eyes. "You could, but you won't."

"Will I not?"

"Of course not. You want to see what happens next." Renala smiled like a hungry predator.

"I absolutely do." She reached into her robes and removed a tattered book.

"Here." She handed it to him. "A gift to an old friend."

The man, having finished rewrapping his eyes and putting the cards away, examined it.

"'An Accounting of the Signing the Daymorian Accord.'" He ran his hands over the book and gave a slight but satisfied smile. "Circa one-twenty Sundered. Very impressive."

"It was written by a knight errant whose name escapes me"—Renala offered a grin that suggested she was the cat that had just eaten the last canary in the world— "but who went on to be a member of the original church and later a founder of the Witchhammer order. I understand that they teach according to his words, even still."

"The Witchhammers have certainly proven resistant to change."

Renala snorted indelicately. "An understatement and behavior that will cost them dearly in the future." She gestured at the book. "It is encoded, I'm afraid, based on a language that died before the Sundering. I recall that Mother War's followers used similar encryption against the Nevaraakese." She cocked an eyebrow. "That won't be a problem for you, will it?"

"Not in the slightest." The man opened the book carefully and ran his fingers across its pages. His brow furrowed in concentration for a moment.

"Interesting. The Witchhammers have indeed changed little. A fundamental understanding of their most basic schools of thought is certainly...useful." His brow smoothed and he put the book down on the table. "I'll decode the minutiae later."

"You're welcome. Now, I must see to it that any survivors from that monstrous debacle they're calling 'the battle of Velasgate'—"

"The '*massacre* of Velasgate,'" Sul interjected, frowning.

"—are proceeding along the necessary path and then I will turn my attention to the village."

The old woman leveled a grave expression upon her companion. "If we lose control of this, Drachaen, the world will follow into ruin."

The man exhaled a final cloud of smoke. "Then we shall see to it that we *don't* lose control."

Renala nodded. "Very well. Now, time is moving, and we are stand-ing still." With a smile she toasted him with her mug before exploding into a flock of birds that dove and swooped out of the tent, soaring high into the sky.

"Good morning, Captain Sul," a level voice called out as someone else entered a few moments later. "How was your sleep?"

"Productive," He turned to regard the Mithrac woman standing next to the table. She was tall, as were most Mithrac, and possessed a full figure that was mostly concealed in the robes that she wore. Her horns curled back on themselves and were tipped with peridot, giving them an emerald sheen. In her hands, she held a tonic, a large book and a supply of quill pens and ink.

"Good morning, Atiya." He drank the tonic and grimaced at the taste.

The scribe opened the book and readied herself for orders. "What is your command, Captain Sul?" she asked in the perfectly even tone those like her were known for.

"Summon the council. We have work to do."

———————————————

THE CAT LAZILY ENTWINED ITSELF AROUND THE LEGS OF the man sitting in the chair. Drachaen Sul smiled and reached down to pet the animal. It purred ecstatically and rubbed against his hand. He straightened, adjusted his black uniform. "Report."

The assembled officers exchanged looks before one cleared his throat and stepped forward.

"Our scouts report that the last of the Taintbrood are beginning to migrate from the field of Velasgate," Lieutenant Pellinore stated in his crisp, concise manner. He ran a gloved hand through cropped blue-black hair which prominently displayed his pointed ears before he straightened his back and held himself at attention.

"Per your instructions, any survivors of the battle were found and collected. Their wounds are being treated and they will be fully debriefed upon their recovery."

"Continue to coordinate with our healers. They are to ensure that these individuals are recovered enough to endure interrogation. I want their information and their support, preferably in that order. Remind those involved that they are no good to us dead."

"Yes, Sir."

"Are the Brood continuing to take prisoners underground?"

To his credit, the other man only allowed his revulsion to cost him a moment's hesitation before answering. However, for his usual unflappable demeanor that faltering moment was telling.

"Yes, Sir, we are getting reports that they are disappearing somewhere in the Wilds. We do not why there specifically yet..."

A high-pitched giggle broke the conversation. It quickly dissolved into nonsensical tittering.

"A vein, a vein of red and gray, built by the dead, kept by the dead and now the way home."

Several pairs of eyes, almost unwillingly, turned to regard the speaker; a diminutive humanoid creature with pale violet skin. It possessed an androgynous beauty and an ageless veneer.

Its eyes were completely indigo save for pupils so contracted they almost disappeared.

Captain Sul turned more slowly to observe the gibbering creature and gestured. "Please, continue."

"The Plague, the Plague, The Plague, The Plague!" It stretched out its body and arched its spine until it was bent nearly double. "We can taste it, smell it, we can hear it! Here! There! Everywhere!" It quickly degenerated into babbling in a variety of languages that none, save Sul, understood.

"Thank you, Chirak." Sul nodded once and turned his bandaged eyes back to regard his Pellinore. "It would appear that there is an entrance below ground to the Underwilds nearby. Assign sentinels to observe and begin plans for a more permanent method of monitoring the location."

"Yes, Sir. And what about the Taintbrood taking captives?"

A moment of consideration as Sul leaned back in his high-backed chair, tapping his finger lightly against his lip.

Chirak wrapped its arms around itself and began to rock back and forth. It looked up at Sul with those blank, dark eyes. "We can hear it singing, down, down, down, down."

"I see," Sul said under his breath, "yes, that would make sense."

"Sir?" Pellinore asked cautiously.

"Deploy a squad of commandos. Make sure they are accompanied by at least two of the Chalicemen. Their expertise in dealing with the Brood should keep our commandos from encountering the bulk of their forces. Their targets are anyone that has been captured alive by the Taintbrood and not yet transplanted underground."

"Should we attempt a rescue?"

"Not unless it's approved by one of the Chalicemen. They will be able to determine whether or not a captive has already been infected at range. I predict, however, that everyone captured by the Brood has already been corrupted past the point of aid."

"May I ask why, Sir?"

"What reason would they have not to begin hastening their captive's corruption?" Sul stated simply. "Our operation shall be solely focused on depriving the enemy of resources. Make certain that their equipment is optimized for combating the Brood...and ensure they have two vials of poison each."

"Yes, Sir. I recommend that we have our forces step up production in our Daymorian mines for additional bloodsilver, if we are going to continue to engage the Taintbrood."

"Recommendation noted, Lieutenant, and already acted upon. The order was sent to our forces before we arrived at Velasgate as well as orders to harvest more herbs for poisons and poultices."

The elf nodded. "Well thought, Captain." He placed his fist over his breast and bowed his head.

"Thank you," Sul replied, nodding slightly. The elf stepped back to stand amongst his fellow officers once more.

"Nadja?"

A female dwarf with short gray hair and an exile's brand marring the skin above her left eye stepped forward. "Bats just got back. This place is done for. The Brood will arrive by dawn at the latest."

"Can they be delayed?"

The dwarf scratched her head and spat. "Sap the place all to blazes, yeah, by a few hours at least."

"See to it."

The dwarf woman bowed and exited the large tent.

"What news from within the village Torvalen itself?"

A nondescript human woman stepped forward. She had dark hair and was dressed like a peasant.

"You were right, Sir." She reported in a thick Nevaraakese accent, "There were reports of a young red-haired woman in the Inn. They're tracking the mages that were in the company of that..." The woman's nose wrinkled in disgust before her professional demeanor fell back into place. "...before the battle. But she and some of her companions have been helping the innkeeper brew poultices to fortify the wounded. Her commander kicked up hell, but she flat refused to move out until the villagers could clear out on their own."

A faint smile crossed the captain's lips. "Of course she did."

"Shall I send word to retrieve her?"

"No, that won't be necessary. They will make their way to us in good time." Captain Sul nodded his approval. "Well done, Scout Mischa. Report back to your unit," The woman hesitated, and Sul arched one eyebrow. "Something further?"

"There is," she began hesitantly, "a child."

"Explain."

"His mother was killed, sir. Goodwife Livia, she was a friend."

"And you wish to honor your friend's memory by adopting her orphan?"

"Yes, Sir."

"I cannot guarantee the boy's safety."

"Yes sir, but respectfully, who amongst us can guarantee the safety of anyone?"

Sul pursed his lips then nodded. "Very well, I'm sure one of our knights needs a page. His well-being then is your responsibility. I assume you understand the gravitas of that?"

"Yes, Sir. Thank you, Sir." The woman handed him a bound scroll, snapped a crisp salute and departed.

Captain Sul turned his attention to the remainder of his officers. "Break camp and prepare to depart. I should like the majority of our forces to be gone before the Brood arrive."

"Yes, Sir." The assembled men and women saluted and departed.

"Captain!" An out-of-breath runner panted, "Our sentries in the Wilds are under attack!"

Sul held up his hand, halting the order that almost issued from Pellinore's lips. "Send for Ravenna and Narl-Shu."

"Captain..." Pellinore's brow furrowed as his lips tightened.

"Let's see what we have." Sul slipped a ring on his finger and waved it over a map. A low hum filled the air as he removed the bindings from his eyes. His glass eyes gleamed eerily, flickering lights dancing within them as he stared at the map.

"Interesting." He peered at the map. A small grouping of bluish light shifted over the map, bringing a faint smile to Sul's lips. "Very well." He nodded, satisfied, and replaced the bindings around his eyes.

A pair of people approached at a brisk pace. The woman was tall, copper-skinned, with streaks of gray through her dark hair. She sported brightly colored tattoos all over her body and gold amulets draped over her throat, rings on every finger. As she swept in, she was preceded by the scent of tea.

The man was squat with short hair, dark robes with a crowned skull emblazoned upon it, and a severe expression. He smelled strongly of cinnamon and pitch.

The dark-skinned woman bowed. "*Saludo, Mi Capitan.*"

Sul tilted his head. "Lady Ravenna."

"Let's make it quick..." the other man barked. Sul arched an eyebrow at the squat man. "...Sir," he finished sullenly.

"Narl-Shu."

The other man stiffened. "Grand Master Narl-Shu," he corrected haughtily.

"Sir..." Lady Ravenna leaned in and whispered to the Captain just loud enough for everyone else to hear, "...if you prefer, I can summon one of the Sanguinaries to assist instead?" She cast a look at her counterpart. "Blood is a much more reliable source of power than scavenging the spirits of the dead."

"Treacherous snake!" Narl-Shu spat...and then nearly jumped out of his skin as the woman *hissed* at him, contorting her body into an accurate approximation of serpentine fury.

Sul suppressed a smile as Narl-Shu's expression slid into outrage and he opened his mouth to protest. The Captain held up a hand. "Peace, Narl-Shu, now is not the time. Your services are required."

"Well, obviously!" The squat man eyed the woman with extreme distrust, making signs of protection over his chest with trembling fingers.

Ravenna rolled her eyes at the other man and shook her head. "How may I be of service, *Capitan*?"

Sul lightly touched the ring upon his finger and whispered something, focusing...

Panic. Short of breath. Sweating through my armor. Riders. Heavy Armor. Barding upon pale horses with dark manes. Right behind us. The scout's thoughts came to him clearly.

Sul returned to the present and nodded grimly. "Witchhammers."

Officers exchanged alarmed looks as Sul picked up quill and parchment. He wrote quickly and handed it to Ravenna.

"Deliver this to the scouts. You'll find them being pursued by Witchhammers near Velasgate, in the Wilds."

The woman bowed her head. "As you say, Capitan." She turned to face the short man standing next to her. "Well?"

Narl-Shu glared at her. "Fine, you old witch!" he snarled, relenting. He brought his hands together and spun them. A swirling green orb of light formed. Within that sphere were millions of tiny motes of light in the shape of skulls. They wailed and shrieked as the ball of light became a spinning blur. With a flourish, he released the orb and it cascaded over the woman.

She flinched as the glow washed over her in waves. *"Mierda,* I hate this part. Like needles and pins!"

The glow faded and Narl-Shu exhaled hard. "Right. I'm leaving, I need a drink." he stormed off.

"Narl-Shu."

The man stopped at the Captain's tone, a bead of cold sweat running down the back of his neck.

"Remember who you are. Remember where you are. And remember who it is you serve."

Slowly, Narl-Shu turned and met the other man's veiled gaze. There was a beat and then the man bowed deeply at the waist. "Forgive me, my Captain, I forget myself."

The Captain held the other man's gaze through the bindings a long moment then he nodded. "Dismissed." Narl-Shu saluted and hurried away. The Captain turned his attention to Ravenna. "Well?"

Ravenna moved her hands, they blurred, leaving a trail of afterimages in the air. Her entire body vibrated as her form began to blur; her movements stretched and exaggerated to face Sul, opening her mouth to speak, "Verywell,*miCapitan*,iamreadytoleavebyyourcommand!"

Sul took a moment to process the accelerated speech and wordlessly handed over the scroll to her. Her hand blurred out and snatched it from him, nearly tearing it. She spun and dashed forward, leaped into the air. There was a burst of black smoke, and a large raven flew away in a blur.

"Will the orders reach them in time?" Pellinore asked the Captain.

"I would not have dispatched them if I believed otherwise," Sul assured his subordinate. Pellinore seemed to be struggling with something. "Speak freely," the Captain said softly.

"Sir, you know I would never presume to question your orders—"

"Peace, Lieutenant, I have no interest in unthinking slaves. Demons, the walking dead, and golems would suffice if I did." Sul turned to face the other man. "What I require are quick, creative minds who can think, reason, and most of all, *believe*." Sul's tone became something sharper, more intense. "We are at war, Pellinore. We cannot afford the luxury of having minds so limited that they cannot expand or adapt to change. Blind obedience and mindless subservience are what the Imperium, their Witchhammers, and the emperor holding their collective leash prefer. Never be afraid to ask questions. It is the only way to gain understanding." He turned to face the horizon beyond the tent entrance. "Perhaps if the church had not forgotten that, its destruction would not be necessary."

"Yes, Sir." Pellinore nodded. "What commands did you issue to the scouts?"

Sul gestured at the map. "I instructed them to split up and dismount and then proceed southwest on foot as quickly as possible while keeping in sight of the Witchhammers."

Pellinore frowned at the map. "Sir, southwest leads directly into the bogs. There's nothing but marshland. Won't they be run down?"

"We shall see." He moved to the far side of the tent and took down a book. "Tell me, Lieutenant...what do you know of history?"

"Ah, very little human history, Sir," Pellinore said, looking surprised at the sudden shift of topic. "I've never really had the time."

"Consider generating both time and interest." Sul lightly caressed the cover of the book and gently opened it. He ran his fingers down the page for a moment and presented it to Pellinore. "'History of the Orders' circa the Reign of Kings during the Second Epoch." He handed the book to him. "Have you heard of the orders of old? The ones that predate the Daymorian Empire and the Sundering?"

"No Sir, I can't say I have," Pellinore replied.

Sul's expression became scornful. "Unsurprising, as much of its history has been suppressed by the Imperium. Too many 'inconvenient truths' for their liking."

"I see," Pellinore answered.

Sul's expression lightened. "Before their submission to the Church of the Imperium, the Witchhammers were a force for good. Motivated men and women of all races and creeds who saw the need for change in the world and set about effecting that change," Sul scoffed. "I find it a supreme irony that those that were heralded as heroes in their age had their legacy erased by the very institution that they fought to protect. The majority of the Witchhammers became part of the Imperium once the lines of kings were broken and the dragons and dwarves were both driven out of Daymore." He paused and waited.

Pellinore shook his head. "I'm sorry, Sir, I'm not familiar with that either."

"You should be. Perhaps I will loan you a few tomes from my library."

"Thank you, Sir."

"With the rise of the Hierophant Emperor, the Witchhammers became the military arm of the Imperium. The Order of the Justicars followed soon after."

"The 'Justicars,' Sir?"

"A poorly kept secret amongst the Imperium, a sect of Witchhammers considered to be the pinnacle of their order; all-knowing, all-seeing, and incorruptible." Sul shook his head. "Much like the Witchhammers, it fails both in principle and in execution,"

"Sir—"

"But what does this have to do with the current situation?"

"Yes, Sir."

"Consider: it is the unfortunate nature of most collectives, especially religious or military organizations, to stagnate over the years. New ideas are ignored or suppressed in favor of the safety of the tried-and-true traditions. They cannot adapt to a changing world and so they work to inhibit that change by whatever means possible."

"Why, Sir?"

"Fear," Sul answered coldly, "fear of losing their power, their place, their privilege. They fear the unknown." His tone became colder still, "and what they fear, they hate and seek to destroy. And so, they fight tooth and claw against any form of change or progress, regardless of the cost to the rest of the world. They are weak and they are cowardly."

"And in regard to the current situation?"

"Strategy, Lieutenant, and an unwillingness to deviate from that which has already been established. In this instance, the strategy of the Witchhammers to travel in full plate mail, complete with Dolor Coursers, into battle."

"Dolor Coursers, Sir?"

"Horses from Eastern Daymore. They are considered the preferred breed of their cavalry. Those who descend from the survivors of the

Witches War in the east make up a significant portion of the Witchhammer Order's command structure. They bring with them their history, their lineage."

"And their horses!" Pellinore said as something clicked.

"Just so."

The officer frowned. "But Sir, I don't understand. Why are their horses important?"

"Patience, Lieutenant. You will see."

An hour later, a cheer rose from the camp and Pellinore nearly jumped.

"You asked why their choice in horses mattered, Lieutenant?" Sul asked, a hint of sardonic humor in his voice.

Pellinore scanned the crowd and his jaw fell open.

"Because they are heavy," Sul answered.

A procession of chained Witchhammers, coated in mud and detritus from head to toe, appeared, led by the jubilant scouts. The Witchhammers raged and spat and hurled insults at their captors as they were dragged towards the command tent, many of them coughing violently. One vomited up a great deal of dirty water and mud.

Barding, plate mail, horses...and it slowly dawned on Pellinore. He spun toward his commander. "You had our forces lead them into the swamp..." He turned to face the bound Witchhammers again. "...and they sank."

"Adapt or die, Lieutenant," Sul said with a predatory smile. "There can be no alternative. Now, shall we welcome our guests?"

NEGOTIATIONS

"Fear, not love, for love is too rare a thing, is the most powerful emotion known to man. Fear is an infection that cripples both armies and nations. Fear of that which is not familiar is what drives a heart to hate. Fear of lack is what drives a man to greed. Fear of irrelevance is what drives a man to arrogance. Fear is your ally. The frightened adversary is the beaten adversary."

—A passage from *Victor Vinguardis* (Way of Victory) translated from Daymorian. Author unknown. Currently banned by the Church of Imperius

AN HOUR LATER, THE WITCHHAMMERS WERE LED TO THE command tent. Their wounds had been bound and their bodies cleaned. They had been granted permission to keep both their armor and blades. The only concession they had been forced to make for their captors was that each of their swords had been peace bound with thin green ribbons.

The tabby cat purred ecstatically underneath Sul's fingers as he scratched under his chin and behind his ears. Sul reached over to a small end table next to his desk, removed a piece of thinly sliced dried ham and dangled it before the cat. The cat sniffed tentatively once before lunging out with a paw, snatching it out of the man's fingers and devouring it whole. Sul's lips curled up in a slight smile.

"Good kitty." The cat turned and looked indignant at the man's patronizing tone. Then it meticulously cleaned itself, running one large paw over its scarred face. The man gently took the cat's face in his hand and rubbed his thumb over the missing eye and scars across its face.

"I'm sorry," he whispered. "I failed you too."

The cat put both his paws on the man's hand, pushed itself forward and began to lick Sul's face, purring.

"Captain," Atiya began, leaning her tall frame down to whisper in the man's ear, "are you certain it is wise to allow the prisoners to keep their weapons?"

Sul gently lifted the cat from his lap and placed it upon the ground. It huffed once and then curled around his feet, resting his large head on paws peering at the prisoners disdainfully.

"One does not strip a Witchhammer of his arms and armor unless you seek to do them a great dishonor." He regarded the group thoughtfully. "Now is not the time for shaming. Now is the time for diplomacy."

Atiya bowed her massive head, tucking a stray lock of auburn hair behind her curved horns and straightening.

"Different faces, different races, different places," Chirak tittered from its position, crouched like a feral beast at the Captain's feet. "But all the same."

"Let us hope not," Sul replied before standing. "I am Captain Drachaen Sul, I bid you welcome to the Phoenix Legion."

"This is an outrage!" One of the Witchhammers, a tan man with more than his share of a nose, roared, "I demand—"

"Oy!" A boot the size of an ox's heart slammed into his back and sent him sprawling. "Shut your bloody gob and speak right to the Cap'n before I gouge out your eyes and skull fuck you to death!" A thick arm wrapped around the man's throat, a second locked behind it and instantly the Witchhammers face flushed as he began to asphyxiate.

"Cap'n Sir!" the unseen assailant barked. "Permission to skull fuck the prisoners to death, Sir!"

"All in good time," Sul replied calmly, "release him."

"Yes, Sir!"

The Witchhammer was dropped in a heap, gasping for air. He rolled over onto his back and gaped in shock.

"An elf?!"

Not a lithe creature of the woods, the elf was easily six feet tall and as broad as a horse, with muscular arms and ham-sized hands. He was covered in scars, the most prominent being a large, puckered gash that might have come from a beast that bisected his face and colored one eye a pale blue whilst the other was a dead black. His hair was gray and resembled the bristles of a wild boar.

He leered at the fallen Witchhammer and spat, "Piss on you!"

"Gentlemen...and lady," Sul amended with a tilt of his head, acknowledging the young woman that was among their ranks. "Permit me to introduce Sergeant Reaper Maul."

"Yeah," Maul grinned. "Name used to be 'Spine-breaker, eye-gouger, heart-ripper', but it wouldn't all fit on the side of me tent."

The Witchhammer that had been assaulted was being helped to his feet, still coughing in an attempt to regain the ability to draw breath.

"Do you drink the blood of your enemies? Are you descended from dragons?"

A younger Witchhammer had spoken; Sul eyed him speculatively. A southerner by his tone and complexion, he couldn't have been off the farm longer than a handful of years.

"Naw!" Maul grinned. "Don't need none of that here."

"Maul's aggressive tendencies and combat abilities are more than sufficient without being further augmented by blood consumption," Sul explained.

Maul jerked his head towards the Captain. "What the Cap'n said!"

"Sergeant."

"Sir!"

"Thank you for your assistance. I do not believe that I shall require it any further for the present."

"Are you certain Cap'n?" He gestured at the Witchhammer he'd nearly choked to death. "That one's a right shifty bastard. I can rip off his arm and beat him to death with it, teach him some manners."

"If you kill him, what use is teaching him manners?"

Maul shrugged. "Fair 'nough." He saluted vigorously but remained standing at attention, ready to serve his master's will.

"Forgive Sergeant Maul," Sul explained, "his tenure in the War Pits left little time for matters of etiquette or protocol."

"He was in the Pits?" The younger Witchhammer gaped, "but he's an elf!"

Sul turned his bandaged gaze back to the young man. "What is your name, Sir Knight?"

"Keiran, Sir. Of House Ehingen."

"Bannermen to the Daymorian nobility themselves." His lips quirked in a brief smile. "You are a long way from home, Sir Keiran."

"Enough of this!" The Witchhammer that had been assaulted had regained his breath and his composure. "By the rules of war—"

"Do not presume to lecture me on the rules of war, Witchhammer." Sul's eyes flashed. "Whilst we are discussing it, however, which 'rules' would you prefer? Those set forth by King Elloran during the Age of Might, or would you prefer the rules of war as proclaimed by Hierophant Corienth and the church of Imperius during its reformation into the Imperium during the Age of Storms?"

The Witchhammer shut his mouth with an audible sound. A pause as he thought before he replied, "The rules of Corienth."

Sul scoffed, "How fitting, given that after his death, those rules were ratified granting exceptional leeway and rights of ransom to officers."

He shifted his focus to the other knights. "The enlisted were not so fortunate."

Chirak threw back its head and laughed. "A cowardly lion! A cowardly lion! A cowardly lion!"

"Enough, Chirak!" Sul admonished the creature. It turned and hissed at Sul but fell silent.

"The Hierophant is now and eternal!" The angry Witchhammer howled back at the man.

"Is he? He is a two-thousand-year-old mortal whose appearance ages and changes regularly?"

"The Lord of the Gods, great Imperius, restores his body as he ages and changes his loyal servant into a form more befitting of him." He spat onto the earth. "As is promised to all his faithful."

"It's astonishing what people will submit to, in order to avoid assuming any responsibility for themselves," Sul replied with a hint of sardonic humor.

"It is promised to the worthy!" he screamed again before glaring at the other man. "Not heretics." His eyes flickered to the woman and the young knight who had spoken. "Nor for those of impure blood or the wretched."

"A poorly veiled reference to those who are not as you are." Sul's lip curled in derision as he settled back into his chair. "Very well then. Custom dictates that the commanding officer identify himself so that formal negotiations may begin. I assume that is you?"

The man stood erect. "I am Knight-Captain Parette—"

"No, you are not," Sul cut him off, his expression predatory.

"How dare—"

"Your armor is of standard Daymorian design, but the plating is merely hardened iron, as is evidenced by the discoloration. Consecrated silver, which does not tarnish, is more traditionally used amongst knights of rank."

Parette moved to object; Sul silenced him with an upraised hand.

"You bear no heraldry upon your shield nor pommel, and the leather of your scabbard is made of common hide, not full-grain leather, as would befit nobility."

Sul leaned in for the kill. "You are what is known colloquially as a 'peasant-knight.' In Daymore, perhaps you could earn your way to a captainship, but hailing from or near the provinces as your accent indicates, you rank no higher than 'Knight-Lieutenant' at best. Perhaps you would like to take a moment to reacquaint yourself with the truth?"

Sul stood and poured himself a goblet full of water. The silence stretched on as he leisurely returned to his high-backed chair and took a measured sip before turning his attention back to the Witchhammers.

"You have violated the third of the five most core tenets of formal negotiation under the Daymorian code: you have misrepresented yourself and your rank and therefore cannot serve as a spokesman to your unit." He gestured to the guards flanking the Witchhammers. "Imprison them. Perhaps they will amuse the Taintbrood after we depart." He turned his attention back to Atiya.

"No, wait!" The young woman stepped forward. "I will negotiate in place of the Knight-Lieutenant!"

Sul turned his attention back to the assembled Witchhammers. "Will you?" Sul asked thoughtfully. "Do you claim greater rank?"

"I also rank Knight-Lieutenant, sir," she replied.

"Do you claim ties to higher nobility?" he pressed.

"No Sir, I do not."

"Can you offer any justification as to why you should be permitted to negotiate instead of your superior officer?"

"Only that I will not sully myself with lies." The young woman looked back at the other Witchhammers. "And that I would lay down my life for my comrades. This I swear on my life and on my honor."

Sul slowly nodded. "Very well. That will suffice."

She hesitated. "Forgive me, my Lord—"

"I am not a Lord," Sul interrupted, "nor am I descended from nobility. I am a warrior, a soldier of Daymore, and an officer. 'Sir' or 'Captain' will suffice. Identify yourself, Sir Knight."

"If you are lowborn," Parette interrupted with a shout, "then you have no right—"

"I do not require 'the right' to pass judgment upon you Knight-Lieutenant Parette, I possess the ability. I am above the mandates of your incestuous nobility and your withered Imperium. I answer to a higher law."

"Which is?"

"*Mine.*" The air between the two men was colder than the empty space between the stars. "If you speak again, I shall kill you. Is that perfectly clear?" Parette said nothing and slunk back amongst his men. Sul returned his attention to the young woman. "Identify yourself, Sir Knight" he repeated calmly.

"Sir Ceyrabeth Vallorin, Sir."

"Now that is a proper, civil greeting." Sul nodded his head approvingly. "You may state your terms."

"Yes, Sir. I would like to have my fellow Witchhammers released without suffering any further harm."

"Perhaps you should refrain from riding several hundred pounds of mount and knight into a bog."

Ceyrabeth's cheeks flared red, and she glared sideways at the Knight-Lieutenant.

"Ah," Sul noticed her discomfort, "you did not. When the order to charge was given, you did not follow into the trap. It was only after your fellows became mired did you enter the bog yourself."

"Yes, Sir. It is how you say."

"And promptly became mired as well."

A quiet sigh escaped her lips. "Yes, Sir."

"Tell me, you've had time now to reflect on your actions, what would you have done differently?"

Ceyrabeth thought for a moment, and then shook her head. "I do not know, Sir. I could not abandon my fellows to death."

"Indeed, you could not. You were in an untenable situation the moment. Your commanding officer allowed his wounded pride to dictate his actions. Given what you had to work with, you showed both courage and loyalty."

Ceyrabeth felt more color rush to her cheeks at the other man's praise. "Thank...thank you Sir."

Sul nodded. "Now, bring me your sword."

She frowned. "Sir?"

"Your sword. Bring it to me. And the sword of your commander as well."

Parette opened his mouth to protest, then quickly remembered Sul's threat to his life and shut it. Glowering at the young woman, he handed over his sword, still bound in its scabbard.

Carefully, Ceyrabeth approached the Captain. Atiya reached out with a large hand and collected the weapons from her. Ceyrabeth frowned at both her eerily still expression and the strange, puckered scars around her lips and eyes.

Atiya presented the weapons to the Captain. He undid the peace binding around Parette's sword and gently removed the blade, examining it critically before rising to his feet, sword still in hand. The assembled Witchhammers moved away from him in alarm, but Sul merely gave the weapon a few measured test swings, tight and precise, and frowned in displeasure.

"Poorly balanced," he commented disapprovingly, "and only a partial tang." He examined the owner of the blade critically. "Too many years guarding acolytes and apprentices. By the quality of this weapon, I can only assume that you have never served on the front line before..."

Sul returned his gaze to the blade. "...against opponents who are permitted to fight back."

Sul frowned at the blade, running his hands carefully along the edges and then down the fuller, rubbing his thumb back and forth against the guard. "You take very good care of this weapon, Knight-Lieutenant Parette. Very good care indeed."

"We're required to make sure our weapons are cleaned after every battle," Sir Keiran provided helpfully.

"Of course. Dried blood is not conducive to the overall integrity of the weapon, to say nothing of Taintbrood blood." Sul pressed the tip of the blade into the dirt and rested his weight upon it. "Inflexible," he noted with distaste. "No give to the steel makes for a brittle blade." He turned his attention back to the Witchhammers. "Quite the liability against the heavier weapons Taintbrood are known to favor."

"This weapon, however, is in exceptional condition, especially considering how poorly constructed it is. There is not a single nick on the edge, or a spot of dried blood within the fuller or encrusted upon the hilt." Sul handed it to Atiya. "Atiya, when was the last time you saw a blade in such a condition?"

"When it was freshly made, Captain, and yet to be used," she answered in her level tone.

"When it was yet to be used," Sul confirmed, taking the weapon back from her and casually tossed the blade at Parette's feet.

"You were at Velasgate. There is no other plausible reason for a unit of Witchhammers in full regalia to be present in the Wilds. I imagine your purpose was to 'protect' whatever mages the church had allowed off their leashes to support the Witchhammer forces and yet I do not see your charges." Sul adjusted his obsidian-colored uniform and retook his seat. Sul turned his attention back to the Mithrac. "Did our Sentinels observing the battle see any mages at the forefront when the army was being massacred?"

"No, Captain."

Sul's expression turned predatory. "Did they see any Witchhammers?"

"No, Captain."

"And what conclusion do you draw from this?"

"That the mages and Witchhammers were somewhere else." She turned her eyes upon the assembled Witchhammers. "Someplace away from the fighting."

"Someplace a great deal away, judging by the condition of their armor and, more tellingly, their weapons."

"It is possible that the mages somehow escaped the Witchhammers and in attempting to recapture them, they could not participate in the battle."

"Possible, if not for the fact that a group of mages could not outrun a full company of mounted Witchhammers on open ground. Even if they had horses of their own, the Witchhammers would have proved to be superior horsemen."

"Perhaps the Witchhammers murdered the mages," the Mithrac woman speculated in the same, emotionless tone, her flat gaze measuring each of the knights in turn.

Sir Ceyrabeth's spine stiffened at the accusation, but it was Sir Keiran who called out, "We would never—"

Sul held up a hand. "Peace Sir Keiran. I am perfectly aware that you did not murder your charges." He gently undid the peace bind to Ceyrabeth's sword and removed it from its sheath.

"Better," he commented, running his hands along the blade's edge. "This weapon has clearly seen battle." Sul held the weapon up and lightly rapped it with a fingernail causing the metal to ring. "Traces of cobalt and silver," he mused. He gripped the sword by the hilt and held it out straight, tip pointed at the woman. "The balance suggests the smith is used to working with denser materials and a lower center of gravity. It is Dwarven-made, then?"

"Uh—yes!" Ceyrabeth replied wondering how in the name of the gods he had deduced that. "It was a gift."

Sul ran his thumb carefully along the fuller. "'Tis a fine gift indeed. But I detect no evidence of mage blood on this weapon."

She frowned. "Sir?"

Sul favored her with a slight smile and took another measured sip from his goblet, wetting his lips before speaking. "Before a major battle, mages will often consume a vast amount of wyrmscale to ensure the potency of their spells. It leaves a telling residue in the blood, traces of wyrmscale that cannot be absorbed more fully into the body." He gently sheathed the weapon and left the peace binding undone. "That residue would be present on this weapon had you run through a mage whose blood was that heavily saturated with wyrmscale. It is impossible to clean off entirely." He handed the weapon back to her and turned his attention to the other Witchhammers.

"As for the remainder of you, your arms were thoroughly scrutinized before they were peace bound and returned to you. There was no wyrmscale residue on any of them." Sul's lips twisted upward at the look of extreme discomfort the Witchhammers exhibited at the knowledge that their belongings had been so thoroughly scrutinized.

He returned his attention to Ceyrabeth. "Therefore, it may be safely assumed that you did not murder your wards." His head lifted back up to regard the others. "Furthermore, during this exchange and based on previous reports, I do not get the sense that there are any amongst you who have the desire or the antipathy to commit multiple acts of betrayal and murder. You possess the courage of your convictions which would prohibit that sort of behavior." His head shifted slightly to scrutinize Parette. "For the most part."

"Then the only logical conclusion is that the Witchhammers released the mages," Atiya stated.

"That is correct." Sul nodded. "And why do you suppose that would be?"

Atiya leveled a dead-eyed gaze at Parette. "Because they stood to gain from it in some way."

"Indeed. Who were the ranking members of the mages in attendance at Velasgate?" Sul asked his advisor casually.

"Archmage Abn Zulkir and Archmage Shiandra," Atiya recited from memory, tilting her horned head quizzically. "Why?"

Sul simply shook his head. "Our information from the Magi suggests that Archmage Shiandra is a modest woman and one of unassailable character." Sul's expression hardened. "But

Archmage Zulkir is a man of means; nobility, I believe." Sul's demeanor became frigid. "As you well know, Knight-Lieutenant Parette." He tossed a small bag upon the ground at the knight's feet. It landed heavily, and silver and gold spilled forth.

"Within one's boot is a poor place to hide a coin purse," Sul said very softly.

"You bastard!" Keiran bellowed and attempted to attack the other man, only to be held back by the guards present. "You SOLD them?! You told us the mages escaped using demonic magic!"

Sul rose to his feet and began to pace, his head lowered in thought. "Zulkir will no doubt return to the Conclave and engage in some form of suicidal stupidity, that's certainly in keeping with his character," he mused aloud before turning to Atiya. "Have our allies been warned to avoid the man?"

"Agent Kelli forwarded the message received from the kitchen staff."

"Let us hope that they can keep themselves intact during whatever insanity Zulkir and his lackeys have in store. The signs all point to something dramatic..." Sul reached into his uniform and removed a pipe and a piece of straw. He carefully set the straw ablaze, using it to light the pipe before crushing the flaming material in his bare fist and lazily dumping the still-smoldering remains to the floor. He took a deep inhalation and exhaled thoughtfully. "...which concurs with the information we have received from our agents amongst the mages and

Witchhammers at the tower."

"Agents?!"

Captain Sul and Atiya both turned to face her. "You have a question, Sir Vallorin?"

"You...you have spies in the Witchhammers? And the Mages?"

Sul smiled slightly. "Tell me: what is the name of the person who prepared your meals at the Tower? The name of the stablemaster's son? The name of the person who cleans the floors of your chambers or ensures that your weapons and armor are polished?" Sul leaned forward. "The person who empties your chamber pots?"

"My squire's name was Abel. He oversaw arms and armor while I was at the Tower. As for the rest...I do not know, Sir."

"The great powers of this world tend to believe they operate in a vacuum; they do not. Behind every great institution is an army of people who assure that it manages to sustain itself day-to-day. Without these people, the societies of Aegreas would collapse and yet their only reward is to remain ignored, unseen." Sul settled back against his chair. "I see them, I know them, and they know me, as do so many other individuals who have been pushed aside and labeled as 'outcasts' or 'pariahs.' And what they see, I see. What they know, I know." He tilted his head toward the woman. "Something to consider for the future."

Her chin lifted, eyes flickering to the others. The unease was almost palpable. "I see by your demeanors that you understand the implications of this." Sul nodded. "As it should be. But there is a more pressing matter to address." He raised his voice, "Knight-Lieutenant Parette, by the Code of the Witchhammers set down by Hierophant Corienth, I judge you guilty of corruption and acting in a manner unbecoming of a Witchhammer whilst in command of Witchhammer forces. Your sentence—"

"You!"

A flurry of movement interrupted the Captain's decree and a young man in robes threw himself at Parette. "I knew it was you! I knew it was you! I saw you!" he screamed. The guards intercepted his frenzied flight and the young man clawed at the air trying to reach the older man.

"Hold!" Sul's command cut through the air. "Bring him forth." The guard carefully lifted the boy up and brought him before the Captain. "Calm yourself. What is your name?" he asked the boy.

"Evric, Sir."

"And you have a grievance against this man?" Sul indicated Parette.

The lad wiped his eyes. "I was an apprentice in the Conclave before I escaped." He pointed a shaking finger at the Witchhammer. "This man...he...sold me to someone visiting there and that man...used me."

"This man—" Sul indicated with his hand. "—was paid by someone visiting you within the confines of the Conclave?"

"Yes, Sir."

"And that person raped you." It wasn't a question. The young man just nodded, wiping his nose. "And then?"

"And then, when it was over, he took me back to the apprentice quarters and told me that if I told anyone, he'd tell everyone I was a Virago!" he cried.

Silence had descended like death upon the proceedings.

"I see," Sul said in a lethally soft whisper.

"This...this is absurd!" Parette shrieked, his voice cracking. "This boy is a liar! He hates all Witchhammers!"

"Is that true?" Sul asked Evric. "Do you hate all Witchhammers?"

The young man looked up at him, no longer weeping but eyes red-rimmed with rage. "Yes."

"And given the chance, would you kill Witchhammers?"

"Yes."

"All of them?"

"All of them."

Sul steepled his fingers underneath his chin in thought then nod-ded. "Very well. You may kill them. Guard, give the boy your weapon."

The Witchhammers cried out in protest as a guard handed the boy his sword. "Hold," came the order from among them. An older knight with one blue eye and one green under his heavy gray eyebrows had spoken and Sir Vallorin nodded hesitant approval. The remaining knights calmed themselves.

The boy looked at the blade for a moment, then back at Sul, then finally on Parette, his expression locked in hatred. He advanced.

"Not him," came Sul's command.

The boy jerked to a stop and looked at Sul, clearly confused. "Sir?"

Sul lazily pointed. "Her."

The boy's eyes turned upon Ceyrabeth. "No!" Keiran cried out and attempted to intervene, only to be blocked by the guards.

"I don't understand..." Evric stuttered.

"It's quite simple. You hate all Witchhammers. This young woman is a Witchhammer. Ergo, it is your desire to slay her." He gestured. "Do so."

"But, she's...innocent."

"She is a Witchhammer, is that not crime enough?"

Evric hands trembled visibly. "I don't—"

"Very well then, another target." Sul pointed again. "Him. The young man."

"No!" Ceyrabeth cried out. "Keiran wouldn't EVER harm a child! He's innocent!"

"So was Evric before he was defiled at the behest of a member of your Order, Witchhammer."

"A member! One man's weakness and cruelty is not that of the Or-der!" she countered.

Sul returned his attention to Evric. The boy was still clutching the sword, but the tip was brushing the ground as though it were too heavy to hold upright.

"You may take your pick then, Evric. Who amongst the Witchhammers shall die first for your suffering? You intend to kill them all, so proceed."

Evric looked into their faces. Ceyrabeth, her face lined with fear and concern. Keiran, looking at him with sadness and pity. The other Witchhammers wore similar expressions; fear, horror, dread.

Sympathy.

The sword dropped from Evric's hands.

"No," he whispered. "They are innocent. They did not do this to me." He pointed a shaking finger at Parette. "He did."

"*A* Witchhammer then, not *all* Witchhammers?" Sul asked quietly.

"Yes," the boy whispered hoarsely and turned away from the Captain, burying his face in his hands.

Slowly, Sul rose from his chair and made his way to the young man. "Hate is a tool for the weak," he stated. "You are above such things."

A hand touched Evric's shoulder. The boy gasped and looked up in shock. "I'm so sorry,"

Ceyrabeth said gently, "but no one else is going to hurt you again."

The boy stood stiffly for a moment and then broke. With a wail, he threw himself into the woman's arms. Ceyrabeth held him and stroked his head as he sobbed. "Shh, it's all right." Sul nodded and then resumed his place upon the chair.

"He's telling the truth," Atiya said simply.

"Of course he is," Sul replied.

"This is all—," Parette blustered. "I demand a fair trial!"

"I have never heard an innocent man say that." Sul commented. "Take note, Knight-Lieutenant Parette: Tears are not the hallmark of a liar. Fear is." He edged forward in his chair. "You stink of fear."

Parette shuddered and drew back as Sul continued speaking, "The Mithrac have a saying; 'The tragedy is not to die, but to be wasted.'" He turned his attention to the androgynous chittering creature perched at his feet. "Chirak?"

Chirak's expression turned eerily somber as it approached Parette.

"Move back!" Atiya called out in a clear voice. She helped the guards herd the other Witchhammers away from Parette.

Parette was well past the verge of panic. Desperately he attempted to find shelter amongst the ranks of the other Witchhammers and saw only condemnation in their eyes. "What's happening?" Ceyrabeth asked, stepping in front of Evric in an unconsciously protective gesture.

"The penalty for your crimes is death, Knight-Lieutenant Parette." Sul stated in a cold tone,

"Chirak, proceed."

Parette was panting like a wild beast. "No, no! Mercy, please!"

"That's what I said," Evric whispered.

Ceyrabeth slowly moved backward, herding Evric into the middle of a protective circle of wary Knights and shifted so his line of sight was obscured.

"We are hungry," Chirak said to Parette.

And then Chirak screamed a horrific wail of pain as it bent itself backwards in half. The scream became a high-pitched screech; grating and angry. A hideous crackling sound filled the air and Chirak's clothing split and fell apart. The blue flesh underneath was bubbling madly as something underneath it writhed and thrashed as if trying to break free. Its torso puckered and burst to become a great fanged maw, drool and bits of its own ragged flesh clinging to it.

"Imperius have mercy!" one of the Witchhammers cried out. The others were cowering away from the bubbling, shifting mass of meat that had been Chirak. Tendrils of flesh and muscle were vomited out of the snarling toothed maw and began to crack and writhe. There was a second eruption of gore and a pair of clawed arms burst out of the sides of Chirak's rapidly shifting torso. Long strips of skin peeled back and fell from the body, the tissue underneath warped, and writhing and it stretched becoming taller until it towered over Parette.

"Oh, gods no!" Parette screamed. He turned and attempted to flee.

The mass of bubbling flesh and teeth emitted a deafening screech and pounced upon him shrieking. The tentacles wrapped around Parette's legs and brought him down, dragging him towards itself.

"No! No! No! No! No!" he screamed and babbled, his fingernails breaking off in the dirt as he clawed for some purchase. The now-vestigial head of Chirak bounced and twitched, loosely anchored to a thin tendril of flesh. It continued to scream and stare blankly ahead, eyes wide and unseeing, locked in a rictus of agony as if horrified by its own actions.

"Noooooooo!" Parette screamed.

The beast sank its teeth into his back and hoisted him up bodily into the air. The tentacles burrowed through the armor and deep into the man's flesh. Parette choked and gurgled as his body was violated. The two arms that had sprouted from the torso were tipped with huge claws that punctured the man on each side of his chest and pulled him flush against itself.

With a final scream, Parette's armor burst. His flesh bubbled and writhed. He looked down at himself uncomprehendingly as his body began to melt and flow like wax.

The gibbering monstrosity opened its deformed mouth wide, and the tentacles pushed the screaming mound of flesh that had once been a Witchhammer in. The sound of his spine breaking was audible over the screams and the wet sound of tearing meat.

Then, he was gone. The mouth closed. For a moment, those assembled saw Parette within the creature's translucent skin. He was still screaming and clawing to escape as he was consumed.

There was a sound like fat sizzling on a griddle and what appeared to be spider legs erupted from the creature's lower portions, covered in fluid. The beast bounded away taking the screaming man within it and the sounds faded into nothingness.

"We shall call a short recess while you and your fellows dine and revisit your terms. Enjoy your meals," Sul stated calmly.

THE BURDENS OF

COMMAND

"Diplomacy is the art of engendering indifference in the hostile and admiration in the indifferent. Use all resources at your disposal to see that those under parlay are treated well. They are not enemies, but opportunities. Treat them as you yourself will one day wish to be treated. Honor their pledges should they honor yours. Respect their oaths should they respect your own. And should they break either pledge or oath, break them in return and scatter their pieces across the landscape so that their annihilation may serve as a warning to others."

—A passage from *Victor Vinguardis* (Way of Victory)
translated from Daymorian. Author unknown.
Currently banned by the Church of Imperius

Ceyrabeth was furious. She had spent most of her life more or less angry, but this was a feeling she hadn't had to deal with in a long time—this pulsing, glittering scratch at the back of her eyes that periodically sent little stars floating across her vision. *That thrice-damned idiot, Knight-Lieutenant Parette*...but he was dead now, and that was half the problem. That creature...Chirak, or whatever it was called...and the master that bound it. What kind of man was this Captain Sul, that spoke with such intelligence and compassion, but kept flesh-eating monsters at his side like a pet?

She wished to the gods that she hadn't had to speak up. It was not in her best interests to have the Captain's eye on her. There was so much she stood to lose if he looked too deeply, and she spoke too indecorously. But it had happened and now she found herself in the rather incongruous position of being the spokeswoman for her fellow Witchhammers.

Between the humiliation of the bog, the uncertainty of imprisonment, and the raw terror the creature Chirak had instilled, they could hardly be called Witchhammers. Even Keiran's unfailingly upbeat outlook was faltering. He sat on the edge of the courtyard, the boy Evric sitting beside him with a bleak look on his young face. The poor mage had simply seen too much, re-lived too much, and he was just plain tired.

Stars hit Ceyrabeth's eyes, and she pulled in a deep breath, her hand automatically touching the pouch that contained her wyrmscale dose. No, she told herself, even though the desire to take it made her muscles clench painfully. She only had one left, having given her spare to Sir Mathias after their supply sank to the bottom of the bog. She would be damned before she would go begging to Captain Sul for wyrmscale, so she had to make it last.

Stars again. She had to get herself under control. The past didn't matter. Now, she had to make sure they all had a future. "We should decide who is going to speak, and what we're going to speak for. Quin, you're technically the ranking—"

"What's the point?" Sir Mathias was still looking a little green around the edges. Ceyrabeth figured that was the result when you vomited up half your weight in bog water. "We're all going to die here anyway. That madman is just playing with us."

"We can't give up..."

"Did you get a good look at his face?" Sir Tregan said ominously before making a sign to ward off evil. "Something's not right there. I think he's cursed..."

Sir Corellan rolled his eyes. "You think everything is cursed, Treg. I'm surprised you don't insist your breakfast be purified every morning."

"Better than being Tainted! I've seen what the Plague does to a man..."

"We were all at Velasgate, Tregan...you don't have to piss your pants over Taintbrood."

Ceyrabeth saw Keiran's shoulders hunch at the mention of Velasgate. It had been his first real battle and it was a good thing that none of them had needed to fight because it was all he could manage to not vomit all over his armor. She was grateful that she had been the one to find him behind the tent, head hunched over his knees and unbidden tears making tracks down his young cheeks. He was steady as a rock against human opponents, but the sheer numbers and monstrous nature of the Taintbrood horde had simply been too much of a shock.

Ceyrabeth had just picked him up, gave him her sash to mop up the evidence of tears, and told him to stick close. Turning her gaze to Evric, she grimaced. She imagined that the young mage who had chosen to accompany her and hers during this break in negotiations didn't need the thought of Taintbrood of all things crowding his already tortured young mind.

"Enough!" Ceyrabeth barked. They all stopped bickering, mostly from the novelty of having Ceyrabeth command them. She was usually quiet, never questioning orders, never drawing attention to herself. Capable in a fight, but never one to boast about it later. "This is exactly what Sul wants. He wants us to be scared and scattered and bickering amongst ourselves. Every shot we take at each other is a shot he doesn't have to take, and it makes us weak. We are not weak! We are Witch-hammers, and we will start acting like it!"

Her speech had the desired effect. Ceyrabeth caught sight of Captain Sul's Mithrac shadow watching them from across the way and Ceyrabeth lifted her chin defiantly.

Then, the food began to arrive. Men and women in impeccable but basic black uniforms set up a long table and set dish after dish upon it. They even brought plates and utensils. With every new arrival, Ceyrabeth's expression tightened.

"What is....?" Mathias began. Quinlan glanced at Ceyrabeth. Everyone else in their little band had been out in the field for most of their career, but the pair of them had spent most of theirs in the heart of Daymore Dolor and all the politics it had to offer. She knew *exactly* what was happening, and so did he.

"He's shaking his dick at us." That surprised a laugh out of Ceyrabeth. It wasn't like Quin to be crude. She moved to the end of the table and took a plate.

"Are you crazy?!" Tregan made the sign of protection over his chest. "He probably tainted it!"

Corellan rolled his eyes. "Again with the Plague...!"

Ceyrabeth interrupted before the argument could really get started. "After what we just saw, what we know about this camp, and our rough start to the day, are *any* of you truly hungry?" She received almost unanimous shakes of the head. "Nor am I. But we should be. It's been over twelve hours since we were brought here. He's testing us to see who the weakest link is."

"I... don't follow," Keiran said cautiously.

"Which one of us is going to let his little display distract us from the fact that we need nourishment?" Quinlan clarified, "because the one with the weakest stomach is also probably the one rattled enough to sing like a songbird when the interrogation really starts."

"Exactly." Ceyrabeth speared a piece of some sort of fowl in a sweet-smelling sauce on the end of her fork, added a biscuit and a spoonful of mixed root vegetables. Quinlan did the same, then Keiran. With some hesitation, Mathias, Tregan, Toliver, and Corellan followed.

"You know," Corellan stated conversationally, through a mouthful of game hen, "as last meals go, this isn't bad. Their cook really knows his way around a spice rack."

Quinlan laughed. "There's the ticket, lad."

"I swear I've had this before," Tregan mused.

"The last time we were captured by a lunatic and his pet demon?" He rolled his eyes at Ceyrabeth. "Something about these spices..."

"It does taste familiar," Quinlan commented.

"Expensive too," Keiran added.

"Got it!" Tregan crowed. "It's saffron! A High Marshal came to visit the Tower way back when, and the kitchens made a whole mess of this in a stew. Turns out he couldn't stand the stuff, so they gave it out to the rest of us. Gods, we ate well that night."

"Saffron? In prisoners' food?" Toliver rolled his eyes. "The man's either showing off or we're definitely all going to get eaten by demons."

"Just eat your food," Ceyrabeth almost snarled. She could feel the tension coming off Keiran and Quinlan like a struck bell. Ceyrabeth was just mopping up the sauce on her plate with a piece of biscuit when Evric finally spoke up.

"He's nice."

"Who's nice, kid?" Keiran asked kindly.

"Lieutenant Pellinore. He teaches us to read when he's not with the Captain. He doesn't hit or yell when you get something wrong." The knights nearest Evric exchanged puzzled glances—Where in the world had *that* little spout of information come from?—But then Ceyrabeth happened to glance up, her hand stilling as she watched Pellinore halt on the edge of their makeshift mess area. His posture was ramrod straight, the epitome of a seasoned soldier.

"Captain Sul wishes to speak with each of you individually," he told them. "Which of you is of the lowest rank?"

Not one of them spoke. Keiran was their lowest ranking soldier, but to answer the Lieutenant would be throwing him to the wolves. Then Ceyrabeth, her eyes flat and cold, stated, "Ceyrabeth Vallorin. Tower of Imperius Militant. Year Three-Hundred Twenty-Five Sundered." It was what every captured soldier was supposed to say, the only information they were supposed to give the enemy; their name, the tower they were accepted into, and the year they entered training.

"Javan Quinlan. Tower of Imperius Militant. Year Three Hundred Fourteen Sundered."

"Bran Mathias. Tower of Imperius Rex. Year Three Hundred Twenty-Three Sundered."

"Davis Corellan. Tower of Imperius Opulent. Year Three Hundred Twenty-Seven Sundered."

"Alyn Tregan. Tower of Imperius Militant. Year Three Hundred and Thirty Sundered."

"I'm the lowest ranking soldier."

"Keiran!" Ceyrabeth hissed, "have you lost your mind?!"

"You don't have to protect me," he stated, even gave them a half-grin before walking to meet Lieutenant Pellinore, following him toward the command tent without a hint of hesitation.

"That curiosity of his will be the death of him," Corellan muttered. He looked around at the others. "Oh, don't tell me you haven't noticed. He's fascinated with that Captain of theirs, how odd he is."

"Odd may be a bit of an understatement..." Ceyrabeth rolled her eyes. "He certainly sees a *lot* for a blind man."

"Aye." Quinlan nodded. "And that accent of his is strange. I *know*

I've heard it before..." They all looked at Tregan, who was the most well-traveled, but he only shrugged.

"Beats me." He gestured to the departing form of Pellinore. "I was more concerned about the damned Royal Elf taking his commands as though he liked it."

"That's....odd?" Mathias asked.

Tregan snorted derisively. "Royal Elves don't do for others unless there's something heavy in it for them. And even then, they're just praying for you to die so they can spit on your grave. If we saw a Royal Elf within five miles of our scout line, we got the Void out. You do *not* want to be left alive in their hands. There was one time...."

"There's a child present," Ceyrabeth interrupt, and he fell silent. She too had heard stories about Royal Elves and their sadistic, xenophobic ways and none of them were suited for Evric to hear.

"Let's look lively," Quinlan interjected, picking up his empty plate and setting it on the edge of the food table. "We've got plenty of clean-up to do. Five tons of mud doesn't do good things to armor."

"He's going to talk," Quinlan murmured to Ceyrabeth as they piled all their gear together.

"He barely knows who Imperius is, much less anything important about the Order," she whispered back. But she was worried. Keiran wasn't stupid, but he *was* trusting. And after seeing what this Captain Sul was able to deduce from the most innocuous of things, he could give away far more than he understood.

Armor cleaning was well underway by the time Pellinore returned. "Alyn Tregan. Your presence is requested."

Ceyrabeth closed her eyes, "Tregan!" she said as he stood. "Strength of Imperius Militant be yours." He nodded, his jaw set, and followed the Lieutenant.

Soon it was Mathias, then Corellan, then Toliver. It became harder and harder to do anything as the time passed. None of the men had returned and Ceyrabeth was next in line. Quinlan had given up and was pacing a path through the dirt. Ceyrabeth examined her reflection in the spot on her breastplate that she had polished a hundred times, displeased to see how pale she was. She pinched some color into her cheeks.

A scream of pain erupted from the direction of the command tent. Ceyrabeth jolted to her feet, breastplate landing forgotten on the ground. "You don't think...?"

"...that he fed someone to that monster?" Quinlan finished grimly.

They were both reaching for their swords when the command tent flap opened. They halted at the sight of Sir Toliver, face puffed up like he had been stung by a thousand bees, being supported between Lieutenant Pellinore and a middle-aged woman wearing a blue habit.

"What in..."

"Apologies for the state of your comrade," Pellinore stated calmly. "He shattered the peace bond we'd affixed to his blade and tried to draw his weapon on the Captain. That was...unwise."

Ceyrabeth moved to intercept and was immediately struck by an unforgettable smell...a mix of crushed greenery and rotten fruit. "Is that...?"

"Rashweed powder," the woman confirmed.

"Toliver, you damned fool," Ceyrabeth cursed at him, slapping him none too gently on the shoulder. "Of *course*, your weapon was booby trapped! How you ever made it past training with your pea-sized brain..."

"Mother Reiko will care for him," Pellinore interjected. "But the Captain requests your presence, Knight-Lieutenant Vallorin."

"Not without me," Quinlan stated firmly. They were surprised to see the hint of a smile touch Pellinore's lips.

"The Captain assumed you would feel that way, Knight-Lieutenant Quinlan." He beckoned them forward and walked the short distance beside them. Graciously the Lieutenant held aside the tent flap for them.

There was a hooded figure wrapped in chains, kneeling next to a huge black iron brazier encasing a towering bonfire. The figure looked up and Ceyrabeth gasped.

"It's Parette!"

"Steady on lass," Quinlan advised quietly, placing a strong hand on her shoulder.

"What?"

"That's not Parette." He gestured with his head. Ceyrabeth scrutinized the figure and realized he was correct. The flesh looked translucent around the face, and the eyes were the color of spit. It resembled nothing more than a not-quite-finished person.

"What sorcery is this?" Ceyrabeth demanded.

"Old sorcery," Sul commented calmly, rising to his feet. The movement to his left drew her eye to Chirak who had now returned to its place at its master's side. She was relieved to see the other Hammers standing by as well, looking a little green around the edges, maybe rattled, but otherwise unharmed. "Older than you can imagine. And as much a thing of nature than sorcery."

"There is nothing natural about that abomination!"

"Perhaps you should spend more time outside your carefully cultivated church gardens before you presume to understand nature." Sul gestured at the creature wearing Parette's face. "Chirak acts as a living catalog to all the forms of life it consumes. Not just flesh, bone, and blood, but also thoughts and ideas...as well as memories."

"Then that...thing..."

"Has all of your former commanding officers' memories and can, therefore, give a very accurate accounting as to whether or not the rest of you were complicit in his crimes," Sul confirmed calmly.

"How can it be Parette and also be part of that?" She pointed at Chirak who chittered. "It makes no sense. And how can anything it says be trusted?"

"If I wished to execute you all, I would simply do so. I would not resort to false testimony. Currently, we all have a common goal."

"Which is?"

"The truth." Sul turned to address the creature wearing Parette's face. "Parette, you stand accused of the exploitation of your wards and corruption of the innocent. Your guilt in these matters is beyond contestation. What knowledge, if any, did your comrades have of your illegal activities?"

The Not-Parette's head lolled on its neck as if the bones weren't fully formed. "Knowledge?" Ceyrabeth gasped. It was Parette's voice; his accent, his inflection, all of it. "Quinlan and Vallorin suspected, meddling fools. Quinlan especially. I had plenty on Vallorin though, and no way was Quinlan going to risk it. He'd slit his own throat to take the heat off his pet." The creature gave a grin, the same sickly crocodile grin Parette always wore when he thought he was getting away with something. It made Ceyrabeth's stomach clench, "Besides, I was very careful."

Sul turned his attention to the knights. "And do all of you swear by this?"

The assembled knights gave their rapid assent.

"A shame none of you had the courage of your convictions to act on your suspicions. I imagine a great deal of suffering could have been avoided. But this is not the same as collusion or willful aiding and abetting." Sul reached down and removed a long metal bar, sharpened at one end. "Very well. I believe that concludes the necessity for any further discourse on the topic."

Without warning, he drove the sharpened bar through the creature's body. It opened its mouth and made a low wailing sound as it struggled against the chains. Displaying more strength than his slim frame would suggest, Sul dragged the impaled creature to the brazier and heaved it upon the flames. There was a loud whoosh, and the creature went up. Its flesh writhed and shifted; a sight mercifully obscured by the fire. Its low wail became a high-pitched screech that set everyone's teeth on edge before it fell silent.

"What did you impale it with?" Keiran asked. He alone looked more interested than disgusted.

"Very hot metal," Sul replied with a touch of wry humor.

"How awful," Ceyrabeth commented.

"Spare no pity for that entity," Sul commented coldly. "It was no more an individual worthy of life than a pustulant growth upon a limb is." He gestured towards Chirak huddled in the darkness. "Chirak has the form of a person, but it is, in fact, a living disease. Even its name 'Chirak' means 'plague' in the old language. It has the power to absorb, consume, infect, and duplicate itself. It creates a grotesque parody of life to sate its all-consuming appetite for the living."

"And what keeps such awful power in check?" Ceyrabeth demanded.

Gripping the bar jutting out of the fire, Sul tore it free from the sizzling misshapen corpse. "I do." He tossed the smoking piece of metal to the ground at the feet of the knights and resumed his seat.

"And when you fail?" Ceyrabeth demanded, ignoring the warning looks from her brothers.

She couldn't help herself; at that moment, the Captain reminded Ceyrabeth of...*her*. The woman whose name Ceyrabeth never said if she could help it: all cold, quiet arrogance and nauseating self-righteousness. "Does your pet consume the world with impunity?"

"If I fail, there are multiple contingencies in place. I am no more a child playing with fire than you are a little girl playing with a sword. We each have our weapons. We have studied them, mastered them, and when they are used with care, respect, and restraint, they serve their purpose admirably. That is the difference between soldiers like us...and men like your former commander."

Another burst of...not anger, that was too tame a word, flooded Ceyrabeth's senses. She wanted to rip and tear and rend; to see his self-assured demeanor lay in tatters at her feet. She wanted to lay into his precious Phoenix Legion with all her strength and shred it as he had done to her Order. They were trapped, demoralized, terrified, and it was all his fault. She glared at Lieutenant Pellinore, who was penning something on a piece of parchment. She could overpower him, she decided. He was older, not as watchful as he should be.

Ceyrabeth didn't realize that her hand was closing over her sword until Reaper Maul's raucous voice bellowed across the tent, "Oi girlie! You're not planning on doing anything bloody stupid are you?"

Ceyrabeth's head swung to face him, startled out of her less-than-gentle thoughts. She flashed him a smile, one that was indistinguishable from a teasing grin unless you happened to look in her eyes. "Would I tell you if I was?" she asked sweetly. "Especially with the threat of being...what was it? 'Skull fucked and beaten to death with my own arm'? Or..." She turned back to Sul. "Is it cleaner to just feed me to a demon? I'd hate to inconvenience you, Captain."

She should have toned down the sarcasm if Pellinore's scowl of disapproval and Maul's throaty growl were any indication. Even the cat on Sul's lap raised its head and narrowed its one eye at her tone. But Sul himself didn't seem to mind; he simply held up his hand and the room immediately fell silent again.

"May I assume you will serve as the speaker for your men, Sir Ceyrabeth Vallorin?"

"If that entails begging for my life..."

"Begging will not be necessary. Your lives are yours, as I've stated already. Now we are simply negotiating the terms of your release."

"Our release?" Ceyrabeth was taken aback.

"Of course. I am not in the habit of executing prisoners to appease my own vanity or bloodlust. We will discuss terms and once we reach an accord, you and your men will be free to go."

"Very well then, Sir." She straightened her shoulders and forced herself to look him in the eyes. Well, where his eyes would be anyway. "And what of Parette's life?"

"Do you claim a grievance, Lieutenant Vallorin?" His tone was cordially amused and again she was reminded of certain, insufferable members of the nobility.

"I do." Ceyrabeth stated. "A Witchhammer bows to no authority save the Church and declaring yourself to be a higher law does not make it so. Thus, I maintain that the right to judge him was not yours, but ours. You robbed us of that right, insulted our authority, and therefore I request recompense for his life."

She was practically calling him a thief. She heard Sir Corellan's groan of dismay, Sir Mathias's whispered, "Divine Majesty, protect us..." But really, what did Ceyrabeth—or any of them for that matter—have to lose? She had already seen the horrors Captain Sul and his pets were capable of and since the combination of wyrmscale deprivation and abject terror was pumping an exorbitant amount of courage-building fury through her veins, she figured that she may as well use it to her advantage. At best, he would reward her for her conviction. At worst, she would be a meal for an...it. And if Captain Sul really was just toying with them and they all died anyway, at least she could stand proudly at the side of her gods in the knowledge that she had not faltered.

All is as They have Seen, and all will be as They Will. The silent prayer brought her a measure of comfort. It was her mother's answer to everything difficult. Her faith in her gods had been completely unshakeable, and if ever there was a time Ceyrabeth needed solidarity, it was now.

The tent had become very quiet. Captain Sul's expression remained utterly inscrutable. *If only I could see his eyes*, Ceyrabeth thought, trying not to shift her weight. The silence continued to stretch, transitioning from uncomfortable to unbearable. Several of the members of the Legion exchanged looks as they contemplated what form the coming apocalypse would take.

Casually, Sul reached for another strip of dried ham and fed it to the purring cat on his lap. He smiled faintly at the sight and scratched the cat lightly under the chin. It was clear whatever the Captain was going to say, he was going to say it in his own way and time. The silence continued to persist on and Ceyrabeth felt her unease reach the breaking point,

"Well?!" she demanded then cursed herself silently for allowing her patience to be broken. Sul calmly turned his attention to her.

"Well, what?"

That bastard. He knew exactly what. "Do you acknowledge my grievance, or don't you?" she ground out as she felt the heat rush to her cheeks.

"I'm curious to know how you intend to pursue your demand. Your circumstances are unique, to say the least."

"I—" The young woman stopped. What in the Void *could* she do about it, really? *Don't let him intimidate you!* she thought and stuck her chin out defiantly. "The Order dictates—"

"Very well then, Sir Knight, I acquiesce to your claims."

"You...wait...what?" Ceyrabeth stopped short again, her eyes narrowing in suspicion.

"It means I'm going to give you what you want."

"I know what 'acquiesce' means!" she hissed. She knew she hadn't imagined the faint amusement in his tone. "I meant, 'why,' which you well know."

"Ceyrabeth, let's not look a gift horse in the mouth, shall we?" Corellan suggested.

"Sir Ceyrabeth Vallorin, if the Order demands justice…if you demand justice," the blind man spread his arms magnanimously, "claim it."

Claim it? Claim what? Did he really think that she was going to draw her sword and attack him in the middle of his bodyguards? How truly stupid did he think she was? Ceyrabeth cast about in desperation. She was missing something, something important. She knew that words meant more than what was on the surface, had had it pounded into her head from the moment she entered that Tower. What was he *truly* offering?

And then, it began to sink in how truly alone her and her brethren really were. She was floundering, and she knew it. "In the name of the Daymorian Empire, I…I demand that you disband your forces and surrender to the rightful authority of the Witchhammers!"

"No."

"No?" Ceyrabeth yelped. "What do you mean, 'no'?! You said…"

"The word is self-explanatory." He stroked the cat at his lap with practiced ease. "I should think that the implications are as well. What the Witchhammer order, or the Diocese of Imperius, or your vaunted Imperial Hierophant himself dictates is not my concern," he explained evenly. "If the gods wish to make a request in person, I will consider it…should you feel compelled in your faith to call down the god Imperius upon us all"—Sul leaned forward in his chair—"your strength no doubt flows from your faith and piety, does it not, Sir Knight?"

Her strength flowed from strategic doses of the powerful, but addictive, wyrmscale but he didn't need to know that. Ceyrabeth narrowed her eyes, "You, Sir, are a murderer and a traitor, and your arrogance boggles the mind."

"I am a warrior," Sul interjected firmly. "And I claim no allegiance to the Imperium, the Witchhammer Order or any monarchy of Aegreas, I have betrayed nothing and no one."

"A child says, 'I did not trip him' when his brother steps on a toy he deliberately put in his way...but still, he is punished for it."

A dark shadow settled across Sul's face. "You may dispense with the platitudes. Do not presume to moralize to me, Sir Ceyrabeth Vallorin."

Ceyrabeth felt a shiver work its way down her spine, as for the first time she clearly understood the kind of man that could command creatures like Chirak and Reaper Maul. The kind of man that she should be very careful of if she wanted to get her brothers out of this place alive.

"I shall share with you a lesson that I have learned," Sul interjected. He had not raised his voice, but for some reason Ceyrabeth found her words withering on her tongue. "Orders and other institutions that feel it within their power to dictate the actions of others tend to have two tools at their disposal: the coin or the sword." Sul reclined in his chair. "You have neither. You and your Order can neither buy me with treasures nor bully me with threats. I will not be reasoned with nor negotiated with in such a fashion."

"Then you lied," Ceyrabeth forced out. "Why are we standing here, if you never meant to listen?"

Sul's expression darkened further. "I never lie. And never under a banner of parlay. I shall indeed listen, but do not think that your position or affiliations can be used to coerce any manner of concessions from me." He rose to his feet, dislodging the cat from his lap. "Here, in this place, before me and before the eyes of the gods themselves, there is no Imperial Legion nor holy Witchhammer Order. There is only the will of the Phoenix Legion. *My* will." He turned his back on the woman and returned to his chair. "You may not believe that we are the 'rightful' authority, but as far as you and your comrades are concerned, I am the *sole* authority. You are alone, Crusader, and you have no power here. The sooner you realize this, the better it will be for you."

And then she understood. He was the king of his particular hill. At this moment, she was the ant at the bottom. He had the power to crush her, crush *them*, and it wouldn't even be hard. What he was asking for was no more than his due; respect. Ceyrabeth sank to one knee. Withdrawal, exhaustion, the weight of her armor, the horrors she and her men witnessed, the weight became titanic, and the burden bore her down.

"Please," she whispered.

"Speak freely," Sul replied, no trace of gloating in his voice. The surprising act of humanity helped her gather up the remaining shreds of her dignity and raise her eyes to face him.

"Please spare my men." She looked back at them. "Parette has paid for his treachery with his life. The rest of my men have been absolved. Spare them. Let them go home."

"You said you had no interest in begging for your life."

"I'm not begging for my life," she growled as her voice took back some fire and she got to her feet. "I'm begging for theirs." She pointed at the other knights. "And whatever price I need to pay, I'll pay."

"You would be willing to do anything for them?" Sul asked, his curious tone oddly respectful.

"Anything," the woman declared.

"They must be men of unassailable valor to warrant such loyalty."

"No. They're not perfect men by any stretch of the imagination. But they're *my* men," she countered. "Surely, I don't need to explain loyalty to the welfare of one's forces to such an illustrious leader as yourself." Her tone was too tired to be caustic, but she was surely trying.

"Indeed." The blind captain actually smiled. "You do not need to explain your devotion to your men." He got to his feet. "You will be given provisions, fresh mounts and set on your way back. I believe we've kept you from your home for long enough."

Ceyrabeth heard the collective sigh of relief, but she knew. She knew that nothing came without a price. "Out of the goodness of your heart, Captain Sul? Because I've learned another truth in my life...that *nothing* is free."

"Ceyrabeth!"

"No." Captain Sul held up a hand and Tregan stilled. "Knight-Lieutenant Vallorin is correct.

Everything has its' price. In this case, your freedom hinges upon the honest answer to one question."

"And that question is...?" Quinlan asked warily. Sul ignored him; his bandaged face riveted on Ceyrabeth.

"Tell me...how long have you been masquerading as human, Lieutenant Vallorin?"

Ceyrabeth felt the world tilt underneath her feet. "I don't know what you're—"

"Do not presume to lie to me." His tone returned to that earlier temperature which spoke of the unfathomable dark void where light cannot reach. Ceyrabeth stopped, unwilling to speak further. A shadow flickered across Sul's features, and he rose and approached her. "Reveal your ears."

"What? No!"

"I am not in the habit of repeating myself." Sul's tone brooked no further argument.

Her jaw took on a stubborn set that was becoming painfully familiar. "No!"

"Ceyrabeth?" Keiran asked puzzled. "Just show him your ears."

"Or, you know"—Maul cracked his knuckles with undisguised malice—"don't."

With a shaking hand, Ceyrabeth drew back her copper hair to reveal her ears. What should have been a normal ear was a roughly cut mass of scar tissue set close to her head.

"Ceyrabeth!" Mathias, startled out of his fear, came forward to examine them. "These...these were cut! Were you tortured...?"

"She was tortured." Sul nodded. He reached out to take hold of her face and she found that she could not pull away. "But the angle of these cuts tells us that it was by her own hand."

Ceyrabeth's breath came faster as she shook her head, mutely begging him to stop. "You docked your ears, like a beast, so that you could be counted amongst the ranks of Imperius' faithful without prejudice, as their wretched ministry dictates."

His touch was feverishly hot and it seared Ceyrabeth's skin like a branding iron. She stared into the folds of his bindings and was certain she saw movement beneath them. "Why must it be thus?" Sul whispered as he ran his fingers lightly over the mutilated tissue. Ceyrabeth noted that his hands appeared oddly smooth and young-looking for a man his age. "Why must they take all that is fair, all that is natural and good, and diminish it for the sin of uniqueness?" The woman was not certain if it was his words or his tone, but he made something wounded inside herself ache in kind.

"This I will not abide." He turned his bandaged gaze away from her, dropping his hands. She gasped as if splashed with cold water. "Chirak?"

"Captain?" Atiya's placid veneer showed concern for the first time. "Are you certain you are strong enough?"

"Master calls and we answer. Master calls and we answer." Chirak scuttled towards the Captain and Ceyrabeth, its hands upraised, palms up. Sul removed a knife from his belt and drew a bloody gash across the exposed skin of the creature. Ceyrabeth retreated at the sight of it, a frightened keening welling from her throat.

"What are you doing?" Quinlan demanded.

"Ceyrabeth Vallorin. Do you still maintain to value your life and the lives of those under your command?"

A beat, then she forced her feet to carry her forward until she was face to face with Sul again. She knew what he was *really* asking—or rather, demanding. This was the price for their freedom.

"Yes," she choked out.

"Admirable." Sul gripped Chirak's thin wrist, and quickly smeared its blue-black blood across his hands. "Then I would advise you to hold still, Witchhammer Vallorin. And brace yourself, this will hurt." Atiya moved to stand behind her, gripping her shoulders in her massive hands. And then Sul put his hands on her ears.

At first, Ceyrabeth couldn't see, couldn't think through the agony that was reporting that the world was ending. Her brain felt as if it liquefied into molten lava. When the world swung back into focus, she could see Quinlan and Keiran struggling to reach her, screaming something over and over...her name? But Maul had one grappled, while Pellinore and two guards barred the other, and neither one could save her from the sickening darkness roiling just at the edge of her mind. Only her unbridled screaming helped, as though the sound kept the beast at bay. Atiya held her tightly in her oversized grip; no matter how vehemently Ceyrabeth thrashed she could not break free. Sul tossed the dagger into a fire and even through the pain, the young woman thought she could hear it...screeching?

Finally, she sagged in Atiya's grip. There was a fresh blast of pain as Sul sprinkled a powdery substance over each side of her head. "Purified Iron to keep the transformation clean." She couldn't even pretend to understand his words, even without the searing agony.

"Ceyrabeth!" With a mighty heave, Quinlan broke free of his captors and wrenched Ceyrabeth free of Atiya's grip.

"No! Don't touch me!" Ceyrabeth screamed. She wrapped her arms around herself for protection and to her shame, she began to cry—hard, painful sobs that felt like they tore her throat with each pull. Nothing—*nothing*—she had ever felt came close to this, this sense of utter and complete violation.

"Ceyrabeth! It's Quin! You know me!" The man shouted into her ear as she frantically fought to regain her senses. Leather. Cloves. The oranges he couldn't get enough of. Yes, she knew Quinlan. The sobs gradually ceased, but not the fury.

"What did you do to me?!" Ceyrabeth screamed at Sul.

"No worse than what you had already done to yourself," Sul replied wearily. "Had you even bled as a woman yet before you carved apart your own body to appease them?"

"Beth," Keiran whispered in shock and pointed at her head. Ceyrabeth's hands hurried back up to her ears. They were long and perfectly shaped, tapering to a delicate point.

"I..." Shock robbed her of her words as she removed the small piece of metal that she kept for sending signals from her tunic and examined herself in the reflection. The metal distorted her image but there was no ignoring the two elven ears that now adorned either side of her head.

"Captain, calm yourself," Atiya's voice broke in. Ceyrabeth turned to look and could not suppress a gasp of horror. The bandages around his eyes were soaked with blood and soon twin rivulets ran down his pained face.

"Why must it be thus?" he whispered, his tone raw and his fists clenched.

Atiya was at his side in an instant, holding him steady. "Captain," she said in her even tone.

It seemed to shake Sul out of whatever reverie he had fallen into. The ghost of his sardonic smirk crossed his features as he wiped the blood away with his sleeve. "The perils of age, I fear, old friend." He placed his hand over her larger one. "I am well, Atiya, thank you. Release me." She did so and Sul continued as if nothing had occurred.

He turned his head. "Lieutenant Pellinore."

"Sir?" The Elven Lieutenant stepped forward.

"See to our friends and then report back to me." Sul turned his attention back to the serene bull-woman. "Atiya, take me back to my tent."

"Yes, Sir." Carefully, Atiya helped the slighter man away, resting most of his frame against her larger body.

"What have you done to me?" Ceyrabeth cried out.

Sul did not turn. "Corrected an error in judgment. One of many such corrections to come."

"You...you...*crownsbane*!"

Sul stopped dead in his tracks. "What did you call me?"

"Crownsbane!" Ceyrabeth spat. She advanced, regardless of Chirak, of Atiya, and of Maul standing near, her dark eyes reflecting the fire as though infused with the blaze. "Forked-tongued, demon-dealing crownsbane!"

It was an insult from a time far before the current age, the deepest kind of vile traitor. One who would stand against all that was good and who dealt in chaos for chaos's sake. And Ceyrabeth would have bet her sword arm that he knew *exactly* what it meant.

Sul stared at her for a moment longer, his posture ramrod straight, apparently undeterred by the twin cascades of blood running down his cheeks like tears. Then he coughed, a deep, hacking sound that sent a shiver of revulsion up Ceyrabeth's spine. The Captain gave her a small bow of his head in acknowledgment or maybe a parting blessing, and turned his back on her, heading back towards the tent.

Everyone has a breaking point and Ceyrabeth Vallorin had reached hers; pain, fear, exhaustion, the terror of what she had witnessed and the horror she had just personally suffered robbed her of her last shred of reason.

"Don't you dare turn your back on me!" she screamed. She tore her blade free from its scabbard, angling it away from her face to avoid the powder trap and charged Sul.

She closed the distance quickly but before she could strike, she heard something growl,

"No...hurt...mass...terrrr!"

A shape streaked out of the darkness, colliding into the woman with the force of a golem and sending her sprawling to the ground. She was dimly aware of claws raking deep furrows into her armor and snapping teeth trying to get to her face as whatever was attacking her hissed and spat. Ceyrabeth thrust her sword out blindly only to have it knocked out of her hand with such force that she felt her wrist break.

She brought her other arm up in a desperate attempt to defend herself, getting her first clear look at her assailant. Sul's pet cat proceeded to plunge its fangs into her armor, penetrating the mail as if it wasn't there. It's one eye glared and began to glow a dim red. Then his other eye opened slowly and revealed a burning orb of roiling fire. Ceyrabeth felt her gauntlet inexplicably begin to heat up. The heat spread to her breastplate, and she couldn't help but scream as she was cooked within her own armor.

Suddenly, the cat yowled deafeningly and Ceyrabeth tore her arm free. She clamped both hands over her ears as the high-pitched scream rolled over her like a wave.

"That will do," came Sul's soft voice.

The cat ceased its attack and turned to face him, its ears flat against its skull. "Kill for Massss-ter!" it hissed. "Eat her face!"

"I am unharmed. Please come here."

The cat turned back to face Ceyrabeth. She hardly noticed through the agony of her flesh beginning to blister. Then the cat swiped a claw across her face, drawing blood, and jumped off her.

This didn't even register to Ceyrabeth—she was more concerned with removing the burning armor from her body. Sir Keiran and Sir Quinlan raced to assist. After a few frantic seconds of blinding pain and fear, the breastplate fell to the ground with a dull sound, her mutilated gauntlet following shortly after. The metal continued to glow angrily in the dirt for a handful of moments before it began to cool.

The cat raced back to Sul and jumped on his shoulder. "I good kitty."

Sul smiled and scratched him behind the ears. "Always."

The cat nuzzled his scarred face against Sul's forehead, purring loudly. Sul stroked his back gently. "Osen; my bodyguard," he offered by way of introduction.

Osen lifted its head and hissed at Ceyrabeth as she struggled to her feet. Ceyrabeth, not yet able to speak, just glared at it with eyes glazed with pain and hissed back. Sir Tregan tried to speak forcefully but he was rattled to the core. "What manner of demon...?!"

"Former demon, if we're being truthful." Sul scratched Osen lightly under the chin before turning to Atiya. "Please send for the White Vanguards and update Mother Reiko as to the increase in the number of patients under her care."

"Yes, Captain."

"And find Osen something large to dismember."

"I have an ox available."

Sul nodded his approval as Atiya looked down at Osen.

"Osen, come."

The cat opened its one eye, eyed the Mithrac with disinterest and closed it again.

"Osen," Sul whispered into his tufted ear. "Meat."

Osen quickly sprang off his lap and rubbed against Atiya's shins. Atiya gave Sul an even look and he shrugged slightly before she and Osen departed.

"I challenge you!" Ceyrabeth cried out. A tiny voice in her head was screaming at her that this was the worst possible idea, and she didn't consider herself to be particularly suicidal...but something had broken irreparably within her. She had held herself back too long and couldn't for the life of her figure out how to regain control.

"Do you indeed?" Sul asked, keeping any implication of mockery from his tone.

"Unless you're a coward! You hide behind your demons and monsters and don't dare raise a finger for yourself!" She caught the scent of alcohol and violence before a voice hissed in her ear.

"Go ahead. Call the Cap'n a coward again," Maul seethed. "Please."

The woman refused to be baited and kept her eyes fixed on Captain Sul. "Well?"

"Oh yes," Sul mused aloud. "I remember. This is when I am to erupt in a display of injured pride and rush forth to challenge a well-trained combat veteran easily more than a decade my junior and trust that my ego will allow me to replace what the inevitable decay of time may have robbed me of." He stepped forward, hands resting lightly behind his back. "I'm willing to admit that your eagerness to fight is inspiring, given your current condition. But do not mistake any regard I have for your courage as stupidity." Sul gestured to Maul.

"Down you go!" Maul gave Ceyrabeth a casual shove and the injured woman's legs buckled underneath her. She crashed to the ground, crying out in pain on impact. "That's for calling the Cap'n a coward, ya moisten wench!" The elf then made an obscene hand gesture at the fallen knight before turning his attention to Sul. "Do you need anything else Cap'n?"

Sul's smile was barely there but it was enough to make the elven woman want to explode,

"No, thank you, Sergeant." His expression hardened as he scrutinized the prone Ceyrabeth. "I believe the point has been made."

"Yes, Sir!" Maul saluted crisply and gave Ceyrabeth a snort of derision.

Ceyrabeth couldn't determine what part of her body hurt most, the claw wounds, the burns, the shattered wrist, or the cracked ribs from being thrown from her horse in the bog, but she struggled to her feet anyway. She would be damned if she would show her frailty to this fiend. "Do you remember what it was to have a conscience?" The rage was receding, taking with it the strength she desperately needed. Her voice was almost pleading once more, her sable eyes looking wider than ever in a face drawn with pain. "Kindness? Decency?"

"More than you know," Sul replied almost too quietly for her to hear. His expression softened, became almost vulnerable. Ceyrabeth couldn't decide what his face showed before the expression was gone entirely. "Perhaps you should ask your former commander about decency and conscience?" Captain Sul's tone remained soft, but the words could freeze lava. "It is said that you can tell a great deal about a soldier by who they choose to serve. You stayed in your Order, knowing the truth of the corruption of those you served. And that, Sir Ceyrabeth Vallorin, is a great failure on your part."

Ceyrabeth went white to the lips. She swayed, trying to find something to clutch for support and found nothing. Nothing could ease the fact that Sul was absolutely right, Ceyrabeth knew it, and could not dispute it. She felt cold wash over her, threatening to drive her to her knees. It was the ghost of an old sensation that coursed through her body—the frigid bite of a blade wielded by a lover as it was driven into her body all the way up to the hilt without mercy or remorse.

"Mother Reiko will tend to you now. Dismissed."

Ceyrabeth dimly felt gentle fingers on her arm and a quiet voice, "Come away, child."

The grip tightened. "This battle cannot be won. Not yet."

Ceyrabeth couldn't walk; could barely think. She just continued to stare wide-eyed at the man who had so easily found the most hidden of her shames and dragged it into the unforgiving light. She didn't know whether she wanted to rip out his heart or throw herself at his feet; pour out her shame and beg for forgiveness.

"Take heart, Sir Knight," Sul's voice slid into Ceyrabeth's thoughts like a stiletto. "You'll have your opportunity for justice...or vengeance, should you so choose."

Ceyrabeth might have nodded, she was unsure. Instead, she allowed Mother Reiko to lead her away from the command tent.

"You appear to have struck the girl a severe blow," Atiya commented tonelessly.

"So, it would seem," Sul replied quietly. "I'm curious to see if she has the strength to recover."

"And if she does not?"

"Then she does not matter."

"As you say, Captain."

"COME, CHILD. SIT DOWN. YOU ARE SHAKING." MOTHER Reiko parted the tent flaps and motioned her to a bunk. "This is my assistant, Sister Stillwater." She gestured to a severe-looking young woman who indicated the arrival of the injured Witchhammers with barely a nod of her head.

"Good afternoon," Sister Stillwater said stiffly.

Ceyrabeth realized with a start that they were in the healer's tent. She was shaking and suddenly her knees buckled. She dimly realized that she hadn't hit the ground because Sir Quinlan had caught her and was laying her down on a nearby cot. "Quin..." Ceyrabeth cried out as the burns made themselves known with a vengeance. "You should have been the one to speak...I never should have..."

"Hush, Ceyrabeth." He opened the pouch at her belt and gave the vial within a gentle shake before uncorking it and pouring it down her throat.

The wyrmscale elixir hit her blood, working its magic just as Mother Reiko placed her hands over her chest and began work on the burns and cracked ribs. She laughed then sobbed at the sweet release of it, the lack of physical agony. But then the rush of emotional anguish hit like a landslide until the combination of two opposing feelings was too much and she finally fell into blessed darkness.

CHANGES

"An army, much like any living organism, must grow to succeed. It must incorporate new elements into itself, however unusual, so that it may continue to evolve. It is only with the influx of new ideas, new imaginations, that a forces' strategy can continue to overcome adversity."

—A passage from *Victor Vinguardis* (Way of Victory)
translated from Daymorian. Author unknown.
Currently banned by the Church of Imperius

YES, THIS WAS FAMILIAR. THIS HAD HAPPENED WHEN CEY-rabeth had gained her lieutenant's commission, one of the youngest in current history to do so. It was the culmination of years of intense drive, study, and hardship...made entirely worth it by the look in Carmilla's eyes.

Pride...lust...love...promise...they had all been there as the Knight Commander pinned the dual star on Ceyrabeth's cloak, marking her an officer of the Order of the Purifying Flame and wielder of the Blessing of Imperius Militant. She had not smiled then, intent on keeping the decorum befitting an officer, and neither had Carmilla, not until later that night when their laughter rang off the walls of her quarters, for once not caring who heard them.

But here in this place of old ghosts and echoes, Carmilla pinned the medal to Ceyrabeth's chest, smiling as she did. Ceyrabeth's eyes widened as the pin grew, lengthened, became a blade that pierced through her heart...and still, Carmilla smiled. Ceyrabeth dropped to her knees, tried to remove the blade but she couldn't.

And suddenly Yulian was there, grinning his enigmatic half-smile as he pulled the blade from her chest. She braced herself for the wound, but he started bleeding in a torrent of red, growing taller with each pulse of his life that spilled on the floor while Ceyrabeth was getting smaller and smaller...the room swirled around her as her heartbeat slowed...

"Child?" Her eyes flew open, and she found herself facing a stone throne in a room covered in dust and cobwebs. The ceiling soared overhead, and frescoes of unfamiliar scenes adorned the walls. The room had probably once been breath-taking, Ceyrabeth decided, but that time was long since passed. "Child?" The voice was familiar, but Ceyrabeth couldn't place it. "You are lost?"

"I don't know," Ceyrabeth replied honestly. "I think I know where I am... but I don't know where I've been. I can't get back."

"There is no going back." A giant rose from the ground. It was a woman, lovely but coarse, aged as though she had lived a hundred lifetimes. "There is only forward...or the end." She reached behind the throne, pulled something out, and offered it to Ceyrabeth. In her left hand, she held a sword and a shield. The shield was scored by a thousand blows and the blade was dull with age. Just looking at them made Ceyrabeth droop with the weight of the battles they had seen. In her right, she held the shattered pieces of what used to be a magnificent crown, gems falling from her fingers. When they hit the stone floor, they immediately turned to drops of blood that beaded and ran toward Ceyrabeth's feet.

"Choose," the woman demanded. "Choose!"

Ceyrabeth jerked upright in the cot with a start. "What?"

"My name is Mother Reiko," a voice at her side informed her calmly. "You are safe."

"Am I?" Ceyrabeth's eyes narrowed. "No fire breathing cat demons, elven berserkers or flesh melting monsters?"

"None." The woman was older, her voice gentle. Ceyrabeth took in the equal parts strength and weariness in her almond-shaped eyes, the thinness in her angular features. She was a Ghen almost certainly, a divided race that hailed from the north, past the mountains. She also concluded that she was a woman who had paid a heavy price for her temperance. "I am a healer. I am also unarmed. If you wish to leave, I cannot and will not stop you, but I urge you to remain under my care until you've recovered completely."

"My men?"

"Are all accounted for as far as I know. You and your injuries have commanded almost all my attention."

"How long have I been down?" She fervently hoped she hadn't spent too many hours in the camp of that blind maniac unconscious and vulnerable.

"You have been asleep for the majority of three days."

"Three days?!"

"Yes, regeneration magic as powerful as the Captain inflicted upon you in his anger puts a terrible strain on the body."

"'Inflicted' upon me." Ceyrabeth was taken aback by her tone. Mother Reiko sounded almost...irritated. "Don't tell me you're not in awe of the Captain like everyone else around here appears to be."

Mother Reiko smiled benignly. "Like 'everyone else around here' I am in awe of him. However, like everyone who knows him well, I am not blind to his faults. There are few things that shake his control or provoke his temper." She pointed toward Ceyrabeth's freshly pointed ears. "The story of your commander's crimes and then the tale of your own personal plight did just that."

Ceyrabeth gently brushed her ears, flinching at their unfamiliar shape. She remembered the tone of Sul's voice and touch, a shiver working its way between her shoulder blades. "I see." Was all she managed. She took a deep breath, let it out. "Is that why I feel so drained? The regeneration?"

"Some..." Mother Reiko's voice was suddenly cautious.

"And what's the rest?"

"Your body was cleansed of its dependency upon wyrmscale."

She froze. "What?" she whispered.

"The strength that the drug gives you helped keep you alive despite the burns and other injuries Osen and Reaper Maul inflicted upon you but the side effects..." The older woman shook her head. "It's too dangerous. The Captain asked that I make removing it from your body a priority."

"The Captain knows?" Ceyrabeth felt sick to her stomach, shame compounding self-loathing. Many Hammers used the Scale to occasionally bolster their powers, before battles and such. But Ceyrabeth had found early on that her gifts were noticeably weak without it. When her teachers had started to notice, she found a way to adapt as she always had; small doses over longer periods of time instead of all at once. She had taken it for so long that it was a part of her. She felt... cold, without the heat of it in her veins.

"Yes, he deduced it from your behavior and physical resilience."

"Who else knows about my...addiction?"

"Your former addiction"—Mother Reiko corrected gently—"was known only to the Captain, myself, and one of your compatriots, the older gentleman who has been demanding regular updates regarding your condition."

"Quinlan." Ceyrabeth's face relaxed into a smile, and she settled back against her cot. "I'd like to see him please."

"Of course, my lady." Mother Reiko bowed.

"And Mother Reiko? Thank you. You're the first decent person I've met in this madhouse."

"I assure you I am not, but you are welcome." Giving the young woman a warm smile, she bowed and exited the tent. Less than a moment later, the tent flap opened again.

"Quin!" Ceyrabeth greeted him with a wide smile, which he returned after a fashion. But

Ceyrabeth could feel the tension in the air as he sat on the foot of her bed. "What happened? What's wrong?"

"You mean other than we're still here?"

"We *are* all here, aren't we?"

"Not precisely."

Ceyrabeth crossed her arms over her chest. "What is that supposed to mean?"

"The others are..." Quin paused, searching for the right word and came up with "...scattered."

"Scattered?" Ceyrabeth repeated. "Scattered like...?"

"Mathias, Tregan, Corellan and Keiran have decided to renounce their vows and not return to the Witchhammers."

For a moment, Ceyrabeth couldn't form thoughts, much less speak. "Toliver?" she asked numbly.

"Already gone. I stayed behind to make sure you were alright."

Suddenly Ceyrabeth found words with a vengeance. "If that eyeless whoreson thinks that he can get away with stealing *my* people out from under me, I will make whatever blinded him seem like a damned *caress* compared to...!"

"Ceyrabeth!" Quin finally broke through. Oddly enough, he was smiling. "I'm so glad you're you."

"Of course I'm me. Who else would I be?"

"An imitation. Something wearing your face."

"An imitat...Quin, are you fully out of your mind?" He had said it so seriously, was still looking at her as though deciding if such an absurdity were true. "Javan Quinlan, do you think I'm possessed?"

"Not after that truly Ceyrabethian speech. But the others..."

"...they think I'm a demon," Ceyrabeth finished flatly.

"Not just you."

"They're turning on each other?"

Quinlan's silence said it all. Ceyrabeth tore her blankets off and planted her feet on the floor. "Where in the Void are my boots? If they think I'm going to let them shirk their vows because some self-proclaimed Captain made their tiny minds believe that they were infiltrated by a demon of all things..."

"It's not as absurd a thought as you're making it out to be, Ceyrabeth," Quin said quietly. "And Captain Sul has had nothing to do with it. We reached, of our own accord, the conclusion that some of us might not...be who we are."

She looked in his eyes, saw the worry lurking there and felt anxiety tingle at the base of her spine. For a veteran like Quinlan to show that much concern...

"Quin, do you think I'm possessed? Or infected or whatever it is?" she asked again.

"Not you. You and I have been together the whole time. Besides... pity the poor demon who tried to consume *you*."

She gave him a lopsided grin. "Then let's get our boys."

They stepped out of the infirmary into the bustle of midday camp. "How many people *does* he have dancing to his tune?" Ceyrabeth muttered.

"I'm sure far too many for comfort," Quinlan replied dourly.

"Hey, it's a Hammer and his pet!" Ceyrabeth looked around at the raucous bellow. A hulking brute of a man easily a head taller than Quinlan stood watching them from across the rough square that formed the center of camp with a lewd grin. "Drop the stiff. I can show you a couple things about hammering, girl."

"Ignore them." Ceyrabeth nodded tersely at Quinlan's words and raised her chin as they continued walking.

"She ain't no Hammer, not with those ears," his companion interjected. He was just barely taller than Beth, broad but reedy, as though he hadn't always been as sure of a square meal as he currently was. Red cheeks and nose hinted long nights and strong drink. "Hey, girlie, are those ears for resting your heels on when you get ba..."

It happened in the span of seconds. Ceyrabeth had stopped walking as soon as she heard him question her placement in the Hammers. She rolled her head on her neck, took a deep breath...and rushed him with a chillingly loud undulation of the throat that could only be described as a yowl. As his back hit the dirt, her fists met his face twice before he even knew what was happening.

"I... earned...every single bit..." she roared, punctuating her words with blows, *"...of my rank, you miserable mud licker!!"*

As he lay groaning on the ground, Ceyrabeth thought to look for his friend. He had his back up against a nearby tree, arms crossed, and a grin plastered over his craggy face. She rolled to her feet. "Don't you *ever* question me, you worthless sack of idiocy," Ceyrabeth stated. Crag-face held his hands up, still grinning.

"Whoo, Maul said you were a wildcat." The big man hoisted his friend up and held him as though he weighed nothing more than a doll. "Now I believe him. She really drew steel on the Captain, Lieutenant Pellinore?"

"She did."

Ceyrabeth whirled to see Pellinore approaching from behind, taking in the scene with his usual poise.

"And you're still alive?" Crag-face commented incredulously.

Ceyrabeth put a hand to her side, wincing. Apparently, not even healers could fix everything. "Mostly."

Crag-face roared with laughter while hauling his friend toward the infirmary tent. "Taarok Limensne," Pellinore supplied. "One of Reaper Maul's...brothers. And speaking of brothers, I'm assuming you want to see yours?" Ceyrabeth nodded. "Very good. Follow me, please. Most everyone should be at dinner."

"Oh, and Berserker Limensne." Pellinore's tone was cool and carried with it the regal weight of what had to be centuries spent as an officer.

"Sir?" Limensne stood ramrod straight, towering over his superior.

Pellinore nodded towards the unconscious form in the other man's arms. "Remind your cohort that Captain Sul insists on civility within the ranks, especially towards those who remain under the banner of parlay, even from berserkers." Pellinore's blue-gold eyes narrowed, "And that a tongue is not necessary to successfully fulfill the front-line duties required. If this is in question, I am certain that the Captain would be more than happy to arrange a demonstration. Do I make myself clear?"

Limensne swallowed around a dry throat and nodded. "Yes, sir. It won't happen again, sir."

Pellinore held the man's gaze a moment longer then nodded. "Very well. Dismissed."

Limensne saluted smartly. "Thank you, Sir,"

Pellinore turned his attention back to Ceyrabeth. "If you are ready to proceed, ma'am?"

The tent that served as the enlisted mess hall was buzzing with activity, loud with the sound of cutlery on tin plates and omnipresent banter. The banter quieted when a young man standing near the door saw Lieutenant Pellinore, snapped to attention, and trumpeted, "Captain's Hand present!"

Benches scraped the dirt as roughly a hundred people rose to their feet and stood at stiff attention; eyes unwaveringly turned forward. "'Captain's 'Hand'?" Ceyrabeth commented.

Pellinore nodded acceptance. "I serve as Captain Sul's second in command; his 'Hand.' Any orders issued by me are from him for all intents and purposes." He raised his voice just loud enough to be heard by all, "Eyes front." One hundred pairs of eyes turned to face them. "I would prefer anyone not associated with these two soldiers"—he gestured to Ceyrabeth and Quinlan— "to vacate the premises temporarily." When people looked at their neighbors questioningly, Pellinore emphasized, "immediately."

It took surprisingly little time for the room to clear and then, there were seven. Mat had been closest to the door, face crimson in shame. He kept his head down and tried his best not to look anywhere near Ceyrabeth, Quinlan, and Pellinore. Keiran and Corellan had been in the middle, surrounded by a knot of people that had left with truly sympathetic looks. Tregan was off to the side, stoic, but tapping his fingers on the hilt of his sword.

It was the sword that did it. None of the others were wearing their blades, but Tregan was— the hilt etched with the Everburning Flame, the one all Witchhammers were gifted with at their knighting. "How *dare* you?!" Ceyrabeth exploded at him with the force of a thousand suns, "how dare you wear that blade, you traitorous..."

"Beth..." Keiran spoke up.

She whirled on him, fists clenched. "Don't you 'Beth' me, Keiran Ehingen! You're just as bad as he is. You sang like a songbird when that eyeless monster put you to the question, didn't you? Watching him like he's the second coming of Baris Longsight..."

"Maybe he is."

"Fairy tales." Quinlan snorted derision.

"What if it's not?" Keiran challenged.

Ceyrabeth glared at him. "Oh, so now what? You're going to follow that...that...*freak*, with delusions of grandeur? Renounce your vows? Everything you've worked most your life for?"

"I am," Keiran stated boldly. "I've announced my intention to join the Phoenix Legion."

"You *what*?!"

"Lieutenant Vallorin, please keep in mind that if you murder someone in the mess hall, the Captain will have no choice but to execute you." Ceyrabeth blinked...Pellinore. Pellinore had spoken. He also had her arm. Quinlan had her other one. She nodded terse understanding and Pellinore released her. She felt something tickle her nose, and when she raised her hand to wipe it away, it came back bloody. Mathias was suddenly at her side with a handkerchief.

"Here." He was no longer sheepishly afraid, but still cautious. "Pinch the middle and push back. It'll stop in a second. You shouldn't be up anyway. Regeneration magic is hard to get over."

"Mat...tell me he didn't convince you to join too," Ceyrabeth pleaded.

"He didn't 'convince' us of anything, Beth," Mathias replied gently. "He offered us a choice. I choose not to spend the rest of my days hunting virago and being set on by demons."

"After what we saw, you feel safer in this camp of horror?!"

Mat grimaced. "I'm not staying *here*, gods forbid. Captain Sul found me a position as a physician's assistant in Daymore Kharas. I was just waiting to see if you were okay." Ceyrabeth was simultaneously heartbroken and touched. "And you?" she asked Tregan.

"Accepted a spot as a guard for the Longmoor Rangers." he replied, naming a prestigious guild known for producing intricately detailed maps of hard-to-reach places. "I want to see it all, Ceyrabeth. I want to prove the world is round."

"Corellan?"

"Dunno." The young man shrugged. "I'd like a break for a while. War and Taintbrood and watching our commander get eaten kinda took it out of me."

"What did you expect it to be, a fancy, dress ball? You all *chose* your vows to the Witchhammers! Nobody forced you to..."

"Chose them over what Ceyrabeth?" Tregan interjected. "Dying in the streets? Getting my hand cut off for stealing food? I was already getting scouted to spy for the gangs...there's no choice there."

"My family gave me to the church," Mat interjected, the sadness in his voice a direct contrast to Tregan's bitterness. "I wanted to repay the church for taking me in. And I have. I've given them as many years as they've sheltered me. But I don't want to hurt anyone else, Beth."

"I was an Acolyte," Corellan stated. "My choice was to put up with filthy hands on me all the time or join the Militant arm. I *ran* to enlist. Hammers got their own living space, you know?"

Ceyrabeth hadn't known, hadn't even suspected. She could imagine what a beautiful child the handsome Sir Corellan had been, what a temptation to filthy beasts like Parette and those whose appetites he catered to. She wrapped her arms around her middle, the ache that had been mere annoyance before threatened to engulf her.

"I joined because it was something so big, so grand," Keiran said, spreading his arms wide. "Saving the world from demons and virago! Cleansing the world from evil! But even good men like Sir Quinlan and a few others can't save something if it's diseased to the core."

"I can sure as hell try," rumbled Quinlan.

"I figured you and Ceyrabeth would go back. But it's a damned waste, Quin! You're both..."

But Sir Quinlan was shaking his head. "Not Ceyrabeth. She can't go back, not now that that wretched demon-worshipping scum violated her."

"You mean her ears?" Keiran asked, aghast. "So, you just explain that it was blood magic..."

"Kei, I'm an elf," Ceyrabeth interjected wearily. "Well, half-elf. The Captain didn't arbitrarily choose a feature to rearrange. This is...how I would look."

"So, you really did...cut off your own ears?"

"That was my fault."

"Javan Quinlan, don't be ridiculous," Ceyrabeth snapped at him. "I knew I'd never be a Hammer with my ears waving like a banner for all to see, and I made it so they wouldn't. And now, it doesn't matter. I'm barred. If Carmilla saw me with these ridiculous pointy accessories"— Ceyrabeth flicked the tip of her right ear derisively—"I'd be lucky if I wasn't executed on the spot. You all can go home, and I never can."

"It's no home to me," Tregan insisted.

"Maybe you're quick to throw away the Order, but you could have at least stood with your brothers!" Ceyrabeth snapped. "You should have been looking out for each other and instead you're scattered like strangers!"

"You're a fine person to be calling us out for being strangers!" Tregan countered. "You've let us believe you were someone different all this time... And maybe you still are!"

"What is *that* supposed to mean?"

And then she saw it. How none of them, save Quin, would look her or each other in the eye, their shoulders were hunched and their faces tense with watching, with worry. This wasn't anger, she realized; this was fear.

"So, it's true," she whispered with a strange ache in her chest. "You've all turned against each other because of the creature."

"We've been separated!" Mathias pointed at Keiran, at Corellan, at Tregan. "They could be anyone! Anything!"

"So could you!" Corellan shot back.

"And you had its blood all over your head! We watched your ears grow right up out of your head, just like it grew Parette!" Tregan snarled, gesturing to Ceyrabeth. "I'm not winding up like that idiot!"

"You spineless lot of damned fool cowards!" Ceyrabeth spat at him. "If you're so scared, why don't you just..."

"I believe I might be of service," a soft voice interjected from behind Ceyrabeth. She closed her eyes and sighed even as everyone else around her went ramrod straight before turning to face the speaker. "I would ask you if the hospitality of my camp finds you well," Captain Sul began. "But at this point, the question would be largely rhetorical."

"You!" The elven woman hissed, low and lethal. "This is your fault! The monsters, the fear, people abandoning their oaths, all of it!" She took one step towards him before the Lieutenant interceded between them.

"Hear the Captain out." And that's when her brain caught up with her. Sul was without his bodyguards and from the look of him, something was wrong. He looked thinner than before. Not frail but spent. His entire demeanor was that of a dry leaf; brittle and curled in on itself.

"What in the name of—" She stopped herself and then tried again, "are you all right?" As soon as the words were out of her mouth, she regretted them. She was far too angry at this human to be overly concerned for his welfare.

"In order to attend to the matters of the camp—including you and yours—certain more personal responsibilities have gone by the wayside. Day and night, there are still only so many hours available."

"What are you doing here then?" Ceyrabeth asked him.

"I'm here because you have all been here long enough to be afraid. You're too perceptive to not be." His voice was a dry rasp, but it still held command. "By now it's occurred to at least one of you that a member of your company or indeed several members may have been consumed and replaced with an imitation by Chirak."

"The thought had crossed our minds," Tregan growled.

"I imagine it's taken hold of said minds and eroded the bonds of trust that you once all held so sacred amongst yourselves." There were enough guilty looks between them to confirm as much. "I've come to remedy that." Sul took the large box Pellinore was carrying and set it on a nearby table. Opening it revealed several vials of what appeared to be clear water.

"Holy water?" Mathias inquired.

"Chirak is no demon. The creatures that it enslaves are not possessed; they are consumed and assimilated. What is spawned has the appearance of a man or woman; their every mannerism, their every facial tick, every gesture. An imitation that knows its subject better than anyone else anywhere. But there is no tormented soul to save. Nothing of the original person remains. They are dead and gone forever beyond all reach and aid."

"By the Hammer..." Quinlan whispered, making a sigil of protection over his heart.

"This is you helping?" Ceyrabeth bit out.

"Chirak is a disease. Those it consumes can leave to infect others like a plague. By now I'm certain the idea of one or more of your infected fellows returning to your watchtower only to transform everyone within has occurred to you."

"It certainly has now," Tregan commented, face pale.

"Fortunately, there is a solution." Sul motioned to Ceyrabeth. "Lieutenant Vallorin, choose a vial and give it to me please." Ceyrabeth raised an eyebrow before choosing one in the middle and handing it to him. "Thank you. Every disease has a cure or antidote of some kind. This is a form of that."

"What will it do?" Mathias asked his professional curiosity piqued.

"If anyone of us is not who we say we are, what we are. This solution will reveal that."

"How?"

A pause. "Graphically."

"Wait. 'Us'?" the elven woman questioned. "What do you mean?"

"I already know that I am not infected just as I know that none of you are. But nothing I will say will make you believe that and so proof is needed. It's not enough that I know this. You must know it." Sul removed the top with his thumbnail, proceeded to drain its contents.

They waited in breathless silence for a few seconds, watched as Sul put the bottle on the table.

"I will not be responsible for the dissolution of your brotherhood," Sul commented in that same dead leaves voice. "If your time here weakens your bonds with the Witchhammers, so be it. But the bonds between each of you is far more important than that and I would not see it consumed by fear or by any action on the part of me or mine."

"That's very...noble," Ceyrabeth admitted.

Sul shrugged. "Even in war, there are rules and room for honor. Perhaps *especially* in war. Try not to sound so astonished at this concept."

Ceyrabeth deigned not to reply to his light sarcasm. If this could convince her friends to not turn on each other and ease their terror, then she was grateful. She removed a vial from the case, took off the top and with a deep breath drank it all. It tasted cold and faintly metallic but that was all. A few seconds of waiting she let out a relieved sigh. "I guess I'm okay."

"If this process can be trusted," Tregan growled.

"Would you prefer to remain afraid or have a bit of faith?" Quinlan commented as he reached for a vial. "To the Hammer and the Shield," he raised a toast before drinking its contents. There was a pause and then...nothing at all. Quinlan extended a shaky breath, "Thank you Lord-Father."

One by one the others took their potions and drank them. Mathias was the last. His hands shook as he tried to open the vial, but he succeeded and quaffed its contents. He counted to ten through trembling lips, his eyes closed before he stopped and opened his eyes and looked around, relief spreading across his face like a deluge. "I'm okay!"

"As I said," Sul reiterated. "It wasn't enough for me to know that you were all right."

With a whoop, Keiran threw himself into Corellan's arms, slammed him on the back. Tregan joined them and soon the whole group was laughing in relief.

"Wait a second." Ceyrabeth pulled herself free. "What about Tol..."

"My spies intercepted him at a nearby tavern and administered the elixir. He's fine and passes this along"—Sul handed her a large ring—"and he reminded you not to eat any snails."

A laugh rippled through the group at the shared memory. "His favorite ring." She smiled a little and some of the ache of his sudden departure abated.

"Pardon me, Captain," Keiran asked. "But what would have happened if one of us had been...not us if we drank that?"

"In all likelihood, claws would have burst out of your skull attempting to slaughter those within reach. Your chest would have exploded with teeth-laden tentacles to devour those who had not been immediately slain. And your arms would have ripped themselves free and slithered like eels into your friends' bodies to consume them from within." Sul considered a moment then added, "speaking only from previous experience."

A long pause. "Oh."

"We have a matter to discuss," Sul informed them. He gestured to Keiran, who straightened.

"This man has petitioned for enlistment into the Phoenix Legion," Captain Sul explained. Ceyrabeth felt tears burn in her eyes, but she simply nodded.

Keiran took a deep breath. A nervous habit, Ceyrabeth knew, before striding confidently forward and prostrating himself at Sul's feet. "I pledge myself to your cause, Captain Sul. My sword and my life are yours."

"Noted," Sul said. "Your petition is refused."

"What?!" Keiran's head whipped up at the same time Ceyrabeth's jaw dropped.

"Your sword and your life are not your own." He nodded towards Ceyrabeth and Quinlan.

"They are theirs, your commanders. And I will not be a party to desertion."

Right then, Ceyrabeth forgot how to talk, and Keiran wasn't much better. He recovered first, "But...but there must be hundreds of people who've joined you that deserted!"

"Those that you speak of did not have their commanding officer present at the time, as one would expect." Sul gestured again to Quinlan and Ceyrabeth. "Your commanders are here, however. If you wish to enlist, you will do so with their permission or not at all." Sul smiled faintly, wearily,

"We are still abiding by the rules of war, no?"

"But...but..." Keiran spluttered.

"I'd just as soon run them all through at the moment," Quinlan commented dryly. "So, I'll leave it up to Lieutenant Vallorin."

Ceyrabeth looked into Keiran's liquid-dark eyes as he looked up at her. Years before, Keiran had posed a question to her, stammering but earnest. If she had answered that question differently then, she might have the right to hold him back now. But she hadn't, and the tenuous link they had as temporary commander and soldier didn't seem strong enough. "I give it," Ceyrabeth whispered.

"You.... What?" It was Tregan who spoke, stunned into the exclamation.

Ceyrabeth lifted her head. "If his loyalty is here, I'd rather he not be forced to bring a diseased heart back to the Towers. Sir Keiran may join the Phoenix Legion."

Keiran smiled, hugged Ceyrabeth before she could dodge. "Thank you, Beth."

She didn't even bother to correct his familiarity or rebuke him for the sudden pain in her aching ribs his embrace caused. "Captain, I..." She swallowed, her next words tasting like ash on her tongue. "I ask the right to stay as well."

This time, every face in the tent locked shocked... Every face except Sul's. "Why?" he asked quietly.

"Because I..."

Sul held up a hand. "Sergeant Maul," he said simply.

"How does he always *know*?" Came an unpleasantly familiar voice as Maul stepped out from behind the tree he'd been watching the entire proceedings from. He stood in front of Sul and saluted.

"Sir."

"Sergeant Maul, I want you to hear this." Sul turned his attention back to Ceyrabeth. "If the next words out of your mouth are not the unadulterated truth, I will have Reaper Maul break every bone in your body. Am I clear, Lieutenant?"

Maul cracked his knuckles, grinning as Ceyrabeth licked lips that had suddenly gone dry before nodding, following it with a "Yes" when she realized that he couldn't see the gesture.

"You may proceed."

"I don't want to join your freak show, gods forbid. But I know you're dangerous and I believe that the best place to keep an eye on you is right here. Know your enemy..."

"...as you would know yourself," Sul finished for her. "First 'crownsbane' and now the teachings of war put forth by King Elloran. Where did you come by your knowledge, Sir Ceyrabeth?"

She frowned at his tone of faint surprise. "I read."

"A lot," Mat murmured.

"Pretty much constantly," Keiran interjected with a grin.

"Curiouser and curiouser," Sul murmured before returning his attention to the elven woman before him. "So, you intend to stay in my camp as a spy for the Witchhammers do you?"

Ceyrabeth shrugged. "Not a spy...a reminder."

"Of?"

"That there are those who have seen your beasts... And still stand." Ceyrabeth shrugged.

"You *did* ask for the truth."

"I demanded it, yes," Sul admitted. "But how far are you willing to go?"

"Meaning?"

"It's your intention to protect the world from me and mine, correct? You are a self-appointed guardian against what you call my 'beasts and monstrosities'?"

"Yes."

"Through any means necessary?"

"Yes."

"Even through my death?"

Ceyrabeth closed her eyes, knowing that her next words could very well be her last. "Yes."

"Bitch!" Maul roared as he stormed towards the girl. "I'm going to fold you in half!"

"Cease," Sul instructed in a calm voice infused with steel.

"But Cap'n!"

Sul shifted his attention from Ceyrabeth to Maul and raised a single eyebrow.

"This hopped-up little boot licker says she's going to murder you because her Order doesn't like you! I'm not going to let—"

"That is correct, Sergeant," Sul's voice cracked like a whip. "It is not your duty to 'let' anything happen. You are a soldier under my command. And if you wish to remain so, you will calm yourself and stand down."

Maul's expression crumpled under Sul's scorn, "Cap'n, I—"

Sul held up his hand. "You are a loyal man, Reaper Maul, and that loyalty is appreciated." He returned his attention to Ceyrabeth. "Take heart; I have no intentions of being assassinated. My duty to Aegreas remains and so I shall remain." His tone became more pointed, "regardless of the wishes of the Imperium, The Hierophant, or a certain ex-Witchhammer, however dedicated she may be." Sul returned his attention to Maul. "Return to your post, Sergeant."

Maul saluted smartly, grinning madly. "Yes, Sir!" He spun on his heels and leveled a finger at Ceyrabeth. "Touch him and I'll make you beg for death before the end. Got that?!"

Ceyrabeth swallowed nervously at the zeal in the elf's expression; he meant it. It didn't halt her conviction, but it did make her aware of just how carefully she would have to tread.

Maul gave Captain Sul a slightly embarrassed shrug and backed off as Ceyrabeth's brain caught up with Sul's words. "'*Ex*-Witchhammer'?" She hazarded.

"Keiran's petition to join the Legion is approved," Sul informed her. "As is yours to remain in camp."

Pellinore spoke up, "My Captain, are you certain that is wise?"

"No," Sul replied with a small smile. "But it should be interesting. Sir Keiran, if you would come with me, please."

Keiran followed the Captain and Pellinore. Ceyrabeth didn't dare look at any of her former brothers but bolted toward the side exit. She would have to face them, eventually she knew, but not right then...

The point became moot as she stopped a moment later to empty the contents of her stomach behind a tree. "'A reminder'," she mocked herself bitterly between heaves. "A reminder of how stupid a person can be, perhaps. Let me just keep an eye on you, oh mighty warlord, but please wait until I can stop hurling my guts out..."

"I told you; regeneration magic is nothing to play with." Of course, Mat had followed her. He gathered her long hair in his thin hand and held it out of her way until the queasiness passed.

"As though I had a choice..."

"I know," he replied, face properly sympathetic. "Let's get you back to Mother Reiko. Davis, you've got her other side?"

The question was answered when Corellan slung her left arm around his shoulder. Both ignored the tears streaking down her face as she heard Quinlan fall into step behind them. Mother Reiko clucked like an old hen when she saw her, but that was okay. Sort of comforting, even.

Even more comforting was the potion she was given that brought beautiful, dreamless sleep.

"I'm sorry I accused you of being a monster..." Mathias was saying sheepishly to Quin, Corellan, and Tregan.

Ceyrabeth smiled as she drifted off.

LEGACIES AND

REVELATIONS

"The greatest weapon is the truth. It undoes all deceptions, exposes the weak and fortifies the strong."

A passage from *Victor Vinguardis* (Way of Victory)

translated from Daymorian. Author unknown.

Currently banned by the Church of Imperius

"MARCH! ALL MARCH!" CEYRABETH'S FEET HIT THE FLOOR before the last notes of the horn blast that had reverberated through the walls had faded. In her groggy state, she had forgotten all about Mother Reiko's potion and would have pitched forward onto her face had the Ghen healer not heard her cry and come to reassure her.

"That is a summons for our people," Mother Reiko soothed her, guiding Ceyrabeth to sit back on the cot. Ceyrabeth's face flooded with color; of *course* she knew the difference between "gather" and "march," but she had been so deeply asleep that she had forgotten where she was.

The sides of the tent had been raised and the door flap stood open to catch the evening breeze. Ceyrabeth could see Sul's Mithrac shadow—Atiya?— raise a large ornate horn to her lips and blast a series of sharp notes. The resonance of the sound made Ceyrabeth's bones vibrate.

"The Captain would speak!" Atiya's voice boomed across the camp. Ceyrabeth winced.

"Is her voice naturally that loud or are they amplifying it somehow?"

"Atiya generally makes herself heard one way or another." Mother Reiko smiled. "You needn't go, child, if you are still feeling unwell."

But Ceyrabeth had caught sight of Keiran, in a dark shirt, pants and boots with edgings of silver, next to Sul and was already rising. She saw Mathias and Corellan standing next to each other off to the side and went to stand beside them.

It didn't take long before men, women, and even a few children huddled around as Atiya led Sul to a raised earthen mound. Pellinore stepped forward and removed a small vial from his belt. He tossed it upon the ground and a large plume of green flame exploded into existence with a loud *whoosh* that silenced the crowd at once.

"Thank you Atiya," Sul said before turning his attention to the vast crowd that had gathered at the green bonfire. "Brothers and Sisters of the Phoenix Legion. Some time ago we were accused of acting in defiance of the Imperium and by default in defiance of the Hierophant of Daymore, and his master: the god Imperius himself. These accusations were levied against us by our newest guests, Witchhammers from Eastern Daymore in service to said god." The crowd began to scowl at Ceyrabeth who kept her face carefully neutral, determined to stand her ground. "I have meditated for several days on these charges and would now answer them. May I speak for you as well?"

A roar of approval answered him.

"Thank you." Sul cleared his throat. "I derive a great deal of consolation that you have decided to allow my voice to represent your will. The severity of these charges cannot be overstated." He bent down to pick up a handful of stones.

"Heresy." He tossed a stone. Coincidentally, or maybe not, it happened to land almost at

Ceyrabeth's feet.

"Blasphemy."

Another stone.

"Treason."

The final stone lay at the elven woman's feet.

"According to canon law of the Imperium, there is only one sentence for these crimes:

immediate execution. A slow death wrought with humiliation so that our suffering may serve as an example to those who would dare follow. No peace in the next world, only an existence in the dark, banished from the sight of the church and Imperius in whom they serve. Unwanted. Unmourned.

Damned. What are we to do about this?" Sul asked the crowd.

The few suggestions offered were extremely graphic. Every word out of their angry mouths made Ceyrabeth stand straighter, her muscles tense. Quinlan, emerging from the shadows of a nearby tent moved to flank her, his mismatched eyes wary.

"Why are we here?" Sul's tone became quieter yet still somehow carried to all assembled.

"How is it that this ragtag band of heretics, pariahs, and outcasts have now come to form the largest privately administered military force in Daymore and now finds itself declared the adversary of the most prominent institution within its borders? Do we fear that if we do not take up arms that those in power will see fit to destroy us for our defiance? Or is it because we have seen the state of this world with eyes unclouded by privilege, hypocrisy, or sanctimony, and have found it wanting?"

He cleared his throat again and Atiya handed her his waterskin from which he took a long drink.

"Thank you." He coughed once. "Here we stand together from all

corners of the world in defiance of tyranny. You are all free people!"
He roared suddenly making those in his vicinity jump. "You have not
been bought or bullied to risk all that you are in this world, not for me,
nor for yourselves, but for each other! For the world itself!" He took
another drink and his tone reverted to its earlier quiet intensity.

"The Imperium, The Order of Witchhammers, The Alliance of
Guilds, the nobility, and every power and order from Daymore Kharas
to the Volca Sea would label us 'rebels,' 'malcontents,' and worse. Why?
What is it they fear? We possess only a fraction of their numbers, their
wealth, their influence. Do they fear our methods? Our ideals? Our
way of life? Or do they fear something far more dangerous than any of
these things?"

"The truth." He turned his bandaged gaze out amongst the assembled throng. "The truth. The fact of the matter is that those who would
condemn us would also have us disregard the truth, even as it stands
there proudly for all the world to see, mighty and unassailable. The
truth which has been obscured and twisted, perverted, and corrupted until it is almost unrecognizable. And not through any foul Nevaraakese plot from the east or unholy alliance of virago and demons,
no. No, not through these means, but by the unyielding arm and unforgiving gaze of the Imperium who has declared the truth to be blasphemy and us damned beyond redemption for believing in it."

The Witchhammers former and present shifted their gaze to their
feet uncomfortably, save for Ceyrabeth, whose fists were so tightly
clenched that it sent jolts of pain through her entire arm.

"I say unto all of you that this is no mere peasant uprising or he-
retical movement, rather that this is the most important crusade since
mankind's united march against the Golden Hegemony of the elven
slave lords from ancient times. Because what it deals with is the very
nature of man and the gods."

Many eyes widened at the boldness of the last statement. Atiya

handed Sul a stack of papers and an amulet depicting a woman holding aloft a flaming sword in a finely detailed ivory inlay. Ceyrabeth
gasped before she could stop herself; the idol was that of Mother War,
a goddess of battle predating the rise of Imperius, now usurped, and
fallen into obscurity. Possession of such an artifact alone was grounds
for excommunication.

"I have here transcriptions of letters, a correspondence between
a Mother..." He frowned and ran his fingers over the letters. "...a
Mother Dario in which she states her concerns about the treatment
of mages and other 'lesser citizens' as they are referred to in other
correspondence, residing in the city of Daymore Kharas. These letters were addressed to Lord Marshal Vijav Forianus of the Justicars.
For those of you who are unfamiliar with this entity, the Justicars
are a form of secret police that answers to only the highest-ranking
members of the church of Imperius. They are tasked with investigat-
ing Witchhammers and other holy knights for signs of corruption or
abuses of power.

"Now, in these letters, Mother Dario cites several cases of miscon-
duct amongst the clergy ranging from harassment and persecution of
non-believers to accounts of rape, torture, and murder amongst the
very people they are sworn to protect. Men, women, and children, too
poor or too frightened to protect themselves. And even against one
another; knights and priests of conscience, of righteousness, murdered
by their own for daring to question those in power."

Sounds of disbelief rippled through the crowd as he continued running his fingers across the page. "Here, Mother Dario quotes a passage
from the Tome of Lordly Might, one of the holy books of Imperius."
He cleared his throat. "'Those in power must maintain their power
through dignity and understand their responsibility. In exchange for
their submission, the faithful and meek shall be protected by the righteous and strong.' Mother Dario quotes this passage and asks the Lord

Marshal why this does not apply to mages, elves, dwarves, and others, asking him 'Are we not all worthy to either protect or to be protected in accordance with Imperius' laws? In his just nature and righteousness?'" Sul looked out among the crowd. "Are we not indeed?"

He took another drink of water, cleared his throat again. "I shall now read to you the Lord Marshal's reply. He starts by quoting a different passage: 'Power is the most sacred truth of Imperius. Those who hold power, either having earned it through their actions or received it as a blessing, are free to exercise that power in accordance with the will of Imperius.' Those assembled here may be familiar with this passage. It is the one that the church cites the most often to justify whatever action they have taken, no matter how brutal."

Sul frowned at the parchments in his hand. "I cannot help but wonder if their actions are what those who fought and died for the freedom of our kind all those ages ago intended or not, but I digress. Lord Marshal Forianus continues with the following, 'What you consider to be compassion is nothing more than naïveté and fool idealism. Mages and others so 'afflicted' cannot be treated the same as people. Every one is a threat to the safety of themselves and those around them. Every one, a virago waiting to happen.'" Sul smiled bitterly. "I'll pause a moment to let everyone ponder that sentiment."

The crowd's mood darkened. Hands tightened on sword hilts, bows, and staffs.

"He goes on to repeat that term 'fool idealism' many times in these letters when Mother Dario talks about caring for those who cannot care for themselves or when allowing mercy or pity to dictate their actions. Well, what ideals would the Lord Marshal prefer, I wonder? Ideals that instead embrace intolerance, violence, and fear? I think so and here is the crux of the matter"—Sul leaned forward in earnest— "what the Lord Marshal wants is for the church and those within in it to behave as The Witchhammers do and as the Justicars do. A church that will do what it is told, a church that does not question, a church that is filled with the devout in perfect lockstep, fueled by nothing more than righteous anger and blind obedience."

"Now these"—he handed the parchments back to Atiya and took from her a letter—"are letters written by a Witchhammer in Daymore Dolor by the name of Yavic ibn Geral."

"Oh, gods, no!" Sir Quinlan expostulated.

"Who is that?" Keiran asked him with a frown.

"An embarrassment,'" he stated firmly while Ceyrabeth nodded grim affirmation. "And an embodiment of everything wrong in our order."

"In these letters," Sul continued, "Sir Yavic outlies his plan for 'The Virago Solution' in which he proposes that every mage in Daymore submit to being confined physically to churches and towers dedicated to Imperius. From archmages, to children barely old enough to walk. Torn from their homes, their families, and made prisoners. Buried in a dungeon as an embarrassment to be forgotten."

Silence descended upon the crowd like a pall, everyone too horrified to speak.

"He asserts that 'Internment and forced concentration of undesirable elements is neither morally wrong nor sinful in the eyes of the Imperius. That throughout the Book of Imperius, submission was the unifying theme, that the ancient goddess Mother War submitted to the will of Imperius when he conquered her and took her power. That Her followers submitted to His will in turn.' He goes on to say here that 'Submission, obedience, and the desire to follow, is intrinsic to faith, to sanctity, and to the very nature of mankind and that by enacting internment of every mage or mage-potential, the church would be acting only as Imperius would, to ensure peace and order throughout the realm.'"

"Ceyrabeth...that's true?" Matthias posed the question, quietly, painfully. She nodded, her demeanor icy, then gestured for him to wait. Sul carefully handed the papers back to Atiya,

"Thank you, Atiya." He turned back to the crowd. "Now it is worth mentioning that Lord Marshal Vijav Forianus rejected the plan as did the current Hierophant—privately, of course. But it is also worth noting that upon that rejection, Sir Yavic was promoted by Lord Marshal Vijav Forianus to the rank of Commander for his 'dedication to the ideals of the church and unfailing loyalty.' A promotion that increased the number of mages and younger knights under his purview tenfold. A promotion that the Hierophant neither censured nor revoked."

Ceyrabeth almost laughed; Yavic had been promoted to the position she had once been groomed for. The rank bastard.

"Those bastards!" A voice screamed out from within the crowd. Others quickly joined, and the crowd rapidly approached a mob that looked ready to storm the capital and burn it to the ground.

"Is he trying to start a riot?" Corellan hissed.

Sul held up a hand and the crowd quieted. "Well, I am afraid that I must disagree with Sir Yavic's views, and with Lord Marshal Vijav Forianus and His Holiness the Hierophant of Daymore who apparently shares those views, however tacitly and instead say that the nature of faith, of sanctity, and of mankind is not in fact submission but instead something far more dangerous:

liberty."

Sul cast a look around the crowd. "I say that liberty and, more than liberty...*freedom*...is the nature of what it means to be faithful, to be sacred, to be alive. Liberty, not blind submission. And as proof, I offer the actions of those who have been deprived their freedom, deprived of their liberty," he shook his fist as he spoke. "They will rise against their captors, they will make war against their oppressors, they will fight and bleed and die, rather than surrender"—he paused for effect—"they will even follow...a woman, an escaped slave with nothing more than a name and claims that she is in fact a goddess, the Mother of War, against the mightiest empire the world had ever known, sacrificing all she held dear in the process so that the races of men and dwarves could be free of elven enslavement of ancient times."

Ceyrabeth let him have his moment, as cheers and accolades rolled in from all sides. She let him stand there and soak it in, while the rage turned hard as diamond in her gut and twice as sharp.

She bent down to pick up the stones at her feet.

"Beth, no!" Quinlan made a grab at her but was too late—she was already as close to Sul as Atiya and Reaper Maul would allow and as the crowd quieted, she deliberately dropped the stones one by one. *Blasphemy...heresy...treason.*

"You. Know. Nothing," Sir Ceyrabeth hissed, her voice quiet. She was not speaking for the masses; had almost forgotten they were there. She spoke straight to Sul. "Nothing of me, nothing of them"—she swept her arm out to indicate her Brothers—"and certainly nothing of the gods. I find it funny, that for all your talk about liberty and supposed disdain for brutality, how you had absolutely no trouble viciously robbing me of a choice I made because it didn't conform to your ideal. My story was not yours to tell and yet, here you are telling it. Will I be fitted for my leash and collar after my hair is shorn, Captain? Will it be struck off when I embrace your 'freedom and liberty'?"

"Your story," Sul gestured at Ceyrabeth. "You're from Daymore Dolor, correct?" Ceyrabeth's eyes narrowed but she said nothing. "Is that your story? You're an elf from Dolor? Is that the summation of Ceyrabeth? No, you're a young girl who grew up trapped, who sacrificed everything she was, to be included in an order who saw fit to cast aside the ancient teachings of kings and dragons passed down by Mother War and work instead to subjugate and discriminate against all followers of other faiths—especially those who are not human. Those who would grind your culture beneath their collective boot. How did that make you feel, Ceyrabeth? Knowing what they did to your people and swearing your allegiance to them. How did your family feel when you told them?"

A spasm of pain shot across Ceyrabeth's features before she could suppress it.

"I see," Sul said softly. "Your family was taken from you. Who slew them? Bandits? Nobles seeking a bit of sport?" He frowned and shook his head. "No..." He pondered aloud, "A young girl does not cut off her own ears simply for acceptance nor security...but for revenge."

"No!" Ceyrabeth couldn't stop herself from crying out.

"A demon," Sul said softly. "Your family, your community, was ravaged by a demon."

Again, Ceyrabeth was struck with a strange sense of familiarity. The way he spoke, almost to himself, working a puzzle out in his mind while his subject stood dumb, unable to stop the forward motion that would leave their secrets bare. The words, the cadence of foreign lands becoming more prominent as they continued, she had heard them before.

"The last time I saw you, Sir Ceyrabeth, you were being dragged out by two of your brothers, you were wounded, and you were screaming for justice for a man you loathed to the woman you cared for more than faith, in front of the Hierophant's Tribunal, knowing it would bring you reprimand or worse. Whoever you believe I am, is secondary to what I *know* you to be...which is so much more than you've become." Sul's face softened with sympathy. "I can't imagine how that must have felt, when her weapon pierced your shoulder and broke your heart."

"My shoulder and the state of my heart are none of your concern, you—"

"I thought it was an old injury, Beth." Keiran asked. "From when you were a child."

"It was."

"Until the Lioness of Daymore reopened it and tossed her to the wolves," Quinlan commented darkly.

Ceyrabeth whirled on him. "Quinlan!"

"The Lady High Marshal? But what does..." And Keiran understood. "You were sleeping with the High Marshal?!"

"Which is none of your damn business!" Ceyrabeth retorted. "As for her..."

Sul smiled slightly as the last piece fell into place. "'Her.' There is only one Hammer that has the conviction, and the hatred of all things demonic and infernal, to lead her company to the aid of elves in Dolor. Carmilla the Lioness. You were the squire of Carmilla Le Fanu, Lady High Marshal of the Tower of Imperius Militant." He reached down to pick up a stone. "Sir Vallorin...catch."

He tossed the stone high and above the elf's right shoulder. Her hand automatically shot up to catch it but then drew short and gasped as pain lanced through her arm. The stone fell to the ground.

"You're right-handed," Sul spoke calmly. "But you draw your weapon with your left, your shield on the right." Sul rubbed a finger across his upper lip in contemplation. "How old were you when you first broke your arm? Old enough for it to heal poorly, young enough to be taught how to use your other arm."

"You have no right..."

"Did the demons that slaughtered your kinsmen do that to your arm?"

"I was lucky it was just a broken arm," Ceyrabeth spat. "After what they did to my mother and siblings...my father..." Her voice cracked, but she plowed on. "My hiding place was good, but I was scared...gave myself away. They tried to drag me out, but I held on. The virago had summoned a demons and one of them brought a damned chair down on my arm. I fought the rest of the night with it cracked. After Carmilla and Quinlan came and took care of the bastards, they decided to take me with them. We reached headquarters, the healer tried to fix it, but it never really set right—"

"You have something to add, Sir Quinlan?" Sul interrupted. He had somehow caught the man's mounting discomfort.

For a blind man, Ceyrabeth thought wryly, *he sees a lot.*

"We didn't 'decide' anything," Sir Quinlan informed them.

"Quinlan, don't!" Ceyrabeth tried to intercept him, but it was too late. Sul motioned for him to continue.

"The High Marshal...she was just a knight then...and I responded to the rumor of virago loose in the Spinner's End of the city." Quinlan stood at parade rest as though reporting to a superior officer, Ceyrabeth noted through the embarrassment creeping through her. He was about to tell her damn life's story to this man and his whole army, so why wasn't she stopping him? "When we got there..." The older man's jaw clenched involuntarily, mirroring the fury on Ceyrabeth's face. "Utter carnage. I've never seen anything like it. There was one person left standing though, fighting like a fiend with an old kitchen knife." She shut her eyes, face flushing as Quinlan continued, vomiting words as though he had held them in too long and couldn't keep them in a second longer. "She couldn't have been more than eleven..."

"Ten," Ceyrabeth murmured.

"But it took four of the undead to subdue her. Not for long...Carmilla saw and cut them down. And when the dust had settled, this little girl asks us, 'What are you?' Not who, what. So, we told her, 'We're Witchhammers.' She said, 'I want to be a Witchhammer.' I told her, kindly, 'Only humans are Witchhammers.' I joked with her, told her... that 'her ears would give her away...'"

"Quinlan, stop!" Ceyrabeth begged. He met her eyes and did stop.

"I see," Sul replied. "I'm sure Carmilla used knowledge of your old injury to full advantage when she ultimately betrayed you, yes?"

"Yes." Ceyrabeth dropped her gaze.

"And when you found yourself alone and betrayed, I'm sure there were compassionate healers present to make sure you were not crippled or worse?" The expression on Ceyrabeth's face said it all. "I see."

"I was *not* alone." Ceyrabeth raised her eyes to Quinlan and stood taller. A smile flickered on the old soldier's weathered face.

Sul nodded, then gestured to Pellinore. "Lieutenant step forward please, if you would." The elf complied unhesitatingly as Sul placed a hand on his shoulder.

"This man is an escapee from the slums in Daymore Merenia after conditions became intolerable. He attempted to liberate his fellow kinsmen from slavery only to have them cut down by members of the nobility. He is the only survivor, having made it all the way to Central Daymore with an arrow lodged in his leg. He is an elf and fellow rebel; we can all see that. But can we see that which is equally true; that he is, in fact, the bravest person assembled here?

If he were human and a worshipper of Imperius and his captors were virago or elves or orcs or dwarves, he wouldn't be standing here now dubbed a 'traitor' and an 'insurgent.' He would not in fact be able to stand at all, he would be so heavily laden with accolades and honors from the

Imperium. They'd write songs about him and sing them as hymns in the greatest cathedrals of the Empire. The most esteemed scribes of our age would fill their books with his tale to be told to our children and our children's children and so on down the ages because we would insist upon it. His name would be as familiar as King Rodham, Emperor Sei-Jung, or Anastasia the First."

Sul approached the roaring green bonfire his eyeless gaze fixed on Ceyrabeth. "Yet, if the Imperium is right, if Yavic ibn Geral and The Hierophant and High Marshal Carmilla are right, what are we to do with that most famous of rebels, Mother War, and those men and women she inspired to break the golden chains of bondage the elves of old had placed upon them?"

He held up the amulet for all to see, the symbol of Mother War glowing a faint green in the light of the alchemical fire. "What of their conceits in defying an empire? Her malcontent in giving

Questor and the other elves who surrendered a home of their own instead of the headsman's axe? It was she who said: 'Let war rise and fall like the tide and when it has fallen, let peace amongst men prevail. Glory in battle, contentment in peace and in all things honor.'," he quoted before raising his voice once more. "What in Heaven's name shall we do this embarrassing truth?" He examined the amulet carefully, running his fingers across the visage of the warrior goddess. "I see only one solution."

He tossed the amulet into the fire where it burst into flame and was consumed. The only sound that could be heard was the crackle of ivory and leather burning and from somewhere the soft sound of weeping.

He continued speaking to the crowd, "The other night, I was speaking to my friend, Reaper Maul, and we were discussing Orcish traditions he learned from them during his time amongst their tribes. He explained to me that the orcs practice a form of ancestor worship. They believe that the most exemplary of their kind once they die become war spirits, ancestral figures from the past that watch over them. These 'spirits' serve as ideals to be aspired to and in doing so they never really leave their people."

He took another drink and cleared his throat, coughing slightly and rubbing his chest. "It made me curious as to who the 'spirits' associate with Mother War and her army of faithful were Talon bin Sahay: the engineer whose mighty creations brought them victory time and time again against overwhelming odds. Mischa Mulah: the swordswoman who could slay a dozen men in a single duel. Velios of the Thunder Hand: the elven mage who defected to the human army and became one of their most trusted and valued leaders. Too long have we denied their wisdom, their insight, their example. Perhaps it is fear that the devotion that we cling to so very dearly would be seen as flawed in their eyes. Perhaps in our fervor we fear that those ancient eyes would look upon our actions in their name and be ashamed."

His expression softened. "There is a truth that I have aspired to, an ideal and it is simply this: We owe our devotion and our allegiance to the future and not the past. That which came before, no matter how sacredly it may be held, is not a guide to the future. Clinging to the past will not make us stronger; learning from it will, and when we have learned all we can from it, then it is to be put aside in a place of remembrance and not reverence." He turned his expression skyward. "I call upon those ancient spirits to hear us, those great and glorious rebels. We desperately need your gentle wisdom and your counsel. Help us overcome our fears, our frailties, ourselves, so that we may finally grow as a people and learn to embrace the future and not the past. And if in doing so we anger the church or the nobility or the Witchhammers and war ensues, then let it come. And may it be finally the last crusade for the freedom of humanity."

Silence reigned in the camp as Sul turned away from the crowd and Atiya slowly led him back to the tent. "He's not long for the world. You know that," Mathias stated to Keiran.

"He looked fairly hale to me." Tregan sauntered over, going to stand next to Corellan when he saw the glare Ceyrabeth was favoring him with.

"Don't be an idiot, Tre. He's tainted. It's spreading fast." Mat turned back to Keiran. "You're really going to pledge yourself to someone who's going to shuffle off into the Void?"

"We all die sometime," Ceyrabeth answered, her voice far away.

"Beth..." Quinlan said cautiously. "What are you thinking?"

"He knew. He knew *me*, knew who I was, and he has from the start," she replied as she watched the crowd disperse. "And I promise you this; he may be courting Death, but he will not shuffle *anywhere* until I know how he knows. This I swear."

Long after those gathered had dispersed, only Ceyrabeth remained standing ramrod straight and staring at the last of the green fire as it sputtered and went out and all became serene and dark once more.

REUNIONS AND

RECOLLECTIONS

"A man will fight and die for a variety of things: his home, his loved ones, his ideals. Create a home for him within your ranks, foster a love for his fellow soldiers and command guided by ideals that speak to him, and he will fight and die for you."
—A passage from *Victor Vinguardis* (Way of Victory) translated from Daymorian. Author unknown. Currently banned by the Church of Imperius

ANOTHER DAMN RECRUITMENT REQUEST. WORD APPARENT-ly traveled quickly in this camp, as Keiran also received several from various battalions within the Legion. The first one for her, delivered by Atiya, had been from the Crimson Vanguard; Maul's ber-serkers, the second from the Sentinels consisting exclusively of Chalicemen. As though she would ever even consider throwing her lot in with a bunch of savages or inbred Palebloods, even if she *was* joining Sul's Carnival of Horrors, which she absolutely wasn't. And now this one from the 'Black Shepherds', whatever the Void they were. At least their commander could spell. Ceyrabeth wrapped the missive around a nearby rock and hurled it into the nearby river. She turned her back on it with a huff and found herself watching her now-reunited brothers interact.

Sir Corellan was a good man, Ceyrabeth mused...well, actually, he was too suave for his own good and too pretty to know it, not to mention thick as stone when it came to cues of subtlety. But he was mostly good-natured and relatively kind...but Evric didn't know that. She watched as her fellow knight sat beside the boy, telling him some overblown story about a dragon he once fought (if one word in ten were true, she would eat her helm), completely oblivious to the fact that Evric was shrinking from him as though he had the Plague. Sir Keiran with his gentle, cheerful demeanor the boy could handle; Sir Corellan was a loud, overwhelming unknown.

She was accustomed to watching for signs of magic, so she noticed when Evric's hair started to stand up with excess static. She decided an intervention was a good idea for all involved. "Alright, Sir Dragon Slayer," she said, sauntering casually toward them. "Quit filling the poor boy's head with lies and go look to your armor. I saw a rust spot earlier."

Corellan jolted to his feet with a strangled noise in his throat before beelining to the tent they were using as a temporary armory. Ceyrabeth smiled at Evric as the cry of "Argh! Gods damned bogs!" reached their ears.

She shook her head wryly. "What a peacock..." Evric finally cracked a smile, and the smell of ozone dissipated. "You don't have to be scared of him," she assured the lad. "In fact, I can show you how you don't have to be scared of anyone ever again."

"Really?" Evric's blue eyes lit like sunshine on an ocean surface, his voice almost crackling with eagerness.

"Sure." She drew her sword from her scabbard and offered it to him hilt first. "First though, why don't you go take a few swings at that practice dummy?"

Evric dubiously accepted the blade. He hesitated for a moment before he lit into the dummy like a berserker, hacking and slashing with reckless abandon, clutching the sword with both hands. He was missing more often than not, but it was when Ceyrabeth realized that he was swinging with his eyes closed that she intervened. "Woah there, dragon slayer," she said. Her dark eyes were dancing as she gently caught his wrist. "You've got the wrong sword for two-handed fighting. Besides, fighting like that slows you down and we must play to your strengths. I'll bet you're fast."

Evric scuffed his toe in the dirt. "Not that fast…"

"Oh yeah? I saw you almost dodge those guards the first day we came in. You came awfully close to getting past them. Besides, there's not much to warriors like us…" She poked him lightly in the belly, then again in the side until he was squirming and fighting giggles. "… so we're harder to hit. Not like that big rock-hands Reaper Maul or Sir Mathias the Sunken."

Both men were nearby, as Ceyrabeth well knew. Good natured, if somewhat explicit from

Maul's side, protests reached her ears from both injured parties. She cheerfully ignored them.

"Fighting for us is like dancing. You've seen dancing before, right?"

Evric nodded hesitantly. Ceyrabeth raised her blade and bowed to him before beginning to hum a popular Daymorian tune. She went through a simple, fluid series of basic sword exercises, all the while timing her thrusts and parries to the flow of the music. "Like that." She handed the sword back and seeing he was still hesitant, she stepped behind him. Ceyrabeth wrapped her right hand around his as it gripped the hilt, tapped his feet into position with her own. With a 'one-two-three' they were off, Ceyrabeth leading him into steps that wouldn't seem out of place in the Palace ballroom—except for the deadly blade in their hands.

Evric relaxed when he started listening to the music and started to get a feel for the way Ceyrabeth was moving. Toward the end, she released him and with a quick forward thrust that would be the envy of any swordsman, Evric skewered the practice dummy straight through the throat. "I did it!" he exclaimed, delighted.

"That you did." Ceyrabeth smiled at him. "With some serious practice, no one will be able to touch you without your permission again."

Evric didn't have the words to thank her, but it was alright. She let him process his newfound strength and teasingly bumped shoulders with Sir Quinlan, who had been watching. He had taught her in much the same way, when she was just a scrap of a girl with big wide eyes and trust for no one.

"He'd have done better if your blade wasn't as heavy as he is," he said with a grin.

"He'll gain his muscle."

"Still..." Quinlan replied. "He should have his own blade."

"If it was in my power, I'd get him one. But I'm certain that my request for weaponry wouldn't be well received."

Hours later, with darkness just starting to fall, Ceyrabeth entered her tent. She had just pulled a brush through her hair when she saw something glimmer on her bedroll. It was the silver hued hilt of a blade. She carefully drew the blade from the serviceable leather sheath, remembering Sir Toliver who had pulled his blade too quickly and gotten a face full of rashweed powder, but she needn't have worried.

The blade was clean, sharp, and just the right length and balance for a boy who hadn't quite come into his full strength yet. She wound the thin green ribbon attached to the hilt around her finger. "So, you were listening..." she whispered into the dusk as a smile inexplicably played across her lips. "Good to know."

"You're going short blade now?"

"Keiran Ehingen!" Ceyrabeth yelped and almost dropped the blade on her foot. "Now look what you made me do! How long have you been there?"

He rose from the single chair at the tiny table in the far corner of the tent with a grin written large across his dusky features. "Long enough to tell that you're losing your touch."

"Yes, apparently being a test subject for dark magic does something to you. Whoever knew?"

He sobered at the ice in her tone. "Beth..."

"No." Ceyrabeth shook her head adamantly. "Whatever it is, I don't want to know. No." She stared at the ground when he tried to catch her eye, turned her back on him when he moved his face into her line of vision. Keiran stood next to her, shoulder to shoulder, turning her around in a slow circle as he moved and she tried to avoid him.

"Beth, I'm getting knighted tomorrow. Captain Sul's knighting me."

"Lovely. Go bother him."

"Be my second."

"No." Ceyrabeth wrinkled her nose. Help him to get ready to be knighted by that...*crownsbane*? The armoring ceremony itself took at least an hour, not to mention the meditation before, *and* the actual knighting....at least half a day in the company of demons and uncouth idiots? Never. "Go away."

"Please Beth? You promised."

"Back when you were a Witchhammer!"

"Neither of us are Hammers anymore. Be my second." He stepped into her path again, moved when she moved. "Be my second. Please."

"No."

"Be my second."

"No!"

"Be my second!"

Ceyrabeth slammed down hard with her heel on his foot, shoved him when he jerked back. Keiran's feet got tangled in the scabbard of Evric's new sword and he went down on his rear with a crash. Ceyrabeth whirled around, fists clenched, ready to unleash *another* vehement denial...when she saw his face, locked in its rictus of comical surprise, and laughed instead.

"You gigantic idiot! Fine! Yes, I'll be your second if you get out of my tent without another word."

Keiran's face lit up as he scrambled to his feet. With a bow and a whistle, he was gone. Ceyrabeth stared after him, unsure of whether to laugh or cry, until she blew out her candle with a sigh and stretched out on her bedroll. She would need all the rest she could get.

"YOU'RE SURE ABOUT THIS?" CEYRABETH HELD THE shoulders of Keiran's surcoat as he finished buckling his vambraces over his tanned wrists.

"Positive. Captain Sul...I know he's odd..."

"Odd?" Ceyrabeth barked a laugh. "Kei, he used the blood of an abomination to regrow my ears and then sprinkled powdered iron on me."

"Yes, but...you heard him talk last night. You can't tell me that it didn't speak to you."

Ceyrabeth had no answer. The truth was that Sul's words had lanced through her, like the first time she had read the Book of Kings and realized the truth of the Order, what a shadow of its former glory that it was. And then came Sul, speaking as the knights of old had, and she...

"You could come too. Pledge your life to a better cause. You know the Hammers just threw you away."

"It doesn't matter, Kei. I'm done with causes," she told him. He raised an eyebrow at her but didn't comment.

Ceyrabeth lifted his coat and he slipped it on over his gleaming new armor. He looked the very picture of what a soldier should be. Ceyrabeth hugged him to hide the growing lump in her throat, then slapped him in the face. "Ow!"

"*That's* for desertion," she informed him. Then she planted a kiss on the cheek she had slapped. "That's for being a good and decent man. And because I'm grateful it'll be Captain Sul dealing with your antics from now on, and not me."

"It's time." Atiya stuck her horned head in and announced. Keiran nodded, straightened his shoulders, and strode confidently out the door. Ceyrabeth counted ten, and then followed into the command tent.

Her first thought was that there wasn't going to be a knighting, simply because there soon wouldn't be a Captain to do it. Sul's skin was chalky, soaked with sweat in the firelight. He seemed to have lost weight even in the short time they had been there. His high cheekbones looked almost skeletal with the gaunt hollows of his cheeks beneath. But still...Ceyrabeth had to admit, he was in full mastery of the moment. Every person in the room waited for his words, his motions. Keiran went to one knee before the man who, even ill, commanded attention.

Sul rose slowly but surely to his feet, "Keiran Ehingen. Tell those present what your intentions are."

"My intent is to swear fealty to the Phoenix Legion, Sir."

"Just so." Sul nodded and stretched his hand over Keiran's head. "Offer virtue without audience, and without compensation. Remain true when all others hide behind lies. Remain courageous when all others falter from fear. Remain loyal when all others betray from greed and envy. Live well and true when others live in dread and doubt. Be the best of all that you are and inspire others to do same. And when you die, die as you have lived: With quality and with honor. Do you solemnly swear this oath?"

"I swear it."

Sul reached into the small silver bowl that Atiya had in her huge hands. "Then be reborn—" He started to cough again, hard wet sounds that sounded like something breaking inside. His fists curled into tight white knuckles, his legs locked, keeping him standing as the painful spasms wracked his body. When it was over, the Captain turned his head to the side and spat, blood splashing onto the ground as he turned his attention back to Keiran.

"Then...be...reborn," Sul said between wheezing breaths as he sprinkled ash over Keiran's hair and shoulders. "From your own ashes into the Phoenix Legion. Are you prepared to receive your first command?"

"I am, my lor—my Captain."

"*Rise.*"

Sul's tone contained something far more powerful than whatever ravaged his body and Ceyrabeth realized that that was Keiran's first command. To rise, to go and do, to follow his oath by whatever means necessary. She gasped as though doused with ice water. For just a moment, she had seen the world Sul was working toward, reborn from its tortured state into something better, braver. Her mind took her back to the moment she had sworn her first oath...

"Beth!" The man with the long white hair beckoned to her excitedly. The little girl threw herself at him and he hoisted her easily up to his shoulder. From there she was able to grab the low- lying tree branch and perch on it lightly as a bird.

"Oh, aren't they beautiful?" she breathed. Imperial Steel armor reflected the sun in dazzling bursts, before glinting richly on the gold embroidery on each aubergine surcoat. The horses tossed their heads proudly, seemingly oblivious to the heavy weight on their backs. No broken-down

plow horses, these; they were magnificent, fiery-eyed animals that would
be the first into battle and the last out.

"Witchhammers are trouble," a neighbor man said worriedly. "If
they're here, someone'll get hurt sure as fate."

"I thought that Witchhammers were supposed to protect us?"

"And so they do, kitkin." Her father shot a quieting look at the neighbor that Beth completely missed because she was too busy trying to identify whether the cloth in the soldier's coats was samite or velvet. She had
seen both in her father's shop but in very small quantities—both were
expensive and therefore in low demand among the denizens of Spinner's
End.

"I'm going to be a Witchhammer, then! I want to protect people."

Young Beth's firmly spoken words brought a ripple of laughter. "You're
raising a dreamer, eh, Vallorin!" called a voice from the crowd.

"Yeah, and I have the Duchesse Meirin in my cellar," laughed another.
A shadow fell over Vallorin's mobile face, and he reached up to lift Beth
down.

They were well away from the road before she spoke again, "Did I say
something wrong, papa?"

"No!" Vallorin took a deep breath, moderated his tone and crouched,
taking Beth by the arms. "No, dearest girl. Never let anyone tell you what
you can and cannot be. If you truly want to protect people, you do it. Just
because they don't have the strength or the drive or the sight to do it, it
should not stop you. You earn your shining armor and your warhorse
and your honor, and never lose sight of what it is that you want. You'll
be afraid, and you'll have pain and sadness on the road, but don't ever
stop. Eh?"

She nodded. Her father was doing it again; sometimes he had a bit
of the seer about him, as Brother Arturo from the Church always said.
When he got so intense, the only thing to do was agree. She had seen it
a few times, always directed at others. This time though, his words sent

strange warmth through her chest, made her scalp tingle and her cheeks heat. She wanted to run and scream and cry and laugh and dance and she didn't understand any of it. Then Vallorin smiled, and the effect broke.

"Calm down, my girl!" He tilted her chin, smiling wider at the sight of the sable eyes that were an exact copy of his own. "You're all eyes."

"Am not," she vehemently denied. The other children teased her for them, called her 'Horse Eye' and other harmless, yet rankling insults that children seem to be so good at.

"Will you promise me then, my Beth? Promise you'll remember?"

"I will, Papa. I swear it."

"I swear it," Ceyrabeth whispered as the past deposited her back into the present. She dashed towards the Captain, stumbling along the way. Osen lifted its head to scowl at her, no doubt concerned about her sudden intentions. Sul quieted the creature as she practically tossed herself on one knee at Sul's feet, her eyes wide and far away. "I swear fealty to the Phoenix Legion."

"Something has changed," mused Sul over the ripples of surprise issuing from the audience. "When you first stated your intentions to stay, you made it quite clear it was to act as a self-appointed safeguard against the Legion and against myself, in the name of protecting the world." His expression shifted. "This is not someone with an agenda upon her knees before we assembled today. I look into you and see only fervor. Something has changed. What is it?"

"I remember," Ceyrabeth replied simply. "My father...he was a seer and a druid, but my mother...she was a warrior. I remember singing the hymns of Mother War set to a different tune, lest we be discovered and executed for treason. I remember her telling stories of the Companions, of the kings of old, the world that was and could be. I always wondered why, why the silence and the sneaking? I hated it, as she did. My father compelled me to earn my honor, my faith, and my strength. But how could I when the breath was being strangled out of me, out of all of us?"

She paused, glanced at Keiran. Suddenly the thought came that she was stealing his moment, his time in the spotlight and she stood, intending to apologize and run, but he grabbed her wrist. His eyes had taken on a strange intensity, as though he could not tear his gaze from her.

"Talk, for gods' sake, Ceyrabeth. Talk. Answer the Captain's question."

She turned her attention back to Sul. "When I was left alone, I saw the Witchhammers, saw their power and knew what they were before, and I heard the call. I mutilated myself and knelt before a god I loathed to be a voice amid people who had it in them to be so much *better* than they were." She felt she was rambling, but she pressed on. It didn't matter if it made complete sense because for the first time in too long, she felt completely genuine.

"Instead, they ruined me. I was crippled, shackled to a slavish, selfish pile of dogma that protected only themselves and their lust for power. I bowed to my gods, prayed my prayers, and worked in silence, choked on it for half my life, working myself to bone just to see good men like Sir Quinlan, Sister Marina, Sir Robert Averis..." Her voice cracked at the last, but she shook her head and plowed on, "...be laughed at and shunted aside and worse. And you...you may be warped, tainted, and the Green knows whatever else...but you gave me back my voice. No, you *commanded* that I speak truth and now..."

Her eyes bored into his face, studying the thoughtful expression it wore. "You will drag your people to hell and back, of that I have no doubt. You also have heard a call and you won't leave a mile untrodden until your purpose is ended. And it won't be a short one, no. It'll be your lifetime, and mine and probably everyone else's here until it is done. No one stands under as much agony as you do for a short, easy destiny. I cannot be silent again, but I would not waste my life screaming at those who will not hear, all on my own. I'm so *tired* of working alone, but I cannot ask anyone to follow me. But this ragtag group of lost ones follow you already, as I will and shall until I can speak no longer, or you become as the Church is now—foul and corrupt and faithless—trampling your people for power. Use my strength, Captain, and I promise I will never allow you to forget *why* you march. This I swear."

For a moment, silence reigned in the tent. And then Sul smiled, faintly, and raised his goblet in toast. "Well said. Your words have swayed me, Ceyrabeth Vallorin. But to be a member of the Legion is to put forth more than words. Deeds are required. Your final trial is a trial by combat." He held up his hand to forestall her already forming protest. "Strictly non-lethal. Two combatants in a ring of sand. Last one to remain in the circle wins."

The elven woman sighed. She could do this. It would be no different than the countless hours spent in the training yard with padded staves. She rolled her neck experimentally. She was drained and the old injury to her arm pained her.

"Battle does not wait for us to be at our full potential," Sul chided gently, once again seeming to read her mind.

"I accept your terms," she announced. What choice did she have really? "Who will I be dueling?"

Sul's smile turned into something dangerous. "Well, we do currently have just the *one* opening." Slowly he turned his bandaged gaze towards Keiran.

"Uh-oh," Keiran muttered.

"I will not," Ceyrabeth said simply.

"Then are words all you have to offer after all?"

"I will not be responsible for denying his chance to be part of something he believes in deeply."

"You would deny it to yourself then?"

"If those are my choices, yes."

"Very well." Sul returned his attention to the lad. "Sir Keiran you will face Reaper Maul in unarmed combat. The only rule is that you must remain conscious and stay in the circle. You may begin now."

"*What?!*" Both Beth and Keiran gaped.

"Heh heh heh," Maul chortled, cracking his knuckles. He took a menacing step forward, the various skulls and bones dangling from his armor clacking ominously.

"No!" Ceyrabeth protested. "I'll...I'll duel him! Better me than that lunatic behemoth."

Keiran looked between the two of them and then slowly nodded, "Okay Beth. Let's do this."

Captain Sul and Atiya led the way out of the tent and to the mound where Sul had given his speech to the Legion just days before. They picked up more people on the way, some chattering in excitement, jockeying to get a better look.

A circle was quickly made in the sand as each of them was given a sword. Ceyrabeth rapped her finger on the edge; dull, blunted, heavy. Sturdily made, but cheap iron. Keiran was swinging his blade experimentally. It was heavier than he preferred, she could tell from his expression, the center of gravity back towards the grip. He opted for a shield, but she declined, knowing that her speed would be a better ally.

And then it just the two of them in the ring, circling each other with trepidation.

"I'm sorry," Keiran said softly.

"So am I," Ceyrabeth whispered in return.

"Begin," Sul's voice rasped.

Keiran came high with his thrust, too high. Ceyrabeth ducked and struck his stomach with the flat of her blade, knocking the wind out of him and causing him to stagger.

"You're not fighting an orc!" she hissed at him. "Adjust your form."

"You're not supposed to be helping me." Keiran swung again and this time his aim was true. She had to parry quickly with no time to riposte as Keiran swung two more times. Whether he was meaning to or not he was striking her wounded shoulder and it was beginning to ache. She could feel the pain and with it her temper rising. He rained multiple blows upon her blade as she fought purely defensively, trying to figure out some way, anyway, that this didn't end badly.

She was *definitely* not as quick, or as strong, without the wyrmscale in her blood. Her guard faltered as her arm wavered and Keiran's weapon connected with her jaw. There was a flare of white pain and then everything went red. "Beth are you all rig..."

Ceyrabeth charged him, her movements going from defensive to all-out attack. She hammered into his shield, holding back just enough to not accidentally kill him but no more than that. Her fury drove her, rode her as she drove her sword into his shield again and again and again.

There was a loud *crack* as the wooden buckler caved. Keiran quickly tossed the pieces, but Ceyrabeth didn't even pause. Three more heavy blows and Keiran's sword shattered. He fell backwards, landed hard on his back a hair's breadth away from the edge of the ring.

"Beth." He held a hand up his other arm pressed tight against his chest.

It would be so easy. She thought to herself. One last blow and he would be unconscious, and she would win...

What in the name of the gods am I doing?!

Immediately, the red haze dissipated. "Keiran." She reached down and helped the man to his feet, hugging him tightly. She couldn't find words. If Sul held to his word and there *was* only one place in the Legion, she had just taken it from him. She put trembling hands on either side of his jaw and rested her forehead against his.

Keiran pressed his cheek against hers, wet with sweat and tears as her own tears flowed down her face. "I yield," he whispered.

Ceyrabeth's hands dropped and they clenched, fury starting to well up. "No, Kei. No. I yield." This was her *friend* and she'd be damned if she'd allow anyone to manipulate her into—

And then, there was applause, slow though not mocking. Sul's applause was joined by others and soon the entire group was cheering.

"The Legion is only as strong as its bonds of brotherhood to each other," he whispered, his breath rattling in his lungs. "You have both shown loyalty to one another, compassion and restraint. You have proven that you are warriors who believe in a code, in something greater than yourselves and not simply automatons to take orders. You have both passed," he rasped. "Well done."

Ceyrabeth whirled to look at him, anger dissipating as fast as it had come. She heard something in his voice she had never expected to hear—relief. Sul had *wanted* them to win.

Both of them.

"I must retire." Sul rose to his feet with some assistance from Atiya. "Enjoy yourselves this evening. Reflect upon what you have learned; about the Legion, about each other, about yourselves."

"I learned something about you as well, Captain," Ceyrabeth declared boldly.

"Oh, this should be good," Keiran muttered, cradling his wrist.

"What did you learn, Sir Ceyrabeth?"

"I learned that it will not be *quite* as much of a chore to follow you as I once thought it would be."

He smiled again, that ghostly smile, like a mirage or afterimage of happiness before gesturing at Keiran. "Have Mother Reiko tend to your wrist and then enjoy the accolades from your new brethren."

"Yes Sir." They both saluted, and then turned toward the healer's tent. Halfway there, Ceyrabeth threaded her arm around

Keiran's waist. He squeezed her shoulders in reply. She tilted her head to listen to his words, then her laugh rang out as it seldom did—a real one, light and almost girlish. Sul's head tilted toward the sound.

"Captain." Atiya was holding the flap of his tent. "I will go fetch the tools."

"Do so, Atiya. Thank you."

SUL HAD JUST FINISHED POURING THE WINE WHEN ATIYA entered his tent, ducking her massive horned frame to clear the entryway.

"Evenzio Vineyards from the age of the maritime kings," Sul explained gesturing to the wine. A friend of mine in Sahath introduced me to it."

"I wasn't aware a man in your position could afford the luxury of friends," the Mithrac replied flatly.

"We are not friends?"

"No, we are not, and we never will be. Your actions made that impossible."

Sul took a sip from the goblet and nodded slowly. "Yes, I suppose they did."

"It's time to clean your wounds," she informed him shifting the conversation to a less loaded topic.

Sul exhaled. "Past time, I imagine." He sat in his chair. "Shall we begin?"

Silently, Atiya unfurled the leather bundle she carried to reveal a bevy of gleaming metal instruments and tools. All manner of hooks, blades, and clamps gleamed dully in the soft light of the tent's vast interior. "I will require more light."

Sul gestured to a small brazier filled with seething coals that glowed sullenly in the dark. Atiya moved to it and gripping it in her large hands, heaved it up and deposited it next to Sul with an audible *thump*. "The solvent?"

"The locked cabinet."

Atiya moved to the large wooden cabinet made of wood so dark it was nearly black and engraved with a pair of dragons sinuously entwined. Their tails formed the large dark handles of the enormous piece of furniture, and she lightly fingered the strange lock mounted into its twin setting: a series of concentric three disks engraved with symbols with a series of small holes.

"Your locks are becoming more intricate," she commented placidly.

"The creeping onset of paranoia as my elder years descend upon me, no doubt."

Atiya shrugged and turned her attention back to the combination lock. She regarded the different symbols for a moment then arranged the different symbols meticulously before placing her fingertips into the holes and twisting hard. The lock snapped open, a variety of bolts retracting back into main body of the lock and the doors swung open silently.

Inside was a dazzling array of vials and bottles of every shape and size imaginable from all corners of the world in a rainbow of different colors, each filled with some strange liquid or powder. Mounted on the inside of the doors themselves were large racks that held every kind of tool and instrument one could conceive of.

"You are always clever," she commented tonelessly as she reached into the cabinet and removed several vials.

"We all have our gifts."

Atiya turned to face him. "Though not all of us keep them."

"Point taken."

Atiya closed the massive wooden doors gently. Instantly the bolts snapped back into place and the lock was once again secure. She stood before the brazier, selected one of the vials and poured some into the smoldering coals. There was a flash of bright, blue light and a small jet of azure fire burst into existence before dying down almost immediately. The now-blue coals gave off considerably more light, bathing the interior of the tent with a strange ambiance that made everything appear slightly unreal.

"The tools must be properly cleansed." Atiya carefully slid each tool from its leather loop or snare and gently placed one end of it into the blue coals. Almost instantly, the metal began to smoke and a strange smell like ozone filled the air. She grabbed several bowls and buckets and placed them near Sul's feet. She then knelt before the older man seated in the chair and carefully prodded the soiled wrappings around his eyes; blood had soaked completely forming a visage as black as pitch. "I will have to cut these off."

Sul nodded and waited patiently as Atiya reached into the brazier and removed a pair of scissors, its twin blades now glowing faintly. Carefully, she snipped at the soiled wrappings. Every time the blades encountered his face, there was the faint hiss of flesh searing. Soon the scent of rotting meat filled the tent's confines. With a final cut, the bandages fell limp, held to Sul's face only by the encrusted blood.

"This will hurt," Atiya stated flatly.

"Yes."

The Mithrac woman took a hold of one edge of the dangling material and began to peel it from Sul's face. Bits of flesh soon detached as the caked-on blood formed a grisly adhesive. Soon red blood flowed followed by streams of black ichor as wet lumps of skin and fat fell into the network of bowls and buckets that had been set up, splattering like wax. Sul's hands tightened on the arms of the chair, but he remained still as strip after strip of tissue was peeled from his face in long gory lengths.

The last bandage was removed and tossed into the brazier, the collected blood and oils of

Sul's skin bubbling and hissing angrily. Atiya dragged the fire closer to see more clearly and her eyes widened.

"For someone of your placid temperament to look so perturbed, it must be grave indeed," Sul said quietly.

"Yes," Atiya murmured softly and took out fresh bandages to staunch some of the blood as she examined the damage. The flesh around his eyes and the immediate area was black and sickly with a pulpy appearance like rotten fruit. Necrotic tissue had swollen to form bloated cysts filled with black pus. Veins pulsed and throbbed over the glistening skin and deep furrows of exposed muscle tissue, riddled with cancerous growths shuddered and trembled with each of Sul's inhalations. As Atiya peered closer, a particularly large mass just above Sul's left eye it abruptly burst and black and yellow pus flowed down his face. She quickly wiped it away.

"The infection has spread," Atiya announced. "The tainted tissue will have to be amputated and scoured clean." Atiya gently took the man's ravaged face. "You must control your emotions—your anger and pain only feed the corruption."

"Noted," Sul replied with eerie stillness. "Proceed."

Atiya removed a small length of leather and inserted it into Sul's mouth. He bit down and nodded his readiness. She removed a large scalpel from the flaming sconce and placed the tip of the blade just above the bridge of his nose. She pushed the blade into his face. His teeth ground against the bit in his mouth and the wood of the chair creaked as he squeezed the armrests. Atiya sawed her way a millimeter at a time until she reached between his eyes.

Flesh sizzled and popped as blood and ichor streamed from the incision as she cut around down the edge of one eye and then the other and then up towards his hairline, forming an inverted "y." Taking a small fishhook, she pierced the flesh in several places and slowly peeled it back, pinning it in place and laying the tissue underneath bare.

Retrieving several small clamps, she meticulously pinned several more pieces of corrupted flesh in place.

"I take it your meeting with Renala went well?" Atiya asked as she took the bit from his mouth.

Sul smiled without humor at her attempts to distract him. "Well enough considering our history. We're confident that Tarah will cooperate, however unknowingly."

"You are playing with fire, Captain."

"How very droll, Atiya. And they say those in your condition possess no wit."

"I possess no emotions," Atiya replied placidly as she continued to meticulously dissect his face. "I still retain wit." Sul's lip curled and then he winced, gripping the chair more tightly. "Are you all right?"

"Continue your work, Atiya."

"Yes Sir." She picked up another. "Tarah is an extremely volatile individual, by her very nature."

Sul grimaced, either from pain as Atiya continued to impale flaps of his skin on hooks and pin them to his face or in irritation at her concern. "I am aware, thank you."

"And yet you insist on involving her."

"She is uniquely qualified for the task that lay ahead us."

"That being?" She began plucking shreds of rancid flesh from around his eye carefully with tweezers.

"The winters in Daymore are more punishing than almost anywhere else save for Reaverlund. Our forces will need shelter from the season as well as our stores replenished before spring."

"And you're confident that the Iron Kingdom can be persuaded to make these things available to you?"

"Exceedingly confident. The dwarves are obstinate, but they are susceptible to the two most basic core tenets of diplomacy."

"Which tenets are those?"

"The same tenets that all sentient beings are susceptible to: greed and fear."

"Innocent people will die," Atiya replied.

"Innocent people will always die," Sul retorted. "And a great deal more are going to die before this is all over." He shifted his weight. "Blood is the currency of change, Atiya, and the change we seek to manifest has a high price indeed." He gestured to his partially flayed face. "As you can see."

Atiya shrugged and removed a large, curved blade from the flames. She forced the edge under the swollen masses that had taken root in Sul's face. With a sharp twist of her wrist, the blade sprang open causing four metal spikes to burst forth. He screamed as Atiya wrenched the spikes as deep into the gory wound as possible and then pulled with all her might. The growth and the surrounding tissue were torn nearly completely free of his skull, dangling by only a thin thread of pitted skin which she severed with the scissors. She peered into the wound, blood bright and red gushed from it and nodded her satisfaction.

Removing a brand from the brazier she stood over him.

"Proceed," he commanded.

Holding him down with one hand, she pressed the glowing brand into the open wound. His entire body shook as the pain robbed him of his ability to scream. After an agonizing several seconds, Atiya removed the brand and examined her work as Sul nearly collapsed out of the chair. A monstrous scar had already formed, angry and red, but clean. She reset the spiked tool, set it into the fire for a moment and regarded him with a critical eye. "Shall we continue?"

Sul raised his head and nodded. Atiya removed the tool from the brazier and examined the next growth.

An hour later, the last of the diseased tissue had been removed. Sul was breathing shallowly, the upper portion of his face a mass of bright red scars and inflamed flesh with smoke trailing away from it in thin foul-smelling wisps.

Carefully, Atiya made a small incision into each puckered scar and nodded in satisfaction as each bled bright red. She critically examined the small shards of glass that formed the latticework replacing the man's eyes. "The shards will also have to be removed and cleansed."

Sul simply nodded as Atiya removed a pair of small round speculums and affixed them into Sul's eye socket. Adjusting the instrument, she examined the shards. "It is fortunate you do not possess eyelids, which makes this easier. Unfortunately, the muscles that would control your eyeball still react normally to external stimulation, so the restraints are necessary."

"I do not require an explanation, Atiya, merely your accommodation. Please proceed."

Carefully, she removed a long thin spike from the fire, half its length glowing blue and smoking faintly and began examining the shards.

Sul's voice was calm, "I assume you remember the correct sequence?"

"Certainly," Atiya reassured him and then she pressed the tip of the needle just under Sul's eye socket, slid the length of heated metal under the bone and began burrowing upward. Sul gasped at the agony and heat. The needle met resistance briefly as it hit bone. Atiya twisted the spike and applied more pressure. There was the soft crunch and Sul jerked once before the instrument finished its trip through the man's face, its tip now lodged behind his eye.

"How does it feel?" Atiya asked.

"It's excruciating," he informed her in a calm but strained voice. "Which means it is firmly lodged in the bone and not the brain itself. It will prevent any shards from tumbling backwards into my skull. You may proceed with extraction."

"Yes, Sir." Removing a small chisel and mallet from the blue flame, she gently tapped experimentally against each shard of iridescent glass in Sul's eye socket. She felt one small piece, near the center of where

Sul's pupil would be had he possessed eyes, shift slightly causing her to nod once. Inserting the very corner of the chisel adjacent to the shard, she tapped it lightly with the mallet: once, twice, thrice and the shard fell free from its mounting.

"Tilt your head forward," she instructed as she removed a small bowl made of obsidian that possessed several small grooves along the smooth, concave surface of its interior. There was a faint sound as a piece of glass, no bigger than a thumbnail fell from Sul's face and landed in the bowl. It trailed a thick strand of viscous black ooze behind it. "Keep your head forward and let it drain."

Sul gave a slight nod of his head to indicate he heard the instruction as Atiya brought the obsidian bowl to the brazier. Carefully removing a pair of tongs, she collected a single coal from the burning fire and placed it within the bowl. There was an angry *hiss* as drops of corrupted blood boiled away. When it was over, she took a small pair of tweezers and with exacting care, arranged the shard into a small groove perfectly shaped to accommodate it along the bottom of the bowl.

"One down," Sul murmured softly. "Twenty-nine to go."

After several hours, the deed was done. Atiya dabbed at an errant drop of black fluid near the corner of Sul's eye socket and dropped the rag into the bucket on the floor, now heavy with a noxious tarlike substance: the extract that had been drained from Sul's face and eyes.

Sul's empty eye sockets looked cavernous in the blue light of the brazier. Atiya carefully maneuvered the last tiny shard into its allocated groove in the bowl. Every piece was accounted for.

"Now to purify," Atiya commented tonelessly. Sul managed a wry smile.

"I'm familiar with the process thank you."

Atiya gently placed the bowl into the roaring azure flames. Soon the bowl began to take on an eerie glow and the scent of ozone intensified.

Piece by searing piece, his eyes were reassembled and reinserted into his skull. When it was finished over an hour later, Atiya wrapped Sul's eyes in clean linen. "How do you feel?" she asked.

"Better." He got to his feet smoothly. "I believe I hear a celebration outside. Let's see how our newest knights are acclimating."

"You wish to study their interactions with the Legion under less stressful circumstances."

"Exactly so."

"Yes, Sir."

CEYRABETH COULD NOT REMEMBER THE LAST TIME SHE had danced. And honestly, that was a pity because she loved it and was quite good at it. Carmilla had hated diplomatic functions, so Ceyrabeth had often acted in her stead.

She had lost Keiran to a grinning, hooting bevy of women early on but found no lack of willing partners to spin her around to the bright, pounding beat that the fiddlers and drummer were currently putting out. When she paused, breathless, Maul slammed a mug of something into her hands.

"What is this?" she asked suspiciously.

"Does it matter?" he asked with a wink.

No, Ceyrabeth reflected. No, it didn't. She drained the mug, grimacing at the taste. It was alcohol, it was strong, and it tasted like spit. "I'll have another." She dropped the mug back into his hands and with his roar of a laugh ringing in her ears, she slammed back another.

She was cradling the same mug in her hands, sitting on the grassy side of a hill and watching the revelry when Sul found her. "It's dwarven ale," he informed her quietly.

"What?" She coughed and rolled the taste of it around her mouth trying to banish it with her tongue. "Dwarves don't drink alcohol."

"Stone dwarves don't drink as a rule, no. They can't afford to have their senses addled when they are surrounded by things that want to kill them. But there are special occasions when they let down their guard and indulge in a little brewing. I managed to acquire a few casks of this after helping them with a crisis in the Iron Kingdom. They needed a good plan and good people to stabilize the region, and I could supply both."

"You've been in the Iron Kingdom?" She nearly choked. Growing up she heard horror stories about that place, *'Be good or the stone people will drag you underground'* had been popular with the parents of her neighborhood.

"Amongst other places." He gestured to the revels. "The celebration is for you as well, Lieutenant."

"Is it still Lieutenant?" she asked.

"Indeed. You earned your rank. I would not strip you of it."

"That's kind. Thank you." She gestured out to the swirling mass of happy people below. "As for the celebration...I was there for a bit. The hors d'oeuvres were tasty but this beer is awful. I guess it didn't pair well with a wounded heart."

"Stronger alcohol is required for that I believe."

She couldn't repress a laugh. "Did you just make a joke?"

"A small one, perhaps." His countenance shifted to something approaching sympathy. "Do you wish to discuss it further?"

"You already know too much about me, Captain." She smiled wryly at him. "Never you mind. Unless you care to tell me why you baited me into telling my life's story when we both know you already knew it." She waited for a beat, shrugged. "Eh, never mind. It doesn't matter tonight. Tonight, you made a loyal, brave-hearted, slightly stubborn young man perfectly happy, and I guess I'd call that a win." She looked up into his face for the first time and smiled a bit. "You're feeling better?"

"I am. Thank you"

"That's good. The screaming worried me. Mathias was furious, said if they'd take better care of you in the first place, you wouldn't have to go through that level of agony... He guessed every four weeks or so. That about right?"

"During periods of calm, yes. During periods of great emotional stress and turmoil such as I've experienced over the last few days, I require attention more frequently to keep my condition in check."

"You mean, times like losing your temper and regenerating an elf's ears with bizarre magic?"

"For instance."

Ceyrabeth leaned back on her elbows and surveyed him for a moment. The alcohol had loosened her tonight, but more than that she felt a compulsion to say the words that were pressing on her tongue. Things could be said here in the soft blending of twilight and dusk that could never be spoken in the harsh, unforgiving light of day. "I'm so sorry for you. You're going to say I needn't pity you, but I do. You're up here on this hill, always watching, so close to them"—she gestured toward the celebration—"but would you ever ask me to dance? Not that you'd want to, but *could* you even if you wanted? Maul didn't even ask, just galloped me away with that huge, splendid laugh of his, and I think that gives him a freedom you'll never have."

There was silence for a long time and then, "You're right," Sul replied. "These are my people and though I am *of* them I can never be *amongst* them. That is the price of power." He gestured with his head. "I lead these people, I command them, I direct them, I even punish them when needed. Their lives and their deaths are in my hands and that is my responsibility. I treasure each and every one of them because they are my men, my Legion...and at any moment I may order one or ten or a hundred of them to their deaths because that's what war demands."

"And me? Would you order me to my death? Or Keiran? Evric?"

They both already knew the answer to the question, but she still felt like she needed to ask.

Another pregnant silence and then, "Yes, I would."

"Of course…"

"And if given the opportunity…I would also ask you to dance."

Ceyrabeth laughed aloud. "But you're much more likely to order me to my death?"

"Just so."

So, he still felt. He would mourn her, aye, but he would also rejoice with her. With them. A commander who cared deeply for his people, against it all. Ceyrabeth felt something loosen in her very soul, like she had been living without air for too long and was suddenly able to take a deep breath.

"Enjoy the rest of your evening, Lieutenant," he said and turned away. "Time with your old comrades grows short. You should make the most of it."

"Thank you, Sir." With a shrug she took a long pull of her drink, and this time the taste made her smile.

NIGHTMARES IN

WAKING

"Warfare is an exercise in deception and truth. To deceive the enemy and yet remain truthful with those who are loyal to you. Trust may be tested with deception, but deception cannot be used to earn trust."

—A passage from *Victor Vinguardis* (Way of Victory)
translated from Daymorian. Author unknown.
Currently banned by the Church of Imperius

CEYRABETH TURNED AND STRETCHED, FEELING A CURIOUS *lack of tension in her muscles. The wind blew soft and warm against her bare skin, scented with salt from the sea and rosemary from the keep's kitchen garden. "Beth." Ceyrabeth turned toward the husky voice with a smile. Carmilla stood by the open window, blonde hair tossed by the fragrant breeze, not a stitch on her strong, fair form. Ceyrabeth propped herself up on her pillows and beckoned languorously with one finger.*

Carmilla came to her with a smile, willowy limbs swaying seductively...long fingers reached lovingly for Ceyrabeth's face...

Carmilla's head split open like an overripe melon before transmogrifying into a ravenous set of jaws. A horrid chittering filled the air.

Ceyrabeth realized belatedly that it was not her lover reaching for her, it was the creature. It was far too late to run, but she fought anyway, ripping off tentacles, gouging the thing's eyes...

And she fell out of bed, flailing, for the fifth time in a week. She lay on the ground, thanking the Gods that it was a short drop, before pushing herself into a sitting position.

"Are you quite alright?"

Ceyrabeth looked up to see Pellinore standing in her doorway. "I did knock," he stated mildly.

"I believe it." Ceyrabeth got up, trying to retain a shred of dignity despite being clad only in her underclothes. "Can I help you?"

"I have a note for you from the Captain." Pellinore handed her a small envelope. Ceyrabeth took it from him, read it, then read it again.

"Is he serious?"

"I've never known the Captain to waste words. It's a standard request to all new recruits, barring restrictions of religion or country of origin. Have you any such restrictions?"

"No." Ceyrabeth tried not to spit the word back at him. It wasn't his fault the Captain was a... She banished the word from her head before it found its way to her tongue.

Pellinore nodded. "I thought you would like an escort. I'll be outside when you are ready."

The morning had dawned cold and gloomy as Pellinore led her across the camp to a small, open-air stall. She could hear the singing before they even got near, the voice of a very young man, clear and sweet and trumpeting an extremely bawdy drinking song. A short, fat figure was hopping from one foot to the other in time to the music around a chair that appeared to be on wheels.

"Don't worry. Bayard's harmless even if he is a little...strange." He felt compelled to reassure her.

"You don't have to warn me of 'strange' in this place, Lieutenant Pellinore."

"You've not seen us at our best." Pellinore caught himself and thought for a moment. "Although, maybe the Captain would say that because you've seen our uniqueness, you have seen our best."

"Yes," Ceyrabeth replied frostily. "His calling dark magic to reshape my ears against my will felt very unique indeed." It was good that it was a short walk to Bayard's stall because it was a very silent one after that.

Pellinore hailed Bayard, who immediately stopped and theatrically whirled around. The little man, with many elaborate bows, gushed his joy to see Lieutenant Pellinore again and to finally meet the young lady that caused such a stir about camp. "Why, it is almost as good as being back at court!" He assured her with a wide grin.

Almost without knowing how it happened, Ceyrabeth found herself seated in the wheeled chair and Bayard was examining her hair with exclamations of delight. "Such shine! Such heft! Why, half this glorious mass alone would bring a king's ransom in certain parts of the Ghenlands!"

"You sell...hair...in the Ghenlands?" Ceyrabeth asked with mild disgust. The Ghen were the people bordering Daymore to the north and were considered to be little more than heretics at best, savages at worst.

"But of course, Madame! You do not think we magic our beautiful wigs from nothing, do you?"

"The majority of it must go. Captain's orders. It's up to Sir Ceyrabeth what's done with it after that," the lieutenant informed him.

"It's all yours." She waved the consideration away. Bayard's face lit like a lamp.

"You are a paragon and a saint, to warm a man's heart as you do with your golden words and generosity. But, ah! I have thought of a small thing." The man's fingers rapidly braided a thin strand about the width of Ceyrabeth's finger. He tied it off at the end then snip! And he handed the length to her. "A souvenir. Now...here we go!" With a slice of his shears, a waterfall of ruddy gold fell to the floor. It didn't take long before Beth was completely shorn, the back of her head a mass of artful spikes and the front just brushing her jaw. "Voila! You are a work of art in any civilized city in the world."

She glanced in the mirror he held out to her to be polite but stopped cold when she saw the face looking back at her. The face of an elf. A face she had never seen before. She touched trembling fingers to her reflection and thought how utterly strange it was that she would not recognize herself.

She looked vaguely tomboyish yet without surrendering her femininity. She looked...good.

Oh gods, save me.

She had to focus on something else and as she saw Pellinore seated at the small table behind her busily scribbling away, an idea formed in her head. "May I?"

Pellinore glanced at her, surprised to hear her voice was calm, even pleasant. "By all means." He handed her a featherless quill and piece of parchment with some ink.

Ceyrabeth scribbled a brief note on the parchment and folded it. "Could you make sure Captain Sul gets this? I'd do it myself, but frankly if I never saw him again it would be too soon."

"Yes yes, you go Lieutenant, and I will escort the young lady safely home!" Bayard stepped between them with another flourishing bow and offered his arm to Ceyrabeth. She took it, though the difference in their heights made her bend to do so, and the last Pellinore saw of them they were heading toward the mess tents with Bayard talking a mile a minute.

He turned away toward where he knew the Captain had laired and though he was loath to disturb him, he knew he would want to know that his orders had been followed.

Atiya answered his gentle knock on the outside post of the tent, thanked him for the information and took the note from him. She ducked back inside and relayed the information to Sul.

"Pellinore says she took it with good grace. Bayard was unmolested in any way."

"Unsurprising. She is of a disciplined nature," Sul replied non-committedly. "Usually."

"Yes, and right now she has turned that disciplined nature against you."

"Sir Ceyrabeth will be tended to in time, but your concern is noted Atiya and appreciated."

He indicated the note. "That is mine, I imagine."

"Yes. I can dispose of it if you'd prefer," Atiya offered.

"Your vigilance is commendable...," Sul's tone was light and only slightly sardonic, "...but unnecessary in this instance. I have never shied away from unpleasant words." In reply, she handed the packet to him. It took just a fold or two to open; a long braid glimmered red-gold in the candlelight as it coiled around a short, simple message:

Calling 12:1

He permitted himself a mirthless chuckle. "Quoting scripture from a god she never followed." He folded the letter up. "Still, a clever choice."

Atiya picked up the paper and examined the slanting writing. "Calling 12:1?"

"I believe the line that is meant to be significant in this case is '*I fear not the Legion, though they rise and set themselves against me.*'"

"Ah." Atiya nodded understanding. "It seems Sir Ceyrabeth likes to have the last word."

"She is welcome to it," he replied tossing the letter into the brazier. "The last word and the final word are not always one-in-the-same."

"As you say, Sir."

"You're going to tear it."

Ceyrabeth glared at Keiran, but she did stop tugging at the hem of her new uniform. The high-collared shirt with its tracings of silver was comfortable but all she could see was Quinlan's face when he saw her wearing it. And that time was coming soon. Quin and the others were to be released tomorrow morning. She had already worked out the details of transportation and provisions for each man with Lieutenant Pellinore. She had told Tregan, Mathias, and Corellan, leaving Quin for last.

"I can do it, Beth."

"What?" She realized that she hadn't heard a word Keiran had said.

"I can tell Sir Quinlan, if you'd rather not."

"I'm not worried." But she was. It was safe to say that without Quinlan, she would not be alive to have this conversation. It seemed like the worst kind of betrayal to send him out to face Carmilla by himself, not to mention joining a group he had severe misgivings about right under his nose.

"Do you want me to come along?"

"No thank you."

She was severely regretting the lack of backup when she was standing at the entrance to Sir Quinlan's tent some ten minutes later. Ceyrabeth took a deep breath, straightened the hem of her shirt once more, and entered.

"So it's true." The disappointment on his normally stoic face made Ceyrabeth's chest ache.

"Quin, don't look at me like that."

"Why not? Seems like you've done nothing but make a scene since you got here."

Her brow furrowed. "That's not fair. We didn't know..."

"But then you did. And you still chose to join up. I expected it from Keiran. But you've seen things, Ceyrabeth. You know exactly what their Captain is." He had been pacing as he spoke, but he whirled on Ceyrabeth. "He's no different than Carmilla, Ceyrabeth. He will throw you away when you don't serve his purpose anymore!"

"We don't know that!" Ceyrabeth defended.

"Don't be naïve, girl. You're chasing power, just like you did with Carmilla."

"I'm not! Quit dragging *her* into this!" Her words sounded like the words of a petulant child, but her stomach was a knot of anxiety. There wasn't one thing Quinlan had said that she hadn't thought herself. But how could she explain the compulsion that led her to pledge her allegiance? That in that moment, when he spoke of honor and duty, Captain Sul had reminded her so strongly of her father that she had seen his ghost? She couldn't. "Don't go back, Quinlan. You could join!"

The words hadn't even fully left her mouth before Quin was talking over her. "Ceyrabeth, have you lost your mind entirely? Never. Never. I took vows to my order, and I will die under those vows. That's what a vow *is*, little girl. Not negotiable, unbreakable."

"But Carmilla will..."

"Give me a little credit, Ceyrabeth. I do have a few friends left that could maybe just maybe stand up to Carmilla the Lioness." The faintest ghost of a smile passed Quin's lips. "Besides, who was my squire at one time?"

"She was..."

"That's right. Don't sulk. You'll wrinkle your pretty face and with eyebrows like that, you'll need to preserve your complexion or nobody's going to want to marry you."

Ceyrabeth stuck her tongue out at him and his smile became a bit more genuine. "That's a girl."

"We'll be enemies Quin. What if he gives me the order to kill you?"

"Then you decide what's more important. What is more important, Ceyrabeth?"

She knew what he wanted to hear—duty. Duty was always more important than emotion. But the words stuck in her throat. "You and the others are to be released. Captain Sul told us to meet at the edge of the bog at daybreak. It's the fastest way to the main road."

"If you say so, girl." Quinlan sat, his broad hands resting on his knees palm up. A hum started in his throat and Ceyrabeth knew he was preparing for prayer. It was a blatant dismissal, but it could have been so much worse. She turned to go but felt a tug on the back of her shirt. Quinlan, still humming the start of the Canticle of Imperius, nodded his head toward the spare chair. Ceyrabeth sat beside him and turned her palms up.

DAWN WAS EARLY ENOUGH WITHOUT HAVING TO FUNC-tion to tell your only friends goodbye, Ceyrabeth reflected the next morning while trying to stifle a yawn. Quinlan hadn't helped by running through the *entire* Hymn of Imperius...they hadn't finished until the shattered moon had faded utterly from the morning sky. Ceyrabeth's voice was a wreck even after the canteen of honey lemon tea that Pellinore had handed her before they had collected Mathias, Tregan and Corellan and started walking.

Captain Sul and his Mithrac servant had met them at the edge of the bog. Ceyrabeth was a bit surprised; he took the time to hand each man directions and a saddlebag filled with provisions. Tregan had just cracked a joke about turning into pack mules when the Captain shook his head.

"I have mounts ready for you." Sul gestured at someone unseen from behind him and continued to speak, "head north along the Imperial Highway until you reach the Danoth Tanis, the Western Road."

"But Mat and I are headed the other way..." Tregan interjected. Sul kept speaking as though the interruption had never occurred.

"You will encounter refugees fleeing from Torvalen in an attempt to avoid the Taintbrood. I would ask that you aid them in this."

"And why would you care about the well-being of refugees?" Quinlan asked suspiciously.

Sul shrugged slightly. "Their deaths serve no purpose and I have no interest in seeing them added to the ranks of the Taintbrood."

Quinlan's eyes narrowed. "The ranks of the Taintbrood? What do you mean by that?"

"A story for another time. You must hurry, however."

A squat man with aristocratic features led several horses out from the trees behind Sul. They were clad in heavy barding from face to hooves yet moved surprisingly lightly.

"Eregost!" Quinlan cried out, overjoyed as he recognized his mount's familiar coloration on the small patch of hide that showed between the gaps in the armor. "I thought I'd lost you in that damn bog." He reached up and under the armor to stroke the mare's nose, then frowned. The horse showed no signs of recognizing him or even acknowledging his presence. "What's wrong girl?"

A thunderous bellow tore through the relative quiet of the swamp as an enormous beast flew over their heads. The flapping of its enormous wings sounded like thunderclaps. It threw back its head and roared so loudly that the trees shook.

"That's a dragon!" Mathias cried out as he and the other Witchhammers dove behind cover, hands on their weapons.

Sul and Atiya by contrast did not appear startled in the least. Sul lifted his face to the sky and smiled. "Good, she got my message."

Ceyrabeth had also stood her ground as she peered intently at the horses. They had remained stock still during the entire encounter and even now, completely unrestrained, remained eerily calm. She approached Eregost carefully.

"Ceyrabeth, what are you doing?" Mathias asked as he tried to clear the ringing from his ears.

Ignoring him, Ceyrabeth reached up to the straps holding Eregost's chamfron to its face. The scent of cinnamon and pitch overwhelmed her, and she coughed, turning her face away.

"Eregost...?" Quinlan whispered, his face going pale as snow.

Ceyrabeth registered the scent of death a moment before she turned to face the creature, "Gods!" she gasped, dropping the horse's helm to the ground.

Eregost's flesh had been almost completely stripped from its head. What little remained was thin and desiccated. Large bandages had been applied over various portions of the creature's face and body which only added to its ghastly appearance. Green pinpoints of light glowed profanely from deep in its eye sockets.

"May I introduce Narl-Shu the Third," Sul offered by way of explanation, motioning to the squat man who was just now coming out from hiding after the dragon had flown by overhead. "An extremely talented necromancer from the land of Nevaraak."

"What have you done?!" Ceyrabeth demanded furiously.

"You are running out of time," Sul countered. "No living mounts could get you to the refugees in time to save any of them. These mounts require neither food nor rest. They will gallop tirelessly for as long as is required."

"They are possessed!"

Sul shook his head and gestured to the Atiya. Placidly she handed him an apple.

"Eregost!" Sul called out and he lobbed at apple towards to

reanimated creature. Eregost leapt forward, nimbly caught the apple, and began chewing on it.

"No demon inhabits these creatures. Each has retained a portion of its original self." "That's not..."

"It's time to ask yourself what you believe," Sul hissed, his tone becoming glacial. "What is more important to you: your lying, timid morality or making it to those refugees before they are butchered to the last child?"

Ceyrabeth swallowed an angry retort, digging her fingernails into the palm of her hand so hard that it drew blood. "I loathe you."

Sul nodded. "You have that right." His tone went colder as he approached the elf. "But you will obey my commands for as long as you serve within the Phoenix Legion. Are we clear?"

If Ceyrabeth could have drawn her sword and cut his head off right then and there, she would have done so with a song in her heart. Instead, she carefully knelt before Sul, "What is thy bidding..." She glared daggers up at him. "...my Captain?"

"You evil bastard!"

Ceyrabeth was bowled over as Quinlan charged Sul, his fists raised. "Quin no!" She tried to call out.

Sul waited calmly as Atiya stepped away from him. When the enraged knight was almost upon him, the Captain pivoted on the balls of his feet and slapped his palm hard against the back of the man's head as he charged past. The extra momentum of the strike was enough to set him off-balance. He overstepped and tumbled forward in a heap of rage and metal, plowing through a thick bed of reeds and landing in a large pool of bog water.

Ceyrabeth clamored to her feet as Sul calmly turned to regard the rapidly sinking knight,

"Quin!" Shooting Sul a murderous look, she raced to the edge of the pool and stretched out her arm.

"Take my hand!"

"I can't..." The rest of Quinlan's words were lost as he swallowed a mouthful of water as Sul regarded the entire drama dispassionately.

"Captain!" Atiya pointed at the pool, her tone suddenly strained. Something that resembled an oil slick was noiselessly gliding over the surface of the water towards Sir Quinlan's flailing.

"Quinlan. Get out of the water. Now!" Sul's voice betrayed a hint of stress that made Ceyrabeth's blood run cold. She had not seen him display the slightest note of anxiety in her presence much less the urgency that that now filled his tone.

She looked past Quinlan and frowned at the oily thing. "What is that?"

"Ceyrabeth, get him out of there." His tone was still carefully modulated but the undertone of urgency was rapidly becoming dominant.

Without a moment's hesitation, Ceyrabeth removed her dagger and with a few quick cuts, slashed the straps holding her armor in place. She clenched the dagger between her teeth and dove into the water towards Quinlan. The oil slick had gathered speed and was writhing back and forth, slowly becoming more substantial as it drew closer to them.

Focus! Ceyrabeth grit her teeth, driving the image of the oily writhing darkness from her mind and directing all her attention to saving her friend. She reached the man and began sawing at the straps to his armor while keeping his head above water and half-swimming, half-wading towards the shore, away from the slithering menace.

"We're not going to make it!" Quinlan cried. "Leave me!"

"Never!" Ceyrabeth dragged the man closer to the muddy earth that marked the edge of the pool. They were so close...

The oil slick reared back up like a serpent and hissed at them, opening something that resembled a wide mouth. Bits of slime and detritus drippled from it, and she was reminded forcefully of her nightmare.

We're not going to make it. Ceyrabeth thought bleakly. *Gods...*

There was a blur of movement and a loud splash. Suddenly, Sul was in the water between them and the malevolent entity in the water. He brandished a large red crystal towards the gelatinous creature.

"Invoco nomine Neriah ille qui stabat coram urente!" The red crystal flashed with light and Ceyrabeth suddenly felt lightheaded and strangely overheated. A pulsing sensation went through her body that set her teeth on edge. *"Voluntas non valebit Vyrantus te!"*

The crystal flashed crimson and the creature shrieked with a sound like a thousand claws across stone as it began to flow rapidly away from the red light.

"Invoco nomine Corin qui prohibuit rubiginem!" Sul advanced relentlessly upon the shrieking entity. The water in the pool had begun to bubble and foam as if it were boiling away. Ceyrabeth hoisted Quinlan out of the water into the waiting arms of the others and turned to watch Sul. *"Voluntas non valebit Krayvan te!"*

The creature shrieked long and loud and rose, looming high above the pool.

"Gods preserve us..." Mathias whispered in dread at the sheer size of the creature towering over them. It lunged...

And with a chittering roar that nearly rivaled that of the dragon and froze the blood in their veins, a writhing mass of flesh and claws burst from the trees.

"You shall not have him!" Chirak shrieked in a chorus of gibbering voices that emitted from all over its contorting body. Ceyrabeth was shocked to see her former lieutenant's head dangling from a stray portion of tissue. His eyes were wide open, and his mouth emitted a steady gurgling wail.

Tentacles burst from Chirak's rapidly shifting form and wrapped around the oily creature, pulling it close. Arms and legs and other limbs that couldn't be identified exploded from Chirak's twisting flesh to propel it forward, colliding into the viscous creature in the pool of water. Sul dove out of the way as gibbering flesh and oily putridness tore and clawed at each other. Mouths and horns tore their way free from Chirak to bite and stab at the thing. Parette's head began wail louder as the flesh bubbled and then split apart, bone and blood spraying the ground as the bisected face became another set of jaws that sank deeply into the other creature.

Chirak wrapped itself around the creature, bones stretching and then breaking before being reabsorbed into its body. Flesh melted and flowed like wax, tearing and then reforming as it coiled around the oily entity which continued to thrash and shriek. Chirak constricted, its prey thrashing within the confines of its prison of flesh and tissue to no avail. It squeezed and squeezed, the sound of skin bursting as jagged pieces of bone erupted from the seething cauldron of tissue filled the air.

And over all of that; the hissing of the dark entity and the chittering guttural roaring of Chirak, deafening in its intensity. With a final wail, both creatures disappeared beneath the surface of the water and silence descended upon the scene like a pall.

Ceyrabeth didn't even have time to steady her shaking hands before she noticed a strange sight; Sul was half-draped over a log, making no effort to pull himself back to shore. And even stranger, neither Atiya nor the necromancer were making any move to help him. She could clearly see the red bloom of his blood spreading rapidly over the water. He was going to be in serious trouble if he didn't get out of there soon. She was just opening her mouth to comment when Sul lost his grip on the log and soundlessly slid under the water. She waited for Atiya or the necromancer to make a move, but neither did. Narl-Shu just shifted from foot to foot, wringing his hands, and Atiya stood there placid as a pastured cow. "He'll drown!" She finally exclaimed.

Atiya nodded. "Yes."

"Let him, and good riddance," Quinlan muttered.

Ceyrabeth felt the moment shimmer with startling clarity; she could let him drown. Just stand and do nothing, walk away from the Phoenix Legion knowing that a dangerous man—possibly *the* most dangerous man she'd ever known—was gone from the world. There were two *extremely* horrifying creatures lurking beneath the depths, an excellent reason to stay on land. But...

"Beth?" She barely heard Quinlan's questioning voice. A thought was screaming at the edges of her consciousness, drowning almost everything else out, a fact, a truth, unavoidable...

She owed him. She owed him her life, and now Quin's too. She teetered on the edge of indecision for two ticks of a second and then...

"Damn it!" she exclaimed furiously before diving back into the vile, malodourous water.

It took three attempts, but Ceyrabeth finally came up triumphant. She hauled Sul up onto the bank, Tregan and Mathias helping her. "He's not breathing," Mathias noted. Ceyrabeth immediately flipped Sul onto his stomach and slammed both her hands down on his back.

"I...am *not*...breathing air...into your lungs!" she informed him between blows. "So you...had better...*breathe*, Gods damn you!"

Almost as though responding to her demands, Sul seized under her hands and expelled a gush of bog water from his lungs, following it up with great, hacking coughs as his body tried to rid itself of the foreign material. "That's it." Unconsciously, Ceyrabeth ran her hand up and down his back in comforting strokes. "Steady..."

"That wound looks nasty." Mathias crouched beside her. He gingerly pulled cloth away from Sul's side and examined what looked to be a claw wound.

Coward though he normally was, the second someone was injured Mathias transformed into a steady stomached, utterly exceptional field medic with a spine of iron. Ceyrabeth threw him her pack before she stood. "Patch him up," she commanded. He nodded acknowledgement but she didn't even see; she was already stalking across the short distance toward Atiya and Narl-Shu.

"What in the *Void* was that?!" Ceyrabeth, delayed fear and rage pumping adrenaline through her veins, exploded with the force of a thousand suns. "You completely, utterly *useless* sacks of steaming bull dung! Traitorous, cowardly, weak-willed...that was your Captain out there! Your leader! And you were just going to let him drown like the moony-eyed, minstrel maidens that you are...by the Goddesses' Ever Holy Tits, I could just flay you both alive!"

"Violette..." The name was almost too soft, but somehow Ceyrabeth heard it through her tirade. "Violette!" She turned and saw that Sul had pushed himself up to a sitting position. He was facing her, and what she saw made the blood drain from her face. Mathias had removed the sodden bandages around Sul's eyes to keep filthy bog water away from a jagged cut on Sul's hairline, and Ceyrabeth caught full sight of the scar tissue that proliferated the top half of the Captain's face. The sight, along with the pleading tone of his voice, drained the rage right out of her. "You shouldn't talk like that...in front of...the baby. Promise me..." The light caught his eyes and Ceyrabeth gasped.

Where she had only seen only bindings over his eyes, now there were dozens of tiny shards of colored glass that morphed into different patterns and reformed. The likeness of pupils and sclera would emerge, assembled from minuscule pieces of crystal before they would swirl and then fade away to be replaced by other seemingly random shapes and patterns. The effect was hypnotic as the prismatic shards spun transformed like a kaleidoscope.

It was bizarre. And alien. And beautiful.

"Violette?"

His voice broke the spell and Ceyrabeth shook herself violently to clear it; he was delirious. She turned her back on Atiya, who had stood like a deactivated golem under her onslaught and went to crouch by Sul. Ignoring the fact that she had no idea who Violette was and there wasn't a baby anywhere in the Phoenix Legion that she remembered seeing, she reassured him. "I promise." "Good." A brief smile flickered over his face. "She learns so fast now...remembers everything. Violette? Why can't I see? It...hurts, Violette!" He seized her hand, and she was completely unsurprised to find it already burning with heat from fever.

"It's time to rest now." Ceyrabeth patted the back of his hand gingerly, nodded when Mathias tilted a vial in Sul's direction. "Just relax."

"When will it stop?" he rasped.

Ceyrabeth felt the change like an electric charge in the air. One moment Sul was talking to the mysterious 'Violette' and the next, she would have bet her left arm that he knew exactly who she was.

The honest truth was that the pain would likely never end in Sul's case, but she didn't have to decide whether or not to tell him that. Mathias waved the vial under Sul's nose and the Captain slipped back into unconsciousness. Ceyrabeth gingerly lowered him to the ground.

"Red poppy," Mathias said to her questioning glance. "It'll help with the pain too, but not for long."

"Help me get him up," she replied. "Quinlan!"

"Here." The answer was a bit sullen in Ceyrabeth's ears, but she let it slide.

"I'm taking Eregost."

"The demon horse?!" Quinlan recoiled.

She rolled her eyes. "Out of all the things we've seen and that's what gets you?" She huffed, "Yes, the demon horse. Help me get him..."

"No."

Ceyrabeth's eyebrows almost hit her hairline. "No?"

"No. You may be willing to jump into a poisonous bog for your new

Captain, but I'm certainly not going to do anything that will prolong his life span."

Ceyrabeth bit her lip against the explosion of fury that sent stars skittering across her vision. "Fine," she replied through the taste of blood, metallic across her tongue. "Then get your *arses* on those horses and ride to Torvalen. Or are you willing to let them die too?"

Ceyrabeth saw the flicker of indecision on Quinlan's face before he nodded consent.

"Torvalen, then Daymore Dolor. What do we tell Carmilla?" he asked.

"The truth, of course."

The truth that would brand both her and Keiran traitors, that would spell the end of the life that she had worked so hard for. Quinlan's face softened with pity as he nodded again and swung up into the saddle of the nearest horse. Tregan and Mathias followed him. "Strength of Imperius Militant be yours, Ceyrabeth."

"And with you all." That was all she trusted herself to say. She turned to try and hoist Sul into the saddle…and found herself face to face with Sir Corellan. She had almost forgotten he was there. He hadn't panicked with the dragon or the horses, hadn't made a sound when the bog monster attacked. But there he was, silently helping her lift the Captain and depositing him gently on Eregost's back before swinging into his own saddle. He briefly clasped her hand before riding away and Ceyrabeth knew with certainty that she would see Sir Corellan again.

But for now… "Let's take you home," she told the unconscious man draped in front of her. And with a loud "Hyah!" they were speeding off toward camp, Atiya and Narl-Shu following closely behind on their own mounts.

WHEN THEY RETURNED, ATIYA LIFTED THE UNCONSCIOUS
Captain from the saddle as if he weighed no more than a child and carried him back into his tent. Ceyrabeth moved to follow. "No," Atiya
said tonelessly. "I will tend to him."

Ceyrabeth opened her mouth to object. "Oh, because you did such
a bang-up job last—" The rest was lost as Atiya dropped the flap to the
tent cutting the elven woman off.

The Mithrac woman lowered Sul onto his cot, his glass eyes wide and
unseeing as she removed something from her belt and placed it beneath his
nose. The effect was immediate; he lurched straight up in his cot coughing.
Atiya placed one massive hand on his back to steady him.

"Report," Sul croaked.

"All transpired as you commanded," she reported. "Neither Narl-
Shu or I interfered when your life was imperiled. Ceyrabeth took it
upon herself to rescue you, then accosted us both. She has a very...col-
orful...vocabulary." She shrugged.

Sul nodded as Atiya handed him his onyx pipe. "I'm pleased to hear
it."

"Who is Violette?"

Sul remained still for a long time. Then said, "where did you hear
that name?"

"You were delirious. The creature's venom had taken hold of you."
She gestured to the claw wound on his side. "Is she important?"

"She is neither your concern nor your business." Sul's tone possessed
the finality of the grave as he lit his pipe. "Are we clear?"

Atiya shrugged fractionally. "It would appear that Ceyrabeth
passed your test."

Sul nodded and ran a hand through his graying hair. "The first of
many."

Atiya tipped her massive head. "To what end?"

Sul's smile would have made the Mithrac shiver if she were capable of processing emotion.

"Why the only end that matters." He blew out a plume of smoke. "Utter, complete and total victory."

That afternoon, dressed and with his wounds bandaged, Sul was poring over a map when a knock sounded outside the tent. "Captain," Pellinore's voice called out. "There's a—"

The tent flap was swept aside, and a tall woman garbed in leather armor pushed her way past the elf.

"—woman here to see you."

"Thank you, Lieutenant, she is expected. That will be all."

Pellinore took his leave as the woman pulled back her hood revealing fine boned aristocratic features, and piercing sea-blue eyes that sought out Sul's with a curious expression.

Her hand snapped out and a metal object flashed from her hand. Just as quickly, Sul plucked the object in mid-air. "Judging from the heft of this coin," Sul commented as he danced a gold coin across his knuckles, "I gather that your mission to Daymore Merenia has been profitable?"

The young woman laughed. "Entirely!" Shaking her head, she pointed. "Answer me this: how does a man with no eyes snatch coins out of mid-air?"

"Practice."

She smirked. "In all the years I've known you, you've never told me what happened to your eyes."

"I misplaced them," Sul replied as he palmed the coin, vanishing it from sight and focusing his attention upon her. "Lily."

"In the flesh."

"It's been a long time."

The woman laughed at the slight censure in Sul's voice. "Captain, you don't send me anywhere where I'll get back in a halfway decent amount of time. Sometimes I think you want to get rid of me for good." She sat in the nearest chair and slung her long leg over the arm of the chair with a weary sigh.

"Perish the thought..." Sul replied without a trace of sarcasm. "Atiya, please bring our guest something to drink." The Mithrac woman bowed once and headed out. Atiya quickly returned with a single goblet of mead, placed it before the woman and departed without a word.

"I have to ask," Lily began, "how does the 'heft' of the coin tell you where I was?"

Sul shrugged. "It's simple. The southern territories are more profitable and therefore have more gold on hand that can be melted down for their currencies, resulting in lighter coins. Coins from Central Daymore, in turn, where gold is sparse tend to be heavier. Even more so where silver is more plentiful and only a token amount of gold is used in the minting of coins."

"We have very different definitions of 'simple,'" she replied in a wry tone.

"The last time I heard," Sul commented softly, "you were fending off Sir Leif and six of his bannermen in the western lands of Daymore near Danoth Ishor."

"Ugh! Don't remind me." Lily covered her eyes with her hand before her brain caught up with her. "Wait! You were there?"

"Peloquin was."

"Well, lovely. Thanks for all the help," Lily drawled.

"You required a lesson in remembering to explore *all* avenues of attack."

"How the in name of the Void was I supposed to know that Leif contracted the Howlers ahead of me?"

"Anyone hoping to conduct business on the Danoth Ishor road should be well apprised as to what the banditry are doing. The Corsairs were taken by fever last winter. That left the White Howlers as the only brigands still operating in the area." He shrugged fractionally. "It was a simple enough deduction."

Lily sipped her mead in sheepish silence. "Yeah, we've discussed this; it's simple for *you*..."

"And it should be simple for you too," Sul countered gently. "You're intelligent and well-trained and I expect a great deal more from you."

"Yes Sir." Lily sat straighter at his mingled criticism and praise. "Well, at any rate, he didn't get the goods. Lady Minaeve sends her regards, by the way." Lily handed Sul an envelope of gossamer thin paper covered in pale forget-me-nots like echoes of the real blossoms. Sul skimmed his hand across it, frowned ever so slightly, and did it again more slowly.

"What?"

"Lady Minaeve is sly and resourceful, but if she attracts the wrong kind of attention—"

"Like Sir Leif," Lily interjected.

"Like Sir Leif," Sul admitted. "She could place herself in imminent peril."

"Want me to keep an eye out? I don't think you have any to spare." Lily grinned.

"No, I have agents in Daymore Kharas, Daymore Merenia and all points in between. I should be able to keep Minaeve out of harm's way and arrange a suitable decoy should those efforts fail."

"What's your interest in her anyways?"

Sul shrugged fractionally. "She's clever and moral. That's enough to garner my interest, especially when it occurs within the ranks of the nobility."

"Isn't that the truth?" Lily rolled her luminous eyes. "I've always wanted to ask you something."

"Then ask."

"Lady Minaeve, myself, Atiya, Reiko, Ravenna—it seems you constantly surround yourself with women." She grinned. "Is it an ego thing?"

"You can do better than that." Sul favored her with an indulgent expression. "Who make the most useful allies?"

"The overlooked. The ignored," she answered without hesitation. She had been trained well after all. "Because if your opponent doesn't know who your allies are then they can't plan for them."

"And therefore?"

Lily stopped for a moment and laughed. "And no one in Daymore is more overlooked than a woman unless a good knob waxing is involved." She shook her head. "You do realize that this wouldn't work in a less obviously sexist environment?"

"Find me a kingdom where it is filled with men confident enough to treat their women as equals and I will consider revising it."

"Point taken." Lily rolled her eyes and shook her head again. "So hopefully I'm not playing bodyguard to Minaeve."

"You are not."

"Great! So does that mean I get to stick around?" she asked, looking excited.

"I'm afraid not." Sul stood and walked across the dimly lit tent with a confidence that belied his blindness. "When I last traveled in Sahath, an acquaintance of mine informed me that there'd been an arrangement made between elements of the rakshasa here in Daymore and the Senate."

"What's some sand cat doing here?" Lily asked, stifling a sigh. She knew Sul would get around to telling her about her next mission when he was good and ready and not a second before.

"Negotiating an arrangement with the Senate under the table to broaden the slave trade. Instead of buying them through the regulated channels, they've begun resorting to mass kidnappings."

She spewed a mouthful of mead out of her mouth, coughing and choking. "They...*what*?!"

"There's a Rakshasa with a pet slaver who has cut a deal with a bloc within the senate."

"How do you know these things?" she asked, aghast.

"I intercepted one of his agents and persuaded him to divulge the information."

Lily shook his head to clear it of visions involving Sul's methods of 'persuasion.'

"Calm yourself," Sul reassured Lily. "There was no need to resort to coercion. Once I supplied him with enough funds to facilitate his departure from the country, he spoke freely."

"Speaking of funds..."

Sul tossed a small pouch to the woman who caught it in her free hand. "Three-hundred gold coins. Find the slaver; an elf named Yvora and her Rakshasa master."

"Where do I start looking? The capital?"

"No, information like this would be disastrous for Praetor Quintus and his allies in the senate if it fell into the wrong hands. Quintus masterminded the bloc and if he's threatened then they all are."

"I'd say it already has fallen into the wrong hands." She gestured at the eyeless man with his wine goblet. "How did that scheming little rodent get appointed a magistrate in the senate?"

"He and Yavic ibn Geral were both contending for the position. The consuls appointed the more political of two evils."

Lily made a face. "Yavic? That madman? I'll wager you a ton of platinum against a bent copper piece that Yavic was offered as a candidate only to make Quintus more palatable to the masses."

"You would win that bet," Sul said dryly. "I can't afford to confront Quintus and his supporters openly. My resources are plentiful and growing, but not enough to challenge the full might of the senate and the Hierophant of the Imperium church together."

"So, what are you going to do?"

"Quintus and his fellow conspirators in the senate will need to establish the logistics of funneling slaves from Daymore back to Sahath. It'll require trial and error. So, they'll take people no one will miss at first until they've established a reliable conduit."

"Meaning Cigany," Lily mused. The halflings were common in Daymore but possessed no centralized leadership, making them easy prey for slavers and criminals.

"If they can find them. Also, elves and dwarves as well as whatever impoverished or lower-class humans they can get away with. They'll start with them and move on to more lucrative slaves once they have their route established."

"That means raiding the ghettos and ethnic communities."

Sul nodded thoughtfully. "There was recently an uprising in the Daymore Dolor ghetto."

Lily scoffed, "Apparently the people living there didn't appreciate being used as sport for the bored offspring of the nobility."

"Apparently so," Sul conceded. "It wouldn't surprise me if additional armed men are discreetly sent to 'reestablish order and ensure public safety.'"

"Slavers?"

"Almost certainly." Sul pursed his lips in thought and then beckoned, "Come." He turned and briskly exited the tent, his stride confident despite his blindness.

The blind leading the... Lily thought for a moment then shook her head as she followed the older man out.

"Light," Sul said softly as he entered the command tent. Instantly, two guards lit torches and placed them inside the sconces within the confines of the enormous tent. Sul paid them little heed as he strode to the massive oaken table.

Lily eyed the enormous fixture appraisingly. "Where'd you get this great thing?"

"Tribute from the Rakshasa, specifically the *Fi'jan* brotherhood," Sul murmured quietly as slowly ran his fingers over the contoured surface area of the map, frowning in concentration. "A token of their esteem."

"The assassins from the north?"

"Assassins and antiquarians. They run the Scarlet Markets in the Ghenlands and along the coast as well as specializing in rare and exotic antiquities."

"And they sent you this…?" Those who operated within the Scarlet Markets, the invisible market where everything from slaves to murder could be purchased, were notoriously stingy.

"Likely to earn my favor."

"Did it work?"

"For the moment," Sul conceded. "Their agents found it in the ruin of an ancient dwarven fortress in the mountains west of here."

"How in the Void did they get a giant table down a mountain?"

"By using a giant to carry it."

"What?"

Sul waved her off and tapped a spot on the map. "Here. From Daymore Kharas along the

Capital Road…" He traced his finger along the road. "…to the Port of Evermere, newly acquired by Quintus."

"If a significant number of the other senators are in league with Quintus—"

"There are."

"—then this whole bit with slaves was a long time in the making. Clever."

"If you say so," Sul replied, his brow furrowed in concentration, the expression looking bizarre with his glass eyes.

"Where's he going to send them?"

Sul sighed and tapped a large kingdom in the far east. "Given that Nevaraak is built upon the bones of slaves that would be the obvious choices. However, you can't sail to Nevaraak from Daymore with a hold full of slaves without half of them starving to death..." His words trailed off as his expression became troubled.

"It's a high-risk cargo. That's why—"

"They are not cargo Lily." A dark shadow settled across Sul's face as he straightened and turned his face towards the young woman. "They are living people. Are we clear on that?" His tone was calm but lethal.

Lily swallowed around a suddenly dry throat as she peered into the crystalline depths of where Sul's eyes should have been. "Yes, Sir."

Sul held the look a moment longer and then turned his attention back to the map, his expression again becoming troubled.

"What is it?" Lily inquired gently.

"There's something about this..." he replied sounding very preoccupied. "Something doesn't feel right." he traced his fingers around the Nymsian Sea which separated the continents Aegreas and Sahath. "Daymore does not have dedicated slave ships. Too indiscreet. So, they make use of converted galleons used for cargo. They can hold between two hundred and fifty to six hundred slaves."

"And?"

"Consider the following: retrofitting ships like that is both expensive and time-consuming. Furthermore, the extensive modifications usually leave the ships far less maneuverable than in their original state."

"So?" The young woman was trying very hard to remain patient.

"So, would you want heavily modified, clumsy ships carrying heavy cargo"—he tapped a spot on the map—"operating in seas dominated

by Raynian pirates who take a very dim view on all things slave relat-
ed?"

Lily winced. That was an understatement. Hailing from Raynia's Rock, the "Suitors of Raynia" were sea-going holy warriors who
worshipped the goddess of the ocean and extolled freedom above
all other virtues. Their wrath against those who dared to traffic
in slaves was both legendary and terrifying. "I see your point. But
if they're not transporting the slaves by sea, then where are they
taking them?"

"I shall have to think more on it. In the meantime, return to the
southlands and keep me apprised of Quintus's movements and those
of his agents."

"Absolutely, o' illustrious Captain!" She snapped a salute at him and
turned to leave, draining the last of her goblet that was held in one
long-fingered hand.

"One more thing, Lily."

"Yes, Sir?"

"Larkin's alive."

The goblet hit the floor and rolled away.

"...what?" Lily managed to choke out.

"Larkin is alive."

"But...but the dragon...and the volcano...and the firestorm..."

"Was apparently insufficient."

"Sweet Gods!" Lily stammered wiping a shaky hand across her
damp brow.

"You'll need a new *senso nomme*."

Lily looked at the Captain with the expression of a woman who'd
been stabbed in the gut. "A what?"

"A Ghen term," Sul explained patiently. "It means 'alias.'"

"Oh." The terrified young woman looked around the interior of
the tent and at the row of banners mounted on the far wall and their

heraldic markings. "How about that?" she asked pointing to one depicting a pair of white swans against a yellow and green background.

"I would advise against masquerading as a member of the de Nalhor family," Sul stated mildly. "Baron Harkon de Nalhor is not a man known for his temperance."

"Well, how about just 'White Swan?'"

Sul pursed his lips and shook his head. "White Swan is the name of a popular Ghen prostitute in Edso."

"How do you know these things?"

"Information is my weapon," Sul offered as an explanation. "'Bright Swan.'"

Lily considered and then nodded. "'Bright Swan.' I like it."

"Good. You have your instructions."

The newly christened Bright Swan nodded and moved to the exit.

"Captain...what should I do if I meet up with Larkin?"

"Swallow your own tongue," Sul stated unhesitatingly. "Because it will be far kinder than anything that madman has in mind if he decides to make you his new plaything."

Lily gingerly rubbed her throat and then nodded once before hurrying out.

Sul listened to the woman's departing footsteps crunch on the gravel before setting his shoulders back with a faint sigh. Time to return to Atiya.

"JUST ONE DAY," CEYRABETH MUTTERED AS SHE PITCHED her bog-sullied clothes outside her tent and donned new, clean ones. "One day without flesh-eating demons, gibbering monstrosities, or daring rescues, is that too much to ask?" She was on her way back from the laundry when, without warning, she was snatched up and spun in the air as a voice boomed in her ears.

"No longer will you fly! My lovely butterfly! Night and Day, I'll keep at bay, and in the dark steal you away!!" A thickly accented voice sang, tossing the elf girl to and fro and around in circles in some bizarre combination of a waltz and a seizure. *"My lovely butterfly. Never shall you die. Day and Night, I will fight the fight. And all your monsters I will smite!"* She was dipped low and found herself bent over backwards staring at an upside-down version of the camp.

"Why, there's life in the young woman yet!" The booming voice called out and Ceyrabeth was yanked forward so hard it nearly caused whiplash and deposited onto her feet. She managed half a step before pitching forward. With a supreme effort she managed to keep her feet underneath her, even as her hand attempted to yank her blade from its scabbard. Then she got a look at her assailant...

...and stopped dead.

He was tall with ebony skin and wore a wide brimmed white hat with gold trim. He was clad in emerald-green leather breeches with matching vest that was cut so high his bare stomach—along with its well-defined muscles—was exposed. Several earrings dangled from his ears, and he was adorned with several straps and buckles around his waist and down both legs, all done in white and gold like his hat. Odd, low-slung holsters hung at both his hips which held a pair of strangely designed curved hilts.

He flashed a grin that could only be described as thoroughly roguish. Ceyrabeth was shocked to see that his teeth were filed to points and capped in iridescent purple which was almost certainly amethyst.

"Greetings and salutations!" The stranger gave a sweeping bow, removing his hat. His hair was an unruly combination of crimson Mohawk and white braids. A pair of horns, one broken off, extended outwards from his skull. "Sir Peloquin of Raynia's Rock, at your service!"

"Peloquin."

The foppish Mithrac replaced his hat and peered past Ceyrabeth. She turned to look. Atiya and Sul were striding forward. The Captain showed no ill effects from his rough morning.

One tough son-of-a-bitch. Ceyrabeth shook her head ruefully.

"My dearest Lady Atiya, my love, *mi amore!*" Peloquin dashed forward and scooped her hand up in his, dotting it with several kisses. "Every moment without you was like an eternity of torment. We must not be parted again!"

Atiya stared at the man blankly and then removed her hand from his grip.

"Peloquin."

Peloquin's demeanor immediately became deferential as he addressed Sul, "*Mon capitan*, I come bearing glad tidings: I'm pleased to announce our mission in Sahath was successful."

Sul nodded once. "Walk with me." The Mithrac swashbuckler offered his arm which the blind man took and led him through the camp. Atiya followed behind and at her beckoning hand, Ceyrabeth shadowed them. Peloquin and Sul conversed as they approached a large group of men, women, and children that looked strangely out of place in the military encampment.

"We managed to acquire twenty slaves from Devon for just under a five hundred gold and—"

"*What?!*"

Peloquin spun around, dropping Sul's arm, and going for the curved hilts at his hips as Ceyrabeth came rampaging up to them. "You're a slaver?!"

Sul turned more calmly. "Never," he replied coolly and gestured. Ceyrabeth focused and saw that several people were working to force metal bracers and collars off their throats, tossing them in a pile of rusted metal.

"You're...freeing them?" Ceyrabeth asked, stunned. "But..."

"I do not keep slaves," Sul replied as they approached the group. "Not now, not ever. They are free and will be offered food, sanctuary and an offer of employment in the Legion."

Peloquin regained his whimsy as he reached forward and scooped up a little girl. "Except for this one!" he roared playfully, twirling the madly giggling child around in a circle. "I am going to take her to Daymore Merenia and make her my bride and we shall go to all the wonderful parties, eat lots of cake and dance all night! *Non più avrai questi bei pennacchini, quel cappello leggero e galante*!" Peloquin sang and dipped, spinning the girl like a top.

"You're not seriously going to put a child on the front lines," Ceyrabeth scoffed.

"An army consists of more than soldiers," Sul replied softly, his tone still chilly. "There is food to be prepared, arms to be maintained, mounts to be tended, supplies to be organized. All of this requires the support of countless people." He indicated the former slaves with a nod. "People like them. They shall receive food and lodging as well as compensation and in turn they will do their part to support the Phoenix Legion."

"All except this one, Captain." Peloquin grinned around a mouthful of purple teeth. "Her and I have to get married right away and eat sweets and cake until we are ill!" He poked the little girl's stomach, causing her to giggle. "Don't we, my little princess?"

"I like cake!" the child exclaimed.

The Mithrac swashbuckler grinned wider. "So do I." He began to twirl the girl around as he began to sing again, "*Quella chioma, quell'aria brillante...*"

"You should be careful!" Ceyrabeth scolded. "She's wounded!"

Sul stepped forward and grabbed Peloquin's arm, jarring the much larger man to an abrupt stop.

"What's the matter Captain, you don't like cake?" Peloquin asked with a cautious expression.

Gingerly, Sul touched the little girl's leg and brought his fingers back smeared with blood. Bringing the blood to his fingers he inhaled once and immediately stiffened. The air around him became almost palpable with menace, causing Ceyrabeth to edge away despite herself.

"She has been violated," Sul stated in a hideous tone, rubbing his thumb and finger together, smearing the blood.

"That she has." Peloquin nodded, his tone still jovial in contrast to his stern expression.

"Where is the one responsible for this?"

Peloquin peeled his lips back into something that might have been a smile if it held any warmth and gently put the little girl on her feet. "Run now, go to mama." She ran towards the group of former slaves. Reaching down, he picked up large sodden bag, reached within...

...and removed a severed head. He casually tossed it to Sul who caught it. The head had been decapitated at the jawline and the flesh from his cheeks was missing, but the wide-eyed stare of terror was still affixed to what remained of his visage.

"Devon?"

"One of his lackeys who apparently cannot be made to follow our very clear instructions on the treatment of the slaves we procure."

Ceyrabeth was staring at the entire exchange with kind of a detached interest; it was almost as if after all that she had already seen, a severed head wasn't all that shocking. In fact, she found the man's grisly fate strangely satisfying.

"Where's the rest of him?" Sul asked.

Peloquin turned his head away and discreetly belched into his hand. "He was a man of very poor taste when it came to decisions, but excellent taste in other regards."

"Fair enough." Sul handed the head back to the Mithrac.

"Whilst we're on the subject"—Peloquin reached into his belt and removed a pouch—"Ghen Black Truffles from the Scarlet Markets of Edso as requested."

Sul took the bag from him, opened it and gingerly placed his nose above the bag and inhaled deeply. An intensely satisfied smile crossed his lips.

"The Captain's table eats well tonight aye?" Peloquin asked grinning.

"Indeed," Sul replied. "I shall make certain to include you in the festivities."

"What is it you plan on making again?"

"Never ask before the meal, it ruins the surprise." He held up the bag. "But these will make a fine addition."

Peloquin licked his chops. "To die for."

Sul handed the bag to Atiya and then frowned, his nostrils flaring.

"Is something wrong, Sir?" Atiya inquired placidly.

"A scent. Something familiar..."

With a roar of rage, a hooded man burst from amongst the former captives. "*Letum inimico! Gloria in Kharas!*" He slammed his fists into first one guard then the other and leapt over them, charging Sul head on.

"Captain!" Peloquin cried out.

Ceyrabeth tore her blade free and moved to intercept the burly attacker.

Sul simply moved out of the way of the first blow and then drove his elbow into his assailant's side. There was a pained howl and the man swung wide. Sul ducked under the blow and rose to slam his palm up under the creature's hood. There was a groan of pain and the other man collapsed upon the ground.

Ceyrabeth took a moment to stare. Whatever frailty Sul suffered from, it was clear he was well trained and could handle himself.

Sul removed the man's hood to reveal flashing green eyes embedded into a broad and scarred face dominated by a sloping forehead and pronounced canines within a wide jaw.

"An orc?" Ceyrabeth asked, confused. She'd encountered their kind in the west of course, but they had been mostly unthinking savages acting as bandits or roaming marauders, certainly not prone to disguises and misdirection.

"Well, well," Sul mused as he examined the strange, raised scars and tattoos that adorned the orc's arms, lightly tracing them with a single finger. The lines began to glow, and a strange humming sound filled the air. "...what have we here?" He looked up from his examination and smiled with a predatory pleasure. "It's been a long time...old crocodile."

REUNIONS AND

RECOLLECTION

"Allies take many forms. Some are expected, some are not. The masterful strategist makes use of all that he has at his disposal but never mistakes the convenience of an ally for reliability. The opportunity that is presented today may be the threat that is presented tomorrow."

—A passage from *Victor Vinguardis* (Way of Victory) translated from Daymorian. Author unknown. Currently banned by the Church of Imperius

THE ORC WAS MARCHED INTO SUL'S TENT BY SEVERAL AN-gry looking guards. One of them was nursing a broken nose; the result of an aborted attempt to shackle the creature. Reaper Maul shadowed them closely.

"Oi!" Maul shoved the orc towards the Captain who was settling into his chair regarding their captive thoughtfully. "Bow your head, you're in the presence of greatness." "I bow for no man," the orc replied icily. "Not anymore."

Maul scowled and opened his mouth.

"Leave us."

Sul's voice was the same even tone that it always was, and Maul knew well enough not to disobey. "All right Cap'n, if you're certain." Maul turned his attention to the others in the room. "Right, clear out you lot! Cap'n's orders." He grabbed Ceyrabeth's arm. "And you luv—"

"She stays."

Calm. Controlled. And totally implacable. Both Ceyrabeth and Maul turned to regard the

Captain for a moment. Then a slow smile crept over Ceyrabeth's face; she plucked Maul's hand off her arm as if it were something loathsome. "You have your orders...Sergeant."

Maul looked outraged; the expression provided the other woman with a great deal of satisfaction. Then he swallowed back whatever he was about to say, managed a haphazard salute and departed.

The prisoner turned to watch them go then turned back. "They've gone."

"Yes," Sul said simply, rising from his chair.

The orc surged forward, faster than he had any right to be. Ceyrabeth dove for her sword, but it was too late. The orc had Sul in his grasp...

...and with a loud whoop he hugged the blind man, laughing.

Ceyrabeth's mouth sagged open as the orc pounded Sul on the back a few times and then pulled away. "I think our performance was convincing."

"I concur," Sul replied with a slight smile, taking his seat. He clicked his tongue a few times and Osen came racing out of the shadows and jumped into his lap, demanding his master's attention.

After a few moments of petting, Osen settled into his lap. "Did you have any trouble getting here, Ulak?"

Ulak shook his head and gritted his teeth. "I tire of ignorant westerners assuming that because I can speak in complete sentences, I must be one of the demon-worshipping orcs of the east."

"And your journey from the Wilds?"

A shadow crossed over his face as pains still fresh moved across his features. "Well enough.

Your man in Raynia made sure I made it to the port. What was his name again?"

"His family name is 'Decius.' His father is a man of influence."

"A senator?" Ulak spat.

"And a bitter rival of Retzel Shen, your former master. It was what ultimately convinced him to leave his family in Daymore Kharas."

"A Daymorian senator as a doting father and husband," Ulak scoffed shaking his head. "I'll believe that when I see it."

"He does tend to dote on his son," Sul acknowledged. "Though not without reason; the young man is a skilled mage but also a principled one."

"Mages! Bah!"

"He's also the man who saved your life and bound your wounds after the incident with the

Emerald Chainmen. Were it not for him the slavers would have taken you."

Ulak stopped short, his fists curled up and his entire posture resembled that of a coiled snake ready to strike. Ceyrabeth's hand moved to her sword again...

...then Ulak sighed and hung his head. "Fair point."

Sul nodded in acknowledgement and gestured to Atiya. "Pour the wine please."

Ceyrabeth released her grip on her weapon and sighed, inwardly relieved. This 'Ulak' radiated barely constrained violence, more a beast than a man.

As if reading her thoughts, the orc whirled around and impaled her with a green-eyed stare.

"Who in blazes are you?"

"Calm yourself," Sul instructed quietly. "This is Ceyrabeth Vallorin. She is a former Witchhammer and newest member of the Legion."

"And you trust her?"

Sul smiled as if enjoying a private joke immensely. "Oh, I trust her with my life."

Ceyrabeth felt something begin to tickle in the back of her mind at his tone, like spiders inside her head. She was missing something again, she knew it, and she gritted her teeth in frustration as Atiya leaned over Ulak to pour the wine.

"Gods!" The orc cried as he noticed the Mithrac woman's scarred features. "A Winnowling?"

"What makes you say that?" the blind man asked mildly.

"Ply your tricks elsewhere, Sul!" Ulak pointed at Atiya's face. "Those scars around her mouth; Mithrac stitching. As they do with all their kind when they lose their minds and become fiends!"

"The Mithrac sewed your mouth shut?" Ceyrabeth exclaimed aghast.

"They did," Atiya replied tonelessly as she finished filling Sul's goblet and took her place behind him. "It is the will of our gods and the law of our tribe. Imposed upon all born with magic who fail to control it and lose touch with their humanity. The Winnowing: the process in which a mage who pushes their powers past their limit goes mad, losing all emotion."

"That's so...barbaric!"

"The Captain said you were a former Witchhammer?" Ulak raised a pointed eyebrow.

"Yes..."

"So, you've only captured mages *humanely* then?"

"Witchhammers don't trap *mages*," Ceyrabeth countered archly. "A Virago and a law- abiding mage are completely different thing."

"Anyone can be a Virago if the Church hates him enough..."

"Former Virago," Sul interjected. "She's no enemy of yours Ulak, nor yours Lieutenant Vallorin. Now, drink your wine, old friend."

Ulak narrowed his eyes over his goblet then took a long pull, his eyes going wide in surprise,

"Is this the...?"

"The same wine we shared last time? Yes." Sul smiled as he lowered his hawkish nose towards his own goblet. He inhaled deeply before taking a measured sip, his expression relaxing. "Taken from the royal vineyards of the last kings of Daymore."

"You know," the orc mused, "I haven't had this since—"

"—the meeting with Praetor Quintus?" the blind man interjected smoothly.

"Stop doing that!" Ulak snarled good-naturedly. "It makes you look ridiculously pretentious."

Sul held up a hand to placate the other man, his lips curled back in a faint expression of amusement.

"I remember that night," Ulak continued. "You insisted that I drink with the rest of you, a slave to sit at the same table as his master." Ulak shook his head at the memory. "You, a senator, an apprentice mage and my master all seated at the table, and you decide to have me join you."

"Former master," Sul corrected gently. "You are not a slave. Not any longer."

Ulak raised his glass in silent toast to that sentiment and chuckled throatily. "I still remember the look on the Lucita and Retzel's faces; they looked ready to have an apoplexy. As I recall, Retzel refused to drink at all!"

Sul nodded sagely. "Praetor Quintus was totally out of his element; attempting to coerce Retzel the way he would a street peddler."

"So why did you do it?" Ulak asked leaning forward eager with curiosity. "Was it just for your own amusement?"

"Deliberately pissing off a powerful senator from Daymore, just for a laugh?" Ceyrabeth interjected. "Sounds like him."

"You can tell a lot of a man from how he treats those he considers his lesser." Sul shrugged. "I wanted to see what I could learn."

"And what did you learn, pray tell?"

"I learned that your former master Retzel is a rat-bastard."

For a moment, silence filled the tent and then Ceyrabeth's jaw dropped. *He swears like a commoner...*was the first thought in her head.

Ulak threw his head back and roared with laughter, tears were streaming from his eyes as he slapped his thigh. "Brilliant!"

"Every now and then." Sul gestured to Atiya. "More wine?"

"Gods, yes!"

Atiya dutifully poured the wine and Ulak took a long pull from it. "That was also the night," he began quietly, "that Lucita's child was found driven mad."

"Virstania," Sul replied.

"That's right, that was her name." Ulak shook his head. "Evil little shit, all six years of her miserable life," he muttered.

"Hey!" Ceyrabeth snapped. "We're talking about a little girl here. A child," she emphasized firmly. "If she was less than kind, the fault rests squarely with her parents."

Ulak's expression curled disdainfully. "I had no idea, Drachaen, that you had enlisted such a moralistic crusader. So eager to play mommy to all those poor, lost and broken children." Ceyrabeth's cheeks flushed crimson and she got to her feet, her face twisted with anger.

"Sit down," Sul's voice cracked like a whip.

She started to obey but instead shook herself and whirled on the blind man. "You condone what he did?!"

"Ulak did nothing."

"Then who—" Her face drained of all its blood. "—you?" she managed to gasp out. "You...drove a child mad?"

"When I first scented blood, I left my meal and proceeded into the courtyard," Sul's voice was soft but devoid of any trace of warmth. "I found Virstania. She had broken the back of a kitten and was busy pulling the eye out of another." Sul's tone became colder still, "I remember that, after I made her stop, I asked her why she had done this. Do you know what she said to me, Lieutenant Vallorin?" She slowly shook her head.

"'Because I could.'"

Ceyrabeth winced. "Ancestors," Ulak hissed, "Then what?"

"Then I kicked the child in the chest, pinned her to the ground with my boot, crushed several of her ribs as well as her arm and proceeded to do what needed be done."

"Why not just kill her?" Ulak asked.

"Her mother required a lesson in what is acceptable and unacceptable behavior. Pain is a useful teacher; its lessons are understood by all and are never ignored."

"I remember Lucita when they found her." Ulak shook his head. "She was beside herself, hysterical. I think that might have been the only time I ever actually felt sorry for her." He lowered his goblet. "You're very lucky that Retzel didn't learn you were responsible."

"Don't be naïve, my old friend," Sul admonished, "Retzel was perfectly aware who was responsible for Virstania's condition."

Ulak's mouth sagged open. "Then why didn't he confront you?"

"Why should he?" Sul shrugged. "He is a pragmatist; what was done was done and he wasn't about to jeopardize any potential dealings we may have had in the future over something as trivial as his apprentice's daughter. What care had he for a child at any rate?" Sul sipped his drink.

"That's cold."

"Such is the way of this world, currently at least."

Ceyrabeth finally found her voice, "Did Lucita—did she have any more children?"

Ulak drained his cup and peered into it unhappily. "No," he finally replied, "Lucita had been pregnant at the time, but she miscarried and her womb was destroyed, though that could have just as easily been from her abuse of sanguinary rites."

"The loss of Lucita's bloodline will not be keenly felt by the world," Sul commented dryly.

"True enough."

"What happened to the kittens?" Ceyrabeth interjected softly. "Did they die?"

"Actually no," Sul replied. "I was able to repair the damage done to the kitten's spine using alchemy and relinquished him into the care of the groundskeeper at the time." Sul leaned back in his chair. "I oft wonder what happened to that kitten."

"And the oth—"

There was a crash of metal outside, screams and Maul's voice booming outside.

"Cap-tain!"

"What in blazes?!" Ulak leapt to his feet and raced out of the tent, Sul rose from his chair more calmly.

"Did you do it?" Ceyrabeth's whisper was raw, "Did you do something to that woman and her baby?"

Sul reached towards a shelf and removed a small bag.

"Have you heard of 'The Tribe of Ecstasy'?"

"Should I have?"

"Probably not," Sul conceded. "They were an orgiastic cult back in Emperor Tiberius's day that believed the greatest form of worship they could offer the gods was to preach love and sensual delight to the world."

Ceyrabeth's expression morphed into revulsion. "An orgiastic cult. Why do I need to know this?"

"In the end, they were hedonists and harmless but that didn't stop The Emperor from exterminating thousands of them down to the last child in his bid to secure his throne."

"They sound like heretics."

"They also happened to be pacifists," Sul countered. "They offered no resistance when they were put to the blade."

"Does this all have a point?"

"Just this"—Sul tossed the bag at Ceyrabeth who caught it deftly—"The Tribe of Ecstasy knew they could not provide for every child that would be conceived during their frequent couplings so the women would swallow one of these seeds. It would, in essence, prevent pregnancy."

"What does that—" She stopped. "What would happen if someone took one of these seeds if they were already with child?"

Sul's calm expression told her everything.

Ceyrabeth's eyes went wide. "How could you?"

"One day you will learn that sacrifices must be made," the blind man replied. "Victory comes with a cost. Do not be so quick to judge one's methods without first considering what is sought to be accomplished."

"I can't—"

Sul reached into his jacket and removed his pipe which he lit with the flame of a nearby sconce. "You need to put your personal feelings aside, Ceyrabeth. Make no mistake; we're at war. Nobody wants to admit it, but the world and all who inhabit it are under attack. Our world is far more fragile than we'd like to think. If the world—*our* world, Ceyrabeth—is to be saved, change must be affected through whatever means we have at our disposal."

There was another loud crash outside followed the sounds of violence. "Sir," Atiya whispered quietly.

"Now"—Sul reached up and removed his bindings, his crystal eyes shifting in a dizzying array of red, yellow, and violet—"let's see who desires the attention of the Phoenix Legion."

They exited the tent to find the immediate area in a state of disarray; two guards were down, one sitting propped upright nursing a badly dislocated shoulder and the other seemed to be barely clinging to consciousness.

"See to them," Sul whispered to Atiya, taking a cloak from a sentry, and drawing the hood up over his face. She nodded and directed men to tend to the wounded. He reached out and put his hand on the dislocated shoulder of the wounded guard.

"Magrom's flaming ass!" the guard hissed. "Watch what you're—" He then looked up and immediately turned fish-belly white. "Captain!" He blanched.

"Be still," Sul replied quietly, giving his shoulder a quick examination. "This will hurt."

"Sir—"

Sul twisted his grip on the man's shoulder and yanked it forward hard. There was an audible *pop*.

"By the gods!" the wounded man gasped.

Sul reached out, took the man's hand in his and heaved him to his feet. Clearly the older man was stronger than he looked. "Thank you, Captain Sir."

"Report to the medics and then inform the quartermaster that you and any other wounded man is to receive two portions each of officer's rations.

"Yes, Sir! Thank you, Sir!"

"Dismissed."

The man started to draw his arm up then winced and saluted awkwardly with the other arm before limping away.

Sul turned to scrutinize the captive; she was a small, thin human with short blue-black hair and dark skin, clad in rags. She was, for all appearances, one of the former slaves. Maul had both her arms pinned behind her back. Ulak had collected a fallen sword from one of the guards and had it trained on her, his green eyes narrow and suspicious. Ceyrabeth flanked him, sword and shield at the ready.

"Well, well," Sul murmured quietly. "What have we here?"

The girl smiled brightly, her teeth bright against her ebony complexion. "Uh, hi! I think there's been a mistake."

Sul smiled fractionally although Ceyrabeth could not discern if he was genuinely amused or simply attempting to disquiet the girl. "That is reasonable," he admitted. "Perhaps if you were to explain yourself, an understanding could be reached."

The girl looked confused at the cordiality she was being shown. Ceyrabeth couldn't suppress a smile of her own. The captain could do more to intimidate with good manners than anyone else could manage with any amount of bluster or threatening.

"Okay well—" she began.

Sul shook his head. "No, first there is another matter to attend to." Sul's shrouded head lifted slightly. "Sergeant, please position her arms upon her chest, fists up tight under her chin."

"Aye Cap'n!" The enormous man grunted and began to push the girl's hands into position. The girl surprisingly put up a great deal of resistance; she was also stronger than she looked.

"If Maul is forced to break both your arms, it will make further negotiations that much more difficult," Sul commented softly.

The girl blanched. "Okay, yeah that's not creepy at all." But she relented and soon her fists were wedged under her chin.

"Thank you Maul. Now, squeeze the underside of both of her wrists twice in rapid succession and then step away as quickly as possible," Sul instructed.

Maul looked confused but obeyed. The elf girl's eyes went wide with terror. "No!"

There was a sharp hissing sound and Maul managed to duck out of the way as a cloud of green powder shot out from the girl's sleeves and coated her face. She began to cough violently and fell to her knees, hunched over as Maul backed away from the toxic cloud.

"I thought so," Sul said gently. "You are a long way from home, yes?"

There was a flash of movement, and a dagger flew from the girl's hands towards Sul.

"Captain!" Ceyrabeth cried out.

Sul's hand lashed out and caught the dagger by the blade, a millimeter from his face, his expression utterly placid.

"Gods!" Ceyrabeth blurted. She had seen duelists who could move quickly before, but that was...*uncanny*.

The human girl meanwhile looked crestfallen. "Oh, well...shit," she sighed. Then she cried out as Maul hauled her up by the back of the neck.

"Miserable little bitch!" he spat. "I'll break you in half!" He lifted the girl above his head and began to fold her. The girl's body began to crack and her eyes were wide, panic stricken at the ungodly strength that had her in its grasp.

"That will do, Sergeant," Sul instructed softly. "You may release her now."

Maul looked at the Captain in shock and opened his mouth to protest.

"Sergeant," Ceyrabeth interrupted, "you heard the captain."

"Sod it!" Maul grumbled and he threw the girl to the ground so hard that she bounced. She cried out in pain and lay still, her spine a howling inferno of agony.

Sul stretched out his hand to the girl. "Are you prepared to resume negotiations civilly or should I ask Maul to break you in two?"

The girl looked up at Sul, unable to see past the darkness of his cowl. "I think I'd like to try talking now," she confessed.

"Wise decision." Sul hauled the girl up to her feet. The girl cried out in pain and nearly toppled over before the man caught her.

"That really hurt!" she exclaimed.

"Yes, I imagine it did," Sul replied calmly.

The young girl composed herself. "Well, I guess I should introduce myself."

"No need." He reached under his hood and removed his bindings though his features remained hidden from view. "You've colored your hair with fermented indigo. I smelled it when you first arrived. Indigo only grows in wettest, hottest climates, such as those found in the south. You are armed with Mindleech poison but have clearly inoculated yourself against its effects as you are currently neither raving nor dying." He held up the knife she had thrown at him. "Your dagger is composed of blue steel and onyx with traces of wyrmscale"—he handed the knife back to her— "and it's a half gram heavy on the back end."

The girl caught the blade looking thoroughly gob-smacked. "How—"

Sul pulled back his hood and his shifting glass eyes stared directly into the girl's face.

"Greetings, servant of the Rakshasa" he said calmly, his eyes transforming into pools of glittering yellow glass.

The girl blanched at the sight; her horrified expression reflected back to her in a thousand golden shards. "*Are Nahin*!"

"Just so. Your name?"

"Janessa," she answered him more by reflex than anything else. "My name is Janessa."

"Very well." Sul gestured to a nervous looking sentry. As Sul locked eyes with the man, the yellow faded from his crystalline gaze and was replaced with shades of green and blue with only a faint yellow at the center. "Issue the command to break down the last of the tents, make certain that all auxiliary personnel have been evacuated and then summon my mount. We ride in a few hours."

"Yes, Sir!" The sentry saluted and immediately began shouting out commands.

"Cutting it a little close, aren't you?" Ceyrabeth commented quietly, her tone dark. "Aren't you even the least bit worried?"

Sul calmly turned to the elven woman, his glass eyes shifting and morphing into shades of red and violet. He raised one eyebrow in an expression of mild interest.

"What I'm saying, Captain, is that there serves no purpose in waiting. It's risky and unnecessary," she added awkwardly.

"All war is risk," Sul replied, crimson shards spreading through his eyes. "I should think you would have come to understand that by now."

"But why—"

"You want to see what the Taintbrood will do!"

Both pairs of eyes turned to regard Janessa. The red and violet faded from Sul's eyes replaced with cool shades of blue and green as he met the young woman's gaze. "Continue."

Janessa swallowed past a dry throat and plowed ahead, "You're not just fighting the Taintbrood; you're studying them. You want to see how they'll act the closer they get to you, if maybe they start doing different stuff?" She bit her lip and prayed she was right.

Sul held her gaze a moment longer; the green fading from his gaze shifting into complete blue with streaks of yellow. "Very good."

Janessa exhaled a sigh of relief as Ceyrabeth eyed first her then Sul incredulously. "What they'll do?! I can tell you what they'll *do*! They'll do what they do to everything else and come in here and kill every one of us! We need to leave, now!"

"Then leave, Lieutenant."

Sul's words and tone caught her like a sword to the gut. "Sir?"

"You are dismissed, Lieutenant. If you cannot follow my orders then your presence is unnecessary."

Ceyrabeth felt the blood pounding in her head. She opened her mouth to protest...but closed it again. Her hands were clenched so tightly the nails were drawing blood from her palms and her knuckles had turned white. She saluted and stormed away, her vision tinted red. She came upon the sentry and without warning grabbed him by his collar and slammed him against a tree.

"We. Are. Leaving. *Now*!" she snarled. "Am I perfectly clear?!"

"Ye...yes ma'am!" He stammered his eyes wide and fearful. Ceyrabeth shook him once for emphasis and released the man who scurried away as if all the demons of the Void were at his back.

She resumed her furious pace to anywhere that wasn't near Sul.

Ulak grunted. "Charming girl," he muttered under his breath watching the red-haired elf stalk away.

Damn him! Damn him! Damn him! Ceyrabeth fumed internally, her scowl and pace doing much to clear any traffic before her. "He's going to get himself killed," she snarled under her breath. "He's going to gamble and he's going to lose and then he'll die and—"

Since when does that bother you?

The thought stopped the woman dead in her tracks, her scowl became deeper and darker. Gritting her teeth in frustration, she stalked toward the stables, her fists still clenched with vice-like intensity. When she finally reached the stables for a final sweep, all of the horses were already gone...except one.

"Eregost, girl, what are you doing here?" It was easier in the dim light to see what a magnificent animal she had been...Quinlan was so proud when he had finally saved up enough to buy her. Ceyrabeth couldn't remember seeing anyone ride higher in the saddle, armor gleaming in the sun, the perfect image of what a Witchhammer ought to be...

She shook the memory off as a familiar squat form walked through the door. "Shouldn't you be helping break down the camp? Or are you specifically reserved for daring bog rescues?"

Ceyrabeth narrowed her eyes at the sarcasm in Narl-Shu's tone. "You need to keep a better watch on your stable hands. They forgot Eregost."

"They didn't *forget* anything. I'm here to take care of it now."

"It? Eregost is a mare..."

"It's a reanimated corpse. It doesn't matter what it used to be."

Narl-Shu rubbed his hands together. A low hum made the hairs on Ceyrabeth's neck stand on end. Eregost backed, rolling her bright pinprick of an eye as the little man approached. It whickered softly, not panicking but definitely unhappy. "What are you doing to her?" she asked warily.

"Sending it back to the Void."

Suddenly it didn't matter to Ceyrabeth that the horse wasn't really a horse or that it had demon eyes or that a good portion of its ribs were visible out of the pale flesh of its torn side. They were just going to end her. Like stomping on a cockroach.

Ceyrabeth grabbed Narl-Shu's reaching hand without thinking about it. She froze as though hit by lightning, a black web spreading through the veins of her hand. There was a loud *snap* as Narl-Shu aborted the spell and she blacked out for a moment. Slowly, Ceyrabeth became aware that he was calling her some very uncomplimentary things, and that Eregost was nudging her shoulder.

"She...is mine." Ceyrabeth interrupted Narl-Shu's tirade through what felt like a mouth full of cotton. "And if you touch her again, I'll break your corpse-raising hand right off, understand?" She didn't wait for an answer but called over her shoulder, "Eregost, follow!" The clip-clop of the reanimated horse's hooves followed her out.

The Mithrac...*what was his name? Peloquin?* she thought to herself, stood with his back against a tree, massive arms crossed over his chest and a smile on his face. "Something to say?" Ceyrabeth snapped at him. The smile got wider, but he raised his hands and shook his head in the negative.

Ceyrabeth didn't stop until she reached the river. She paced, fuming, furious at herself as she watched Eregost crop the tender shoots of grass at the water's edge. It was the next thing to a *demon*, for Green's sake! A monster. She was trained to *end* monsters, not adopt them. Narl-Shu would have even done the work for her and she just...

Something hit her lightly in the back. She whirled around...and saw no one, nothing except a tiny glimmer of gold at her feet. She gingerly picked it up and immediately recognized the symbol on the wrapper as belonging to one of the premier confectioners in Daymore. Another little gold missile hit her leg then tumbled onto the ground next to her. She sighed. "You can come out." She addressed the trees.

"You're sure, Beth?" Keiran popped his head out of the branches. "You'll eat the chocolate?

Not bite my head off?"

"Positive."

The young former Witchhammer looked good, she noted as he dropped athletically to the ground. The diverse population of the Legion was doing him some benefit—he was already walking with more confidence. He didn't even flinch when Eregost turned her open side to him, simply sat on the hill and patted the grass next to him. She sat beside him with a huff that just narrowly escaped being a sigh.

They sat in silence for a minute, just watching the camp break and condense.

"The guards are saying that you're the reason for the quick breakdown," Keiran said casually. "Said they're used to moving efficiently, but this is the fastest they've ever broken camp."

"Yes, well, if the guards have an issue with the way—"

Keiran popped a chocolate into her protesting mouth with the ease of former practice. "You promised."

Ceyrabeth bit down with a roll of her sable eyes and felt her anger drain as the tart sweetness of raspberry flooded her tongue. Her very favorite, and almost impossible to find. "Did you save these all the way from the city?"

Keiran nodded with a grin. "For emergencies."

They watched the river for a moment. "So," Keiran finally said casually, "You decided to keep Eregost huh?"

"Yes, I decided to keep the *free* horse that can run for days without needing food or drink.

Problems?" Ceyrabeth asked coolly.

Keiran shook his head with a smile. "I'll bet the Captain was happy about it."

"He doesn't know yet."

"He knows." Keiran stated with conviction.

"Speaking of the Captain Who Knows," a voice behind them called out.

Ceyrabeth and Keiran whirled around at Pellinore's mildly amused statement. "He requests that you three"—he swept his arm to include Eregost—"rejoin him at your earliest opportunity. The Taintbrood are almost upon us." Pellinore didn't seem overly worried about slavering hordes descending upon them, unsurprising in her opinion, considering the power that dwelled within the camp to oppose them, but Keiran had turned a very telling shade of pale.

"I should grab my mount," the young man managed.

"I'll come with you," Ceyrabeth assured him. Soon they found themselves heading back toward the four semi-permanent shelters that housed the Legion's mounts. Surprisingly, there was a large crowd around the shelters. *Last minute stragglers*, she thought. And then, a piercing shriek froze the blood in her veins. She and Keiran both went for their blades.

"What in the name of the gods was that?!" Keiran managed to

choke out. Slowly the assembled ranks parted to make way for Sul. He was astride a great reptilian beast, its leathery hide bone white and heavily scarred. Its eyes were bright pink and it emitted a strange cackling purr as it peered at the people around it.

"That," Ceyrabeth said with strange wonder coloring her voice as her sword arm dropped, seemingly without her noticing, "is a wyvern!"

"It is indeed," Sul replied. He was wearing what appeared to be armored robes; layers of wool and pale leather accented with mail and plates of dark metal split up the center to accommodate riding.

"What breed is it?" she asked, still riveted on the beast.

"An eastern breed born without wings and deemed too unruly to be made into proper mounts."

The wyvern took that opportunity to raise its head and emit another ear-piercing shriek that caused Ceyrabeth's teeth to rattle.

"The Shrieking Stalker?" the elven woman asked as soon as her ears stopped ringing.

"The same," Sul patted the creature on the neck. It gave another cackle purr. "They are not a well-known species. You're very well-informed lieutenant."

Ceyrabeth felt heat rush to her cheeks, and she quickly averted her gaze. "As I've mentioned, I used to read a lot when I was young. A Church brother named Arturo set up a research station in Dolor and gave me access to his library in exchange for running his errands." She coughed once and affixed a glare on her face to banish the blush from her features before addressing him. "What? You don't have a monopoly on reading."

One dark eyebrow lifted slightly in a now-familiar gesture of interest. "I have acquired all of Brother Arturo's works and contributed to a few as well. He is an insightful man."

Ceyrabeth gestured at the beast. "What's his name?"

"Her name," Sul corrected gently, "is Banshee."

Keiran frowned up at the creature. "Banshee? What does that mean?"

"It's a very old word, from a time long before the Ancient Age."

"There's nothing before the Ancient Age," he said confused.

"That depends entirely on who you're asking. Now, report to your unit soldier."

Keiran immediately stiffened and gave a crisp salute. "Yes, Sir!"

"For the record," Ceyrabeth commented sourly, watching her young friend go, "he's never saluted me."

"All in good time, Lieutenant."

"Yes Sir." Ceyrabeth straightened and saluted. "Have I orders as well, Sir?"

"Shadow Lieutenant Pellinore for now." Sul nodded as Pellinore detached himself from the crowd on Sul's right. The two elves exchanged nods. "There is much for you to learn."

"Sir," Ceyrabeth acknowledged. Pellinore seemed a decent sort. She could at least be grateful that she wasn't taking her orders from the foppish Peloquin or the berserker Maul.

Sul nudged his mount forward and nodded to someone she couldn't see. A raucous horn sounded along with the command to "Move out!". The words were picked up and reechoed until they were lost in a thunder of hooves and wagon wheels.

INTRODUCTIONS AND

FAREWELLS

"A campaign is fought on many fronts. A battle won or lost in one location will have serious ramifications throughout the entire theater of war. Therefore, one must be kept appraised of all that would affect his strategy. Ignorance is neither safety nor bliss but rather assured destruction."

—A passage from *Victor Vinguardis* (Way of Victory)
translated from Daymorian. Author unknown.
Currently banned by the Church of Imperius

"THE CAPTAIN'S GIVEN THE ORDER TO HALT CAMP."

"Thank the Green," Ceyrabeth breathed at Pellinore's words. She shifted in the saddle, grimaced. It felt like her saddle sores had saddle sores. Over the last weeks, the Legion had effectively split with the slower riders, such as the heavy cavalry who were defending against Taintbrood stragglers from behind, and the faster riders scouting ahead and running interference for those refugees unfortunate enough to still be on the road. In classic military formation, both groups were responsible for protecting those in the middle; women, children, the wounded, and the noncombatants.

Ceyrabeth had already pulled her share of guard and patrol duty, finding to her surprise that she enjoyed the people she worked with even though they had little time for idle chit-chat. Captain Sul pushed the pace hard and no one could blame him; hard travel was much preferred to being consumed by the Brood.

But the reports coming in from the southern arm of the Legion had gotten more and more favorable the farther north they went. It was time to regroup. Ceyrabeth fully expected, as one of the newest recruits, to be doing the grunt work inevitable in making a large camp. So, when Sul called her into the newly pitched command tent, she was surprised to have him offer her a seat. Latrine duty didn't really require much except a 'go dig there' and certainly the Captain didn't need to be the one giving *that* order.

She had politely refused a glass of wine and was watching him survey her over the rim of his own cup. "May I be of assistance, Captain?" she finally asked.

"Yes." Sul set his glass down. "A mission has come up that you are... uniquely suited for, Lieutenant. Tell me... how much do you know about the mages fortress of Arcus Meier?"

"Umm..." Ceyrabeth had to think; she hadn't been outside the towers for a long time. "It's led by the archmage Meier Cyn, with Marshal Aeneas commanding the Witchhammers stationed there. They've worked together for a long time. Arcus is widely considered to be one of the most stable institutions for magic in Daymore."

"It appears that is no longer the case. The Witchhammers are on the march to destroy it."

"What?!" She shot to her feet. "Why?!" Sul waved her back down. She sat reluctantly on the edge of her seat. Sul opened his mouth to speak but was drowned out by a titanic roar that practically imploded the canvas walls.

"Dragon!" Ceyrabeth cried out as she dashed out of the tent, sword in hand, cursing the sentries that hadn't alerted them sooner.

"There's nothing to fear," Sul said, coming to stand behind her.

"Nothing to..." She gestured at the enormous, winged creature. Its scales shone an iridescent crimson and the smell of scorched rock hung heavy in the air. "That's a red dragon. A *dragon*!"

Sul smiled faintly as he rose to his feet. "I can assure you she has no interest in violence."

Don't even ask how he knows. He wants you to ask so he can show off more. Just don't. Ceyrabeth coached herself. *Don't even...* "And how can you possibly know that?" *Damn it.*

"Because dragons are expert spellcasters and master strategists with centuries of experience and allies to call upon." Sul turned his bandaged gaze to her. "If she were here to kill us, we'd all be dead."

That was news to her. The Imperium painted them as beasts in all their sermons and scripture...cunning, certainly, but animals for all that. And then her brain caught up with his words, "She?"

The dragon landed with more grace than a creature its size should have been capable of. Its sleek form was no less impressive on the ground than in the air. Its clawed feet crushed rock underneath it as it approached the camp, hissing and snarling. Men's hands tightened on the hilts of their swords and their bows.

"No one make any hostile actions towards her," Sul said in a voice of bared steel. He waved everyone back and approached the creature. Its red and orange eyes were vertical slits of contempt and its nostrils flared. The scent of burning rock and ash increased.

"Look out!" Ceyrabeth cried out. "She's going to—"

The rest of her words were drowned out by a sound like an enormous bellows filling and then a roaring conflagration of fire exploded out of the creature's mouth.

"No!"

The flames raced towards Sul...and terminated less than a foot away from him. She could see that the sheer heat of the flame had scalded his face red, but he remained unmoved.

"Are. You. Finished?" His words were calm as he addressed the enormous beast looming over him.

The dragon snuffed once. "For now, I suppose so." There was a flash of light, a crack like thunder and where the enormous red dragon had been stood a pale skinned woman with white-blonde hair, a lithe form and orange eyes. "Hello...Uncle."

"Uncle. Well, that explains a lot." Ceyrabeth's tone was dry, but every sense was on high alert. Somehow, even though she was every inch the perfect replica of a human, the woman reminded her of a dragon still. Something in the way she held her neck, how she stood leaning slightly forward as though she would drop to all fours at any second. Ceyrabeth got the sense that dragon though she was, this "woman" was about her age, if not younger.

There was something fascinating about her eyes, as though if you looked long enough you could see beyond the dimension of mortal ken. Ceyrabeth realized she had been staring and shook herself, focusing instead on Sul who was answering the dragon's greeting.

"Lieutenant." Sul gestured. "May I present Tarahjhunkaiel; conqueror of the white wyrm Scylis, defeater of the lich necromancer Kressius Krul and companion to her majesty the Winter Queen."

"You may refer to me as 'Tarah'," the woman informed her haughtily.

"'Companion' to the Winter Queen." Ceyrabeth frowned. "Does that mean—"

"It means I *accompany* her. Her dearest friend. Keep your assumptions to yourself, elf."

"And yet, you did not arrive with her," Sul interjected smoothly. "Does she know where you are?"

Tarah's chin took on a defiant set. "She knows what she needs to know."

"And do your parents know where you are and what you're doing?"

Tarah's orange eyes narrowed. "Don't push it, Uncle."

Don't ask, don't ask... don't...damn it! Ceyrabeth shook her head. "All right, I give up." The elf turned to face the blind man. "Are you actually her uncle and if so, doesn't that make you a dragon as well? Is Drachaen your name or your title? It means 'dragon,' doesn't it?"

"It's a term of affection." Sul gestured to the other young woman. "I helped raise Tarah, and she helped me through...a difficult time in my life."

"If you call being tortured to death over and over for centuries on end 'difficult'," Tarah commented with an air of disdain.

"Wait, what... No. You know what? No, I don't..." She was about to say 'I don't want to know' when she realized that it was a lie. She was intensely curious about Tarah's statement. "You were tortured to *death*?"

"I was."

"Over and over? As in you died more than once?"

Sul sighed, clearly not enjoying being the topic of discussion. "I did."

"For *centuries*?"

"Longer."

"So, you're a reanimate? Like Eregost?"

"No. I am simply a man."

"Nothing 'simple' about you, dear uncle," Tarah commented dryly.

"How did you surv—" She turned her gaze towards the dragon. "You?"

"My parents. I just gave him his name." A smile flickered across her regal features, dispelling some of the cruel lines of arrogance that otherwise dominated it. "He showed the strength of a dragon. He deserved a fitting title to go with it."

"You didn't come all this way from the north to rehash the past," Sul commented.

"Perhaps I simply wanted to see you."

"Perhaps you did, but more likely you want something."

Tarah sighed. "Is there someplace we can talk?"

Sul nodded. "Right this way."

After a short walk, Sul opened the door to a large wooden caravan. Ceyrabeth was surprised to see the unmistakable form of Peloquin already lounging in the wagon. Despite the bulk of his size, the foppish giant managed to fit comfortably inside the confines of the wagon without it seeming crowded. Ceyrabeth's eyes finally adjusted to the dimness after the bright light outside...and she immediately revised her initial assessment. This wagon was *far* too small to hold her, Sul, Tarah...*and* a completely naked Peloquin.

"Good morning, all. Quite the wake-up call, no?" He grinned his purple teeth at Tarah, completely comfortable despite his state of undress. "My dear, may I say you look simply *ravishing*..."

Tarah rolled her eyes so hard Ceyrabeth was surprised they didn't get stuck in the back of her head. "One more word, Mithrac, and I will eat you. "Why is he here?" Tarah asked as Sul helped her into the wagon.

"Peloquin is my spymaster. I imagine what you have to say he should probably hear."

"Okay," Ceyrabeth spoke up, looking at the lamp, the desk, *anywhere* else but Peloquin's knowing grin. "But why am *I* here? I truly don't need to be here. Shouldn't Pellinore be here instead?"

"The Lieutenant is minding the men. I need someone to take notes and observe." Sul flashed a rare smile. "I assume both of those requests are within your capabilities?"

"Entirely." The elven woman's expression was completely deadpan, unless you happened to look in her eyes.

"I'm relieved to hear it." Sul turned his attention to Tarah. "So, now will you tell us what brings you here?"

"The news from the Reaverlund is dire—" Tarah began.

"It usually is," Peloquin commented wryly.

Tarah emitted a guttural growl that was far too deep and resonant for a human frame to be capable of.

"That'll do," Sul stated calmly. "Please continue Tarah."

"The Farcold is progressing farther and faster than we anticipated."

"'Farcold'?" Ceyrabeth frowned.

"By the Great Flame, they really don't teach you southerners anything of any use, do they?" Tarah sneered.

"The Farcold is a sentient disease upon the land of Reaverlund," Sul explained, holding up a hand to stave off Ceyrabeth's inevitable retort. "It is a pattern of weather, the most frigid lifeless winter you can imagine that is working itself slowly down the northern continent, killing everything in its path. It renders entire swaths of land uninhabitable, ravaging them with unending storms of snow and ice."

"I still put no stock in this fool notion that the Farcold is sentient," Tarah said dismissively waving her hand. "I believe it to be some form of freak magical occurrence, no more no less."

"It seems drawn to inhabited areas," Sul replied. "That would suggest at least a rudimentary intelligence."

"Regardless, it is showing signs of growth and acceleration." The woman's face was grave. "The kingdoms of Icefire Peaks and Wintercrown have already fallen, and the rest of the north is in peril."

"I imagine that's disrupted the balance of power in your homeland considerably."

"You don't need to 'imagine' anything. It's fact."

"Not to sound callous," Ceyrabeth began, "but what does this have to do with us?"

Tarah opened her mouth, her expression dark and angry.

"It matters because the north keeps the southern kingdoms in check," Sul interjected. "If they weaken, you may be certain that Daymore will start considering the advantages of conquest."

"That's absurd," Ceyrabeth scoffed. "He'd have to move an army all the way through the Ghenlands to even reach the northern coasts and *get* to Reaverlund."

"Not if he uses his navy."

That comment drew the elven woman short. "The Daymorian navy is large enough to move an *army*?"

"It is," Sul confirmed. "And, even if it weren't, the Emperor of the Ghen could be convinced to allow an army to move through his territories without lifting a finger."

"How? They hate each other."

"Large piles of gold," Peloquin answered dryly.

"Just so." Tarah turned her attention back to Sul. "And if the southern armies do start aggressively expanding north..."

"Then we could be under a great deal more scrutiny than we are currently equipped to handle." Sul nodded. "Fair point."

Sul rose from his seat and moved towards a map. "We need to work to bolster the northern kingdoms."

"How are we going to do that?" Ceyrabeth asked. "Gold?"

"Oh, please," Tarah scoffed. "The Northern kingdoms are almost as wealthy as the dwarves." She took in Ceyrabeth's look of surprise with contempt. "Why do you think your Hierophant and his precious church wants them?"

"Information then," Peloquin put in. Sul nodded. Something rustled in the far corner of the caravan where Peloquin's bed was. Intercepting Ceyrabeth's questioning look, he reassured the elf, "don't mind her." Ceyrabeth's face flooded with understanding just as another rustle came from the pile of cushions and blankets. "Don't mind *them*," he amended, laughing at Ceyrabeth's groan of dismay.

"Detailed reports," Sul emphasized quietly, immediately bringing everyone's attention back on track, "on the movements of the southern forces could help ease the minds of the remaining royalty in Reaver-lund."

"Not as much as you being there in person to help them shore up their defenses against the Farcold or invasion from the south, Uncle," Tarah put in. Ceyrabeth swore she could hear a spark of hope in her usually sarcastic and callous tone.

"I'm afraid that's not possible. We're contending with the Taint-brood here." Sul turned his bandaged gaze to her. "If the Brood crosses into the Ghenlands, they'll spread like wildfire and very easily make it to the northern coast, leaving you vulnerable to attack on two fronts."

"I do have some information about that," Tarah said, looking resentful at being refused. "The Brood isn't behaving like a swarm any longer."

"Explain."

"They seem more organized. As if they have united behind a single purpose beyond simply slaughter."

"I surmised as much." Sul nodded. "Which is why I've been observing them." He sighed and rubbed his temples. "I cannot say for certain but based on the patterns of their behavior I'd say they've united behind a single leader or at least a single group."

"That cannot be good," Peloquin commented glumly.

"Agreed. The question is what to do about it." He frowned for a moment then turned to Ceyrabeth. "Lieutenant?"

"Sir!" She straightened her back.

"I have a task for you." He turned to Peloquin. "Peloquin, I want all our reports on the movements of Daymore's army and navy over the last six months compiled and ready to go in an hour."

Peloquin placed a hand over his heart. "Alas, the curse of being as talented at your job as I am—being asked to do the near impossible."

"Will that be enough to appease your liege?" Sul asked Tarah.

"I suppose it will have to do for now," the dragon grumbled.

"Captain," Ceyrabeth began cautiously. "What exactly *is* this task?"

"In a moment Lieutenant."

"May I get you a cold glass of water while we wait, Lieutenant?" Peloquin rumbled. Ceyrabeth could hear the laughter threatening in his tone. "Your face looks...flushed."

"You should see the healers. Your eyesight is obviously failing."

"It is as I was saying before, Lieutenant," Sul addressed Ceyrabeth and pointedly ignoring the banter. "Arcus Meier will soon be under attack. Your mission will be to delay the strike."

"...excuse me?"

Sul just looked at her.

She shook her head in adamant denial. "Marshal Aeneas is a legend! We literally learn about him in training. He's considered the paragon of what a Witchhammer should be. If he's calling for the Witchhammers to come down in force, then there must be a damn good reason!"

"I imagine so. And I very much want to know what that reason is. Furthermore, I have need of the mages there and having them exterminated to the last runs counter to my goals."

Ceyrabeth nodded reluctantly. "Yes, Captain. Will I be going on this mission alone?"

"No, Lieutenant. I have a team in mind for you. They should be arriving any moment." As though in response to his words, a knock sounded on the caravan door. Ceyrabeth lunged for it, even though it was technically Peloquin's door to answer. Keiran, Evric and Scout Mischa stood outside.

Ceyrabeth gratefully stepped out, closely followed by the Captain.

"This is it?" Ceyrabeth asked incredulously.

"Thanks for the vote of confidence, Beth," Keiran commented sourly.

"I'm sorry," she sighed. "But how exactly am I supposed to accomplish this mission with three people who, put together, have less combat experience than I do?"

"Keiran is a capable soldier as you are well aware," Sul explained. "Evric is a talented mage despite his youth and Mischa is one of the finest infiltrators one could ask for."

Ceyrabeth sighed, finding herself missing her former comrades amongst the Witchhammers. They could get this mission done with ease.

"Have you any objections to my choices, Sir Ceyrabeth?" Sul's question intruded on her thoughts.

Resigned, she saluted. "None, Sir."

"Excellent. See Lieutenant Pellinore for your requisition orders."

"Yes, Captain!" Ceyrabeth snapped to attention.

"For the Legion!" Keiran, Evric and Mischa declared.

"For the Legion," Sul replied.

"For the Legion." Ceyrabeth sighed once more before saluting. The mission she could handle, and even her team. But one thing bothered her to the point of distraction: *When had Sul called the team together and how did they know where to meet?*

She sighed again. Another one of the hundred mysteries she would probably never understand.

"THAT'S HIM."

Evric's whisper came to Ceyrabeth's ears from off to her right. They sat at the dinner table of a rough but clean inn, in the Daymorian province of Corbray. She cut into an apple with her dagger and brought a piece to her mouth before turning around and crossing her legs casually. She immediately found the subject of the whisper; a tall, handsome man with dark brown hair streaked with gray and pulled into a half-tail. "You're sure?"

"Believe me, I know Josef," Evric replied with a roll of his eyes. "He used to give the Hammers a right proper time when I was at Arcus. He'd always find some way to try to escape. He managed it seven times...well, eight if you count this one."

"He sounds like he'd be very helpful," Ceyrabeth replied. Along with arms, armor and travel rations, Captain Sul had thoughtfully provided dossiers on people who may be helpful in case they needed a hand. The first portion of their mission had gone off without a hitch but that was *before* Keiran had been recognized in a stroke of insanely bad luck. It was only a matter of time before the local Witchhammers descended on them in a shrieking hoard, out for his "traitorous blood." Keiran was currently lying low, but they desperately needed someone who knew both the lay of the land and the local faces.

Ceyrabeth watched Josef move about the inn, stopping here and there to chat with a villager.

He seemed to be well-liked, if the smiles and nods directed at him were any indication. For a moment, Ceyrabeth thought about going up and asking to speak to him in private, but then she rejected the idea. He was going to be cautious, over-watchful. "You said he was a healer?"

"Yes." Evric nodded. "At least he was back at Arcus...Ceyrabeth!"

Ceyrabeth cried out in pain as her dagger clattered to the floor, its edge now stained with blood. *Her* blood, point of fact. She had grasped the blade and drawn it across her palm hard enough to leave a gaping wound. Josef looked around at the unmistakable sound of distress. Evric had grabbed a cloth from the table and was pressing it against her hand before Josef could make his way over. He was careful to keep his head down, but Josef didn't even notice him.

"What happened? Are you alright?"

"I...it was on the bench," she breathed, doing a very convincing approximation of a maid in distress. "I wasn't paying attention."

"Let's see." Josef took her hand, examined it carefully. "You're going to need stitches," he informed her. "Were you using this dagger to cut this?" He gestured to her half-eaten dinner. She nodded hesitantly. "You don't want to risk blood poisoning. Follow me."

"Are you a leech?" she asked, using the peasant's term for one who tended wounds. Josef smiled at her.

"Of a sort."

He led her up to his room, gesturing her to the chair before removing a small sewing kit and bottle. "This'll sting," Josef warned her as he poured a splash of the liquid onto her palm. It did sting but much less than she expected. Josef still cradled her hand in his as he began sewing the wound, which was also less painful than expected, and she focused in. She realized that he was slowly healing her hand, the stitching just a blind for his real actions.

"Thank you," she said sincerely as he bound the freshly cleaned and stitched hand in a length of new bandage. "How can I repay you?"

"You can stay right there. *Manere*!"

Ceyrabeth recognized the mage's spell to paralyze a split second before it hit her. Her limbs seized up and she went rigid in her chair. "Sorry." Josef moved about the room, rapidly stuffing things into a small bag. "I'm sure you're not a Witchhammer, but I can't be too care—"

But Josef had made a serious mistake; he had only paralyzed her from the neck down.

"*Eluo*!" Ceyrabeth spoke the command to cleanse magic and her limbs immediately unseized. Before Josef could react, she had tackled him to his bed. Electricity blazed across his skin, but she was expecting it. Most mages immediately thought electricity as defense.

"*Silence*!" she cried out and Josef yelped in dismay as his magic abruptly ceased.

He heaved her off bodily, desperation giving him strength.

Ceyrabeth threw herself forward and grasped his ankle, tugging him down with an almighty crash. "Josef!"

"You won't take me back!" He kicked at her once, twice and by sheer blind luck he caught her in the forehead. The skin split and blood poured into her left eye. He scrambled up once more and made for the door.

"Just listen!" she roared, pouncing on his back. They slammed into a wall with crushing force. "I'm not...a...Witchhammer!"

"Those sure as the Void *feel* like Witchhammer abilities!" Josef slammed her into the wall again. She gritted her teeth. She hadn't wanted to hurt him, but he was really giving her no choice.

She tangled her fingers in Josef's hair with both hands and, dropping her weight, she wrenched back on his head. He slammed to the floor and tried to roll but Beth was already straddling his chest. Her fist connected across his face with the force of a mace, backed by an ability that her trainers called "Arcane Binding." It not only caused physical pain but drained a mage's magic reserves. His hands shot up, tried to block her, tried to strike back but it was no use.

Evric burst through the door just in time to see Ceyrabeth roll off Josef's chest. The mage was bleeding from his nose and a split lip and was just lying dazed on the floor. "Lord's Mercy!" he exclaimed as he took in the scene.

"He's been silenced," Ceyrabeth told him, rummaging for something to staunch the flow of blood from her head. She eventually found a towel and pressed it to the wound. "I didn't want to, but he paralyzed me. Help me get him onto the bed."

She and Evric pulled him as carefully as possible onto the mattress. Evric rummaged around in Josef's healing bag until he came up with a greenish vial. "Healing potions. Excellent." He popped the cork from the vial and drained it into Josef's mouth sip by sip. The young mage's eyes fluttered, then opened.

"Josef, can you hear me?" Ceyrabeth asked gently, doing her best to appear as anything other than a terrifying Witchhammer bound to drag him back in chains. Josef side-eyed her warily and nodded, wincing. "I'm going to dispel the Ward of Silence." Ceyrabeth told him. Evric's eyes flew to her face, but he didn't object. "We just need you to listen. Please."

She whispered the counter to the Silence and Josef sighed in relief. "Hi, Evric."

Evric nodded at him with a sheepish smile. "Hi, Josef. Sorry if we scared you."

Josef shrugged. "Where did you learn all that?" he asked Ceyrabeth curiously. "You're an elf."

"Half-elf. It's a long story." She sat next to him on the bed. "Short version: I posed as human for a lot of years to train as a Witchhammer." Ceyrabeth started talking quickly, just trying to get the words out before he decided to set her on fire. "I defected, along with others in my squad. Now, we're trying to halt a Witchhammer assault against Arcus Meier—"

"Arcus is under siege?!"

"It will be. My friend, Keiran Ehingen, was recognized by someone on the road and it's only a matter of time before the Witchhammers come in force. Evric heard your name in town, and we thought you might help us. The word is that you're good at escaping." Josef smiled a little at that, but

Ceyrabeth was too much in earnest. "Josef, please. They'll kill him."

"I've seen Sir Keiran's wanted posters." Josef tapped his index finger against his chin. "And now that I think about it, I've seen *yours* too. Sir Ceyrabeth Vallorin; Wanted for Treason and Defection."

"It's pronounced *sara-beth*, not *say-ra-beth*, but yes. That's me." A twinge hit her. So, Quinlan had made it back and informed on her to Carmilla. She squelched the pain that rose from the part of her that had hoped he would come back, would protect her once more. This wasn't the time.

Josef considered. "If I *were* to help you, and I'm not saying I will... what's in it for me?"

"Freedom. The man we work for, the one that's stopping the assault, he's...the most diabolically brilliant mind I've ever come across. You can stay with us, and I promise you, you'll never have to even *consider* if there's a Witchhammer nearby for the rest of your life. He has already given safe haven to quite a few mages, including one from the Daymore Merenia massacre. *Or*, if you want to disappear, start over entirely, you will have that option. Assistance given and no questions asked."

"*What* in the Void is going on up here?" The proprietress of the inn burst through the door. *A little behind*, Ceyrabeth thought cynically. She stiffened as Josef put his arm around her before flashing a charming smile at the woman.

"Sorry, Stella. My girlfriend got a little...excited." Ceyrabeth glanced sharply at him before plastering a wide smile on her face and winking at the shell-shocked Stella.

"Oh. *Oh!*"

"You don't have to worry. Evric will patch me up. Thanks for checking in."

Evric gently herded the woman out the door and shut it firmly.

Josef chuckled at the expression on Ceyrabeth's face. "You can't say you didn't deserve it."

"We're even then," she replied.

"For now." Josef ran his hands through his hair, retied it. "Alright. I'll help you."

———————————

"*THIS* IS WHERE YOUR CONTACT LIVES?"

"You aren't a snob are you Ceyrabeth?" Josef asked with only a trace of mockery. "Because I don't work with snobs."

Ceyrabeth heaved a sigh and looked at Evric. She had wanted to get Keiran, but Josef had adamantly vetoed the idea. He was already outnumbered, he said. So Ceyrabeth had yielded.

She sincerely wished she hadn't when she heard the ungodly yowls coming from inside the hovel.

They burst through the door, weapons drawn. "Where's Gaetano?!" Josef demanded of the terrified woman cowering by the fireplace. She just pointed a trembling finger toward the back.

They charged back...and stopped cold. An elderly elven man lay firmly tied to the bed while a tall, dusky-skinned human man stood near the window, fiddling with a crystal cube that was casting strange shadows on the prone figure. "That was close..." the human muttered. "How about...this?" The shadow changed and the elf screamed. "Ah! There it is."

"What are you doing to that man?!" Ceyrabeth demanded.

The human glanced up briefly. "Josef! Welcome back."

"Please my lady, don't let him hurt me anymore!" The old man turned his head, tears streaking down his face.

Ceyrabeth's expression hardened, and she leveled her sword at the human. "Step away from him. *Now!*"

"Look, precious, I don't have time for..." The human turned his exasperated attention to Ceyrabeth...and in that split second, a wave of magic lashed out that sent them all flying.

Ceyrabeth reacted instinctively. "Shield!" Blue light shimmered around herself, Josef and Evric, but she was disgusted to find that it was weak. She had used too much energy trying to subdue Josef.

Ceyrabeth shook her head, trying to clear it. "*Con—*" she started, but the human picked himself back up.

"Don't worry about that Witchhammer nonsense," he said contemptuously as he picked himself back up and climbed on the bed. Ceyrabeth took note of his features; fine-boned with short dark hair and a thin mustache along with his accent marked him as Eastern, possibly Nevaraakese.

He removed a vial started to shake a clear substance onto the elf, who screamed earsplittingly with each drop on his skin.

"What's he doing? What is that?" Ceyrabeth asked Josef doing her best to tune out the ungodly shrieking and the memories of the monstrosity Chirak it brought oozing to the surface of her mind.

"It's holy water; sanctified waters from a sacred well that—look, I've got no interest in explaining all this to you so just shut up and stay out of the way."

"Holy..." Then it clicked. "The man is possessed!"

"Give the girl a prize!" the dusky man drawled. He hopped off the bed, braced his arm on the headboard. "You hear that?" he asked the elven man conversationally. "You're possessed. Now, I knew that, and you knew that. It's time to hear which demon you are. Well?"

The elf hissed something at him that Ceyrabeth didn't understand but seemed to make total sense to the human. "Now, now," he admonished. "There are ladies present." And he tipped half the bottle of holy water onto the possessed man's head. The creature hissed and screamed, pulling at ropes that Ceyrabeth devoutly hoped were well tied. "Try again?"

The elf glared at him hatefully. "Of course, you want to do it the hard way." The human withdrew a knife from his belt. It gleamed unusually bright even in the muted light. "You learn anatomy in Witch-hammer school?"

Ceyrabeth took a second to realize that he was talking to her. "Of course!"

"Great. There's this fantastic little nerve cluster in the shoulder... hurts like all the Void if you hit it just right." He offered her the blade's hilt. "Like to demonstrate?"

"No!"

"Witchhammers." The man rolled his eyes. "Never want to get their hands dirty." And with that, he yanked the elf's arm out straight and plunged the knife deep into the ball and socket joint of the elf's shoulder. Smoke rolled off the wound as the man howled in agony. "Well?"

"*Hux...Huxenlem*!!" The voice that bellowed from the elf's throat wasn't even close to mortal.

"Of course, Huxenlem!" The man withdrew the knife and the demon sagged back. "Now, was that so hard?"

"One of the Forbidden Ones?" Ceyrabeth asked.

He looked at the elf and snorted. "You're remarkably well informed for a Witchhammer."

"*Former* Witchhammer," she corrected frostily.

"Uh-huh, sure. Anyhow he's a *servant* of one of the six 'Forbidden Ones.' Doesn't quite possess the power to be counted amongst them, but don't hold that against him." The man slapped the possessed creature's shoulder in something almost like camaraderie. "He's the best cellmate a man could ask for," the human replied caustically. "Ok, Huxy. Time to go."

The effect was instantaneous. The elf strained against his bonds with the strength of the desperate and another wave of dark magic lashed out, filling the room with the sick scent of brimstone and pitch. It impacted against Ceyrabeth's shield and they staggered, but the shield held. It gave the human just enough time to finish fiddling with his cube. The elf screamed and they all could hear the difference; this was not the screams of the damned, but of a mortal being in excruciating pain. The human man ripped the shirt away from the elf's chest.

His ribs were breaking through his flesh, leaving multiple puncture wounds. Ceyrabeth and

Josef both readied their weapons as they saw the area of the man's stomach roil with the terrifying visage of the demon within. "Got it!" the human shouted and placed the cube directly into the worst of the wounds. One more agonized scream, a blinding flash of light...

....and then it was over. Evric, at Ceyrabeth's nod, rushed to the elderly elf. "He's still breathing," he informed her.

"Good."

"Yes, rumpy-pumpy triumph," the human man said breathlessly. He was brushing pieces of ash off his clothes as he reached over to retrieve the crystal cube, which was no longer clear but smoky gray and covered in blood. "Josef, sweetness, go and get the woman, would you?"

Josef obeyed. Ceyrabeth pulled the sheet of the bed over the elf's chest just in time; nobody needed to see that, least of all what she assumed was the man's wife. "OK, so here's the rub," the human started in as soon as the woman entered the room. "Demon's out, grandpa's alive. I don't work for free. What do you have?"

"What does she...?" Ceyrabeth asked, too shocked to be angry.

"Lucre. Recompense. Remuneration. *Payment*, precious." He rolled his eyes at her. "I saw a girl earlier. Bring her in."

The old woman scurried out as Ceyrabeth worked on trying to form words. She was back before Ceyrabeth could say a thing, towing a doe-eyed slip of a girl behind her. The dusky-skinned human surveyed the girl critically. "No tits, even for an elf," he commented. Then, he casually reached out and patted her groin. Ceyrabeth suddenly and explosively found words.

"Get your hands off her immediately!" she roared, placing herself between man and girl.

"No need to breathe fire," the human replied. "If I wanted veal, I'd head over to the tavern. I like a little thatch on my roof if you know what I mean. Besides"—looking over Ceyrabeth's shoulder to the girl, who was now trembling and whimpering, he sighed—"I've had all the fear I feel like dealing with for now." He re-focused on Ceyrabeth. "What about you, precious? You look reasonably shapely of breast and firm of thigh. No? Too bad." He turned his attention back to the old woman. "Alcohol, then."

"We...we have none, Sir," the old woman informed him tremulous-ly.

"By the Succubus' infernal tits!" the human expostulated. "Is it too damn much to ask for a cup of tea? No? Well then, go make it and take your babe in arms with you!" Both women hurried out the door. Ceyrabeth slammed both her palms into the man's chest, sending him reeling back.

"Hey! Mind the goods!"

"You...you pig!" she spat out. "Knave! Warped, fool-born Void rotter! Who do you think you are?!"

"Gaetano, meet Ceyrabeth Vallorin. Ceyrabeth, this is my contact Gaetano," Josef interjected dryly.

"You *cannot* be serious!"

"'Fraid so, precious." Gaetano sent her a charming smile that made her want to punch all his perfectly straight teeth back into his head.

"Don't call me 'precious'!" Ceyrabeth shook her head. "No. Not happening," she told Josef. "I will slit my *own* throat before I'll work with this man."

"Maybe we should take care of the person who just suffered life threatening injury before we work out any other arrangements." They all looked over at Evric's sharp words. He had torn a blanket into strips and was working to staunch the old elf's bleeding wounds.

Josef hurried over to his side, looking properly abashed. "Here, let me." The healer reached his arms out over the man, and he was suddenly bathed in gentle, blue light. The ribs reset themselves before their eyes, wounds knit cleanly, and some of the gray receded from the man's features. He even breathed deeper.

"Ok, I'm going to pretend for a second that I care why you're here," Gaetano said to Ceyrabeth as they watched Josef work.

"I was going to ask for your help. Now, I think I'd rather feed myself to the archduke of Hell."

"Feisty. I love feisty. Who's in trouble?" She shot him a sideways look. "I know your name. It's plastered all over the wanted posters. But you're moving around freely. So, it must be someone else."

"My comrade, Keiran."

"Ah. Keiran Ehingen? Between the two of you, the reward is..."

Ceyrabeth grit her teeth. "Your head will adorn a central place on my wall before I let you..."

"Your tea, Sir."

Gaetano took the rough mug from the old woman's hands and sipped. "Finally. Something good. Why are you with Josef?"

"Because we thought he would help us get out of the city."

"Help...Witchhammers?" Gaetano hooted. "By the by, however *did* you learn those abilities? I imagine your lovely, pointed ears and distinct lack of curves gave you some trouble."

"Less than you'd expect."

"So...you *were* a Witchhammer raised and trained then? Blessing of Imperius, vigils, all that?" Gaetano pursed his full lips. "But not anymore?"

Ceyrabeth didn't see how it would matter but she nodded. "No, not anymore."

"Who are you working for now?"

"Why in the Void should I tell you that?"

"Because you need me."

"Like I need a rotting hole in my chest..."

"Come on, precious. Indulge me a little, and I might just give a little back." Gaetano grinned. "On my honor."

"Fine. Have you heard of a group called the Phoenix Legion?" Ceyrabeth felt the change in Gaetano the second the words left her mouth. His expression became darker, colder.

"You work for Drachaen Sul?"

"He's our Captain, yes." She was puzzled. She hadn't met anyone yet who'd even *heard* the name let alone had such a strong reaction to it.

"I can't believe that Tainted bastard is still alive."

Ceyrabeth bristled. "I'll thank you not to speak of him with that tone. The Captain is professional, efficient and considerate...unlike some I could mention."

"He's got you dancing to his tune sure and certain." Gaetano's lip curled. "He always was good at swaying the faithful into breaking their vows."

"How dare you!" she spat. "I won't listen to you a second longer. I would rather throw myself to the Brood than work with you...you..."

"Ceyrabeth!" Evric, who had been standing at the window, beckoned her over.

Ceyrabeth moved quickly to his side and felt her heart seize. A heavy cart pulled by a pair of speckled drays rattled by the hovel, two guards in heavy armor riding atop behind the horses. And behind its chained and barred rear door...

"Mischa..." Ceyrabeth breathed. She had just caught the young woman's face as they passed. If Mischa had been caught their chances of success had just been cut drastically.

A heavy weight on her shoulder made her look around. Gaetano was leaning against her, body tight against her side. He was grinning all over his handsome face. "So...what was that you were saying about Taintbrood?"

"JUST SO WE'RE CLEAR..." CEYRABETH COULDN'T BEAR TO look at herself in the mirror. The dress she had been forced into mortified her life out; cheap silk and too much skin. "...I'm going to kill you as soon as your usefulness has run out." Evric and Josef were both affecting interest in other points nowhere near her, like true gentlemen, but Gaetano had no such qualms; his eyes took her in from full, painted lips to high heeled shoes.

"Oh, you're going to have to work on your sweet talk if you want to convince the guards that you're the soiled dove they've been waiting for." Gaetano laughed.

"Why are we not just breaking the door down again?" Ceyrabeth asked.

"Hey, you want to charge into a prison full of guards, be my guest..."

"Because you want to rescue your friends, not kill a whole bunch of people." Josef interjected.

"And why me?"

"Because the sad truth is that not everyone is as equal an opportunist as I am." Gaetano reached to fix a bow on Ceyrabeth's hip; she knocked his hand away with a glare. "These boys are all about their girlies. And lucky for you, they've got a thing for pointy ears. Must be that whole subservience thing...'yes, master, no master...'"

"You've got that blade, right?" Evric interjected. Ceyrabeth patted her thigh. The strangely bright blade that Gaetano had used on the demon was the one thing that gave her any sort of comfort.

It felt odd against her skin, colder than a normal blade. "Let's go then. Better now than never."

On the walk to the prison, Gaetano grasped Ceyrabeth's arm. "Now, you're sure you can take care of the two at the doors? Because we're not going to be charging in to save your skin, so if you get pinned down or whatever..."

She just rolled her eyes at him. "I'm not completely helpless."

"Sure, precious." He made a gesture to Evric and Josef, who immediately turned to the right. They would meet up with them after she and Gaetano were inside. "Alright," he whispered, "now's the time to bat those pretty eyes. Tits out. Howdy, gents!"

They had reached the prison. "Gaetano! What have you got for us tonight?" One of the guards hailed him.

"Boys, meet Lorelei. Brand new skin, not even in rotation yet." Ceyrabeth, newly christened Lorelei, felt her cheeks flush but she swept her eyes up, blinking her lashes at them in a motion that felt ridiculously coquettish.

"Lorelei," the younger of the two asked, "like the song?"

"And, oh, will she make you sing Sir Brandon." The boy, he couldn't have been much more than eighteen, flushed to the roots of his blonde hair. Gaetano saw and immediately capitalized.

"What's this I see? Blushing like the most vestal maiden I've ever seen! Could it be...a *virgin* I see before me?! Oh, oh my sweet Lorelei." He braced one hand on her shoulder, put one hand over his heart. "Go and make this boy a man, I beg you!"

Ceyrabeth just barely managed to not roll her eyes again as she followed an awkward Sir Brandon into the prison. They stopped in an empty block of cells near the entrance; he still couldn't manage to look her in the eye. "Look, I'm sorry, I'm just not..."

But the woman was already moving. Taking hold of his head, she planted his forehead squarely into the iron bars and Sir Brandon was down. She tied his hands and feet together and relieved him of his keys before skimming the prison log, sighing in relief when she saw Mischa and Keiran's names. "Block C."

She sauntered back out through the door. "Back so soon?" Gaetano raised his eyebrow.

"You know boys." Ceyrabeth let the Dolorian accent she had spent years trying to rid herself of back into her voice. "A slip here, a squeeze there and pop!"

"I guarantee it won't be slip, squeeze, pop with me girlie," the other guard leered. "Where is the little bastard now?"

Ceyrabeth glanced at Gaetano, thought fast. "I may have...left him a little dazed. He was having trouble with his legs."

"I'll go get him..." Gaetano offered.

"You know that you flesh peddlers don't go into the prison," the guard said. "I'll get him. You come with me, girl. I'm not wasting my time because some kid can't control himself. I'll fuck you on top of him if I have to."

If looks could kill, the man would be not just dead but flayed alive. Luckily, in his haste to get through the door, he didn't notice.

"There you are," Gaetano said as she returned a second time a few moments later. She was spattered in blood and carried a short sword and small targe, plus another, taller sword and shield and a mage's staff. "He gave you a little more trouble than the kid?"

"No," was all Ceyrabeth said. She pursed her lips and whistled. Evric and Josef emerged from the corner of the building. Wordlessly she distributed the weapons and led them into the prison.

But as they passed Sir Brandon, who was just waking up, she found her voice. "You..." She smacked him none too gently across the cheek and he looked at her with wide eyes. "You are *much* too nice of a boy to listen to this idiot!" She flung her arm out to indicate his very battered comrade. "The next time something like this comes up, do yourself a favor and don't do ridiculous things like *almost sleep with a woman you don't know*! Train hard, find better friends, and make your family proud! Don't let *anyone* bully you into *anything*! Got it?" The young man was gagged but he nodded.

"Good. I'm going to leave you there. Start kicking up a fuss and you'll end up like Sir Pummeled Pig-Shit, am I perfectly clear?"

Another nod and Ceyrabeth stalked away, Gaetano sniggering behind her. "By the Six...did you walk off the damn recruiting posters?"

"Shut up," she muttered. Now that they were a force, they could afford to sacrifice silence for speed. "Knockouts only." She commanded. She had always been good with using her shield offensively, and all it really took was a quick feint and a well-placed shield bash to subdue the few guards they came across.

"Do you even need us?" Josef asked sometime later after the third guard fell.

"No," Evric answered for him. He had been training with her since she became an official part of the Legion and had seen her fight before. "Just stay out of her way."

"Lazy," Ceyrabeth muttered. She unlocked a heavy wooden door. "This should be it."

"Ceyrabeth!" Mischa lurched up to the bars, frowning through a split lip. "You have to go get Keiran! The Witchhammers just took him!"

"Where?" Ceyrabeth asked her. She pointed out the far door. "Evric, see to Mischa." Ceyrabeth freed her before wrenching open the door, Josef and Gaetano hot on her heels a moment later. She heard their voices before she saw them; they were discussing something that made her stop in her tracks.

"Why in the Void did they send that thing *here*? Why didn't they send it by bird straight to Arcus?"

"You don't send a Call-To-Arms by bird, you idiot! What happens if they get shot down? It's hand to hand from the clergy to the Witchhammers until it gets where it's going."

"But why is it *here* in the ass-end of nowhere?"

"I dunno. Some problems along the line, I guess. We have to take it up to the Archbishop when we're done with our pal here."

The Call-To-Arms; the order of assault on Arcus Meier. The actual writ was not two feet beyond that door. No order, no assault. "Josef...Gaetano..." she hissed. "For love of the gods, stay behind me."

"Shield," Josef replied, and a violet dome shimmered up and around them. Ceyrabeth nodded her thanks...and kicked open the door with a bloodcurdling screech. Between Ceyrabeth's rapid assault and Josef's magic the Witchhammers were completely overwhelmed.

Keiran was strapped to a table, battered and bloody but alive. "Hey," he slurred up at Ceyrabeth as she moved to release him. "You look great."

"Don't you even start," she told him.

Josef stepped up, looked into Keiran's eyes. "A concussion. I should have *just* enough power left to help."

"Gaetano, find the orders," Ceyrabeth commanded, and the man immediately obeyed, coming up with a very official looking piece of paper from the older Witchhammer's belt pouch. Ceyrabeth took it... and handed it to Josef. He cocked his head at her. "I thought you might like to do the honors."

Understanding flooded Josef's gaze and suddenly the writ of assault disintegrated with blinding, white-hot flashfire. He spat into the ashes on the floor.

"So, I really hate to rush you..." Gaetano interjected, holding something that smoked and hissed firmly wrapped in a cloth. "But we gotta stick this somewhere *now* or we're gonna have a pissed off demon on our arses!"

"And you didn't know this before?!" Ceyrabeth slung Keiran's arm around her shoulder and hauled him off the table.

"Well, excuse me, precious!" Gaetano shot back. "There wasn't enough sunlight when I sealed it!" He moved to one of the downed Witchhammers and opened the cloth to reveal the crystal cube. It was no longer clear but black as pitch with flickers of violet lighting striking angrily inside.

"What are you doing?!"

"Deporting the demon!"

"Not them!!" Ceyrabeth grabbed the cube from him. Gaetano went to protest...and caught sight of her hand. The left was normal but the right was webbed with black lines. She took off running toward the entrance, Gaetano following close behind, a look of consternation fixed on his features.

"Him!" Ceyrabeth commanded, pointing at the knight she had dubbed Sir Pig-Shit.

"Fine!" Gaetano took the cube from her again, started manipulating the symbols on the side. "Make me an entrance!"

"What?!"

"The blade, the blade!" he yelled. "Use the bloody blade! *Now*!!"

Ceyrabeth didn't give herself time to think; she pulled the blade from the sheath on her thigh and plunged it into the knight's belly. His eyes flew open, too surprised to even try to scream. Gaetano slammed the cube into the wound and backed far out of reach. "Get out of the way!" Ceyrabeth obeyed, dragging the terrified Sir Brandon with her.

They watched in horror as Gaetano started chanting...then the ground below the frantic knight opened, roiling and seething with tendrils of black smoke that formed hands and dragged him into their embrace. Inch by inch, with the eerie sounds of Gaetano's chanting and the infernal wailing coming from the pit assaulting their ears, Ceyrabeth and Brandon watched the knight get dragged into the Void.

Ceyrabeth got the gag off Sir Brandon's mouth just in time to watch him heave the contents of his stomach all over the prison floor.

"What in the Void happened to him?" Evric asked as he, Mischa, Josef and a very unsteady Keiran approached, but Ceyrabeth just shook her head. Gaetano cautiously approached the blackened circle where the knight had disappeared and retrieved the cube, which was crystal clear again.

"Whew, that was a close one!" He grinned.

Ceyrabeth stood, her hands shaking, and slammed him by his collar against a wall. "Get us...out of here...*now*."

Gaetano held up his hands in a placating gesture. "Sure thing, precious. One safe exit, coming up."

LIEUTENANT PELLINORE WATCHED THE BAT FLUTTER down from the sky. It was one of the animals they sent with agents in the field, and unless he missed his guess, it held news of Ceyrabeth's mission. He had held some qualms about sending Ceyrabeth, especially with the other former Witchhammers added in; could they be trusted to act against their former comrades? But he had kept his concerns to himself. The Captain seemed to trust her and that was enough for Pellinore. As he skimmed the note, which was two lines on a piece of paper in a slanted, feminine hand: *Strike entirely halted...leaving Corbray immediately. C.*, he found himself smiling.

He reported the letter to the Captain immediately. "Adjusting for distance and the speed of the bat, if she left Corbray three days ago, her team should be back tomorrow."

"Yes." Pellinore couldn't tell if the Captain was pleased or not from his tone, but that was no real surprise. "I wish to see Lieutenant Vallorin the moment she arrives back in camp."

"Yes, Sir."

"And what of the rest of the army?"

"All present and accounted for, Captain." Pellinore's was the last satellite unit of the Legion to check in, point of fact; the army was once again whole. Now, they could begin the not insignificant task of setting permanent camp.

Sul nodded his approval. "Thank you, Lieutenant. Dismissed."

"Yes Sir." He spun on his heel and departed.

Ulak took that opportunity to emerge from behind the tent's rear curtain, pulling at his new, unfamiliar armor. "Are you certain that this is entirely necessary?"

"Does it not fit well?"

"It's fine. But are all these spikes actually useful?"

"It presents an image. All of warfare is deception, Ulak. And a fearsome appearance can serve as a preemptive measure. It helps you avoid unnecessary confrontations and keep a lower profile, at least more so than open violence would."

The orc frowned and looked down at the armor then back up at Sul. "So it...really makes me look fearsome?"

Sul smiled and nodded his assent.

Ulak frowned and peered past Sul at Janessa for confirmation.

"Oh definitely!" Janessa piped up. "Seriously, I have chills."

"Really?" Ulak considered and then nodded. "Well then, thank you Captain."

"You'll still need a weapon." The blind man reached down by the table and with a heave dragged an enormous sword onto the table. It landed on the hard wood with a definitive *thud*.

Ulak eyed the weapon incredulously. "You can't possibly be serious."

"It's called 'Harkon's Tooth'," the other man informed him. "Use it in good health."

Ulak took hold of the massive weapon and heaved it off the table. "Gods, how am I supposed to fight with this thing?"

There was a sudden hum in the air and the armor on Ulak's body began to glow faintly. Suddenly the sword weighed nothing at all. He heaved the blade up in one hand and began to twirl it experimentally.

"The armor acts as a conduit," Sul explained, "much like water conducts lightning, the metals in the armor and the way it is cut and etched corresponds with residual magical energy a sort of sympathetic resonance."

"A what?!"

"The armor powers the sword, and the sword returns that power to the armor."

"Why didn't you say that in the first place?" Janessa commented wryly.

Ulak looked stunned as the power of his new arms allowed him to do the impossible. "How did you do this?" he breathed in wonder.

"With great care." Sul gestured at him. "Put that down for a moment. I want to show you one other useful talent." The blind man walked around the table to face the other man, stopping only to pick something off the ground. "You spent enough time in the company of Retzel to understand the relationship between wyrmscale and the astral plane?"

"All too well," Ulak growled.

"In sufficient quantities, wyrmscale can be used for rites to enter the astral plane physically."

"Yes, yes," the elf bristled, "so what?"

"So this."

Sul thrust a large snake into the orc's face. Ulak shrieked and lashed out blindly...

...and his hand passed through the snake. In a flash of blue light, the serpent went rigid and then completely limp.

"I see you're still afraid of snakes." Sul tossed the dead creature to the ground.

"Don't you ever—" Ulak couldn't speak as he tried to catch his breath. "What in the name of the Ancestors' Tusks was that?!"

"That was awesome!" Janessa cried out.

"The armor is tempered with heavy quantities of various types of wyrmscale powder. It allows portions of yourself to enter the Astral Plane for a few moments. It makes a useful first strike weapon or interrogation. In time, you'll gain enough control to augment your combat skills; making yourself more resistant to magical assault or become more difficult to hit." Sul smiled faintly. "A useful talent for a fugitive. And helpful considering where you'll be headed." "Yes," the elf murmured. "You haven't actually told me where I'm going."

"Daymore Merenia by way of the Carnifain Passage," Sul replied.

"And what's in this Daymore Merenia exactly?"

"A ship that will take you to Gloomvale, in the eastern part of the empire. From there you'll make your way to Daymore Dolor."

"Daymore Dolor," Ulak scoffed. "You're sending the former mage's slave to the city known as 'The City of Curses'?"

"I'm sending the former slave of a mage to a city where there are enough Witchhammers to give even Retzel pause."

"...All right, fair point."

"When you arrive in Dolor, you'll be meeting with one of my agents; a dwarf that goes by the name Piotr."

Ulak grinned ruefully. "Ah, some sort of master assassin or spy no doubt."

"Piotr possesses a singular ability to appear completely ineffectual. He plays the role of a buffoon expertly."

Ulak frowned. "Why would I need a buffoon?"

"There are many uses for a man who can appear much more foolish than he actually is."

"That's actually true," Janessa pointed out.

"I'll take your word on that," Ulak replied skeptically.

"Take this as well," Sul placed a heavy pouch in his hand. "That will cover all of your expenses in addition to procuring room and board in the city."

Ulak gaped at the pouch; it contained more coin that he had ever seen in his entire life. Then his train of thought caught up with him. "Eastern Daymore," he spat.

"Is that a problem?" Sul asked politely.

"If the rest of the world turned into orange slime, I would still prefer that to living in the Eastern Empire." His voice slipped into a bad Eastern accent. "Oy! I'm a bloody idiot with the brains and table manners of a sodding goat!" He shook his head disdainfully.

"Hey, that's pretty good," Janessa laughed.

"I'll grant you that Daymore Dolor isn't a bastion of intellectualism," Sul admitted, "rampant ignorance and barbarism seems to be symptomatic of pervasive Imperium influence."

"Huh?" Janessa said frowning.

"Stupid people are easier to control, especially if they're too busy fighting each other to fight the people in charge," Sul's tone dripped with spite. "And the Imperium does so love having control."

"Oh."

Ulak smiled and shook his head. "You've chosen a worthy adversary; I'll give you that much." He cleared his throat, "Thank you for all your help. Is there any way in which I may repay you generosity?"

"There is," Sul said softly and held up a small vial filled with a purple liquid. "I need you to drink this before you go."

Ulak frowned. "What is it?"

"It is an elixir, one that will erase a very specific set of memories."

"Are you joking?" the orc exclaimed.

"No, I am not joking."

Ulak scowled. "Which specific set of memories exactly?"

"This elixir will erase all recollection of a single individual from your memory."

Ulak's brow furrowed as he tentatively took the vial. "Which individual?" he asked as he held the bottle up to the light and peered within.

"Me."

Ulak nearly dropped the bottle. "What?!" he asked, aghast.

"The elixir will remove all memory of me from your mind. To you, it will be as if we never met."

"But wh—"

"Retzel will not stop hunting you Ulak. We both know that his ego is too large to allow him to simply cut his losses." Sul gestured at his people, caught in the bustle of setting camp. "If the unthinkable should happen, he will not hesitate to ravage your mind to uncover how you managed to escape." Sul's tone became regretful, "As much as our friendship means to me, the lives of those I am responsible for must take priority."

For a long time, Ulak regarded the man before him and then the vial. Sul held out his arm and Ulak grabbed his forearm without hesitation. "I have never known a truer friend, nor a nobler soul," the orc rasped.

"Take heart, Ulak," Sul offered him with a solemn smile.

"*Varghak shen shiel,*" Ulak whispered.

"And you as well," Sul replied releasing the orc. For a moment, the two men simply looked at each other.

"Does it speak ill of me that I am afraid?" Ulak asked.

"Only the dead are without fear," Sul replied. "But there comes a time when you stop running, when you turn and face the tiger."

Ulak smiled faintly. "I like that. I will remember that, if nothing else."

"If anyone could…"

There was another long moment of silence between the two men. Then the orc bowed deeply, his hand over his heart, turned and departed without a word.

Sul remained where he stood watching as Ulak faded from view and a prolonged silence followed.

"What did that mean?" Janessa asked curiously, seeking to break the pall that had settled over them. "*Varg—*"

"*Varghak shen shiel,*" Sul corrected.

"Which means…"

"Boundless glory," the blind man answered softly. "A pledge between brothers who are to enter battle and do not expect to see each other again in this life."

"…oh." She looked down at her hands and then back to regard the man. "He was important to you."

"He was...my friend."

A long pause and then Sul turned away. "Come, we have work to do."

"Yeah, about that," Janessa rubbed the back of her neck sheepishly. "It's been fun and all, but I really need to be on my—"

"You are directly responsible for the injury of two of my soldiers and have incurred a debt to the Phoenix Legion," Sul cut her off, his tone utterly devoid of the humanity that had been present a moment before. "That debt will be repaid. Follow."

"Aye, aye." Janessa swallowed noisily and, repressing a shiver as she got to her feet, followed the blind man from the tent.

THE TRUE THREAT

"It is under adversity that the weak and slow minded are broken and the strong and quick-witted flourish. These opportunities may come from unexpected places but must be capitalized upon. The wise warrior does not question potential because the form is unfamiliar. They find the best way to turn it to their advantage."

—A passage from *Victor Vinguardis* (Way of Victory)
translated from Daymorian. Author unknown.
Currently banned by the Church of Imperius

"Lieutenant Vallorin, welcome back."

"Hello, Lieutenant Pellinore." Ceyrabeth smiled down at Pellinore and Keiran from atop Eregost. She was rather surprised at how much seeing them, and the rest of the Legion, felt like coming home. "What's the news?"

"The Captain wants to see you in the command tent, Lieutenant. Immediately."

"Immediately. Of course, he does." Ceyrabeth sighed. She had ridden hard for days. A bath had been the only thing on her mind for roughly the last hundred miles. She felt like less than half a human. But...it was Sul, and she could not defy him. She handed Keiran the reins. "Take Eregost for me, will you?"

Ceyrabeth followed Pellinore through camp, astonished at the number of smiles directed at her, and the number of times she heard "Welcome back Lieutenant!" or "Glad you're back, Lieutenant!"

Sul echoed the trend. She found him in his usual place; poring over a map in the command tent. "Welcome back, Lieutenant," he greeted her without looking up.

Ceyrabeth bowed at the waist. "Thank you, Sir."

He straightened and folded his hands behind his back. "Your report?"

"Yes Sir." Ceyrabeth thoroughly laid out the events of the last weeks. When she mentioned Gaetano's name, she was surprised to see Sul's lip curl with scorn. "He doesn't think much of you either, Captain," she informed him dryly.

"No, I imagine he does not. Is he in camp?"

"No, Sir," she replied with a grimace. "Thank the gods for small favors."

"Indeed." Sul steepled his fingers. "Still, I'm curious about this artifact he's managed to acquire."

"I'd just as soon never see it—or him—again," Ceyrabeth huffed. "So, if my next mission is to retrieve it Captain, I respectfully submit my resignation."

A smile flickered over Sul's lips; just a second before it was gone, but Ceyrabeth knew it had been there. "No, Lieutenant. We have bigger issues."

Ceyrabeth frowned. "Sir?"

"Follow me," he said, turning without even waiting to check if she was following, and striding away from her, a heavy cloak of dark purple flaring out behind him.

"Yes, Sir," Ceyrabeth muttered and with a sigh trudged after him. At the stables, the Captain ordered Banshee saddled and the shell-shocked stable hand had it done in less time than it took to blink. They hadn't even had time to unsaddle Eregost as Ceyrabeth swung back up.

They rode out of camp to the south, the road packed firm by the tramp of many feet. It made for easy riding and after about an hour, they were facing a steep incline. Sul dismounted and so did Ceyrabeth. "Leave Eregost," he commanded. "I would rather not have your mount spooked."

"Yes, Sir," she said automatically, but then a thought nudged its way into her mind.

"Wait...how do you spook the undead?" Sul made no reply. "You know," she puffed, cursing the fact that she was being forced to march uphill in armor, "the Taintbrood have to be close on our heels."

"You are mistaken, Lieutenant," Sul replied, not sounding the least bit out of breath as he crested the peak and gestured out to the vista. "They are already here."

Ceyrabeth's eyes went wide, and the blood drained from her face. "Green preserve me." The Taintbrood were swarming over the ground like an upended ant hill, clamoring over everything that moved. They were a hissing, snarling mass of horror and her stomach turned at the sight of them. Even as she watched she could see the ground and vegetation wither and blacken from their blighted presence. The smell slammed into her with the force of a war hammer; heat and rot and decay, like a bloated corpse left to putrefy in the sun.

"Their scent was on the winds a day and a half ago," Sul stated impassively, giving no outward indications of discomfort. "But you can feel the presence of the horde from further still."

"Fe...feel?" She swallowed back bile.

Sul turned to regard her coolly, his eyes hidden by the samite bindings. "What you're experiencing right now? That feeling of filth that never washes away? Anyone who cares to, can detect it, at a cost."

"And the cost is?"

"For the remainder of your days, Ceyrabeth, you will never be able to forget how the horde got inside you blood, wormed its way behind your bones...and made you experience their corruption." He looked back out upon the roiling mass of filth and carefully began to unwind the samite bindings around his eyes.

"What are you doing?"

"Tarah told me that the Brood's threat was greater than any realized." The final wrapping came undone, and Sul looked at Ceyrabeth with eyes colored yellow, streaks of green and violet running through them. "That the evil behind it is the true threat." He removed a small ornate half mask from his cloak, adorned in blue and yellow jewels.

"What is that?" Ceyrabeth asked. The mask looked like something out of a royal masquerade ball. It seemed very out of place here.

"A gift." He placed the mask over his face. "Something to increase one's perceptions and reveal that which is hidden."

As the seconds passed, Ceyrabeth got restless. "Is your plan for us to stay here until I can experience the worming corruption for myself? Because I have to tell you, that would really—"

A scream, agonized and bestial, cut her off. Sul was stumbling about, his hands over his face. *He* was making that awful sound, like all the pain in the world was being inflicted upon him.

"Captain Sul!" Ceyrabeth cried out and reached out for him.

"Don't touch me!"

Ceyrabeth gasped. His eyes were pools of swirling blackness. The blackness quickly overflowed from his eyes to spread through his face; his forehead, his cheeks, through his nose and down his neck, across his lips and mouth...*in* his mouth... she could see it forcing itself down his throat like liquid tar and his throat bulged obscenely. He pushed himself away from her and stumbling, he pitched forwards...

...and fell from the precipice.

"*No!*" The elven woman cried out and she lunged and dove, her armor scraping across the dirt. Frantically she clawed forward and nearly threw herself over the edge after him. By blind good luck, she seized his wrist and he jerked to an abrupt halt. Beneath him, not fifty meters from his feet was the roiling horde of the Taintbrood, ravenous and bloated, teeth and claws and swords and death.

"Give me your other hand!" she screamed, dangling over the edge at the waist. The scream was as much pain as urgency. In the heat of the moment, she had reached with her dominant hand, her wounded shoulder howling agony as the injured muscle ripped under Sul's weight. Ceyrabeth set her jaw against the pain. "Please, hurry!"

Sul's mangled features peered back down at the Horde and then once more into Ceyrabeth's face.

"Release...me," he croaked.

"No, I've got you! Just give me your other arm!" The weight of her own armor was starting to drag her forward toward death.

"Release me," he commanded again, his voice stronger. "You can do nothing for me."

"I can save your flaming life!"

"The life of a heretic? A vile blasphemer? A man you yourself swore to kill?"

Ceyrabeth gritted her teeth, her wounded shoulder on fire with the strain of supporting his weight and trying to stop her own descent. "This is *not* the time for this conversation! For the love of all that is Holy, give me your other arm!"

"By all that is holy, as decried by the Imperium, release me!"

"*To the Void with the Imperium! Give me your arm!*"

Time stood still in that moment and for the first time Ceyrabeth could recall, she saw surprise register across Sul's mutilated features. With a grunt he swung his free arm up. She reached and made contact...

...and the ground beneath her legs gave way.

"No!" she screamed. She slid forward...and jerked to a stop, something pulled tight around her ankle.

"I've got you!" a voice called out from above her. Ceyrabeth dared to look back, the angle giving her vertigo.

It was the girl, Janessa. She smiled as she wove a stout length of rope through the waist straps of Ceyrabeth's armor, another length already wrapped around Ceyrabeth's ankle and anchored somewhere above. "Have you out in a lick." And then her face vanished from view and Ceyrabeth felt the rope near her waist pull taut. Her armor dug into her shoulders and neck, but Ceyrabeth felt her center of gravity begin to shift as she and Sul were hauled back from the cliff. As soon her torso was on solid ground, Ceyrabeth focused on pulling Sul up, every muscle in her body on fire.

There was a snarl and a jerk, and Ceyrabeth gasped; a scrambling, chittering Taintbrood had broken away from the hoard, scrambled up the cliff, and attached itself to Sul's leg. She howled as the motion ripped against her injured shoulder again, spots dancing across her vision.

"Janessa!" Ceyrabeth screamed. "They've got him!"

"One moment please," Janessa said in a voice that spoke of tremendous strain yet attempted nonchalance. There was a brief pause, "Alley-oop!" and then, "Look out below!"

With a heave that made her choke on another howl of agony, she brought Sul up far enough that he could throw his left arm around the back of her neck, grasping her pauldron for purchase.

Ceyrabeth twisted her head around as far as she could to see what was about to...

A dagger soared up into the air over her head, lazily spinning end over end.

What is that girl—

The dagger finished its ascent and began to plunge down towards them.

She couldn't possibly—

Gasping, Ceyrabeth jerked her head to the side quickly as a familiar dagger with a heavy looking pommel plunged past them and collided hard into the creature grasping at Sul, shattering its nose. It shrieked and clutched its face as it plunged back into the teeming mass below.

"We're clear! Pull!"

"*Quatas*!" Janessa swore as her body flexed. "What in the name of Seeress Edaya do you think I'm doing?!"

Ceyrabeth hazarded a look back. Janessa had the rope holding her and Sul slung over the branch of a tree, forming a crude pulley. She had it wrapped around both arms and was pulling down with her entire body. She clutched it like the lifeline it was, her feet braced against the solid root that the rope was anchored to. She looked far too small to be holding so much weight, but with a growl and a curse she heaved and brought Ceyrabeth back onto solid ground. The other woman wasted no time, even as she felt Janessa's hold go slack, to hoist Sul all the way up. She dragged him a solid two feet away from the edge before releasing him.

"Not...giving me grief about that dagger's balance, now, are you?" Janessa panted as she sagged to the ground next to Sul, shaking out arms that were already starting to show bruises. "What happened to him?"

"I'm...not sure." She was suddenly leery about the Captain's privacy.

"I'm fine," Sul said calmly and got to his feet. Ceyrabeth was shocked to see that his features had returned to normal, his glass eyes now a combination of yellow with streaks of violet and green.

Suddenly something occurred to Ceyrabeth. "Janessa...don't think I'm ungrateful," she started, "but what in the name of the Green Lord were you doing all the way out here?"

"The stable boy and I are…friends," she said with a wink. "I asked him to keep me up to date on who leaves. I thought it was weird that you and the Captain would be heading out alone, so I followed you. I didn't think I'd be running a rescue mission. So…really though. What happened?"

"I was told by someone that it was the evil behind the Brood that was the true threat," Sul reiterated as he turned his gaze back out to the edge of the cliff, careful not to look directly at the Horde again. "And she was right." He turned back to face the women. "Our plans must be accelerated. This faction of the horde cannot be allowed to rejoin the rest."

"This isn't the whole horde?" Janessa asked agape.

"No, this is but a single arm of it." He turned his glass gaze to Ceyrabeth. "You know it well, Lieutenant; it was the faction that decimated your forces at Velasgate."

The woman's eyes narrowed dangerously. "So, what do we do about it?" she asked.

Sul considered a moment. "I believe that the time to engage our enemy upon the field of battle is drawing near."

"Finally." Her expression transformed into one of predatory glee.

"Come." Sul started to descend the hill but then stopped as he ran his hands over the rope.

"Sir?" Ceyrabeth asked, still concerned for his health.

Turning, he faced Janessa. "Two people plus armor. How much would you say that weighed?"

The girl shrugged. "I don't know. Maybe a few hundred pounds or so."

"And how much do you weigh?"

Janessa laughed. "Come now, you know better than to ask a girl her weight—" The rest of her joke died as she watched his face. "Less than a hundred pounds."

"You sound confident of that answer."

"I am." She smiled a little. "I was always good at figuring these sorts of things out. Helps to know by heft whether something is brass or gold when it comes time to make some quick coin."

"I would imagine so," Sul replied his tone taking her by surprise with its complete absence of the judgment she'd always received regarding her methods from everyone else. "And the dagger? Throwing it blind up into the air and having it come down exactly where you need?"

"Wasn't blind." She tapped her head. "I remembered where you were and the rest of it was just, you know, making sure I picked the dagger with the right heft and got the right kind of throw."

"You mean calculating weight, trajectory and angle, all from memory?" Sul's tone took on an admiring note.

Janessa blushed. "I...guess? They taught us a lot about how to fight without seeing our opponent back home."

"How is that possible?" Ceyrabeth gaped. "I thought for sure that was magic!"

"'Magic' is just a word for knowledge we have not yet encountered." Sul looked thoughtful.

"You've shown initiative by having the stable boy provide you information." He gestured at the rope.

"The way you set up the pulley and anchored the rope to precise points on Lieutenant Vallorin's armor demonstrates both ingenuity and expertise, especially given how little time you had to come up with it." He smiled faintly. "And your skill with a dagger is certainly above question."

"Umm..." Janessa gave a little laugh. "Thank you?"

Sul nodded. "Thank you for saving the life of someone I value greatly." He nodded towards Ceyrabeth. Her copper eyebrows furrowed, and she studiously avoided Janessa's gaze.

"Not to mention yourself." Janessa winked. "Or do you not value your own life as well?"

"Not particularly." The matter-of-fact coldness of his tone brought both women up short.

"Oh," Janessa managed.

"You did well today, Janessa. The Phoenix Legion has need of quick and creative minds." His tone thawed slightly, "If you are going to insist on being so useful, then I am under an obligation to find use for you."

"That sounds...nice?" The young girl's voice vibrated between bewilderment and a giddy awe.

Sul nodded once and turned his attention to Ceyrabeth. "And as for you, Lieutenant, you disobeyed a direct order. You were commanded to release me. Your priority was to return to the Phoenix Legion and warn them."

Ceyrabeth's features flushed, this time with anger. "Yes, and I'd do it again! What in the Green do you think I could warn *anyone* about?! That the Hoard is moving and ravenous? Things we already know?" She raked her fingers though her hair. "Shit, Osen would probably eat me thinking I threw you off the cliff myself! *You're* the one with the knowledge, you're the one with the plan, and your life had better well start meaning something to you because it means something to the rest of us!" She stopped for a moment before adding, grudgingly, "... Sir."

They stared at each other for the span of a few heartbeats. "Ceyrabeth, you are insubordinate, reckless and you question my decisions relentlessly. Your actions today only prove what I have already long known."

"Do they? And what is that?" She blinked hard, once, then again, her chin tilted just a shade higher than it needed to be, despite her practiced look of stubborn surety.

"That I chose my lieutenant well." A slow smile crept upon his lips.

"I...what?"

Reaching out, Sul placed his hand upon her shoulder. "Thank you for saving my life and for your continued loyalty to the Phoenix Legion. Rest assured, it has not gone unnoticed."

With that, he strode towards the waiting Banshee below.

"What just happened?" Janessa asked as the pair of them started after him.

"I have no idea," Ceyrabeth replied.

"Me neither...but I really want to find out."

"Same here. Let's go."

With that, both women hurried behind the departing form of their enigmatic Captain.

They headed down the hill to where their mounts were tethered, a bay gelding joining Eregost and Banshee. Janessa swung up into the bay's saddle as though she weighed nothing, the Captain only slightly less agile as he mounted Banshee and began rewrapping his eyes. That left Ceyrabeth, flat footed and staring at the side of a horse that suddenly seemed miles tall.

She could not raise her right arm. Bringing it a few inches up made her want to howl. The other side wasn't much better; not injured but weak with strain. There was no way she was going to be able to haul herself onto the horse's back with one semi-working arm. If she ordered Eregost to belly down, they would know she was injured. For some reason, she did *not* wish to show weakness in front of Janessa.

"I believe," said Ceyrabeth with carefully studied nonchalance, "that I will walk."

"Walk? Ceyrabeth, there is an *army* of Taintbrood right on the other side of the hill and..." Janessa studied her carefully. "You're joking? Is she joking?"

"I think not." Sul turned his rebandaged gaze to Ceyrabeth, studied her a moment, and slipped off Banshee's back. Ceyrabeth stiffened as he came to stand beside her, almost close enough to bump elbows.

"Do ghualainn?" "Your shoulder?"

He spoke Draith, oddly enough, his voice barely a whisper. Ceyrabeth had learned the dying Druidic language as a little girl. How he had come to know it, or how he *knew* she knew it, she had no idea.

"Yes." Ceyrabeth replied, matching his tone.

She felt something small and cold press into her hand and then, with a swirl of aubergine fabric, Sul was settled on Banshee again. "If you're certain, Lieutenant. Come, Janessa."

They were almost out of sight when Ceyrabeth looked at what Sul had handed her. A tiny crystal bottle, stoppered with a unique filigreed silver rune. She uncorked it and a glimmer of light welled up, making her fingertips tingle.

"Healing potion..." She was barely aware that she had spoken aloud. And not one of the cheap, wyrmscale knock-offs that kept the Dolor city patrol so busy—no, this was the real thing. She'd seen legitimate healing potions only a few times in her life. The one in her hand probably cost more than she and Eregost put together, with her sword thrown in for good measure.

The second it hit her tongue she wanted to laugh. She could practically *feel* the torn muscles knitting themselves together. The pain was eradicated instantly. No longer did the horse seem an insurmountable obstacle—she could leap over his head, in full armor and suddenly walking didn't sound like such an idiotic plan after all, really, or maybe she'd just run the whole way...

"Good of you to join us," Janessa said dryly as Ceyrabeth came galloping up. The other woman shot her a two fingered salute, nodded at Sul and dropped back into her place, just behind Banshee's shoulder on his left side.

When they returned to camp, Sul acknowledged no one. He dropped out of the saddle at the entrance to the command tent as Ceyrabeth and Janessa followed suit. Sul stalked in, his purple cloak billowing behind him like a storm cloud with the woman flanking him in his wake.

Janessa's eye caught sight of the bejeweled half mask still clutched in Sul's fist as he moved to the opposite side of the war table. "Those are blue sand sapphires and royal topaz," she whispered to Ceyrabeth, "it's worth a small fortune..."

Wordlessly, Sul hurled the mask full force to the floor, slammed down his boot, and the delicate piece of art detonated into a shower of gold and shards of jewels.

"Goddess!" Ceyrabeth gasped, stopping in her tracks. She felt her emotions shutting down, her mind clearing in the defense mechanism that had served her well in her time with the Hammers and especially with Parette, who never spoke moderately if he could lose his temper instead.

Meanwhile Janessa stared at the pile of twisted metal and broken gems that had once been a priceless artifact. "That hurt me on so many levels," she murmured forlornly.

Sul's hands were gripping the edge of the war table so tightly the women could hear the wood creak and his fingernails scraping against its surface. His head was hung but his shoulders remained hunched and tightened like a coiled snake ready to strike.

"Captain..." Janessa reached out to touch him and froze as Sul jerked his head up to face them. The expression on his face could only be described as a feral mask of fury and anguish. If he'd had eyes, she was certain that they would be filled to the brim with murderous intent. As such, they were twin pools of yellow glass.

"Janessa, to me," Ceyrabeth ordered, her voice carefully neutral. The young human wordlessly did as she asked, slowly, as one would when backing away from a dangerous animal.

Sul took a long, deep breath exhaling slowly and stood up straight. His expression became calm once more. "Atiya?"

"Sir?" The Mithrac woman appeared at his side with such speed that she may have teleported there.

"Double the sentry patrols and summon the war council. I want the inner council, the highest-ranking officers, the division commanders. Everyone."

Atiya frowned slightly. "Everyone, Sir?" All the women in the tent wore identical expressions of confusion.

The air in the room abruptly went cold again as Sul locked his glass gaze on his servant.

"*Eve-ry-one,*" he emphasized each syllable, and his tone was lethal.

Atiya blinked and then nodded. "Yes Sir."

"Well," Janessa whispered to Ceyrabeth, "I certainly don't need to use the privy any longer."

Ceyrabeth was too engrossed in what she was witnessing to comment. "He looks *pissed,*" Janessa continued.

"He certainly does," the other woman admitted. The part of her that was *not* responsible for holding her unease in careful check could not help but wonder how the man would channel his rage.

She suspected it would not bode well for the Taintbrood.

Or for anything else that got in his way.

Fifteen minutes later the spacious tent was packed full. Sul sat at the head of the war table. Atiya stood behind him. To his left sat Lieutenant Pellinore and then arranged around the table was Peloquin, Ravenna, Narl-Shu, Maul, and a man that Ceyrabeth did not recognize who wore the emblem of the Chalicemen. Ceyrabeth, her face carefully and thoroughly blank, sat across from Pellinore on Sul's right. The rest of the tent was filled with various men and women who represented the leadership of the Phoenix Legion in its entirety. The elven woman only recognized a few faces, but every person there radiated both competence and confidence.

Sul held up his hand and all idle chatter ceased as those assembled awaited the commands of their leader.

"There has been a miscalculation on my part," Sul began softly. "I have underestimated the strength of the enemy's forces. This mistake is mine and it is my responsibility to correct it."

Everyone in the tent exchanged mute looks of shock. It was possible that few of them had ever seen any evidence that the brilliant strategist that led them was in fact capable of *making* a mistake let alone being willing to admit it in front of his subordinates.

"We will implement evacuation protocols upon the conclusion of this meeting."

There were more than a few gasps of shock from those assembled. Ceyrabeth and Pellinore exchanged looks of stunned disbelief. *Evacuate?* Ceyrabeth frowned and fought down a rising tide of confusion and frustration. *Hadn't he just said we were going to* engage *the enemy?*

"We will withdraw to the northern regions. The foothills there will provide additional cover against the Brood and by keeping to the river we will be able to move more quickly and keep our provisions well stocked."

"Those lands are the territory of Duke de Chalon," Peloquin spoke up, his tone lacking its usual mirth. "If we're going to be moving our forces there, we need to make certain that the ruling nobility is amicable. May have to grease some palms...or slit some throats," he finished his statement with a grin and a chuckle.

That chuckle died before it was halfway done as Sul focused on him. "Then grease palms and slit as many throats as is necessary. You will have access to as much funding and personnel as you require but you will succeed in this mission by whatever means necessary. Am I clear, Peloquin?"

The one horned Mithrac swallowed and nodded. "Perfectly clear, *mon capitan.*"

Sul turned his attention to the unfamiliar man displaying the sign of the Chalicemen.

"Wallach."

"Sir?" He was a middle-aged man with a prominent mustache, his head shaved to the skin. He looked to be about twenty years older than Ceyrabeth, maybe more. Normally competent, Ceyrabeth decided, but now he looked very nervous.

"You and your Chalicemen know more about engaging the Brood than anyone else. I want you to assemble your most proficient riders and rangers. Arm them with bows and enough provisions to survive on their own for an extended period."

"Skirmishers, Sir?"

"That's correct. Your men will act as a rear-guard diversionary force. It will be their job to draw the Brood's attention away from the Legion whilst we make our way north. Under no circumstances are they to attempt to engage the main force directly. Harassment and diversionary tactics only. I expect you to have multiple routes of attack and twice that many routes of escaped planned out in advance."

"Yes Sir. When do you want them by?"

"Within the hour."

"Sir that's—" Wallach's protest died in his throat at Sul's demeanor. "Yes Sir, a plan within the hour. How long do I have to assemble my forces?"

"One day."

"Yes Sir."

Sul held his gaze a moment longer then nodded before shifting his attention. "Narl-Shu."

The necromancer managed a shaky smile. "What are your orders..." and then as an afterthought, "...Sir?"

"Our route will pass through the barrows of Valak, Jenhyme, and Corrus."

"Yes, Sir. The entombed remains of men and dwarves who fought together against the Nevaraakese incursion of the previous age."

"I want them."

Narl-Shu looked confused for a moment before his mouth fell open, "you mean, you want them reanimated?"

"I do."

"With all due respect, Sir, you're talking about hundreds of entombed dead. It would require every necromancer in my cabal and even then, it would be almost impossible."

"Then I expect you to use every last necromancer at your disposal and achieve the impossible."

The Necromancer opened his mouth, but no words came out.

"The penalty for breaking into those crypts is death," Peloquin said softly. "If they are discovered, it would mean war with the dwarves and several of the prominent noble families whose relatives they would be stealing away."

"Then they best not be discovered," Sul said calmly. "I want these corpses reanimated and instruct them to head south."

"You want them to cover our escape," Ceyrabeth spoke up suddenly as Sul's plan became clear to her. "That's why we're headed through this region; you need disposable forces to defend our rear ranks."

"Just so, Lieutenant."

"Breaking into those crypts in broad daylight"—Narl-Shu shook his head—"I don't believe it's possible."

"Anything is possible," Sul countered as he shifted his attention to Ravenna, "with the right support."

"Sir?" The bronze skinned woman looked confused and more than a little apprehensive.

"Gather your best illusionists and have them accompany Narl-Shu and his cabal."

"You want us to use our spells to make Narl-Shu and his graverobbers more difficult to detect?" she purred in sudden comprehension, endlessly excited by the man's cunning.

"Cloak them in whatever enchantments they will require to access the barrows without drawing attention to themselves."

"Aren't hordes of undead shambling their way out of the earth going to attract attention as is?" Ceyrabeth asked.

"Not if we do it one barrow at a time," Narl-Shu replied as understanding flooded him. "We move from burial mound to burial mound. Ravenna's illusionists cover us. We reanimate those interred and send them south. In small groups of five to twenty and then we move on. If we keep their numbers small, they should be able to avoid notice."

"What are bands of five to twenty undead going to do against an army? Such small numbers, any attack is doomed." Scout leader Mischa shook her head.

"Because those bands will all meet in one place, someplace hidden, perhaps underground. Once we've got enough assembled, we'll send them to attack the Brood and keep the attention focused on themselves instead of our living forces," Narl-Shu explained, his tone bordering on contemptuous.

"Remind your people not to take any unnecessary risks beyond gaining access to the burial mounds," Sul instructed. "Raise the dead, send them south. At no point should you or anyone under your command be within sight of the Brood itself." Sul nodded at the necromancer. "Get your forces together, plot your route to the barrows, select the most promising ones and find a rendezvous point where the dead can assemble in secret before sending them against the Brood."

"And how long do I have to put this together?"

"Two hours to plot your route. Another twelve to assemble your cabal and start heading south. Take a detachment of rangers to accompany your forces; you'll need their help navigating the wilds."

Narl-Shu relaxed slightly, even as he and Mischa acquired similar looks of irritation at being stuck together. The prospect of his group of mages stomping through the wilderness in search of the burial mounds without any kind of support had seemed like suicide. Having a company of experienced woodsmen made the entire idea much more palatable.

"Beggin' your pardon Cap'n," Maul rumbled, "but is all this necessary? They're the Brood; mindless bloody rabble of ugly and the like. Just massacre the lot of them and send them packing."

"You are mistaken, Sergeant," Sul explained calmly. "These are not a 'mindless rabble' as you put it. The Taintbrood have gained a focus and a direction I cannot fully explain. Until I find out how—and I *will* find out—I will not waste troops or resources on an enemy I am not prepared to defeat."

Maul held the Captain's eyeless gaze for a few heartbeats, then slowly nodded. "Okay boss, where do you want me and mine?"

Sul pointed to a spot on the map. "Here. You will serve as the forward vanguard traveling at least a day ahead. You will eliminate any threats you come across and take special care that Shu's and Ravenna's forces do not encounter any unwelcome surprises."

"Shouldn't Maul and his men stick close to us if they're supposed to be our escort?" Narl-Shu asked, concerned.

"Cap'n knows what he's doing," Maul offered. "My berserkers and I do better given free run of the battle instead of leashed to a single spot." He gestured to the necromancer. "Me and mine can outpace you lot three to one. We can cover more ground and we can take out anything that gets in our way before you ever see them." Maul turned his attentions back to the Captain. "I assume that's the plan, yeah? Wipe out anything nasty on our way?"

"If they can't be reasoned with, yes." Sul nodded before adding, "You have a keen grasp of the tactical capabilities of your warriors. Well done."

To Ceyrabeth's astonishment, the enormous elf *blushed*. "Umm, yes Sir, thank you, Sir." He kept his flushed grin focused on the table.

"Obviously speed is of the essence. I will not waste time going through an unnecessary chain of command." He turned his attention to the Royal Elf sitting beside him. "Lieutenant, I am hereby promoting you to the rank of commander. You will coordinate our retreat and act with my authority during this matter and other such matters that may arise in the future. You may assemble your staff at your discretion."

There were more than a few gasps—including from Pellinore. "Yes Sir!" The elf swallowed hard. "I—Thank you, Sir."

"Congratulations Commander Pellinore." Sul turned his attention to the assembled officers and the stunned silence of the tent. "Janessa, Lieutenant Vallorin, remain. The rest of you have your orders. Dismissed."

With crisp salutes the assembled officers filed out of the tent, some offering congratulations to Pellinore, who was still in a state of shock.

Soon only Atiya, Janessa, and Ceyrabeth remained. "I know you," Janessa murmured.

"Do you?" Sul asked smoothly.

"Yes. Amongst my people we have a legend of a maimed chieftain who could see into the souls of friends and enemies alike and was unbeatable on the field of battle. We call him '*sipahasaalaar*.'"

"Which means?" Ceyrabeth inquired.

"Warlord," Sul answered on her behalf, he looked back at Janessa. "As apt a title as any I suppose."

Janessa was grinning wildly. "Then you *are him*! The siege of Quhath. The defeat of both the djinn and lithmorte armies. The liberator of the slave citadel at Yhen-Naga. The—"

Sul nodded. "Yes, I am," he interjected to stem what seemed to be an endless tide of accolades.

"That is so..." Her grin threatened to split her face in half. "This is such an honor." She gave her best military salute. "Where do want me?"

"You'll be assisting Ceyrabeth in her efforts with Pellinore."

"I'm what now?" Ceyrabeth demanded.

"Pellinore is going to need staff. I expect you will be amongst them. You can both give and follow orders, you understand the enemy we face, and you have a talent for making the most of various opportunities other, more traditional minded individuals may overlook and ignore." He nodded towards the tent exterior. "Put them to good use and assist the commander. In turn, Janessa will assist you."

The younger woman flashed Sul a bright grin that showed up even more brightly against her dusky skin. *"Aap ek kalaakaaravaadee maut mar sakate hain!"* she recited and spun on heels heading out of the tent.

"And you as well," Sul answered.

"What's going on?" Ceyrabeth asked.

"An old expression from the deserts of the south. It means 'May you die an artistic death.'"

The elven woman made a face. "Charming, but not what I'm talking about." She sat across from the man. "I mean *why me*? Out of everyone in this camp, why am I suddenly third in command?"

"For the reasons I stipulated earlier. You instill confidence."

"In the men?"

"And their leader."

Ceyrabeth felt a touch of warmth flood her face. "That's...unexpected. Thank you, Sir," she said quietly before turning a frown towards the tent exit. "But do I really need *her* help?"

"I leave that entirely up to you, but I would not dismiss her out of hand. Like yourself, Janessa enjoys the luxury of non-traditional thinking."

"If you want to call it that," the elven woman muttered before looking down at her feet. Right next to her boot was one of the jewels from the shattered mask. This one was fully intact.

It increases one's perceptions and reveals what is hidden.

More out of curiosity than anything else, Ceyrabeth discreetly reached down and palmed the jewel. It was the size of her thumb and shone a piercing royal blue. Carefully, she raised the gem up to her eye. The room was cast in azure as she scanned it. She peered at her own hand in wonder; it showed up in vibrant shades of orange, green, violet, and red. When she focused on Atiya she saw no colors at all, only a shadow that permeated her entire being. Then she focused on Sul, who had his head down studying the map.

Screaming. Hooks and chains. Ropes caked in gore. Sharpened spikes and blades. Carving, cutting, shredding, impaling. More screaming. Wailing. The cries of the damned. Flesh being torn, flayed. So much blood...

Ceyrabeth cried out and yanked the gem away from her face; her heart pounding, eyes wide as she gasped for breath.

"Was there something else you had to add Lieutenant?" Sul inquired calmly.

"No...no, Sir. Sorry Sir." She cleared her throat, and then again. Barely trusting her trembling legs to support her she stood and made her way to the door.

"Lieutenant?"

"Yes—" She swallowed around what felt like a mouthful of cotton. "Yes Sir?"

"The gem currently in your possession is dangerous." He gestured at the tabletop with a quill. "Leave it upon the table."

Ceyrabeth licked her lips as she nodded hurriedly and rushed to the table, casting the stone upon its surface as if it were a poisonous creature. "Yes Sir."

Sul looked up at her, his eyes an intense, sickly shade of goldenrod. "Thank you. Dismissed."

She didn't trust herself with any other words as she hurried out of the tent.

"What do you think she saw?" Atiya asked stoically.

"Enough," was the Captain's only answer.

Ceyrabeth made it ten paces outside the command tent before her stomach emptied itself in a torrent of vomit and bile.

"Goddess…" she swore. She grabbed a canteen from a passing soldier and drained it in a single gulp. "More," she rasped, shaking as she pressed it back into his hands. The soldier hurried away as the elven woman bent double, the heels of her hands pressing into her eyes. *Green Lord, Mother War, spirits above, oh…*

"Child, are you quite alright?"

The soldier was back and he had brought back Mother Reiko. Ceyrabeth looked up at Mother Reiko's question. "You know. You know what was done to him?"

"Roland, thank you. You go ahead." Reiko gently dismissed the soldier who wasted no time following her order. Reiko slipped an arm around Ceyrabeth's waist and urged her away from the command tent. "Yes, Ceyrabeth. I know he has suffered greatly."

"Suffered greatly?!" Her angry howl sent birds winging from the trees. "Tortured! Mutilated! You…you cannot stay sane. You cannot! And yet he is here, and you follow him. You all do, even with that hellscape behind him and *MOTHER*! How do you do it, and know, and still follow?!"

"I do because I must. Whether sane or not, he rescued me from my own Void. Now I must help deliver him from the Void that he carries within." The older woman smiled, sadly. "I have managed to put my torments behind me, but the Captain? I believe his suffering is the closest thing to a constant companion he has ever known."

"What a terrible life you must have led." Ceyrabeth stumbled along next to Reiko, her pale skin flushed and feverish. "Alone, always forgotten except when they forced you to...."

"Do not look too deeply." Reiko's voice cut through the haze at the edge of Ceyrabeth's vision. She sat her on the edge of a bench, placed a cool hand on Ceyrabeth's forehead. The elven woman leaned into it, almost desperate in her need for the small comfort offered. "Was someone in your family a seer, child?"

"My father," she murmured. "The gift died with him."

"I wouldn't be so sure of that." Reiko replied with a gentle roll of her dark eyes. "Just focus here. What do you hear?"

"Screams. Tearing flesh. Metal on metal..."

"No, Ceyrabeth." The healer's voice was sharp. "Here, in this camp. What do you hear?"

Frogs. They were still near a bog on the opposite side, and the chorus was nearly deafening. The shrill, droning whine of mosquitoes coming out for their nightly blood hunt. A soft whicker from the stables. People moving, hurrying but hushed, trying to move as fast as they could under the grim authority of their Captain and so many being called to stand by. Be ready to march, any second...

Ceyrabeth's eyes snapped open. "I need to help break down the camp. We need to move, now."

Reiko smiled as Ceyrabeth stood and offered a hand to help her up. "Indeed. Captain's orders."

Ceyrabeth nodded, her sable eyes no longer sharp with fear but steady and determined.

"Captain's orders."

"Before you do"—Reiko reached into her robe and removed a vial with a small note—"this...may help you."

Ceyrabeth took the vial and the note and studied it.

That which is seen cannot be unseen. Thus, it must be forgotten and cast aside. The flowing handwriting, crisp and precise, could only have come from...

"This is from Sul," Ceyrabeth murmured.

"His creation, yes," the elderly woman confirmed. Ceyrabeth held up the vial. It was filled with a purple substance that made Ceyrabeth feel dizzy and sick to her stomach as she watched it shift and flow in the light.

"What is it?"

"Something to help you forget. You now carry a terrible burden. This will relieve you of it."

"What happens if I don't drink it?"

"Then you will carry a piece of the Captain's Hell with you. A bond will form, forged of shared agony and either your compassion, strength, and mercy will temper this bond...or it will become a cancer within your soul that will consume you completely."

Ceyrabeth un-stoppered the vial. The scent that wafted from it was sickly sweet and it made her light-headed. She couldn't focus. Shaking her head to clear it, she cast Reiko a wary look.

"It's your decision, Ceyrabeth. The burden is yours to bear or cast aside."

The elf regarded the contents of the vial. It would be so easy to forget...

Screams. Blood. Shrieking torment. Endless and terrible.

Wordlessly, she tipped the vial over and poured it upon the Earth.

"If you can bear Sul's Hell, so can I." Ceyrabeth took the older woman's hand and squeezed it, giving her a brave smile. "And I think it's time someone helped you carry the burden."

Reiko took the young woman's face in her frail hands. "You remarkable child." She kissed Ceyrabeth's forehead gently.

The other woman smiled a little. Then, taking a deep breath and pushing aside the horrors that now dwelt within her thoughts, she got to her feet and stood straight and unbowed. "Come on Mother Reiko. We've got work to do."

"As you say, Lieutenant."

THE BATTLE OF TARGESTE

CEYRABETH TOSSED AND TURNED. THE NIGHT HAD turned sultry, heavy with the promise of rain, but until it fell it made sleeping nigh unbearable. She scrubbed her hands across her face with a growl of impatience and rose from her cot.

She made her way to the tent that Sul had set up as a mobile library. Rows of chests containing neatly sorted books of all varieties stood stacked atop each other, each chest with a small latch that could be closed and locked at a moment's notice. She would have bet her sword arm that the chests also contained enchantments to protect against fire and water. She knew for a fact that they were warded against theft. She chose a volume—Brother Arturo's celebrated treatise 'Peoples of the Underwild'—and sat at the desk where Commander Pellinore could usually be found writing letters, organizing orders, and doing whatever else Sul required of him.

She blew lightly on the fist-sized stone that rested atop the desk and it flared to life, bathing the tent in a gentle white light. What had Pellinore called it? "Bioluminescence," Ceyrabeth tested the word on her tongue. Like everything in the Phoenix Legion even a simple lamp had a greater meaning attached to it.

And like as not the words: 'The Captain found it on his travels' attached to it. She thought with a sigh.

Sometimes she'd like to drag him down to the Underwild, just to see what would happen.

He'd probably find the fabled fortress of Roth Relas and then persuade the Five Thousand Wraiths to join his army. The thought made her sigh again.

Underwild. She told herself firmly, banishing all other thoughts from her mind. She had little enough time to prepare for the coming battle against the Taintbrood, and one thing she had absorbed from her time at Sul's side was that knowledge is power. The Brood hailed from this blighted region after all and so she would learn what she could.

She quickly lost herself in the tome, smiling at the occasional turn of phrase. It brought her back to when she was young, listening to Brother Arturo talk to himself as he tried to find the right words, the right way to phrase a passage. She hoped she had told him how much those times meant to her; how grateful she was that he took the time to take a half-blood under his wing.

The wind was rising. Ceyrabeth slapped her hand down on the book's pages with a jerk and looked around. She was no longer in the library tent. She and the book were lying on the grass by the moat of a tremendous fortress that towered so far above the ground, its battlements were obscured by the clouds above. She sat up, frantically looking around, her mind trying to remember the disconnect.

She had been reading, interested, awake, even taking notes...and then she was here.

Carefully, silently, Ceyrabeth stood and made her way to the drawbridge which was, blessedly, down. She could feel magic singing all around her, so she stepped cautiously onto the planks. They held and she made her way across. When she reached the door, she looked up...and up...and *up.* Closed tight, unscalable, even if she *had* the proper equipment, which she didn't. No handle. No bell. No attendant.

"Merowr?"

Ceyrabeth looked down. There was a cat, the largest cat she had ever seen. It had a long, expressive face, a coat of midnight fur that seemed to catch all the light around it and enormous iridescent eyes. Currently it was eyeing her from around the corner. Ceyrabeth crouched.

"Here kitty kitty," she soothed, rubbing her fingertips against her thumb in an effort to call it to her. "It's ok." The cat came a pace closer but remained out of reach, watching her with eyes that seemed almost far too intelligent. "Are you hungry, kitty?" Slowly Ceyrabeth reached into her pocket and withdrew a bundle wrapped in a clean handkerchief. She carefully withdrew the cheese from her snack and placed it an arm's length away.

The cat edged toward her, walking Ceyrabeth noted, with a clearly defined list to one side.

She watched him as he ate. He didn't favor one paw or act in pain, but his back had a funny twist in it, as though he had been put together just ever-so-slightly crooked. "Well, you certainly have good manners," she informed him as he sat up and washed his face with one paw. He tilted his eerie, rainbow hued eyes in her direction and sashayed toward the door before disappearing though it.

Ceyrabeth gasped. *Where in the world...?* She trotted to the door near where the cat had gone, and then she saw it. A crack in the wood, hidden inside the seam that was *just* big enough for her to slip through, nearly invisible in the watery gray light.

The cat was waiting for her on the other side. He rubbed his cheek against her ankles and when she reached down to lift him up, she felt the thrum of his happy purring all the way up her arm.

"Where is everyone, kitty?" The keep was huge, she noted as she wandered, the vegetable beds well- kept and growing beautifully, the rooms that she peeked into clean and in good repair. Many of them even had food and drink on the tables, as though the owners had sat down for dinner and just remembered a pressing need to be elsewhere.

But other than herself and the cat, she saw no other signs of life. No animals, no people, no sound at all. The strange stillness made her want to tiptoe, and even her breathing sounded deafening to her ears. And there was something else.... She sniffed at the air and rolled her tongue around her mouth trying to figure out what was wrong. It finally came to her. As a child she often helped her parents with their gardens. She could remember how the air smelt of rich soil, how the vegetables left a scent in the air that she could taste: onions, carrots, cabbage. Here though, there were no scents in the air, no tastes upon her tongue even surrounded by all these living things.

Ceyrabeth avoided the front door with its austere height and thoroughly forbidding glyphs and instead followed the line of greenhouses to the side of the keep. She was rewarded with a small servant's door in the stone...and it was unlocked. The door was strangely shaped, as if it had been made to blend into the surrounding wall. And yet it was ill-fitting; the door did not sit completely in the doorway almost as if it had been added without the careful precision that the rest of the castle seemed to exhibit.

She kept her ears open as she made her way down the hall. Still no sound—not even the sconces on the wall crackled, even though she could clearly see they were lit with merrily burning flames. The cat seemed perfectly content to settle into the crook of her arm and purr, occasionally chirruping when he saw something he liked. It made her jump every time.

She was standing in an opulently furnished living area, her hand trailing on the brocaded arm of a very plush looking armchair set in front of a warm fire, when she finally heard something that *wasn't* her feline companion. A thin thread of sound, but it was enough to make her perk up. "Well, kitty, maybe we're not alone after all." The cat narrowed his brightly colored eyes, and the purring stopped.

She followed the sound all the way down the hall, through a cavernous arming room, a well-stocked kitchen, and an impressive wine cellar. She felt it tugging her deeper into the keep, and after she had gone
down a few flights of stairs, she could hear it clearly. It got louder with
every step and with it came an emotion she knew all too well—fear.
She had borrowed a sword from the arming room and as she turned
into the corridor, she carefully set the cat down and drew it.

Ceyrabeth blinked, rubbed her eyes; her face locked in an irritated
scowl. Ever since she had hit the bottom floors, the lights were playing
funny tricks on her eyes. Spots flitted against her vision, doors were
and then weren't there, and everything was bathed in an increasingly
shadowed mix of red, purple, and yellow iridescence. Here in the bow-
els of the castle the darkness seemed to be a living thing. Smothering.
If she closed her eyes, she could almost hear a sound like deep, slow
breathing.

Finally, she reached the end of the corridor. She was there. Even if
the door hadn't been covered in runes and ornate carvings, she would
know. She felt the pull in her chest as surely as she could feel her sweating palm on the hilt of her blade. She went to open the door and pulled
back her hand with a start; the handle was freezing.

Ceyrabeth could feel the cat crouched at her feet, clearly unhappy
yet not willing to leave. The animal flattened its ears against its head
and hissed its displeasure. She looked down, ready to move quickly,
but the angry outburst wasn't meant for her; the animal's attention
was fixated on the door. *Why am I not leaving?* She asked herself as she
wrapped her hand in her shirtsleeve and reached for the door again.
The compulsion to go forward, to open the door despite the sounds of
despair on the other side, was irresistible.

"Don't," a voice whispered to her, but it was too late. She was already
through and headed toward the figure in the center of the room. It was
a man; she could see that clearly now. He was suspended in mid-air by

very thin wires that bound his naked body from head to toe. Blood ran freely from his body as his bindings cut into him. He had been flayed and she could see the wet slick of exposed muscle, the yellow of bone. Ceyrabeth wasn't sure he was still alive.

There was something disturbingly familiar about him.

"Hold on," she whispered. "I'm going to get you out of there." She slashed her sword down against the wires, but the moment her blade made contact the metal was shattered, and the wires began to vibrate with a high-pitched whine. With horror, she saw them constrict tighter on the man. Blood poured out of his body. She examined the wires at the ground but as far as she could tell they were fused into the floor with absolutely no release points. She gingerly gripped the wires, then jerked her hands back with a gasp; they were razor sharp and barbed with tiny hooks.

Don't give up! The plea touched Ceyrabeth's mind like a caress. The cat yowled from the doorway. The man lifted his head.

It was Sul.

A younger version of the man she had come to know, his features twisted in agony and his eyes... His eyes were just gone; gaping sockets that wept blood continuously. The wires that were sawing slowly into his flesh inexplicably emerged from within their cavernous depths.

"Please...help me..."

More wires burst from his skull to press into his mouth, working their way down his throat.

"No!" Ceyrabeth screamed, reaching for him.

"*Mira*, wake up!"

Ceyrabeth jolted awake, her heart pounding, a thin sheen of sweat soaking her shirt. She frantically tried to catch her breath, her eyes wide but not completely seeing the waking world yet.

"*Mira*. It's alright. Just a bad dream."

Mira. The low elvish word for sister, also used between two fellow soldiers, but never amongst Royal Elves. Pellinore's thin hand rested on her heaving back, and in direct contrast to his upbringing, he was calling her sister. She must have startled him...well, as much as the unflappable Commander Pellinore could be startled. *"Athelen, mireth."* She smoothed shaking hands over her face. *Thank you, brother.*

"Is it the Brood?" he asked sympathetically, his eyes falling on the still open book by her elbow.

"No," was all Ceyrabeth offered. Her back straightened; her breathing slowed. "I'll be alright, honestly. Have we been given the order to march?"

"Not yet." Pellinore clasped his hands behind his back. "You are requested at command. The time is coming to make our stand."

Wires bound, digging into flesh. Eyes weeping blood. The soft rumble of a small life purring in her hands.

Just a dream, she told herself sternly.

Pellinore offered his hand to help her up. She took it without hesitation, but immediately pulled back with a hiss of pain. Ceyrabeth turned both hands up...and froze at the sight of the angry welts bisecting both palms. "What on earth did you do?"

"I'm...not sure."

"You'd best check your new gauntlets." Ceyrabeth smiled faintly as Pellinore spoke; his voice was dangerously close to full-on fussing. "I've never known Yevvon to do shoddy work but if this is the first time..."

She nodded in reply, outwardly agreeing as they made their way to the command tent. But she knew that it wasn't her gauntlets as sure as she knew her lungs drew breath. As she looked across the command table at Sul, listening to him give his orders, something had changed. Ceyrabeth felt it in her bones. Well, she would know what she wanted to know whether the good Captain wanted to tell her or not, she promised that to herself...but first, they had a battle to win. Banishing all doubt and fear from her mind, she made her way to the field.

"LIEUTENANT VALLORIN?" A VOICE CALLED UP FROM ground level, "The last of the scouts have reported in!"

Ceyrabeth repressed a sigh. The younger officer was typical of The Phoenix Legion; eager, long on enthusiasm but short on a working knowledge of proper military protocol. Amongst the Witchhammers with whom she had previously served, it would have been inconceivable for a boy as green as Laro to hold an officer's rank. But Ceyrabeth was forced to admit, the Legion was about as far from the Witchhammers as one could get and remain on Aegreas.

"Sergeant Laro," Ceyrabeth growled, her freshly minted dragon scale armor creaking as she leaned forward from her saddle, bringing all the authority that serving in the Tower of Imperius Militant had afforded her to bear. "You are an officer serving on the front lines of a major engagement. Information is not to be simply bellowed in the general direction of the recipient. Do I make myself clear?"

The young man paled. During her time in the Legion, Ceyrabeth's reputation for ruthlessness against those that displeased her had become nearly as dire as the Captain's. "Yes sir." He drew himself to proper attention; straight backed, head held high, and snapped off an abrupt but acceptable salute. "Apologies, sir."

Ceyrabeth held the moment a while longer, then leaned back in her saddle. "Now, report."

"Yes ma'am." The sergeant cleared his throat. "Our scouts report scores of Taintbrood entering the field."

"Their point of origin?"

"Our rangers predict an access point to the Underwilds somewhere in the wilderness."

She nodded and unconsciously tucked a lock of coppery hair behind her pointed ear. "That would fit with our earlier assessments."

She surveyed the sunlight draped landscape. Flat terrain for the most part, sparsely wooded with elevated ground on the Western borders that eventually became the foothills of the Bannoth Thor Mountains.

The realm was called Targeste, and as far as geographical features went, it was thoroughly unremarkable. Which made the Captain's insistence on it being the staging ground for their attack upon the Taintbrood that much more of a mystery. The last few weeks had been spent herding them, strike by carefully coordinated strike, to this very location. She shook herself from her reverie. All would be revealed when the Captain was good and ready. It always was. "What are the Taintbrood numbers?"

The sergeant swallowed. "A quarter-score at least, lieutenant."

"That's five to one." Ceyrabeth repressed a shudder as fear began to settle into her bones.

"Their composition?"

"Infantry, Brutes, and Skirmishers. The same creatures that were seen at Velasgate."

And there it was, the name no one had wanted to speak; Velasgate, where her order of Witchhammers had fought their first and last engagement in open warfare. Her comrades had fought bravely there. They had fought honorably there. They had fought valiantly there.

And they had died there.

Now, here she stood with only a fraction of the men that her former colleagues had fielded. Here on open ground, in broad daylight, outnumbered many times over in an army comprised of rebels, mercenaries, and other malcontents. Here under the command of the greatest military mind the world had ever seen.

The thought instantly replaced the chill of fear in her bones with a burning anticipation. No, they were not the same doomed men and women that had stood at Velasgate. They followed a different kind of a leader now—a better kind—and led by him they would give the Taintbrood something new to fear.

"Very well sergeant. Report back to your unit and prepare your forces."

"Yes ma'am!" Offering another salute, the sergeant took the reins of his horse from a waiting attendant, mounted and galloped away, kicking up dust and dirt as she did.

Out of reflex, Ceyrabeth placed a steadying hand on her own mount to calm him, but the motion was halted before it barely begun. Eregost was one of the undead. She did not require food nor water or rest, and certainly did not require calming from a bit of dust and dirt being kicked up.

She pulled his reins and steered her past the Honor Guard that was maintaining a vigil on a higher western outcropping that offered a good view of the field of battle. The Honor Guard were the elite of the Phoenix Legion, easily identifiable by their plate mail consisting of mystical alloy and dwarven steel. The armor gleamed copper and bronze and was etched with various motifs depicting falcons, hawks, and other birds of prey. Ceyrabeth's own armor was a match for theirs but significantly lighter, a peregrine falcon chased into the reinforced pauldrons.

The choice of bird had been the Captain's and for some reason it seemed to amuse him. Ceyrabeth added it to the list of things she wanted explained. None offered challenge as she rode into their midst to confront their ward and their lord as well as her own; Captain Drachaen Sul

He sat upon his own mount; the albino wyvern Banshee, her bone white scales reflecting the glaring sun. She didn't look any happier about the oppressive heat than Ceyrabeth was. The beast offered her a nod of recognition as she approached.

"I still don't understand why we're launching an attack during the hottest part of the day," Ceyrabeth commented sourly. "Our men must be baking in their armor."

The tall figure astride Banshee turned to regard her. His own armor was a blend of metal, silk, and leathers done in multiple layers. It all looked extraordinarily complex which made a certain amount of sense as the Captain himself had designed it. The Legion's master smith, the golem Yevvon, had complained about it incessantly for weeks.

"Consider the Taintbrood, born in darkness. To fight in the full glare of day offers them a greater disadvantage," Sul commented in that tone that was equal parts calm and culture that would have been suited for a man sitting upon a throne and not a war mount. If he was experiencing any tension at all about the upcoming battle, it did not show in the slightest. Of course, when he was wearing his helm—featuring a large faceplate that left only his mouth exposed—it was impossible to get any kind of accurate read on the man. The only indication of any kind of feeling at all was the rhythmic tapping the tips of his fingers upon the pommel of his saddle, each finger alternating but maintaining a steady beat. Not quite fidgeting, but there it was.

"The scouts have reported in; standard horde makeup as far as troop composition and numbers well into the several thousands," Ceyrabeth reported.

"As was expected," Sul replied. "This is a different arm of the Horde then and not the main bulk which I imagine remains in the Under-wilds amassing under the command of the Taintbrood leader, if the Nevaraakese documents we recovered are accurate."

Ceyrabeth's nose crinkled in distaste. All things Nevaraakese, especially matters pertaining to their foul demonic masters, were *not* things Ceyrabeth, in her devotion to the Green Lords that sought to heal and rebuild the ruined world, understood.

"Those things that hold power over us only do so at our allowance through our investment," Sul commented softly turning his blank-faced helm towards her.

"Yes Sir." Ceyrabeth just barely managed to not roll her eyes.

He beckoned and a small map adorned with several different figurines floated towards him. The map depicted the region and Ceyrabeth could safely assume that the figurines represented the various forces, both under their command and arrayed against them.

"All the Taintbrood need to do is push forward with their forward vanguard, outflank us with their reserves and they'll surround and consume us," she reported darkly, gesturing at the multiple enemy figurines on the map. "At least at Velasgate, we had the ability to funnel the Taintbrood forces into a bottleneck. We could direct the enemy."

"At Velasgate, the Witchhammers had dominance over the terrain," Sul acceded. "An advantage that they failed to capitalize upon or retain." He turned his attention back to the map before him. "They had spent the entirety of their lives at the feet of the Imperium training how to win the *last* war and at their back stood a leader too blinded by holy doctrine to adapt to fighting something other than mages and other 'heretics.'"

It was then that the shriek of a horn cut through the air off in the distance and a massing shadow began to form and spread, surging like a swarm of something alive. Vile and hungry.

"Those are not heretics," Sul finished and Ceyrabeth could not refute his argument. "Steps have been taken to ensure not just dominance of the terrain, Lieutenant, but mastery of it. There are many ways to direct the enemy's movements," his voice took on a sly tone, "or have you forgotten how you first came to be in service to the Legion?"

Ceyrabeth's already heat-flushed cheeks burnt a little hotter. She and her fellow surviving Witchhammers had been led neatly into a trap, involving nothing more complicated than some fleeing scouts as bait and several pools full of deep bog water. The trap had ensnared an entire company of trained Witchhammers without a single weapon drawn or arrow loosed. It was doubly painful to remember that she *had* seen the trap, and had to walk into it regardless, to save her brothers.

"No Sir. I have not forgotten."

Pellinore removed a strange device from his belt—a "spyglass," he called it—and handed it to Ceyrabeth.

"What do you see?" Sul inquired.

She brought the device to her eye and sighed, "I see the horde. They are coming for us." She fussed with the device for a moment. It too had been designed by Sul and allowed one to see far further and more clearly than the average sailor's glass.

"Do they march with any recognizable formation?" Sul asked, his tone intensifying. "Grouping based on arms, breed or ranking?"

"Not that I can see." She shook her head. "They approach as a swarm, much as they did at Velasgate. Does it matter?"

Sul permitted himself a thin smile. "Understand the Taintbrood, Lieutenant, and you will understand how to destroy them." Sul's fingers were still tapping out their strange patterns against the horn of his saddle. "Five hundred and closing. It's time." One of his fingers immediately ceased tapping and he turned aside. "Commander Pellinore."

"Sir!" The elf snapped a crisp salute.

"The count has been reached. Sound the first wave."

"Sir!" Pellinore reached for a horn on his belt. It was oddly constructed and adorned in runes that glowed and hummed. He blew hard and a booming note rolled forth from the instrument to reverberate across the entire landscape.

"And this is how it shall begin," Ceyrabeth mused grimly, watching the vast hordes of Taintbrood arrayed against them. Answering calls from various horns echoed up and down the ranks of armored men and women on either side of them.

"Begin?" Sul shook his head and smiled a smile that would have frightened the blind. "No, Ceyrabeth. This is how it shall end."

An arcing ball of fire from her left caught Ceyrabeth's eye. She turned just in time to see it climb high over the ranks of her men, hurtling towards the masses of Taintbrood. It was soon joined by a second and a third in rapid succession, each from a different position just behind their forward ranks.

"I wasn't aware we had brought siege engines," Ceyrabeth commented cautiously.

"We didn't," Pellinore replied. "We brought Yevvon."

Ceyrabeth's confusion still showed on her face before her brain caught up with her.

Pellinore allowed a tight smile. "Do you know how far and how rapidly a golem can throw a large flaming stone, especially when augmented with a spell of haste?"

"Five hundred…" Her voice trailed off as the first of the flaming rock impacted upon the Taintbrood. And with a whoosh that was audible even clear on the other side of the battlefield, the entire stretch of land that the Taintbrood trod upon exploded into fire.

"Gods!" Ceyrabeth cried out as the following rocks landed and detonated amongst the Taintbrood. Walls of flame sprouted up surrounding the Taintbrood, dividing their ranks, cutting off both advance and retreat in seemingly random patterns. Soon an entire third of the eastern field was a roaring conflagration; a labyrinth of fire from which there seemed to be no escape for the Taintbrood whose death cries were audible to the entire army as they burned.

"Burn you motherless bastards!" someone cried out and there was a roar of approval from the assembled army.

"How?" she asked.

"Spellcasters have often combined spells that saturate oil into the earth and spells that can ignite them. Our rangers just substituted pitch and oil for magic and…" Pellinore gestured at the results.

"There is dominance of the terrain," Sul said softly, "and there is mastery." Another finger on his right hand stopped tapping. "The count has been reached, Commander. Artillery may fire at will and sound for archers."

"Sir!" Pellinore reached for the strange looking horn and removed a disk of metal contained within the body of it, sliding in a thinner disk with a series of holes in it. He blew the horn three times, the tone higher pitched. Down the line, similar horns sounded, and flags were raised.

"Orders received, Sir!" Pellinore responded.

"You can't hope for accuracy at this range," Ceyrabeth protested. "It's far too great a distance."

"The objective is not to slay, Commander," Sul responded, "but to spur." He turned to Pellinore. "Ready a volley."

Pellinore blew the horn emitting the same high-pitched rapid sound. Flags were lowered and raised again, and men took up their weapons, nocked and drew even as great flaming stones continued to pelt the Taintbrood.

"Loose."

Pellinore blew a single sustained note, and a cloud of arrows darkened the sky and soared towards the Taintbrood.

"Taintbrood armor is thick, but in poor condition; corroded by their own acidic blood and a lack of maintenance," Pellinore commented. "We can afford to use lighter arrows sacrificing penetration for range."

The arrows fell upon the burning Taintbrood in waves of black, like a swarm of wasps. Few fell, but almost none escaped without an arrow lodged into an exposed arm or leg triggering even more chaos.

And then they started to fall to their knees, choking and vomiting.

"And the poison doesn't hurt either," Pellinore finished mildly.

"Poison? Clever." Ceyrabeth commented dryly. Poison was forbidden as a weapon of warfare amongst most civilized nations as well as the Church. Sul, by contrast, did not seem perturbed by the taboo of such things and its efficiency could not be argued.

"The Taintbrood now only have two options," Pellinore replied, nodding. "Remain where they are and burn whilst being shot full of arrows and crushed by flying rocks, or march through the flames and take even more losses."

Ceyrabeth was forced to admit, it was an elegant trap. She watched the fires burn...and then gasped as they suddenly started to flicker and go out.

"Captain!" Ceyrabeth shouted and pointed.

"Finally," Sul commented.

"Without the fire, how do you intend to control the terrain?" Ceyrabeth asked.

"There are other ways to maintain the advantage in battle. In this instance, knowledge."

"What knowledge does having our trap fail grant us, pray tell?"

"Our trap has not failed," Sul retorted coldly. "In extinguishing those specific flames, the Taintbrood reveal two vital pieces of information; where they intend to move their troops and, more importantly; the location of their mages." Sul turned his eyeless helm towards her. "*Their* god does not forbid them from making use of magic on the battlefield." He settled back against his saddle to watch as the Taintbrood began to advance through the freshly extinguished paths of scorched earth.

"Fortunately, neither does mine."

Pellinore frowned. He'd not heard the Captain discuss matters of religion on a personal basis before. "Begging your pardon Captain, but which god is that?"

Sul smiled again, that chilling smile that would have looked like madness on the face of anyone else but him. "Why, the only god that matters in war, commander—victory."

Sul handed the spyglass to Ceyrabeth. "What do you see?"

She took the instrument and adjusted the lenses until the front lines of Taintbrood snapped into focus. "The first few ranks of Taintbrood are in bad shape between the arrows, the fire and the giant flying rocks," she reported. "But the ones behind them are looking fresh and angry."

"Range?"

Ceyrabeth checked which lens was in position and counted the notches on the side of the spyglass. "Three hundred and closing." She brought the instrument up to her eye again, frowning. "Their Brutes and heavy infantry are closing fast but I don't see any mages."

"Mages are well hidden in any army, but sorcery is rarely a subtle thing," Sul replied evenly as the third finger on his hand stopped counting. "The count is reached commander. Issue the next command."

"Sir!" Pellinore adjusted the horn and added a thicker, heavier disk into the body and blew out a single long, low note followed by a short note that was even lower in pitch. The reaction was instantaneous; archers exchanged bows with the men behind them and took up shorter, thicker curved bows and readied larger arrows with oversized tips that gleamed wickedly in the sun. The men in the ranks before them readied great shields and spears and arranged themselves in a formation that Ceyrabeth had never seen before.

"It's called a 'phalanx,'" Sul answered her unspoken question softly. "I came across a reference to it in a dwarven manuscript dating back to the fall of their last kingdom. There the dwarves arranged themselves in such a way as to delay the encroaching Taintbrood and buy time for the refugees fleeing the city."

"They're sitting ducks, grouped together that closely!" Ceyrabeth countered. "One good blast from a mage—"

"Your anxiety belies a curious failure to understand the ways of formal warfare," Sul commented in an almost lazy tone. "No doubt an oversight in your ecclesiastical education."

Ceyrabeth turned on him, dark eyes snapping. "Witchhammers are *not* soldiers." She informed him frigidly. "We are *not* cannon fodder. We are highly trained and specialized professionals that can bolster armies, destroy demons, or remove dangerous idiots with delusions of grandeur before they hurt people as the case warrants it. Idiots like—"

"Have you found any enemy mages?" Sul asked calmly.

"Not since they extinguished our fires!" Ceyrabeth got the hint and brought the spyglass up to her eye, scanning the swarming ranks of the Taintbrood. It was impossible to see anything through all the smoke and chaos, their sheer numbers were giving her a headache. Thinking quickly, she traced back the line of trajectory from where the last wall of flame had been extinguished hoping to find its point of origin...

...and found a dead Taintbrood mage, distinctive for its ornate headdress, its throat neatly slit.

"How?" She scanned again and found a second body, an arrow buried in its eye. A third with the same, a fourth with a sword buried in its side. A gloved hand materialized out of the chaos of the horde to wrench the weapon free of the body and neatly sliced off its head before diving to the ground, disappearing amidst the dirt and smoke.

No, not disappearing...blending in with the surroundings with a dirt and grass colored cowl and cloak, patterned to the shapes and hues of the wild.

"Camouflage," she whispered softly. Ceyrabeth lowered the glass, turning to Sul. "How did you get rangers that far into—a stray memory clicked. "You didn't!" she gasped. "You just had them lie in wait for the Taintbrood to arrive after they finished spreading the pitch and oil about!"

Sul's helm tilted fractionally to the side. "Well done Ceyrabeth," he said. "Very well done indeed."

Ceyrabeth could not keep the warmth from spreading within her. The Captain's compliments were rare as diamonds. "Thank you, Sir," she mumbled and was grateful that he couldn't see the furious blush spreading across her cheeks.

"And Ceyrabeth?"

"Yes, Sir?"

"My soldiers are not cannon fodder."

She swallowed once and nodded. "Yes, Sir."

A roar, echoed several times over, tore her from her thoughts and back to the present. She brought the spyglass up to her eye and gasped, "those hulking Brutes will be on us at any moment." One had succumbed to its injuries from fire or arrow but three more continued to rampage forward, seemingly undeterred by the multitude of burns covering their body and arrows protruding from their enormous, deformed bodies.

"The phalanx formation will not hold against a combined onslaught by three Brutes," Pellinore cautioned their Captain.

"Fortunately, they will not be called upon to do so," Sul answered evenly. He turned his attention to Ceyrabeth and continued tapping his fingers rhythmically. "Range?"

"One hundred and closing awfully flaming fast," Ceyrabeth cried.

"Do I give the order Captain?" Pellinore asked.

"Hold," Sul instructed. Tense moments went by as fires burned in the distance and arrows descended upon the ravenous horde bearing down on them. "Sound the count."

Ceyrabeth couldn't spare the seconds to remove the eyepiece from her eye, she just twisted the device until things came into focus and counted the notches on the side by touch.

"Eighty."

"Seventy"

"Sixty!"

"Captain!" Pellinore cried.

"Hold," Sul replied calmly, continuing to tap his finger at a steady pace.

"Captain, the ogres will be in melee range of our front ranks in seconds," Ceyrabeth cried. "Fifty!"

"Sir!" Pellinore shouted.

After what seemed an eternity, "The count is reached commander," Sul said softly. "Sound the charge."

"Forty!" Ceyrabeth shouted. Pellinore brought the war horn to his lips and blew three short rapid bursts.

The forward archers raised their bows and fired level to the field directly into the oncoming Brutes whilst the rear archers continued to rain death upon the advancing Taintbrood infantry.

"They can't stop them!" Ceyrabeth cried as she readied to charge to their aid.

"Hold, lieutenant. Your courage does you credit, but what you lack is patience."

"Patience?!" Ceyrabeth spat. "Those men will be slaughtered!"

"That is possible," Sul conceded. "All war is risk and in every battle losses are inevitable."

"I won't stand by and allow my men to die needlessly!" Keiran was down there somewhere. Even Evric, boy though he was, had been assigned to a battalion. The thought of them falling to the Taintbrood made bile rise in her throat.

The Brutes were upon the forward ranks, their war clubs raised high, and their red eyes filled with hatred.

"Yer mother was a half penny whore!!!!!!" a familiar voice called out.

Ceyrabeth jerked her head back and gaped at the sight of Reaper Maul riding some sort of wheeled vehicle being pulled by a pair of enormous bears clad in barding. He was screaming at the top of his lungs and the forward ranks stepped deftly aside, granting him and those that followed him, a clear shot at the approaching ogres.

"Neither will I," Sul answered her coolly.

The brutes managed a look of bestial astonishment before Reaper Maul plowed headlong into the largest one. The two bears pulling the vehicle savaged the brute with their massive paws as Maul leapt from the vehicle, landed upon the ogre's chest and began to pummel the creature senseless with his fists, which were encased in massive, spiked gauntlets.

Ceyrabeth's mouth opened and closed several times as she attempted to form words.

"Our berserkers have been successfully deployed," Pellinore exhaled with more than a little relief.

Sul nodded. "So it would seem."

Ceyrabeth exhaled hard as she observed four wheeled carts, each loaded with men and women howling for blood and wielding enormous weapons, descend upon the Brutes and run them down. "What are they riding?"

"An older form of transportation," Sul replied. "It is called a 'chariot.' I learned of the design from a children's toy in the east and adopted it for combat."

"I've never seen one before."

"They are rarely used now. They require flat terrain to be most effective."

"Targeste accommodates them rather well," Pellinore commented. "Especially with the ground freshly scoured by fire or frozen over by Taintbrood frost magic."

Ceyrabeth watched the onslaught in awe. The chariots bore several large men and women painted in strange designs and garbed in clothes made of animal hide, adorned with blood and the gory trophies of former victories. "Who are they?"

"The Crimson Vanguard; Berserkers and warriors adept at war frenzies," Pellinore answered.

"In addition to growing stronger from their injuries, they have the power to inflict a type of curse upon the feeble-minded that paralyzes them with mortal terror." He turned in his saddle to address Ceyrabeth. "The Captain discovered that Brutes, whilst physically powerful, are vulnerable to any form of mental assault."

"Why not use mages?"

"Our mages are otherwise occupied and not so numerous that we can afford to pit them against Brutes in such a direct manner," Sul replied patiently.

The death-cry of the final Brute falling to the weapons of the Berserkers drew Ceyrabeth's attention and she could not repress a grin. "That's the last of the Brutes," she said, then frowned.

"What are they doing?" Rather than retreating, the charioteers formed up and were pushing deeper into the ranks of the Taintbrood. "They'll be overrun," she commented. "And our archers can't offer any support without running the risk of hitting them."

Sure enough, the Taintbrood converged on the charioteers, swarming their position. For every two or three slain by either the bears or the enormous weapons the soldiers wielded, more swarmed to fill the void. The horde moved with a singular purpose.

"They're going to die!" Ceyrabeth cried out and though her feelings towards Maul were mixed at best, he had proven himself a valiant companion and worthy of a better death than this.

"A possibility faced by all warriors," Sul commented calmly, still rhythmically tapping two of his fingers.

"Damn it!" With a growl of equal parts frustration and anger, she brought the spyglass up to her eye and found Maul amidst the swarm of Taintbrood. He was covered in wounds yet still grinning madly as he brought up his war horn, carved from the skull of the first dragon he had ever slain he had once informed her, and blew a last call of defiance and tribute befitting his courage.

And then the forward ranks of the Phoenix Legion answered the call with their own and charged the distracted Taintbrood.

And she understood. Maul's vanguard was not just a single strike against the Brutes; they were a *distraction*.

Ceyrabeth gaped as the forward line charged the spawn. The front line collided into them with the force of a storm; shields bashing aside the confused spawn and swords drawing blood with every blow. Arrows arched up and rained down on the heads of the Taintbrood infantry, well short of the charioteers who had reached the rear echelons of the Horde.

The Taintbrood quickly adjusted to this sudden attack and surged against the Legion. The Legion responded in turn by digging in their shields as the next line of troops fell into position behind them bearing those strange bows. The spawn charged the phalanx formation, and the second line released a volley of arrows that streaked through the gaps in the line of soldiers before them to strike the Spawn head on.

Undeterred, the Taintbrood collided with the phalanx formation, drooling and clawing at the shields trying to get to the men behind them. The soldiers held their ground against the Horde, held against the crushing momentum of the beasts. Held and continued to hold.

And then there was a moment of near silence as both man and monster realized that the line would not break.

The silence was broken by the howling of beasts as armored hounds raced through the ranks of the assembled Legion and streaked towards the Taintbrood.

"War hounds!" Ceyrabeth cried out.

"War hounds cannot stand against frontal assault," Sul commented. "As the army at

Velasgate learned."

There was a single cry and the front line shoved with all their might, knocking the Taintbrood back. The soldiers pivoted sideways in unison and a second volley of arrows streaked out from the line behind them and cut down the spawn. The front line then reformed and surged forward with their blades and cut the disoriented brood down.

"However," Sul continued, "when used in conjunction with close-quarter troops, they can force the enemy to divide their attention between two separate angles of attack; high and strong from the men, low and fast from the beasts and the end results are as you see."

Ceyrabeth did see, as the hounds dragged the Taintbrood down to meet the blades of the soldiers, hampering the movements of the creatures so that the soldiers of the Legion could deliver the killing blow, before bounding away back behind the forward line. The Taint-brood regrouped and charged again only to be met with the solid wall of shield and muscle.

At that moment the war horns from the rear of the Spawn sounded and Reaper Maul led his chariot vanguard directly into the backs of the Taintbrood bringing death to the spawn with axe and claw, sword, and fist.

Chaos erupted as the Taintbrood struggled to adjust. They turned their backs to face Maul's onslaught. The Legion's infantry took advantage of the Taintbrood's state of disarray and pressed the assault, forcing the enemy to face them on two fronts.

Slowly the forward line funneled into the main body of the Taint-brood horde, digging in their shields and providing cover for additional troops who penetrated the ranks of the horde and fortified their position with spear, sword, and shield. Whenever a point within the formation looked to be overwhelmed, Maul would sound his horn and his charioteers would race to intercept and draw the enemy to them whilst the archers would focus their fire on that point with assistance from Yevvon's carefully aimed boulders. When Maul or his charioteers were in danger of themselves being overrun, they would speed away and the infantry formation would push forward. Man and hound would work in unison to push deeper still into the ranks of the enemy.

Inch by inch, the Legion invaded the Horde and fortified their ranks within the enemy army; shield and spear creating a corridor in which poured the remaining infantry. Ceyrabeth watched the battle unfold and a grin slowly spread across her face. *Leave it to Sul to—*

Her thoughts came to a crashing halt as she watched the Horde, still vastly outnumbering the Phoenix Legion, begin to reshape its ranks in response to the incursion. She understood their plan and her blood ran cold.

"The Horde is attempting a pincer!" Ceyrabeth yelled. "They're going to try to outflank our forces!"

"With the main body of their infantry divided and their superior numbers, a double envelopment is the only sound tactical option the Taintbrood have available to them," Sul commented calmly. "Fortunately—"

The arrow came from somewhere off to their left. It struck Sul in the shoulder, knocking him from his mount.

"Drachaen!" Ceyrabeth cried out, drawing her blade as a group of Taintbrood materialized out of the shadow. Pellinore was already off his horse and tending to their fallen Captain. That left her and the other elite to defend. "For the Legion!" she roared and bore down upon the charging Taintbrood. She didn't bother to count how many they were. It didn't matter—they would all die by her hand this day.

"Die, you vile bastards!" she hissed, bringing her curved sword up.

"Hold!"

The command from Sul came suddenly and she jerked the reins on instinct, causing Eregost to rear up before the oncoming monsters. Suddenly there was a click followed by sudden cracking noise...

...and the entire Taintbrood platoon tumbled into a concealed pit that Ceyrabeth had missed by inches.

The smell of pitch and oil overwhelmed her senses just in time for her to comprehend the plan. She gripped the flask containing the firebomb at her belt. It was standard issue for all horsemen, and she hurled it into the pit. With a crackle and a scream of tortured wood and flesh the entire trench went up, consuming the Taintbrood within and blocking those infiltrators that had attempted to follow. Ceyrabeth couldn't help but laugh as adrenaline and admiration coursed through her veins.

"Archers: Loose."

Ceyrabeth stayed perfectly still as the royal guard unleashed their bolts into the oncoming creatures. Without the element of surprise, the spawn could not withstand against the withering onslaught of fire and bolt.

"Osen," the same voice called. The cat appeared out of seemingly nowhere, ignored the Captain on the ground, instead hopping onto the shoulders of...

...one of the royal guardsmen, his features concealed by his helm.

"Mas-ter?"

"Kill."

The one-eyed cat hissed with glee and dove into the flames of the trench, tearing the beasts apart.

"Won't he burn?" The "Captain" being propped up on the ground asked in a voice that was distinctly high pitched and feminine.

Ceyrabeth dismounted and came bounding back to the scene, placing her hand on Banshee's flank. "What is—" She pulled her hand back. It was simply white paint covering the brown scales of the far more common Highland wyverns "—all this?" She also noticed that the saddle was a fabrication, made of wood and plaster and designed to increase the height and girth of whoever sat upon it. The guardsman assisted the "Captain" in removing the faceplate of the massive helm to reveal:

"Janessa?!" Ceyrabeth exclaimed.

"The one and only," she smiled painfully. "Ow! I don't think I want to be the decoy anymore."

"Are you badly injured?" The guardsman inquired before removing his helm to reveal Sul garbed in his samite eye binding.

"Lords of Earth!" Ceyrabeth exclaimed. "How did you—"

"Some cheap theatrics and minor enchantment all geared towards misdirection," Sul said waving her question away. "Janessa?"

"I don't think it penetrated the undercoat." She managed a brave smile. "Yevvon does good work."

"He does indeed." Sul hefted Janessa up in his arms.

"Oo!" Janessa squeaked. "You are stronger than you look." She pretended to trace the cord like muscles on his arms. Ceyrabeth pretended not to notice.

"Captain!" Pellinore yelled over the noise. "The count is breached. The Bulwark will not hold!"

"Sound the final charge. Send left and right lancers against their targets and deploy the mages. Pellinore, lead the left charge, Lieutenant Vallorin the right," Sul replied calmly.

"Sir!" Pellinore strapped his helm on and readied his flail. "For the Legion!"

"Osen!" The cat, coated in flames and blood and yet none the worse for wear appeared out of the trench licking its chops. "Clear the way. Fire and death."

"Fire! Death!" the demonic tabby cat roared, its mutilated eye now open and displaying a rolling ball of flame as he bounded into the darkness ahead of the knights.

Ceyrabeth meanwhile was trying to make sense out of what was happening. "What Lancers? What are you..."

She noticed then that no less than forty knights had materialized from out of the gloom behind them, armed and ready. The entirety of Drachaen's honor guard split amongst themselves between Ceyrabeth and Pellinore's command.

"You'll be defenseless!" she hissed at Sul.

"The gods watch over us all child," came the response as Reiko took the wounded Janessa, who released her grip on Sul somewhat reluctantly. "And if the gods are busy..." She gestured behind herself to the forms of Atiya, Peloquin and a masked individual who she had heard referred to as "Arcuse" once before, who had lurked in the darkness until now, but were prepared to provide their Captain with all the protection he could require and more.

"You have your orders Lieutenant," Sul said.

Ceyrabeth snapped on her ornate war helm. "One day," she muttered to a grinning Peloquin under her breath as she passed, "I am going to be too angry by his cleverness to be impressed by it and I am going to kill him."

"Perhaps, *mi amor*." He offered the elven woman a wink. "But not this day. Mind the glyphs."

"Yes Sir," she growled, drawing her sword in one hand and her shield in the other. She may have been ignorant of a massive battlefield and formal warfare, but rally a small group to glory? *That* she could do. "All on me! We are the Fire Risen!"

"For the Legion!" the soldiers cried out.

"We are the light against the darkness!"

"For the Legion!"

"They will see us and see their death!"

"*Death*!"

"*Death*!" she roared back and charged down the hill, her knights rampaging after her to fall upon the divided Taintbrood forces. She caught Maul's eye as he and his charioteers headed straight to the nearly overwhelmed infantry.

And then, they sliced the harnesses of the bears clean from the chariots and leapt free from the vehicles.

"What in the name of..." Ceyrabeth stared.

The bears ran full speed at the Phoenix Legion bulwark. The bulwark held firm as the first of the bears reached them. The bears leapt over their shields...

...and with an explosion of black smoke the bears were no longer bears, but wolves.

Our mages are otherwise occupied and not so numerous that we can afford to pit them against Brutes in such a direct manner, Sul had told her.

"Shapechangers!" she gasped.

Suddenly, the chariots that had been abandoned within the ranks of the Taintbrood exploded into arcing blue lightning, coursing through the all the water that had been created from the snow and ice from the Taintbrood mages' efforts to put out the flames from earlier. They added to the confusion and allowed the wolves behind friendly lines to become robed men and women. Maul and his berserkers were not idle; using their great weapons and ability to induce fear to drive the Horde back whilst the mages booby-trapped the front lines of the bulwark.

Mind the glyphs.

The various mages had shed their wolf forms and were now desperately laying down glyphs as fast as they could before the men standing at the fore of the three-way bulwark. Ceyrabeth watched as the glyphs glowed green and blue forcing the Taintbrood to back away from the infantry. Where two glyphs overlapped, there was an explosion of kinetic energy that knocked the Taintbrood back and directly into the lances of herself and Commander Pellinore. The flanking Taintbrood were suddenly outflanked themselves, caught between those glyphs, the spears of the bulwark, the weapons of the berserkers, and the lances and flails of the cavalry.

The Taintbrood ranks broke. Deprived of their mages and Brutes, they fled the only way they could; away from the flames and arrows of the Phoenix Legion, away from the battle and deep into the open wilderness far from the sanctuary of the Underwilds that had spawned them.

An hour later, it was all over.

THE CELEBRATION WAS AN UNUSUALLY MUTED AFFAIR. The Captain had prepared roasted boar, spiced wine from the

Ghenlands, stag on steel and other traditional dishes; all manner of delicacies that often graced the Captain's table were now being shared amongst the men freely. But no man drank more than a second cup of mead or wine, and all eyed the horizon as darkness fell.

"I...have a question," Ceyrabeth put forth to the table with some hesitation.

"Caution does not suit you lieutenant," Sul said not unkindly. "Speak your mind."

"It's just...it could be a ridiculous question to ask a practically omniscient master of strategy..."

Sul made a sound then, before taking a long sip from his goblet. Ceyrabeth could see his lips pulled up around the rim the wine glass. That sound...

Did he just...snort?

"I make no claims to mastery, I assure you," Sul replied, his tone still light and amused. "Please ask your question. My ego is not threatened here, and I should prefer to clear up any confusion rather than allow one of my officers to remain ignorant."

"Fair enough." Ceyrabeth took a deep breath and braced herself. "You have a dragon at your command—"

"No one has a bloody dragon at their 'command' girl," Maul scoffed. "Stop being daft."

"—*however*," Ceyrabeth shrugged his words aside. "You didn't call her into battle. Why not?"

There were a few chuckles from around the table and Ceyrabeth's face flushed. The chuckles died as Sul rose to his feet and silenced them with a look.

How does he do that with no eyes? Ceyrabeth found herself thinking as Sul began to speak.

"What do you know about dragons, Lieutenant?"

The elf woman searched her mind, trying to remember everything

Brother Arturo had taught her about them. "They are...very powerful," she began cautiously. "They are extremely accomplished magic users, they can fly, and their breath weapons contain the power of nature's elements. They come in different colors and are rare."

"They certainly are in this age." Sul nodded. "Since the line of kings was broken in Daymore, the Imbued have retreated from the affairs of man and the Primordials have very little interest in working with the mortal races."

"I'm not sure I follow."

"I'll spare you a lengthy lecture on history..." Sul began.

"There's a first," Narl-Shu barked with a laugh.

Ceyrabeth leaned forward, a brittle scowl on her face. She had had just about enough of the man. "One more word and I'll tear your ears off and feed them to you. Do you understand?"

Narl-Shu sat back. Ceyrabeth could practically see the wheels turning in his admittedly intelligent head. Would he test her, or wouldn't he? Finally, he made the right choice—muttering an obscenity, he turned his attention back to his drink.

Sul gave her an appraising look and to her surprise, his lips curled in a small smile before he continued, "Primordial dragons are made from the forces of nature: flame, cold, decay, growth and so on. They are creatures of supreme ego, each one born with the unshakable belief in their own innate superiority in the face of all other 'lesser' creatures."

Ceyrabeth rolled her eyes. "Meaning everything else that *isn't* a dragon?"

"Primordial dragons in general, and red dragons in particular, do not bother justifying their actions to anyone or anything else. They aren't interested in equality or understanding. From the first moment of their existence until their very last, they will do what they want, when and where they want, however they want. They do not compromise. They do not cooperate. They do not accept the command of another."

Ceyrabeth nodded. "Which means they can't be relied upon in a battle."

"A thirty-foot creature, weighing over a ton, rampaging across the landscape throwing spells and incinerating everything in its path is not conducive to any kind of strategy or achieving any kind of long-term conquest."

Ceyrabeth sat back down feeling an odd sense of contentment; she had learned something new. She had always been curious by nature. It had been real, soul-crushing work to put a damper on that desire to learn for so long during her time amongst the Hammers. "I see. I appreciate you taking the time to explain."

Sul sat back down in his chair and raised his goblet in toast to the woman and this time it was Ceyrabeth's smile that curled over the rim of the glass.

"Do you believe the Brood will return?" Pellinore asked gesturing to the massive war table draped in maps and marked with flags and icons designating various agents and factions.

"I am uncertain," Sul confessed. "We have given them a way out. If they possess enough sense to do so, they will take it."

"I still don't understand why we gave them a way out at all," growled Narl-Shu. "We have them fleeing for their miserable lives."

"And if we had forced their backs against the wall with no escape, they would have been fighting for those said miserable lives," Sul countered softly. "The objective here was to deny them the southern regions, which we have done. More importantly, we deprived them of easy access to the Underwilds. Our victory serves to remind the Horde that not all the forces of men will fall as easily as they did in previous engagements. Even the Horde understands morale. This battle should throw them into a state of confusion."

"And if the Horde should take our presence more seriously and dedicate a significant force to destroy us?" Pellinore asked cautiously.

"You mean more dedicated than the several thousand Taintbrood that already attempted to?" A faint smile quirked on Sul's lips. "Be at peace Commander. After tonight's revels, we head northwest into the Bannoth Thor mountains. Our tributes to the dwarves of Iron Realm have not gone unnoticed and the seasons are changing. Whatever state of flux the current state of queenship is in, the ruling matriarchs are perfectly aware that they're in need of the supplies we bring, however grudgingly they accept it. Between the terrain, the token dwarven sentry presence, and the dragon cult, the mountains should be safe enough for the time being."

"Dragon cult?" Ceyrabeth interjected. "What dragon cult?"

"My people," Reaper Maul answered, grinning broadly. Even with half his face bandaged and his arm in a splint, he still looked capable of disassembling the remainder of the Taintbrood forces with his bare hands.

Ceyrabeth gestured at Maul's mangled visage. "Your people? The last I heard you were an elf from the dwarven gladiator pits."

"After my daring escape, I wandered into the mountains and was taken in by a fine group of people. They taught me all kinds of useful things, but I was never what you'd call a 'true believer.'"

"Why not?"

"Because they worship a dragon as the living manifestation of their god…" Sul explained quietly whilst peering at his maps. Ceyrabeth chuckled and sipped her wine. "…who defends the Glass Tower. It is the last known resting place of the remains of the Crown of Daymore."

Clang!

The cup dropped with the elven woman's jaw.

"What?!"

"Oh aye!" Maul grinned running a hand against the boar-like stubble upon his head. "Keys to the bloody kingdom and the rulership of man."

"But this is the discovery of a generation! A lifetime! It must be—" Ceyrabeth heaved a frustrated breath. She couldn't find the words. She would cut off her ears all over again for the chance to see the Crown.

"You're right," Sul commented readily before looking up. "It must be. But it will not be made by the Phoenix Legion. It is not our place to unleash knowledge of this magnitude upon the world. That responsibility shall fall upon those who would benefit more from the prestige."

"I don't understand."

"Nor are you required to at this juncture, Lieutenant. For now, all that needs to be established..." Sul moved a heavy phoenix figurine to cover a marking over the Wilds, "...is that these lands are no longer a point of access for the rest of the Horde."

"We could just finish them off," Ceyrabeth commented darkly.

"I will not waste time nor commit resources attacking an enemy I am not prepared to defeat."

Sul looked back at his maps. "Our men are tired, our arms in need of repair and replenishment, and the enemy marches upon unfamiliar ground. The Legion is not prepared to go to war with the Taintbrood on their own territory." He ran a length of black silk from the phoenix figurine to a large, squat figurine located within the Bannoth Thor mountains. "We will establish a barricade here."

"We may not have the manpower for that," Atiya commented in her monotone.

"We don't," Sul agreed. "But the wild men amongst the Seven Tribes do and have a vested interest in keeping the Taintbrood from rampaging across their sacred hunting grounds."

"I'll have messenger bats sent out," Atiya confirmed.

"Between the barricade here, within the southern lands, and the one at Bannoth Thor, the Taintbrood in this region are cut off. They can't cross open territory and any Brood trapped in those tunnels will remain trapped." Sul smiled slightly. "Severed from the rest of the

Horde and the call of their Hivelord, either they'll starve to death or tear each other apart. We'll see."

Sul traced his fingers across the war table. "The remainder of the Horde will be forced to march across the open countryside of Daymore without the majority of the Underwilds offering safety or shortcuts."

"And that's a good thing?" Ceyrabeth asked.

"It is if you want to motivate various warring factions to cease quarreling and unite behind a single leader," Pellinore commented.

"The Hierophant's position of authority is tied to his assertion to be able to defend Daymore against the Taintbrood without the assistance of the Chalicemen or anyone else beyond the Church.

We'll see how many ravaged fiefdoms it takes for the Imperium's reputation to crumble."

"And how many farmers, soldiers, and innocent people will die in the process?" Ceyrabeth commented icily.

"As many as are necessary." Her eyes narrowed but she held her tongue. He could be as ruthless as he wanted, but Ceyrabeth would keep reminding him, regardless of whether he wanted to hear it or not. At this point though, she didn't have the energy for another one of Sul's humiliating verbal eviscerations.

"Blood! Death! War! Rumpy-Pumpy! Triumph!" came the roar from outside.

"Aye!" Maul toasted from within the tent, hoisting his flagon.

"What in the name of all that is holy was that?!" Ceyrabeth choked out as she released the death grip on her sword.

"Just the lads having a bit of fun," Maul answered with a grin. "Our Crimson Vanguard, blowing off the last of the battle lust." The scarred man gave her a wicked grin. "Care to join us?"

"Um—"

"The answer to that question is 'no'," Sul replied without looking up from the map.

"Seconded," Pellinore commented hoisting his own glass in silent tribute. "The Vanguard fights hard but tends to play rough with their..." He eyed Ceyrabeth warily. "...'toys.'"

Ceyrabeth's eyes narrowed. "I am no one's toy, Commander."

"Which is why I recommend against participation."

"Think I'll join my mates," Maul said, nosily draining the contents of his mug and tossing it outside the tent before making his exit...

...and jerking to a stop as Sul took ahold of his splinted arm with an iron grip.

"Boss?" Maul swallowed a yelp of pain. "Something I can do for you?"

"Your former kinsmen of the mountains are, or soon will be, coming into contact with a person of great personal value to the Legion and to me. He is to be kept intact until such time as he is taken into the custody of our Outrunners."

Maul swallowed. "Begging your pardon, Cap'n, but will my 'former kinsmen' be expected to *live* through taking possession of this man?"

"That depends entirely on their discretion and your ability to ensure the man in question is of sound mind and body when we arrive."

Maul exhaled hard. "I'll be heading north then, if that suits you Cap'n."

"Enjoy your evening. You'll receive further instructions by bat."

Maul gave the shorter man a grave bow and Sul released him without word.

"So, who is this person of great value?" Ceyrabeth asked.

"A historian, scholar and writer of unparalleled insight and talent." He paused for a moment. "And he is a friend."

"I wasn't aware you had any 'friends,'" Ceyrabeth scoffed, still provoked by Sul's earlier ruthlessness.

"Not many."

"So, you'd wipe out a village for a friend?" The silence that answered spoke volumes.

"Of course, you would." The elven woman refilled his glass, even though she much would have preferred pouring the wine into his lap. "How do you sleep with all that blood on your hands?"

"The same way you do I imagine," Sul rejoined. "Fitfully."

Ceyrabeth slammed the wine pitcher down with a *thunk*. "My sleeping habits are absolutely none of your—"

"If I may"—Pellinore cleared his throat diplomatically, returning focus to the matters at hand— "after Reaper Maul has successfully completed his assignment, where should he reconnoiter and await further orders?"

"Send him to the Winking Wererat and remind him not to kill any of the patrons in drinking contests. He can assume the responsibilities of whomever we currently have stationed there."

"Yes Sir." Pellinore made a note. "With Reaper Maul gone, we will need someone to coordinate the removal of our dead from the battlefield so they can receive proper rites."

"I'll do it," Ceyrabeth volunteered. It was a hard, thankless job but it would be easiest for her; since she hadn't been with the Legion long, she wasn't as close to the fallen as the others were. She knew she wasn't imagining the relief in the other's faces.

"The White Shepherds and many of the Chalicemen are already on the field searching for survivors," Sul replied. "You may join their efforts, Lieutenant. Report to the stable for the necessary equipment."

"Sir!" Ceyrabeth stood, snapped a salute, and exited.

Hours later, Ceyrabeth heaved yet another body on to a broad cart. She took a moment to straighten, stretch her aching shoulder. Between Sul's healing potion and Mother Reiko's strengthening exercises, it was getting better but still was not up to full use. She had given up hope long ago that it ever would be, so the thought didn't crush her. She would just find a way to work around it as she always had.

She surveyed the battlefield thoughtfully. The fighting had been intense but, crushed between the infantry bulwark and the cavalry charge, the Horde had broken and fled. Once she and Pellinore's lancers had met in the middle of the field they could have chased them all the way back to the Underwilds if they'd been so inclined, but the order had been to let the Taintbrood quit the field after they retreated past the range of the Legion's distance archers.

She took stock of the battlefield with a critical eye. She saw the familiar faces of good men and women amongst the dead; mostly within the ranks of the infantry that had held the phalanx against the Horde. The Crimson Vanguard had lost nearly a third of their berserkers (though not, she remembered with a rueful smile, Sergeant Maul) and she herself had lost a pair of knights to a combination of Taintbrood ferocity and simple bad luck. But such were the fortunes of war and not outside the realm of expectation.

What was unexpected was how relatively few injured and dead they had suffered and how catastrophic the Taintbrood losses had been. Some of the injured members of the Legion had to be almost dug free from the crush of the enemy dead; in some cases, the corpses of the Horde were piled five or six high. It was as complete and devastating a defeat for the enemy as any military engagement she had heard of or participated in.

Outnumbered five to one and it was a massacre. Ceyrabeth would not have believed it unless she had seen it herself. Like Velasgate in reverse. What would have happened if it had been Sul in command of her brethren that day?

"I would have waited for the reinforcements from The Ghenlands as well the remainder of the Daymore's forces from the outer provinces."

She started at his voice but congratulated herself silently on not jumping. "How could you possibly know what I was thinking?" she asked without turning around.

"It is the most common thought of those who have survived a terrible defeat in one battle and then stand upon the field of victory in another."

"And that is?"

Sul stood beside her now, ramrod straight hands clasped behind his back. An effigy of perfect military poise. "'What if?'"

She just smiled and shook her head, past the point of being impressed with his deductive reasoning. Instead, she focused on the rapidly approaching dusk and the post battle chaos around them. "How did you find me in the dark amidst all this?"

"Were I cast into the Void, I would still find you." He shrugged slightly.

She felt a flush of heat come to her cheeks but was determined to not allow herself to be affected by his words. "Your magic glass eyes would make such a task quite easy I should think."

Sul turned his head slightly, and the intensity of his presence was palpable. "Radiance can be felt upon the skin; it can be smelt in the air and tasted upon the tongue. So, it is with the light of the sun, the cast of the moon and the brightest of stars." He turned his attention back to the field. "And so it is with individuals such as yourself. Eyes are not required. Merely the ability to perceive radiance and experience the warmth it brings."

This time she could not prevent an electric current from running through her body. She squeezed her hands into the fist so tightly that the dragonhide creaked. She felt the twinge of her old wounds and the pain grounded her.

"Thank you, Sir," she whispered.

"It is a simple truth. Much like that final battle of your former fellows itself."

"How so?"

"That battle was lost before it was ever fought."

Ceyrabeth frowned and shook her head. "The Church and the forces of Daymore—"

"The high clerics of Imperius had no business being upon the field of war. Certainly not in addition to a *legatus* of Daymore," Sul interrupted coolly. "When you are given command, it is total and complete. One leads or one follows, and it is the man...or woman"—he added with a nod towards her— "with the ability to strategize, maintain long term focus and discipline amongst both himself and the forces in his charge, that is in command." He shook his head slightly. "And not simply a man born with his god's 'blessings.'"

"Meaning the clerics?"

"I am curious to know precisely what they would have done if the Daymorian leader had not made himself such an easy target for assassination by the enemy," Sul considered before turning his attention back to her. "But no, the clerics was not fit to lead either."

Ceyrabeth bristled a little. "They had many victories against the Ghen and helped protect the independence of Daymore."

"They fought against the Ghen," Sul acknowledged evenly. "And grown complacent after a ninety plus year occupation of that province and lead by a man who was both universally despised by the people of the land they were tasked with ruling, as well as being incompetent in all matters military. A petty despot who cared more about the trappings of rulership than its proper execution, who deferred most matters to a mage whose only interest was practicing magic outside the scrutiny of the powers that be." Sul's smile was scornful. "No, Ceyrabeth, the only advantage the Ghen had against the 'Divine Commander' of Imperius was numbers."

He nodded towards the decimation of the battlefield. "An advantage that is far from a guarantee of victory." He turned to face her. "And that was is why The Church, for all its cunning, reputation and confidence is doomed against the Taintbrood: they are beyond them.

The clerics are not kings, as much as they may want to be, there are not even leaders."

"What are they then?"

"They are zealots; forever seeing the world as an opposing heresy to be smote," Sul answered in that calmly modulated voice. "Much like a hammer sees all the world as a nail...," His tone turned slightly sardonic. "...whether that happens to be the case or not. But the Horde...I have seen their will now. It is singular, united. One could almost admire its 'purity' if such a word could be used for them; survival, conquest, consumption, unclouded by an enforced conscience, manufactured remorse, or an imposed sense of morality from an obsolete and burdensome religious institution."

He removed a small pipe that he lit with bit of tinder. The embers caused the glass fragments of his eyes to glow scarlet and golden as he inhaled. "I imagine if The Church had ten divisions of such men who possessed such conviction, then perhaps they would stand a chance against the Horde." He exhaled slowly; a cloud of smoke trailed away lazily. "But that isn't what I see, not in this world as it is."

He paused a moment in his musings. "The kings of old saw things differently. They were leaders for they saw the world both as it was and how it could be."

"And you, Captain Sul," Ceyrabeth challenged, "what do you see when you see the world?"

Sul was quiet for a long time, so long that she feared he would not answer her question.

Then, slowly he scooped up a handful of dirt.

"I see discord, Commander." His voice so soft it was almost lost on the wind. "Targeste, the Underwilds...I see battles that extend beyond this one and wars that extend beyond all of them." He turned to face her, his foot resting near a freestanding puddle of blood, whether human or Taintbrood, Ceyrabeth could not tell in the fading light. "I see struggle and dispute beyond one man's bid for the throne, one nation's struggle for survival, or even one Horde threatening to consume an entire continent. I see The Ghenlands, Reaverlund, Nevaraak and Sahath. I see Daymore, Raynia's Rock and Al-Salahd."

He stared past the horizon to points that Ceyrabeth could neither see nor fully understand. "And I see death, Lieutenant, and such terrible suffering. I see all the world on the precipice of change ready to plunge into the flames to either be consumed whole or remade." He gestured to the battlefield. "This? This isn't the sweeping victory you believe it to be, Ceyrabeth. This a step forward in a long journey many years in the planning and years still in the undertaking." He tapped out the pipe, his face shrouded in darkness. "And there is only one direction that leads to any point beyond extinction: forward."

It was in the stillness of that moment that Ceyrabeth contemplated the awful truth of the man she had chosen to follow; there would no peace, no rest in his world and there never would be. He had received some vision so terrible to behold that it propelled him towards a destiny that he could neither deny nor even share, a road of ash and fire and scorched earth that he was forced to trod; unceasing, unending, and unyielding.

Alone.

But...

He is NOT alone. Ceyrabeth told herself firmly before speaking aloud, "As you say, Sir. And speaking of forward...if we are to finish before nightfall, I should get back to it."

Sul nodded agreement and Ceyrabeth took Eregost's reins, leading the reanimate and his heavy burden back toward camp. When she was out of sight, Sul turned to his left with a faint sigh.

"You can come out now."

Tarah emerged from the shadows, skin still glimmering as she shed her shielding magic.

"Answer me something, Uncle. What is your plan for that one?" She nodded her head in the departed Ceyrabeth's direction.

"The same plan I have for all of my soldiers."

Tarah rolled her eyes. "Really? So you tell all your soldiers that they're radiant and you could find them if they were cast into the Void? I never knew."

Sul turned his eyeless gaze to Tarah "Pray tell, Niece: what is your sudden interest in my Lieutenant?"

She shrugged. "Just trying to discern your mind. You chased her and her squad to you deliberately. You manipulated her into joining the Legion. You took her to view the Brood, at great peril to your secrecy. And then"—she motioned out over the field— "this battle. Pellinore could have led forty lancers by himself well enough, and yet you handed her—an unproven Lieutenant—half. You kept her in your inner circle while you put her fellows down in the lines. I'm concerned, Uncle. And others are starting to notice."

"Ceyrabeth Vallorin is one of the most competent soldiers I have encountered, and she is a valuable asset to the Phoenix Legion." He turned to face her "Do you or these 'others' have some concern with the military efficiency of how I am waging this campaign?"

"Your strategy is sound enough, as always. It's your personal actions..."

"I endure your concerns because we are family." His tone became quieter, colder. "And because of who it is you protect and hold dear."

"You needn't bristle at me." Tarah met his bandaged gaze fearlessly. "I just hope you're not forgetting what you went through to get this far for a doe-eyed lightning rod for disaster. Especially *not* when you could crook your little finger and have someone who could hand you the means to achieve your goals, fight beside you while you do it, and has no parallel for beauty besides. You should go to Reaverlund. Meet with the queen. She is *most* anxious to see you again."

Sul scoffed, "You're a terrible liar Niece. The queen has not given me a thought since she was a babe. Whatever impression I may have left upon her then, I'm certain her ambition and the appetite for domination left such things cold and ashen."

Tarah snorted a dark chuckle. "And they say dragons are out of touch with the emotions of man..."

"She has much larger concerns than nostalgia over a dead man," he interjected. "A man whose deaths and executions you witnessed firsthand, lest you forget." Tarah blanched just a little...but enough that it proved his point had hit home. "And we do as well. We've wiped out a large force of Brood. As noble a goal as that is, several thousand Brood turning up as corpses on the open field will generate significant attention. Power, like nature, abhors a vacuum."

"I suppose you're insinuating that I should—" Tarah stopped mid-sentence, and her head whipped around. Her nostrils flared. "What is..."

"*SILENCE.*"

The word rumbled through the air, made the ground below them shake with the force of it, underscored with the angry scream of what might have been a horse. Tarah grimaced when the spell hit, hissing her displeasure, and suddenly a red dragon stood where she had been. For a second, Sul was truly blind as the shards in his eyes went an ominous smoky gray. He reached out a hand, steadying himself on Tarah's broad side. Then the glass shards in his eyes reformed, exploded into a rapidly shifting tapestry of gold, ruby, and emerald.

Tarah lowered her neck without being asked and Sul quickly climbed aboard. Her broad wings ate the distance across the battlefield until they were directly over the tableau that had brought them there. "Land now!" Sul commanded, and Tarah, with the briefest hesitation, complied. On the way down, he wrapped his eyes with quick, sure motions.

"Captain!" Ceyrabeth looked up with a start as he strode toward her. "Stay back! The creature could be dangerous!"

The creature was a Taintbrood. On its knees, it was almost level with Ceyrabeth's head, but she showed no signs of fear or faltering as she held her blade on it.

"A Taintbrood mage?" Tarah was back in her human form, staring at the creature.

"I don't know if it's a mage or not," Ceyrabeth replied, eyes back on her prisoner. "But it's certainly a Taintbrood."

"But the Silence..." Tarah studied the elf's profile. "*You* cast that muting spell?"

"Well," Ceyrabeth's voice was even, but the corner of her mouth was twitching with the effort of suppressing her amusement at Tarah's surprise. "It surely wasn't Eregost."

"Why a Silence, Lieutenant?" Sul asked her.

"It *speaks*, Captain. Actual words, not hissing and growling, like the rest of his kind."

"And so, you muted it with the force of a thousand suns?" Tarah scoffed. "How very...Imperial."

Ceyrabeth's eyes narrowed but Sul cut her off with a gesture. "What did he say, Ceyrabeth?"

"I haven't the faintest," she replied haughtily. "I couldn't think of anything good a talking Taintbrood *could* say."

"Dispel the Silence, if you please."

Ceyrabeth opened her mouth to protest, but one look at his face convinced her to obey. She whispered the counter and stepped back as the creature got to its feet. Ceyrabeth stood directly in front of Sul, ready to defend him.

"*Na via lerno Victoria*," the Taintbrood spoke in a rumbling voice. Its visage was distinctly human despite its deformity and its posture was as regal as any lord or lady that ever walked Aegreas.

The Taintbrood was broad shouldered and a whole hand span taller than the Captain. As it shifted, there was the rustle of cloth and the clink of metal.

"Stand aside, Lieutenant," Sul commanded. Ceyrabeth reluctantly shifted to the side a bit, but her sword remained ready.

"Sir, we still don't know anything about...it."

"We know from its speech that he hails from Nevaraak," he replied. "And he is listening— and comprehending—every word we're saying." Turning his attention back to the Taintbrood, Sul continued, "he's been captured by a foreign force bearing a standard he does not recognize so he is exploiting the ignorance of his captors and hoping to learn as much as he can about us by playing the part of the savage and studying us until he has learned what it is he needs to know; in this case, who is in command of these forces." Sul turned his bandaged eyes towards the Taintbrood. "*Hoc est rectam?*"

The Taintbrood's distorted features twisted into a smile. "Entirely." His gaze flickered to Tarah, watching and wary, to Ceyrabeth and Eregost standing ready to do battle, then back to Sul. "Your Nevaraakese is strange, but I understand it."

"There is much that you must find strange in the world as it is now." He beckoned, "come and we shall discuss it.

"Captain! You're not thinking of bringing him into camp?"

Sul turned to her, the corner of his lips quirking in a dry smile. "I believe that things have been...normal, for quite long enough." He inclined his head to the Taintbrood. "Shall we?"

Ceyrabeth watched them go, worry warring with indecision on her face. "Ceyrabeth." Sul turned before they had taken too many steps and smiled at her. A *real* smile, not sardonic, not a ghostly image of happiness. It was small, but it was there. Ceyrabeth felt her heart slam hard against her chest. "Are you coming?"

She nodded, inexplicably relieved, and whistled for Eregost who trotted up behind her. "By your command, Captain."

"The most important virtue a warrior must embrace is love. Love of conquest. Love of the cause they are fighting for. Love for your brothers in arms. Find something to love and you will find the path to victory."

—Passage from Victor Vinguardis *(*Way of Victory*)*
translated from Daymorian. Author unknown.
Currently banned by the Church of Imperius.

ABOUT THE AUTHORS

 ALEC PETERSON has been writing for several decades. His work includes urban fiction, dystopian fantasy, horror, and poetry. He won a Hugo Award for Best Related Work in 2019 alongside his sister. He is currently a reclusive author who is slowly making his way to Tangier by way of Florence and Kyoto to live out the classical author's life of overindulgence and consorting with the spirits of those storytellers more talented than himself.

 CHARLOTTE FARIS is a Hugo Award-winning author and a born and raised Wisconsin native. When she's not agonizing over dialogue or plot points, you can find her slinging scripts as a Certified Pharmacy Technician, causing mischief with her son Jonah, or re-reading *The Green Mile* for the millionth time with one (or all) of her three cats on her lap.

You can follow updates about Charlotte and Alec's latest projects on their Facebook page: www.facebook.com/LastWarlordChronicles.